Sub Rosa
The Lost Formula

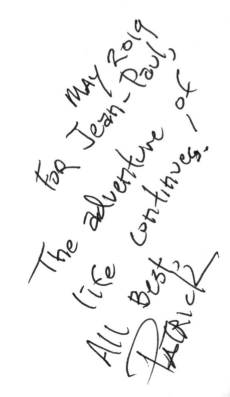

MAY 2019

For Jean-Paul,

The adventure of

life continues.

All Best,

Patrick

ALSO BY PATRICK SEAN BARRY

Sub Rosa – Sanctuary's End

Sub Rosa
The Lost Formula

Patrick Sean Barry

Cover layout by Caitlin Barry
Map and Cover Photos by P. S. Barry

Published by Sator Rotas Press
A Division of P.S. Barry Enterprises
Newbury Park, CA 91320

Trade Paper ISBN: 978-0-9960809-2-7
Kindle ISBN: 978-0-9960809-3-4

For Brigitte, Caitlin and Brian—
Who make it all worth it.

And in memory of my uncle,
Monsignor William J. Barry—
One of the Good Ones.

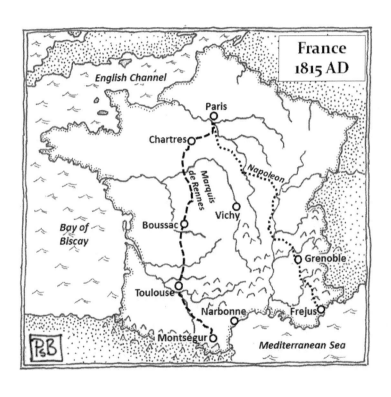

France
1815 AD

English Channel

Paris

Chartres

Napoleon

Marquis de Rennes

Vichy

Bay of
Biscay

Boussac

Grenoble

Toulouse

Narbonne

Frejus

Montségur

Mediterranean Sea

*"There are two levers
for moving men –
interest and fear."*
Napoleon Bonaparte
Emperor of France

*"Through her extreme sensibility and the mobility
of her own bodily fluids, the woman is to a certain extent
in a favorable position to cross to the higher level...
She stands, therefore, on the right-hand side of the arcana."*
Armand Barbault
Alchemist

i

The Sky Over Central France
1 March, 1815 AD – Midday

Not far from Vichy, in the Auvergne region, she had just crossed high above the last river, the Allier. The afternoon light drew long shadows across the fields below. Radiant mustard plants cultivated to create brilliant lemon-hued patches on the gently rolling landscape were turning amber as the day's colors grew more somber and muted. She scanned from side to side as she flew on, following the inner compass that had been so reliable for her kind for eons.

Her wings felt the fatigue of the long passage. Her rests along the way on the occasional tree limb had always been brief, something inside always pressing her on, to complete her journey. Two days before, at the beginning of her flight, she had barely avoided a falcon's talons, but one of her companions was not so fortunate. That peril long forgotten, the relentless ancient instinct pushed her further on.

The landscape became more familiar to the ingrained patterns in her primitive brain. Her internal compass told her the flight was almost at an end. Drawn to a hillcrest ahead, one which overlooked the countryside, an edifice resembling a small barn stood atop the hill, but including a feature which set it apart from other structures in the vicinity. Off to the side of the barn, a tall wooden tower stood three stories in height. The top two stories hosted numerous small rounded openings with short wooden platforms. She headed for one on the top level, and finally landed. Upon entering the small portal, she brushed across a thin copper bar mechanism which tripped a bell that jingled in the belfry of the tower.

Down below, in the mottled darkening shadows of the ground floor, amid a symphony of persistent avian cooing, Maryse Bertrand had been tending to feed the carrier pigeons in their wooden cages when the bell rang high above her. As usual, the thirteen-year-old hiked up her long cotton patterned dress to facilitate easier movement, and she lithely climbed the extremely wide wooden ladder-like structure up to where the light gray carrier pigeon had just come to roost. Maryse smiled with affection and care as she reached out to take the bird gently, cradling her protectively, and then climbed back down the ladder with deft athletic familiarity. When she reached the bottom, she smiled at the bird.

"Oh, my little one, have you had a long trip?" Maryse inquired lovingly, almost as though she expected an answer. As she petted the pigeon lightly, Maryse spied the petite leather case tied securely to the pigeon's right leg. The girl dutifully carried both the pigeon and her precious cargo from the roost tower and over to the farmhouse nearby. She knew she was not to open these message packets, or even to untie them from the bird, without her father's direction or permission.

Inside, Maryse's father, Yves Bertrand, was busy writing a precise and microscopic message on a small and very thin piece of special paper, copying it from an original. Once complete, he then tightly rolled the communiqué and inserted it into a tiny leather case much like the one which had just arrived on the leg of the carrier pigeon. He glanced up to see his daughter, not yet noticing the pigeon cradled in her hands. He picked up the leather case, along with three more like it, and handed them to Maryse.

"These must go to the Mayor of Poitiers. It's important, so we'll send four, hoping at least one gets through. Prepare the birds and call me when they're ready. I'll check them before release," he directed her with a sense of distracted purpose. It was only then, based on her hesitation, that he saw Maryse had a pigeon with a message. Yves gestured for her to hand it over to him.

Yves Bertrand studied the knot tying the small tube-shaped leather case onto the pigeon's leg. "This is urgent," he observed. Yves glanced briefly at his daughter with concerned distraction, then motioned her away slightly with his index finger.

Maryse knew this signal meant her father needed to be

alone with whatever information this sachet contained. She took the four missives her father had prepared and returned to the roost to discharge her duties as directed.

Yves Bertrand petted the carrier pigeon with professional respect, and then carefully untied the minute leather case. Before opening it, he studied all the details of the exterior to assure he did not miss any part of what was being communicated. From the inside, he extracted a small thin piece of scrolled paper which he unrolled onto the table, and then read the brief message. In disbelief, he needed to read it again, and again.

"*Mon dieu!* It cannot be!" he muttered in private astonishment.

Yves Bertrand quickly went into action. He took ten small prepared slips of thin parchment paper and painstakingly copied the message over and over. He knew this one message might be the whole reason he was here, and that his family had chosen this avocation. This was destiny and history in the works, and he was part of it. He copied the message in a tight, crisp script, and he intended to have these on their way to Paris within the hour. Hopefully, they would reach the destination before the end of the day tomorrow.

Time was truly of the essence.

Hotel la Comtesse de Narbonne
16th Arrondissement, Paris, France
2 March, 1815 AD – The Dinner Hour

From the balcony of this stately and well-appointed city manor, a small coterie of elegantly dressed socialites had gathered around two men: all were excited with the demonstration about to transpire. Despite the candle lighting, the entire group stood fundamentally in the shadows, which brought an added sense of mystery and exclusivity to their activities.

As one dandy onlooker, dressed in opulent green velvet vestments, flirted with one of the elite society maidens in attendance, most remained focused in anticipation of the promised entertainment.

One man held a large round object—something like a misshapen ball. He stood poised by the edge of the railing where a panoramic view of the city lights sprawled out below them. The second man took a long candle from its stand and brought its flame closer to the object and handed it to the first man. The luminance of the flame revealed the focus of everyone's attention: a miniature replica of an ornately crafted and working scale model of a hot air balloon. Complete with intricate colorful painted decorations festooning two sides of the silk balloon itself, its bulbous shape was supported by a framework of thin wire ribbing.

"Ah, the moment of truth! I predict the entire contraption shall burst into flames before us!" the dandy quipped, hoping to impress the young beauty next to him.

"Silence! Let the Marquis de Rennes concentrate!" commanded the hostess of the event—La Comtesse de Narbonne—revealing a trace of impatience with the impertinence of the loud-mouthed scoffer in her otherwise exclusive soirée.

The marquis, meanwhile cautiously delivered the candle's flame to a wick in a receptacle located in what would traditionally be the passenger basket on a full-scale balloon. Made of the thinnest gauge brass wire, the receptacle had been crafted to work as a small lamp-torch; and a substance housed in a small cup, soaked with flammable oil, immediately lit.

The small crowd held their breath for what would happen next. Roger Rosier, the assistant to the marquis—a charming and handsome man in his own right—took back the candle as the marquis allowed the bottom of the balloon's basket to rest on the palm of his hand, his fingers lightly holding the base. Illuminated from within by the flame and now clearly buoyant in the air, the small pear-shaped balloon remained tethered by the marquis's fingers.

"The miracle of flight is now in all of Mankind's grasp, my friends."

The marquis opened his fingers, releasing the brass basket below the balloon. The miniature craft immediately rose, caught by a light buffeting of wind, and began to drift out over the city. The balloon itself, illuminated by the flame radiating up into its heart, brought the colorful hand-painted decorations to life: a man and a woman in elegant dress, holding hands in a representation of love. It had a magical effect on the party there on the balcony as the balloon moved out over the expansive cityscape below them. The entire clique applauded loudly, offering 'bravos' and congratulations. One woman flirted with the marquis.

"I would very much enjoy going up in one of those, monsieur le Marquis. I am told you are quite an experienced pilot of these fantastic inventions."

"Indeed, mademoiselle, I own two. And if you were ever to visit my château in the south, it would be my honor to host you for a journey which I dare say would be the defining moment of your life."

"I would love to ride with you, *mon beau* marquis, and I would hope I could provide some definition for your life as well!" the young maiden replied, her double-entendre blatant and fully intended to hint and entertain the group. All laughed, as some drank champagne; others simply gazed at the balloon as it drifted further off into the distance.

In time, it floated to a point out above the city where it

became difficult to see clearly. With the novelty and excitement of the moment having passed, the group gradually migrated back to the heart of the festivities inside the manor house, to the salon.

The Marquis de Rennes stepped through the doorway leading inside, and the ambient light made his features easier to discern, as was the case with all partygoers entering from the balcony. Dressed in an elegant plum-colored velvet waistcoat, frilled white shirt, violet silk leggings with white stockings, one feature in particular gave the clean-shaven and strikingly handsome man a special and distinctive look. In contrast to his long flowing dark brown hair gathered in the back, his right eyebrow had the appearance of being predominantly bleached white.

As he and his valet Roger entered, the hostess, la Comtesse de Narbonne, dressed in a sumptuous emerald-green silken gown, made sure they were offered a fresh glass of champagne, which both men readily accepted with charm and poise.

At this moment in history, the salons of Europe were where the heartbeat of culture pulsed, and the salons of Paris were not only the nerve center of France, but in fact the most influential on the continent. All of the latest news of the world and local gossip emanated from here. All artistic tastes, the trends and fashions, were defined here. And, as well, all the political opinions and cultural attitudes were forged in the cauldron of the passionate debates and brilliant conversation found here. Both before and after the Revolution, the salon of the Comtesse de Narbonne, in her grand city mansion overlooking the Seine River and the Île de la Cité, held the vaunted status of being one of the undisputed elite centers of Paris society.

Tonight the Comtesse's festivities celebrated the debut of her new, sumptuously appointed grand drawing room, designed and furnished with what had been, until ten months before, the newest rage of Paris society: the neo-Egyptian style inspired by Napoleon's military campaign into the mysterious and exotic lands of the pyramids, which had taken place over a decade before.

Undaunted by the overbearing and *de rigueur* environment of the new political correctness, where the head of the re-installed Bourbon dynasty wore the king's crown of France, her newly debuted drawing room—complete with all the finest details of Egyptian-inspired décor—expressed an unambiguous homage to France's recently departed emperor.

Selected Egyptian antiques, as well as newly crafted furniture, statuary, and beautifully commissioned wall and ceiling murals, created an ambiance which was certainly not ancient Egypt, but something else redolent, unique and elegant. It boasted an idealized hybrid of styles which took the best of late Baroque craftsmanship, blended with the neoclassic influence, guided by the evocative stylistic lines of ancient Egypt, resulting in a subtle quasi-mystical and stylish environment which provided hidden details of refinement, accomplishment and charismatic mystique at each juncture and niche in the room.

Special attention was also given to the large balcony off the salon where the balloon demonstration took place. Here two small white marble Egyptian obelisks—especially custom-made in the finest Carrara marble—framed the view of the Île de la Cité, where history cites the birthplace of

Paris. There as well, esoteric tradition teaches that on this small island in the Seine River, over a millennium before Notre Dame was built, a temple to Isis herself stood in ancient Roman times. And this temple, ancient tradition reveals gave the city its name, taken from the age-old Pharos lighthouse of Alexandria, and the dominant worship of Isis in this city—hence Pharos-Isis became shortened to Paris.

Even Napoleon revised the seal of Paris, adding the star of Sirius, symbolizing Isis, hanging over the prow of the boat in the crest which represented the ship-shaped Île de la Cité. The insertion of the star caused great displeasure among the Christians and royalists. Yet this version of the Paris crest remained proudly displayed and prominently emblazoned on the wall of the balcony near the 'Cleopatra obelisks,' as the Comtesse had affectionately dubbed them.

Beyond the spacious main salon chamber—where the latest Vivaldi string quartet composition was being performed in front of a large well-heeled gathering—a grand two-storied octagonal private library housed hundreds of rare volumes on dark hardwood shelves, along with all the classics. The truly rare tomes were only accessible along the bronze and iron-railed second floor balcony which overlooked the heart of the main floor of la Comte de Narbonne's library.

A number of paintings hung not only on the two-story high walls, but also on various easels—the theme of tonight's library art exhibition: the great Dutch masters. Pieter de Hooch, Adrian van de Velde, Van Dyke, and of course the prerequisites for any comprehensive Dutch master collection—Rubens, Vermeer and Rembrandt—were on display. Landscapes, portraits, still life pieces, and more, delivered a feast for cultured and appreciative eyes.

The jovial and corpulent Comte de Narbonne, an avid and wealthy collector, had much to be proud of with his impressive collections of paintings and many more *objets d' art*. He was also especially proud of his finely crafted esoteric and mysterious works by Nicolas Poussin, as well as two new politically powerful paintings from the Spaniard Goya, which sparked lively discussion and debate in his circle.

This exclusive realm of well-dressed gentlemen of high station, a selection of nobly born and men of distinguished accomplishment, smoked ornate carved ivory pipes loaded with the latest blend of imported tobacco from the young nation of America. Expert opinions, and a fair share of priggish bloviating, bandied back and forth amid sometimes self-satisfied pooh-bahs who had distinct opinions about the merit of the paintings and various bronze and marble statues, some antiques, and other *objets d'art*, which adorned this impressive library.

The splash of colors of the gentlemen's satin and high-collared silken waistcoats, red, bright blue, emerald green, violet, with intricate golden embroidery and more, created a rich rash of hues in movement. Combined with the host of over sixty paintings, the riot of vibrant color and design made it difficult for the unaccustomed eye to focus on any one piece in particular.

The 'Egyptian Room,' as it was immediately titled by one of the early elite arrivals, however, was the center of activity. Here both the gentlemen and the women mingled and flirted, and this locale hosted the most impactful activities of the evening. A demonstration of the latest technology—the steam engine—had been shown to the gathering in a miniature representation, foreshadowing the arrival of the nascent Industrial Age. Included, as well, a presentation of new scientific phenomena—the exotic and mysterious magnetism and static electricity.

Now, as the music played, a card game of chance, with a life's fortune at stake, was being decided in one corner. At other tables, however, the whims of cultural influence and political authority of the land swayed in the balance of the evening while fresh Normandy coast oysters—packed in Alpine ice—and the finest champagne were consumed with ravenous gusto.

Other exotic cuisines originating from the southern shores of the Mediterranean enhanced the Egyptian theme, as the eclectic mix of luminous guests sparked lively and intelligent discussion in the broadest range of topics.

To the untrained eye, nothing might necessarily distinguish one set of circumstances from another; however, from two closely situated tables in the corner, opposite the card game, the fate of France was being politely debated. And contributors to that debate were significant and influential players in the destiny of the nation.

In the background of this powerful and stylish discourse, while seemingly innocuous to a casual observer, one particular transaction worthy of note occurred. A distinguished guest, upon his arrival and welcomed warmly by the hostess, presented the Comtesse with a neatly wrapped sheaf of papers tied with a wide vermillion silk ribbon. The Comtesse accepted the package with charming appreciation, casually covering it from further view with her pale blue silk fan. As she chatted breezily with the man who delivered the parcel, she gestured to one of her servants. She handed the package to the attendant and whispered quietly in his ear as he nodded acknowledgment of his duties, while the Comtesse led the new guest into her husband's library.

The servant, meanwhile, traversed the crowded salon to another guest who had observed the entire exchange with veiled interest. Seeing that the Comtesse had led the guest into the library and was hence out of direct line of sight, the servant then passed the package over to the well-dressed nobleman, the Marquis de Rennes. Taking the package with a thankful nod, he then turned to his valet, Roger. He spoke quietly to the valet as he passed the package and then watched as his valued assistant exited the party straightaway. Yet the marquis also noted that, before he left the soirée, Roger could not resist flirting and pinching the cheek of a particularly attractive maid serving for the Comtesse and the soirée.

After the valet finally exited, and seeming to be relieved of a burden, the guest with the white eyebrow sat by a beautiful young woman who had saved a seat for him at the table next to which, at the neighboring table, a spirited, yet polite political discussion, was taking on a new tone.

On the surface, the discussion at the adjacent table explored the topic of the Congress of Vienna, currently in session, where the allied nations who defeated Napoleon debated the future of France. Since Napoleon dismantled the Habsburg dynasty's centuries-old claim on the Holy Roman Emperor title, speculation at the table explored how the Pope would react to the new balance of power which now tilted back in favor of European royalty.

A small cluster of voices welcomed the restoration of 'sanity' and described the scenario where Europe could finally return to its destiny of a unified Christian culture, rejecting the abominations of the liberal and pantheistic thought which the Revolution ushered in, and which Napoleon facilitated in some measure with his following regime. Opposing voices noted that these new values and freedoms—fought for in the Revolution, embraced by Napoleon, and fundamentally accepted by the new king, Louis XVIII, as well—were sacrosanct.

"These principles must be regarded as permanent changes and part of the newly recognized foundations of the Universal Rights of Man and the Enlightenment. France has led the way in an historic step in the progress of civilization," one well-heeled advocate proclaimed behind the smoke of his small clay pipe.

"Humbug! All this nonsensical blather is destined for the trash heap of history," declared the brash, handsome and fair-haired duc Henri de St. Pré, notorious for his rude, abrasive sarcasm, short temper and a member of the royalist minority in attendance at the gathering.

In response to the elite societal caliber of the scorn's author, other guests attempted to redirect the discussion at the table to a potentially more neutral subject: the discoveries in the New World and how Baron Von Humboldt's recent explorations brought to light an important study of the exciting and mysterious pyramids in Mexico. A prevailing view of many at the table expressed how these monumental structures most certainly provided evidence of the ancient influence of the Universal Intelligence which also guided the storied and legendary Egyptians in their millennia-long legacy of glory and accomplishments along with their own building of the venerable pyramids.

Reflections on the recently achieved independence of Mexico from Spain also sparked observations of lost opportunities for this young culture of the New World to gain from the advantages of sage wisdom and guidance from the Old World. Adding to this point, another participant observed the missed opportunity for Mexico to enjoy the benefits of achieving liberty, equality and fraternity, and the ideals of the French Revolution, carried forward by Napoleon's vision, and now being 'supported and shepherded' in France by Louis XVIII.

In stark contrast, and in counterpoint, this discussion gave way to the duc de St. Pré's didactic report on the important developments of Hegelian philosophy currently being inculcated into and across the Prussian culture. He specifically noted the critical role of Hegelian thought being incorporated into mass education, its part in re-formalizing and rigidly stratifying class distinctions, as well as focusing the guidance of the 'ignorant masses' properly so they dutifully fulfilled the roles and responsibilities that were expected and required of them.

The duke's point emphasized that the State was inherently the presence of God in the modern world and must be obeyed without question. Rapidly gaining in recognition, acceptance and popularity in the German principality states, this philosophy carried an exhaustive organized system of thought which promoted the concept that the ideal ruling class held positions of power without the tedious distraction of democratic elections. This new system would benefit from the authoritatively directed labors of the underclass, which were ultimately meant to benefit the world in a grand vision of proper and ordained order.

The duc de St. Pré pushed this discomforting view further. He pontificated: "This educational model would be most suitable for France to facilitate the culture's return to the fold of the Christian kingdoms within the Holy Alliance. Implementing this philosophy of governance in France will be an excellent first step to rehabilitate the collapse of the Holy Roman Empire which Napoleon recklessly dismantled during his rule."

This extreme royalist perspective stood in direct opposition to the general sentiments being expressed at the table. The noble personage imposing so patronizing and didactic a line of discussion, the brilliant and privileged duc de St. Pré—a close confidant of the newly re-installed Bourbon king, Louis XVIII—was rumored to be part of the King's closest circle of policy advisors.

Notoriously handsome, he was supported in his assertions by two well-dressed companions: a heavyset British member of minor nobility, Lord Cornelius Bluefield, and a dark, lean Russian noble of comparable social stature, Count Vasily Petrovich Kotrouzko. The Cossack noble had been in command of one of the Tzar's cavalry battalions which marched into Paris after Napoleon's defeat almost a year ago. Most at the table knew this, and so his presence brought with it some understandable discomfort.

These members of minor European nobility, as well as a

few other noble Frenchmen, part of the duc de St. Pré's entourage, and accompanied by their valets, represented in total a sizable party of over a dozen people. And in point of fact, the duc de St. Pré, who perpetrated these antagonistic pronouncements, had not actually been invited to the Comtesse de Narbonne's salon. Yet when he appeared at the door with his entourage, it seemed virtually impossible for the Comtesse to gracefully turn them away. Instead, she behaved as though nothing was out of place and welcomed him and his clique with charm and hospitality. The consummate hostess, she also directed her staff to assure food and beverage were offered in ample supply. Currently ordering more oysters and champagne, the duke and his cronies consumed the countess's hospitality with an entitled sense of predatory satisfaction.

Sitting at the 'main' table of the salon, the duke enjoyed ensuring the royalist point of view was expressed with overbearing confidence, in an insinuated exercise of unlimited power. Indeed, while the new king was considered a 'good man' for supporting and ratifying the essence of Napoleon's socially inspired changes, many of those who returned to royal power with him, however, did not maintain the same perspective. Far from it. The duke emphatically disclosed he aligned with the latter classification when it came to his political stance.

"With the Congress of Vienna currently in session, and all the *rightful* crown heads, or their suitable representatives in attendance, His Royal Highness expressed to me that he is confident the divine order will ultimately be restored so that *all* of the royal and noble families may rightfully execute their righteously anointed powers and finally return the continent to the proper order of affairs. These Hegelian measures present an intelligent and appropriate means to an end, to forging a new Holy Roman royal alliance, where the masses finally understand their proper and subservient place in the divine scheme of things, exactly as God wills it. This obscenity of the Corsican artillery officer's rule will merely be recalled as an aberrant and bad memory. Nothing more," the duke declared officiously.

Many at the table took clear offence to the duke's imperious remarks. The majority, however, remained hesitant to confront these statements. While the Bourbon king was initially perceived to be the 'good man,' who accepted and adopted many of the social reforms implemented in the Napoleonic Code, the message the duke conveyed was that these would eventually be swept away in the King's name.

Bringing undue attention to one's opposing view, here in this setting, could later result in misfortune. Many in attendance could confirm that perception since numerous accounts in circulation described the King's ministers enacting vindictive measures, some directed as clear revenge on individuals, for which no recourse was possible. Openly challenging the duke's declarations risked putting oneself in the sights of some vindictive royalist vendetta. Yet to sit in silence, however, expressed a spirit completely counter to what everyone there was about—a free and open exchange of ideas.

One attendee at the table took it upon himself to respond with reason, as respectfully and as articulately as possible. "Excuse me, and with all respect, duc de St. Pré, but is this truly King Louis's view? Having affirmed the

'Rights of Man' just back in October, would this not suggest he fully supported the people's work, the social progress, a sacred concept for which so many sacrificed their lives defending the ideals of the Revolution?" Pierre de Molay, a friend of the Comtesse, suggested politely.

The duke glanced at his two noble companions with a wry sense of vexed entitlement and venomous savor before he turned to his deferential challenger. They rolled their eyes with dismissal as they continued to consume Normandy oysters and wash them down with champagne. The duke viewed de Molay with thinly veiled disdain. "And you, sir, would have the courtesy of giving me your name?"

"Pierre de Molay," the man replied after a pause, somewhat intimidated, but unwilling to be completely cowed by the royalist's manner. The duke nodded to one of his attendants nearby, who pulled out a small leather secretary, opened it to retrieve a pencil, and proceeded to dutifully record the name, offering a glance at the unfortunate target of the duke's attention. The duke gave de Molay a withering stare.

" *'De Molay'*… Now why does that name sound so familiar, and yet so disagreeable? Monsieur de Molay, the king is a realist. In the short term, he allows the *perception* of sustained social progress, as you quaintly call it. However, once he consolidates power throughout all the provinces, and he has finally replaced all the old corrupt ministers and military leaders with those who can be completely trusted, then you shall see a true rebirth of the Bourbon line and the rightful destiny of the noble class of France. I'm telling you all of this now, so you can become part of the new divine plan which is inevitable for the entire continent. To oppose this, of course, would risk the complete extinction of one's family."

An oppressive silence ensued. The threat was palpable. Those present did not wish to engage the duke further at the risk of seeing their name entered into this nobleman's little black book. Satisfied he now commanded the spirit the evening in the salon, the duc de St. Pré continued his casual imperious rant. He breezily pointed around at the neo-Egyptian décor of the salon with dismissive disgust.

"And the Inquisition, which as you all know has recently been reinstated by our blessed Holy Father, the Pope in Rome, would view this extravagant abomination and display of pagan paean, with very grave concern indeed. I too would share that very, *very* grave concern." The duke drank deeply from his champagne, enjoying the impact of his words, as he glanced across at his two companions with a lofty and satisfied pursing of his lips and arching of his eyebrow.

Another dreadful pause hung over the table, none in attendance seeming willing to venture an intellectual retort or challenge to the duke. Yet as this uncomfortable moment extended, boisterous laughter came from the adjoining table. Those who sat at the duke's table first assumed this merriment was part of a separate discussion concerning the next table. This perception, however, dispelled completely when the duke observed one of the guests at the second table mimicking him in an exaggerated *commedia dell'arte* theatrical styling of the duke's gesture of pursed lips and arched eyebrow. And more laughter came forth. Infuriated upon recognizing this insult, the duc de St. Pré stared coldly, with a direct lock of eyes at the man with the white eyebrow who clearly ridiculed him.

Seeing the duke's threatening gaze, the Marquis de Rennes merely stared back, blithely. He then turned to the guests at his table, mimicked the cold stare, bulged his eyes in a grotesque mockery and shook his head side-to-side in a crude clownish gesture, then finally stuck his tongue out and puffed his cheeks. And the entire table again burst out laughing. The duke's eyes widened as he blustered in indignation and signaled to his secretary to get ready to write another name.

"*Excuse* me, sir?" the duke challenged.

"I sincerely believe, sir, there is *no* excuse for you," the marquis at the adjoining table countered promptly.

"Do you *know* who I am, sir?" the duke challenged the stranger with the most implicit threat his voice could deliver.

"I know *what* you are. The critical question is, I believe, sir, do *you* know who *you* are, sir?" the marquis replied casually, taking a drink of sparkling water from a stemmed crystal glass.

With a huff of officious body language the duke delivered what he intended to be the big weapon: his title. "*I*, sir, am *the* duc de St. Pré, close confidant of the King, Louis XVIII, and advisor to the future of the kingdom. And you are…?"

The duke clearly intended to convey threat and dreadful consequences to the man who dared to laugh at him in such a public and critical social setting. Everyone present knew this was no place to lose face, since gossip spread like wildfire from salon to salon.

"I, sir, am… unimpressed and frankly disappointed."

"Excuse me, sir!" the duke quickly replied indignantly, trying to reinstate his sense of threat in the room. The marquis, who graciously thanked a servant who just refilled his glass, glanced at the imperious duke with sincere patience, and spoke slowly as though he might to a child, or an imbecile.

"It would appear, sir, that I repeat myself when I state that there seems to be no excuse for you at all. Was I not clear? You arrive at a salon without invitation. Our hostess gracefully allows you entry without objection. While drinking her finest wines and eating her exquisite cuisine, you proceed to intimidate and insult her guests with impunity—here in the house of a family whose noble bloodline goes back more than six centuries. In stark contrast, *sir*, your modest line of nobility only goes back as far as your father. And he bought his title after great success in the slave trade. While your representations of proximity to the royal house might indeed intimidate some, your behavior and breeding reflect nothing more than a common thug… sir," the marquis replied with calm confidence, as he then took another drink from his glass of sparkling water. He smiled at the beverage and commented, "Ah, yes, how refreshing!"

The main table tittered with guarded laughter, and as the duke's rage built, his eyes narrowed.

"I take offense, sir! And you may not quite understand the gravity of your actions here tonight," the duke intoned with as severe a sense of threat as possible.

"Unfortunately you are painfully easy to offend. I suspect you would take offense at someone simply sneezing in your presence."

At which point, the man with the white eyebrow proceeded to muster a theatrical sneeze and then roll his eyes for the benefit of those looking on who all remained rapt with attention at what might happen next. Following his sneeze, the man's smiling gaze calmly returned to the duke who was turning red, apoplectic with fury.

"Indeed, I do believe my sneeze has offended you!' the marquis observed with bemusement.

"Sir, I *demand* your name!" the duke ordered as he stood in a threatening manner.

"Is it because you are so very unhappy with your own, sir?" the marquis quipped. "Sorry, but mine is taken already."

More laughter ensued. Before the duke could respond and certainly escalate the exchange, the Comtesse de Narbonne swept into the space between the two tables, having been summoned by one of her dutiful servants. At this same moment the Vivaldi quartet completed their performance and the uneasiness at the duke's table had become all the more accentuated by the silence left following the polite applause for the musicians. With deft wit, timing and decorum, the Comtesse immediately redirected the energy of the room with the dramatic flair of a hand gesture which featured her elegant fan.

"And now, dearest friends, we arrive at one of the much anticipated features of the night's festivities! Coming direct to you after his studies in Germany with the world-renowned Dr. Anton Mesmer, pioneer in the art of hypnotism, I present to you the Marquis Jean-Marc Baptiste de Rennes. He will present to you a demonstration of the mystical art of hypnotism and explain the practical principles of human science at work in the process. And without further ado, I proudly introduce my dear old friend:

the Marquis Jean-Marc Baptiste de Rennes."

The Comtesse proceeded to clap, and all guests in the room followed suit. The man with the white eyebrow stood, then leaned slightly over to the duke, with a charming smile, which he also shared broadly with the entire room.

"Now that you have my name, sir, I hope you may enjoy the rest of the evening without further agitation or distraction," the marquis bantered to the duke.

This statement, of course, only irked the duke further, as he glanced over at his valet to assure he had dutifully recorded the name of the duke's newly chosen nemesis.

As Jean-Marc now stood before the assemblage, he saw his presence also drew the men from the library, curious to see how this new diversion might enhance the evening.

"First, I extend my heartfelt thanks to the lovely Comtesse de Narbonne for inviting me to this elegant soirée. I think anyone *invited* here tonight should feel deeply honored. And if you're here, and you were *not* invited, might I ask, 'Have you *no* shame?' "

Light laughter rippled through the gathering; and some knowing guests glanced at the duke, who scowled silently.

"Tonight it is my honor to present to you a demonstration of what people currently call 'hypnotism', but which has been a practice of the ancients for millennia. Only recently here on the Continent has an interest in the art gained some sense of growing popularity. May I see with a show of hands, how many of you are familiar with the term 'hypnotism?' "

Most of the people in attendance raised their hands.

"And how many of you have witnessed a demonstration of this modus operandi?"

Only a smattering of hands remained up in the air.

"Excellent! I only hope I might humbly provide some service to you all in demonstrating one set of practices related to this much talked about, yet little understood, phenomena of the human experience."

The marquis then provided additional context to his presentation, indicating that, while Dr. Mesmer had indeed pioneered a European system of technique and application, the general practice of hypnotism had roots in ancient Egypt, India and China, where the technique was employed for very practical and useful applications. One specific example was the invaluable medical treatments which, in selected cases, had been powerfully effective. And with that, the marquis asked if anyone in the audience had been suffering from consistent pain either in their legs, or arms, which made their lives more difficult, and which had possibly persisted for an excess of six months. An embarrassed pause ensued. It seemed among this elite crowd a common hesitancy to admit to pain or any sort of vulnerability. Yet after a short pause, where the guests casually glanced from one side to another, one man who stood in the door of the library raised his hand as he walked toward the marquis.

"I have had a condition which forces me to walk with a cane; and it has been with me for more than five years, sir. Are you saying you can do something for me?" the guest challenged as he approached Jean-Marc. While stylishly dressed, and somewhere in his early sixties, he clearly depended on his ornately carved cane, with an ivory and gold handle, to make his way toward the marquis.

"I hope I can be of assistance," Jean-Marc responded as

the man arrived. "But first, I must state, sir, that we have never met before. Would you be so kind as to confirm that?"

"If we had, I certainly have no recollection. But enjoying my fifth glass of the good Comte's private reserve of port, what I recollect is now open to challenge!" the old man quipped, to which Jean-Marc and the guests laughed heartily.

"Good enough. And while you are in some ways feeling less pain from the port, your condition nonetheless still persists. May I ask where your malady troubles you, sir?"

The distinguished guest with the cane described an intense and persistent pain in his hip and right side, shooting through his leg, which made walking very difficult, especially in damp and cold weather.

Jean-Marc nodded, studying the man with an empathic intensity. From his velvet jacket pocket, he withdrew a golden chain with a large diamond setting at the end. The marquis instructed the guest to stare into the diamond's luster as he gently swung the gem back and forth, and quietly guided the man with the cane into entrancement. Once achieved, Jean-Marc placed the suggestion, that once out of the hypnotic state, the man would experience no pain, that indeed he would feel ten years younger, and even be compelled to spontaneously hop a jig to demonstrate his vitality of youth and the departure of his infirmity.

Once the hypnotic spell was released, the elderly man acted as if he had not even been under the spell. Yet as he stood, he expressed surprise at the absence of pain in his hip and leg. He spontaneously hopped slightly in the air, testing his right side, and then with a sense of surprised jubilation, danced a jig in celebration. The ecstatic crowd applauded enthusiastically—all except for one: the duke.

"It's all a scandalous fraud! A disgusting disgrace!"

A palled silence descended as all eyes fell on the imperious duke. He stood, pointing his accusing finger at the marquis as he spoke through his teeth with venom. "This's nothing more than a carnival sham and an insult to the intelligence!" the duke continued, as he began to advance toward Jean-Marc. "And despite claims to the contrary, I submit forcefully that a connection will ultimately be established between the subject and the perpetrator of this fraud. It is disgraceful that none of you can see this and that you accept these charlatans at face value," the duke snarled in a shrill contemptuous pitch.

"Sir, among all the guests here tonight you display the most unfortunate set of manners. And under the circumstances, I of course use the term 'guest' lightly, since you attend without benefit of an invitation. And I must declare, here and now, in front of all the Comtesse's guests, that my honor has been impugned, and I feel there can only be but one true recourse," Jean-Marc protested with a surprisingly casual tone. Yet the declaration of 'impugned honor' and 'true recourse' had an unmistakable and resounding resonance in the room. The marquis let the pause hang, for many in the room took this to be a challenge to a duel. Yet to undercut this perception, the light smile which hung on the marquis's face displayed an enigmatic and playful demeanor as he continued.

"If you claim I am an imposter, sir, then the only proof possible is for you yourself to submit to my hypnotic suggestion. If I am unable to deliver results, then I shall publically apologize to you and the gathering. And to further that point, I shall put in your possession, this diamond from ancient India along with its solid gold chain. It is a duke's ransom, and which I have used for years to aid me in this procedure," Jean-Marc announced.

"I fully expect the diamond to also be a fake, sir. But if you desire this manner of satisfaction, I counter your suggestion. If you are unable to hypnotize me, then you will surrender yourself for arrest by the authorities, with charges against you as a sham, a charlatan and a troublemaker. This would presume the likelihood of your spending many months in prison for your fakery, while a complete investigation into your background and activities is performed. At which point, depending on what is revealed in this investigation, you may never leave prison until you are a very, very old man. For I am certain we shall find ugly perfidy hidden behind your pretty clothes and distracting parlor tricks. Are we agreed with the contract, then, with all these good people in witness of it? Sir, do you agree, or are you a coward, a liar and a fraud?"

Excitement murmured through the room, abuzz with the high stakes nature of the wager. Jean-Marc, however, remained unfazed. His serene smile remained on his face, seemingly exuding a sense of bemused satisfaction.

"Sir, one might observe you have biased the wager from a gentleman's bet to one more weighted to a vindictive design. A wager to stake one's very life on the line, isn't it? So to balance the scales, I suggest one additional condition of this bet. If I am able to hypnotize you, then you must agree to allow me to place the suggestion in you that you run naked through the streets of Paris, yelling 'I am the fairy princess of the sacred goddess Isis and I pray to her undying glory daily.' I think that would make the risk and the stakes comparatively even on both sides. You must also follow my directions during the procedure and do exactly as I say while undergoing the hypnosis, or this will all indeed be a sham, but one of your making, not mine. Are we agreed, sir?"

The room remained stone silent as all eyes now focused on the duke, who came to realize on some level that he just might have bitten off more than he could chew. If so, it was the smaller, more silent, part of his consciousness, because the dominant personality facing this social setting now craved blood. The thought of seeing this man in the king's prison, without ever again seeing the light of day, was too much a temptation to let more reasonable thoughts intervene. Though he secretly knew a hasty, abrupt and rude departure now could still keep his social status intact, the thought of losing this wager remained inconceivable to him. Granted, to lose this bet, and be required to honor the debt, would result in public humiliation he might never live down. Also, to lose the bet and not fulfill his agreement would besmirch his vaunted honor, which would most certainly affect his standing in the king's circle. Indeed, only a quick retreat now would assure the safest and most sensible route. He was, however, certain this charlatan had no hope of hypnotizing him.

"Agreed," the duke declared boldly.

Jean-Marc smiled slightly. "Very well then, sir. We have a duly witnessed wager. Prepare to be hypnotized."

The marquis then requested the duke approach him, in front of the entire salon, for all the attendees had now assembled to eagerly witness whatever might take place next. With the duke standing before him, and his eyes directed where the marquis instructed him, Jean-Marc then held the diamond pendant and swung it slowly in front of the duke's eyes. At first the duc de St. Pré looked away, around at the gathering, and sensed on some level how deeply he had ventured into uncharted territory. Jean-Marc calmly and insistently encouraged the duke to re-direct his attention to the diamond pendant, which glittered enigmatically in the salon candlelight.

Before long, despite his iron-willed determination to resist any possibility of falling under an unintended influence, the duke became hypnotized. The duc de St. Pré's body relaxed and Jean-Marc explained to the audience that he could not place a suggestion against a subject's character or will. For example, one could not hypnotize someone to commit murder, unless the subject was already inclined toward violence. With the duc de St. Pré, Jean-Marc explained, it was critical to demonstrate the fact that the duke had indeed been hypnotized.

The marquis queried the audience for what might be a suitable suggestion. Some guests joked, while others offered serious recommendations. And finally, Jean-Marc took one suggestion, and modified it somewhat.

The original idea had been for him to have the duke run around the room bare-chested. As a result, Jean-Marc observed to the duke that it was extremely warm in the room, and he might want to remove his elegant coat to help make him more comfortable. The duke complied. Continuing with the suggestion, he told the duke it was still quite hot; and ventured it might be more comfortable for the noble to remove his shirt, mentioning as well that many people would most certainly admire his manly bare-chested form, especially the women present, if he were willing to grace them with this elegant display of "virile magnificence." The audience stood spellbound, expectant at what would occur next. The duke's entourage shifted uncomfortably, already dreading the outcome.

De St. Pré smiled in a preening way as he disrobed his fine silken blouse and showed his chest, flexing for the audience, who applauded. He of course took the applause as an affirmation of his extreme manliness, and encouraged by Jean-Marc, took a flourishing bow.

The marquis then whispered something very specific in his ear, to which the duke nodded pleasantly in agreement. Stepping back, he then spoke to the duke indicating the temperature in the room was cooling down, quite quickly, and it would most likely be advisable for the duke to re-don his clothing, to which the duke complied.

Once dressed, and again standing in front of the audience, Jean-Marc explained that when he clapped his hands the duc de St. Pré would return to his normal state and have no memory of what had just transpired. Indeed, the marquis suggested, it would seem as though, from the duke's perspective, that the duke had successfully resisted any attempt at Jean-Marc's hypnosis. And with that, the marquis clapped his hands.

The duke reassumed his imperious manner, staring at Jean-Marc with impatience. An expectant silence gripped the room.

"**W**ell, sir? Will you attempt this charlatanry or not? The wager has been placed. It's too late to back out of it now," the duke declared with clear and threatening irritation.

The audience burst into applause, to which the duke glanced around quickly and observed, "It would appear any applause is premature, since you have yet done nothing, sir."

Jean-Marc bowed gracefully and stood again with a smile. "I have done what I can, my lord. You have indeed shown great strength of body and will. To attempt any further endeavors with you would, I fear, only bring about the same results." And he bowed again, to which the audience renewed their resounding applause, some offering "Bravo!" to their approbation. Any who did not stand before did so now, some coming up to him to shake his hand.

"Our wager, sir: You must submit to me," the duke insisted indignantly over those congratulating the marquis.

"Indeed, the results of this unfortunate bet are confirmed, sir. And all will certainly expect the loser to honor the wager. All in due course, sir."

Jean-Marc turned his back on the duke as the noble's valet immediately approached and conversed with him very quietly and confidentially. As they spoke, an elderly and elegantly dressed woman in her eighties approached Jean-Marc with a sense of wonder and confusion.

"Is it really you? That is not possible... Sir, do you have a close relative, possibly your father, who is known as the Comte de Saint Germain? For the resemblance is exact and uncanny," the Countesse d'Adhémar exclaimed with intense curiosity.

Jean-Marc turned to her; and after the shortest moment,

he smiled, then took the elderly lady's hand and kissed it.

"Countesse d'Adhémar, I am honored to see you again, after these many years."

"But it cannot be! The Count de Saint Germain I knew forty years ago looked exactly as you do today, sir." The countess seemed disoriented at being in such close proximity to this sphinx-like character.

"Indeed, if my humble memory serves me correctly, we last met in Venice. You had been considering the purchase of a property overlooking the Lago di Garda. You had concerns about the welfare of your daughter, Camille, who was twelve at the time. She suffered from symptoms of a high fever combined with uncontrollable shaking in the lower limbs. I recommended a selection of medicinal herbs, as well as the proper way to prepare them for her. I did not see you after that occasion. I trust Camille fared well with her malady," Jean-Marc expressed with sincere concern.

"Why, yes, your medicinal treatment was the perfect remedy. She recovered completely within a week; and she has since brought me five beautiful grandchildren, one of whom has married, and we expect our first great grandchild in the fall. But, sir, all this is simply impossible. Our meeting took place at least forty years ago, and you have not changed at all."

"We all change, Countess. For some the changes are less apparent and slower in being evident to observers. The changes, however, endure nonetheless."

"But you should be my age, if not older. I don't understand."

"So much in this world holds mysteries we fail to comprehend, and it has been one of my goals to dispel that absence of knowledge. I am indeed quite an old man, Countess, but one hopes it does not make you think any less of me," Jean Marc replied gracefully.

Behind Jean-Marc, the indignant duke had impatiently waved his valet aside, ignoring the aide's deferential counsel, and advanced to press his point, intent on claiming his victory in the most public and humiliating way possible with Jean-Marc. His two noble companions of the evening, the Russian and the Brit, however, pulled him aside to strongly advise him to reconsider. Jean-Marc glanced over at the duke and noted a widening of the duke's eyes in disbelief as the King's man listened to his companions. The duke responded in a quiet agitated denial to their disclosures. Meanwhile, another gentleman guest of the salon approached Jean-Marc and offered his hand.

"I am not sure you remember me, sir." The elegantly attired gentleman spoke respectfully, but with a clear sense of wonder and amusement at the evening's festivities.

Jean-Marc peered at him briefly, then smiled and bowed. "Ah, yes, Baron Dominique Vivant Denon. You accompanied General Napoleon with the *Commission des Sciences et des Arts* with the *Armée d'Orient*, and your illustrations of Egypt, as well as your excellent descriptions in *Travels in Upper and Lower Egypt*, stand as invaluable resources and treasured contributions to the knowledge of Mankind. Your first volumes of *Descriptions of Egypt* left me eager to see the final outcome of your efforts. I possess the complete collection of your prodigious authorship. It is an honor to see you again, sir," Jean-Marc spoke as he shook the baron's hand.

To the side, Jean-Marc noticed the duke ordering his

valet to go on some errand, to which the marquis frowned slightly.

Denon, meanwhile, expressed equal pleasure with seeing Jean-Marc and described the circumstances of their last meeting. "As we moved on with Napoleon and the main body of his army, south to the grand and mythic location of the Great Pyramid outside Cairo, you stayed behind in Alexandria. Do I recall correctly? You were with a detachment of surveyors and excavators, engaged in what I felt was a most unfortunate and possibly unexciting task, to map the location of the underground canals of the city and evaluate their condition. We, in the meanwhile, went on to see the rich treasures of Upper Egypt. I remember feeling sorry for you and your loss of opportunity. Being so close to the great venerable temples, but compelled to stay behind in Alexandria, which is barely even being in Egypt. Were you ever able to see the great pyramids and the Upper Nile, sir?"

Jean-Marc smiled with gratitude. "Yes, Baron Denon, it has been my good fortune to have seen most of the great structures of ancient Egypt. Unfortunately, however, my original goal in Alexandria remains unfulfilled. I shall one day hope to return to that mythical port city to study its mysteries in more intimate detail."

By this time, the duc de St. Pré's attendant had returned, and with him, a dueling sabre, which the valet handed to the impatient duke. Armed and dangerous now, the duke spoke loudly, finally gaining the complete attention of all in attendance.

"Sir, I demand satisfaction! You have insulted me, and this wrong cannot, nor will not, be ignored!"

Jean-Marc peered over at him casually and at the

sheathed sword in his challenger's hand.

"Indeed, sir, I have done my best to ignore you, yet this method of dealing with your vexing and irritating pretense was obviously misguided. We all make mistakes. Luckily, mine has been comparatively minor. As it relates to satisfaction, sir, I submit that your departure now would satisfy the majority of those in attendance tonight. And if you do so with a pledge never to return to this household, I will forgive you the debt you owe me," Jean-Marc offered magnanimously.

"I owe you nothing but the cutting edge of my sword! I challenge you to a duel, sir! And if you refuse, you shall reveal yourself as the coward you are!" The duke took a pair of gloves from his attendant, stepped across to Jean-Marc, and attempted to slap him across the face with them. Jean-Marc's reactions, however, were startlingly swift. He caught the duke's hand well before the blow landed, quickly relieved him of the gloves, threw them over his shoulder with one hand and kept control of the duke's wrist with the other. The marquis's light manner darkened noticeably as his eyes riveted on the duke's. Yet he did not lose control of his emotions, nor did his winning smile depart. His eyes narrowed, and he spoke quietly as he released the duke's hand from his surprisingly powerful grasp. The Marquis Jean-Marc Baptiste de Rennes's voice resonated across the rapt silence of the room with unequivocal eloquence.

"Sir, you are a man completely without honor. You have lost a wager and owe a debt in front of all present who will bear witness to that simple fact. Yet to attempt a clumsy cover-up regarding your undeniable obligation to me, you in turn claim to be wronged, when indeed you are the offending party. You bandy about inane claims of how you would fix the French education system, based on your nitwitted perception of the Prussian-Hegelian model, which reduces humanity to little more than obedient slaves. You have wormed your way into the King's circle and bullied your way into this salon. At some point, someone must stand in your path and simply say 'enough is enough.' Your claim to noble blood is merely the byproduct of a financial transaction less than ten years old, where your father rescued a deeply indebted viscount from Picardy and gained a noble title in the bargain. Your family's wealth came from illicit smuggling with the English enemy at the time France was at war. You and your family have never been loyal to France, but only to your own selfish interests of power and privilege. You, sir, are unworthy of the company you keep with the King's friends, and anyone who recommends you to His Royal Highness should be marked a fool or a traitor. And after tonight, I expect that perception to become a widespread reality."

The room surged with commentary over Jean-Marc's brave speech opposing someone who stood so tall in the King's circle, at least up until this point. The moment of truth in the conflict, however, drew near; and all knew that brave words might not be enough for the stakes which played out now.

"Your brazen and foolhardy words only delay the inevitable. I repeat: I challenge you to a duel, sir, and I will not allow refusal!" The duke gestured impatiently at one of the Comtesse de Narbonne's servants. "Bring the dueling swords from the count's library."

A moment of indecision ensued as the servant looked to

the countess questioningly. She in turn put her hand on Jean-Marc's arm. "Jean-Marc, this has gone much too far. If you apologize…"

"My gracious hostess, and dearest friend, you know as we all do, that the apology should come from an individual who has made it clear that shall not come to pass. I therefore must accept his challenge and this duel."

The excitement in the room pulsed with electricity as two dueling swords were brought from the library. Jean-Marc tested the sabres with a demeanor that revealed to the observant eye a manner very familiar with these weapons; and he finally chose the one which suited him best. As Jean-Marc did so, the duke removed his elegant jacket, eager for blood.

"You have tangled with the wrong lion, sir. A ruthless lion who has known the satisfaction of challenger's blood on his sword more times than I care to describe," the duke boasted. "I would also have you know in advance that I studied with Master Armand-Philippe d'Onsange. And I am considered a master of the blade by many. If you concede immediately, and surrender so I may hand you over to the authorities I'll spare your pitiful life. For this offense has gone far beyond first blood, sir," the duke declared with wild-eyed intensity. "This duel is to the death. And I frankly hope you do not concede. For I am in need of some exercise tonight, and slaying you now would be just the thing to give this wasted evening some meaning."

"My, my, you're indeed long-winded. And yet on the

point of exercise, I agree it's a good time. It helps with the digestion of all these wonderful foods our hostess has offered to us tonight."

Jean-Marc gazed at the duke casually as he too took off his jacket and spoke with knowing bemusement. "And yes, I know Master Armand-Philippe d'Onsange; not a bad teacher. But, sadly, he is hardly a shadow of the true sword master, his great father, Michel-Philippe d'Onsange, with whom I trained extensively some years ago. But I confess I came to Master d'Onsange's training hall somewhat later in my growth as a swordsman, having studied the many ways of the sword for quite a few years in India, China, and Japan as well. And before long, my tutelage with Master d'Onsange became more of an exchange of techniques among equals. He was a man who recognized skill in others and carried no ego, nor pride. Yet from what I hear, his son did not benefit from that mold of wisdom, and has been preoccupied with social position and training only those who advanced his perceived place in the hierarchy of society. He's also something of a shameless sycophant for hire, as I understand. As a result, the quality of his teachings, I must confess, has been gravely compromised in my view. You studied under a flawed master, and so I suspect what you bring to this challenge will only deliver further embarrassment to you and your family name. You may still withdraw, sir, with the proper apology."

"You're bluffing, sir! If you think these cheap claims will save you from the bite of my blade, you're more of a fool that I thought!"

"My purpose in telling you this, sir," Jean-Marc spoke patiently, "was to offer you one last chance to save any vestiges of dignity you have left. Whatever techniques you use, will certainly be familiar to me, and they might even be ones I taught to your master's father. But you, sir, will most likely be unfamiliar with the wealth of technique I possess. And I will draw upon my vast knowledge as I see fit to prevail in the moment. You have one advantage, however, sir. And that is that I have pledged never to take a life, nor to draw blood in anger.... So if I do indeed cut you, and make you bleed, please recognize that it's with the most pleasant and humorous disposition that I do so," Jean-Marc mocked. A number of people laughed at the remarkable display of blithe spirit in so deadly a setting.

The two men, now in shirt sleeves, stood opposite each other at sword's length; the duke eager for blood, Jean-Marc relaxed, yet observant.

"This is to the death, sir!" the duke declared loudly, intending to intimidate.

"To the death of your reputation, I would concede that, sir, however specifics of the rest remain to be seen." Jean-Marc smiled, studying his opponent's stance, sword held wide and low at a curious angle, knees bent in an anticipatory lunge. He observed: "And judging by your stance, it appears you intend your opening attack to be the 'Swooping Sparrow Cut', sweeping the opponent's point aside with a swift circular upward block, and then a quick downward point strike to the right jugular. Very bold and quite impetuous, I dare say, intending a mortal blow at first strike."

This uncanny and astute observation infuriated the duke, who immediately lunged into his assault, which indeed he had already committed to in his mind, instead of reassessing his prey. The attacking strike's technique unfolded exactly as Jean-Marc predicted.

Jean-Marc's response was masterful and lightning-fast. First he let out a robust and startling shout, side-stepped simultaneously and executed a deft, tight and powerful circular upward parrying movement which resulted in the disarming of the sword from the duke's hand as it flew into the air among the enthralled gathering, who quickly stepped out of the way as the sabre clattered unceremoniously to the floor. Jean-Marc's sword point, however, now rested directly on the duke's throat.

"Indeed it was the 'Swooping Sparrow Cut', and as you saw a demonstration of one of the many effective defenses against this sadly outdated technique."

Wild applause broke out in the gathering.

Keeping the point pressed on the duke's neck, yet not breaking the skin and drawing blood, Jean-Marc smiled to his audience and elucidated. "The shout is termed a *'kiai'* in Japanese. Its function is delivering a simultaneous attacking energy to both the spirit and the body of the opponent. As you see, it momentarily stunned my adversary with distraction while I engaged in my defensive technique."

Lowering his point, Jean-Marc then turned to the duke and offered his hand in a good-natured shake. "Unfortunately your choice for an opening foray was gravely ill-considered under the circumstances, especially when so clearly anticipated. Hopefully you'll now see room for improvement, and possibly consider a new teacher. I can offer you recommendations."

The crowd laughed and applauded loudly, emboldened by the duke's humiliation, as he heard 'Drooping Sparrow' and 'Stooping Rooster' jokes already echoing through the assemblage.

Infuriated, the duke gestured with dismissive hostility at the offer of a hand shake from Jean-Marc, as he barged on with belligerent and aggressive talk.

"You cheated, sir! You used cheap carnival tricks to gain advantage! Had I had a proper start, you would be lying on the floor in a pool of your blood. Enough joking and cheap lucky stunts! If you're man enough to continue this contest, you may have a remote chance at winning my respect."

"Winning your respect is the last thing I seek, sir; for this is an unattainable and frankly unworthy goal. However, assuring the fundamental and undivided loss of your respect within Parisian society—your complete humiliation—holds great appeal for me. And it appears the only way to stop this irritating fly is to slap it. So, take your weapon, if you insist. And now, I shall only use the scant few methods of swordplay to which your diminutive experience is limited. I shall only use techniques from the younger Master d'Onsange's paltry repertoire, for you are apparently incapable of greater challenge. Let's see then, what you are *not* made of… *sir*."

Never before in the experience of those attending this elite salon had they heard the word 'sir' spoken to communicate so profound an insult.

The duel began in earnest. The duke pressed every advantage, to which on each attack, Jean-Marc parried, within the techniques of the younger Master d'Onsange's training. The marquis even bantered with various guests as the duel progressed—observing the techniques both contestants used, with encyclopedic knowledge and authority—which only fueled the duke's rage further. And finally the duke succeeded in penetrating Jean-Marc's defenses so that he slightly cut the marquis's arm. In response, Jean-Marc burst out laughing, without anger, but spoke in a chilling taunt.

"So now we have reached blood for blood. So be it, but without anger," Jean-Marc announced. "Instead, with love and joy!"

With lightning moves, all within the repertoire of the younger d'Onsange, which he had not shown up to this point, Jean-Marc succeeded in easily penetrating the duke's defenses, cutting his shirt open, and slightly drawing blood on the chest. He then used the side of his blade to slap the duke with resounding force on one side of the face, leaving a deep red welt, and then on the other side of the face, leaving another welt. Then he swiftly cut the belt to the duke's breeches; and, with one final swoop, he again disarmed the duke, who now stood shirt open and with his breeches at his ankles before the salon, in momentary shock.

"Remember: 'Blue Apples Feed the Hungry Soul,' " Jean-Marc quoted specifically to the startled duke, who then instantly succumbed to a post-hypnotic suggestion. His manner changed to an almost effeminate saunter as he broke into a sing-song voice.

"I am the fairy princess of Isis, and I kneel at her feet! I pray to her daily!" the duke chanted again and again with melodic affectation while he wiggled his hips suggestively allowing his shirt to fall off his shoulders as he stepped away from the breeches at his feet, now leaving him completely naked, sauntering before the gathering.

The room burst into laughter and applause, with the

duke, fully naked, bowing to them, responding to his perception of their appreciation of his singing. His valet and companions witnessed this fiasco in total mortification.

"I believe the debt has been paid, and we may consider this matter closed," Jean-Marc announced to further resounding applause and pats on the back. He then turned to the duke, clapped his hands three times, and shouted. "Get dressed, duc de St. Pré. Your social downfall has only just begun."

The duke snapped out of his hypnotic state and stared at all the faces laughing mirthfully as he stood stark naked before the cream of Paris society. His valet ran to cover him with clothing. The duke glared back with impotent rage at Jean-Marc before being quickly led out of the room by his valet and companions, to which Jean-Marc waved in a friendly manner.

Without warning, a voice called loudly and urgently from the doorway of the salon: "Napoleon is on the march with thousands! He will be in Paris in a matter of days!"

All attention turned to a young man in the doorway—the Viscount René de Narbonne, the son of the count and countess—who appeared disheveled, having ridden some distance straight to the salon. His mother crossed to him, looking very concerned.

"What are you saying, René?" she inquired urgently.

"Mother, Napoleon has escaped from Elba and landed near Cannes with eleven hundred men. He marches north to Paris. Legions join him along the way. Some say he already has a force of over five thousand. Some say more. The news is less than two hours old. It just arrived by carrier pigeon."

The room burst into pandemonium. Some guests

cheered; others found themselves stunned and clearly disturbed by the news. All knew that conditions in the city would be drastically different in a very short time. The salon quickly dispersed, with guests taking their leave to attend to new matters of urgency.

At one table, members of the *Trois Frères* lodge of the Freemason Society conversed in a lively exchange with members of the Nine Sister Lodge. The discussion at this Freemason table ranged from the recent edicts of the new Bourbon king, and what that meant with this new development of Napoleon's reappearance onto the capricious stage of history.

Republicans and Bonapartists debated the royalists. They confronted the inevitable variables of politics and power now actively thrust back in play: Would Napoleon even reach Paris? Might it truly be possible he could take power again? With so much ill-will generated by the royalists in the Bourbon return to power, could Napoleon's reemergence re-enforce the precious Rights of Man for which so many had fought so hard? Might the end result be a constitutional monarchy like England? How would this development affect the Pope and the Church of Rome with its newly resuscitated Inquisition? How would the combined forces of Europe, who had joined together before to face Napoleon, respond now? Those as well as a host of other issues were argued back and forth offering no clear resolution, with many unanswered questions still in the air regarding this seismic development.

With the subject of the Pope's influential power in European politics a relevant theme of the discussion, the talk digressed onto the topic of the Vatican Archives, which had been housed in Paris since Napoleon's seizure of this invaluable trove of documents during his occupation of Rome some years before.

One participant observed the Vatican Archives contained documents and artifacts the Church did not want people to know about, and that the Pope's representatives continued to work tirelessly, with the cooperation of the Bourbon royalty, to get the thousands of crates of volumes safely back to Rome.

Another Freemason in attendance recounted that the famed occultist Count Alessandro di Cagliostro, founder of an Egyptian esoteric Masonic chapter had made repeated claims that rare age-old records existed in the archives— ancient papyri dating back to Egypt and the time of the pharaohs which originated from the legendary Hermes Trismegistus. Count Cagliostro had repeatedly petitioned the Napoleonic authorities to gain access to these files, but to no avail.

And with the Bourbon leadership more recently in control, and overseen by clerics of Rome, all activity at the palace where the Vatican files were stored was directed at cataloging them properly before transport back to Rome—a mammoth endeavor, months long in the undertaking. One member ventured that with Napoleon coming, maybe all that would change and Count Cagliostro might renew his quest for these mysterious alchemical documents.

Another participant—a distant cousin by marriage to the Comte, who remained silent for most of the conversation and known to have close ties to various royal families—observed: "They will send a force to meet Napoleon. He will not get north of the Auvergne, if he gets that far. He cannot succeed in this madness." He then placed his hand respectfully and affectionately on the Comtesse's arm and offered the following advice, as he pointed out a small bronze bust of Napoleon—set on dark green marble sitting on a nearby table. "At this point in time, I suggest it might be advisable to store such pieces of artwork as this in a safe place. Displaying it so openly at times like these may bring unwanted attention."

Smiling inscrutably in reply, the Comtesse exhibited grace, as always, as she stood over the table, then took note of Jean-Marc, who had been standing more in the background, listening politely to the conversation. He came to her, bowed to her and kissed her hand.

"It appears the perpetual march of history has taken yet another turn down a new road. The next days will reveal themselves as interesting ones indeed," Jean-Marc offered.

"Well, I suppose if one's soirée is to be interrupted unexpectedly, this is most likely among the best of excuses," the Comtesse observed with a breezy humor concealing a sense of distracted concern.

"At least we achieved our primary goal of the evening, to neutralize the duc de St. Pré," Jean-Marc replied, attempting to brighten her spirits.

"I cannot believe you played him with such ease. You read his character like a book, Jean-Marc. He could not resist imposing himself into my party once he heard how socially desirable an invitation to attend this evening's festivities was. Planting the seed of awareness by a pair of wags at his social club made him burn with determination to attend by whatever means. Character is fate. His own selfish drives compelled him to this humbling outcome which you designed and predicted so aptly."

"And with the duke's neutralization within the King's circle, and negation of his undue influence, so too passes his ugly plan to transform France's system of education into a program essentially supporting slavery. If I never see him again, that will meet with my satisfaction. I'm sure, however, he will not let this humiliation rest. He'll seek revenge. Tomorrow I would expect."

"You must take care, Jean-Marc. Even if his position at court stands severely compromised, he remains quite capable of directing serious harm your way. He certainly now wants you dead."

"It would not be the first, nor will it be the last time I must contend with such lethal hounds of rage," Jean-Marc remarked lightly. He then took her hand more earnestly with gratitude. "And I must thank you as well for the delivery of the documents you helped procure. They'll be invaluable to our work, and most timely indeed."

Jean-Marc indicated his imminent departure, while repeating his gratitude.

"When will we see you again, Jean-Marc?"

The marquis smiled enigmatically. "My dearest friend, the winds of destiny are most difficult to read."

Marquis de Rennes Apartments
4th Arrondissement, Paris, France
3 March, 1815 AD – After Midnight

Jean-Marc returned to his lodgings with a sense of great urgency. The unexpected news of Napoleon's dramatic escape from Elba and bold march on Paris represented a potentially overpowering threat to the status quo, and immediately altered Jean-Marc's plans. While he remained essentially neutral to the news of Napoleon's audacious act, Jean-Marc was concerned how the consequences of this development might cause unforeseen and potentially detrimental complications for his current painstaking preparations.

Upon entry to his apartments, he made his way to a back

room, which had originally been a kitchen, now set up as a laboratory of sorts, with glass beakers, as well as a sizable kiln oven. Here he found his valet, Roger, in a back corner at a worktable with lantern and candle lighting, putting the finishing touches to a project he had been working on. The packet with vermillion velvet ribbon lay open beside him. Three official documents with large red Vatican wax seals at the bottom, as well as other sundry official French documents, were laid out and arranged on the workbench beside Roger. Jean-Marc picked up the Vatican papers with a sense of sober distraction.

"How goes it?" Jean-Marc inquired.

"I completed the lost wax copies of the two seals they use, created the clay mold, and I'm baking it in the kiln. It will be ready soon. I can then pour the copper original in short order," Roger replied, gesturing to the small iron cauldron of molten copper which steeped in a fire he had burning in the large fireplace nearby.

"And the transit documents themselves?" Jean-Marc asked.

"They're all drawn up. As you know, finding the right paper was something of a challenge." Roger smiled, proud to share his account of an accomplishment embellished by his personal habit of myth-making wherever possible. "But I happened to know a sweet little woman who works in a paper shop. After bit of charm and persuasion, she let me into her master's secret stash of parchments which he only intended for his customers of the noblest station," Roger reported—more bragged—with a telling smile.

Focused on business, Jean-Marc did not respond to the implication of Roger's extracurricular activities which had seemingly facilitated achievement of his goals.

"Once this is done, we must remove everything essential here. And then tomorrow you must place yourself in the location we discussed. Time is of the essence. I expect the duke to respond with some vindictive action before the coming day has passed. We must remain in movement from this time forward," Jean-Marc counseled.

Roger spoke as he worked at the bench, putting the final touches on a parchment document with his pen. "Your ploy with the duke was successful then?"

"Success in any endeavor tends to result in an equal and opposing reaction. Judging by the success of my plan, I expect a quite forceful and emphatic response. I believe, though, our goal was achieved. The duke has been neutralized politically and he's now the laughing stock of Paris society. He has no way to contain the gossip which will ensue as a result," Jean-Marc assessed.

"I regret I had to miss the humiliating festivities," Roger commented with an amused smile.

"I will share with you the details when we are at leisure to do so, Roger. But for now, we must maintain our sense of urgency."

Jean-Marc then shared the news of Napoleon's reported march north to Paris and its potential effect on all their planning. Roger immediately shifted his focus to a more professional and urgent workflow, as Jean-Marc began to sift through the personal papers he needed to burn, and those he must take with him.

After some time, during which he packed all his essential belongings, Jean-Marc checked with Roger on what progress he had made. Roger's work to craft lost wax copies of the seals which appeared on the Vatican documents—and in turn fashion clay copies from the lost wax versions which he refined with expert touches of a sculpting tool before he baked the molds in the kiln—ultimately resulted in the creation of two hard clay molds to receive molten copper for producing the needed Vatican seals. Roger also produced an official-looking document with a small printing press that had been set up in the corner of the apartment. Jean-Marc studied the documents and nodded with satisfaction.

The apartment, which faced out over a back street, stood about a half mile from the Seine River. While he had turned down an offer of lodgings in a much more prestigious and picturesque part of the city, overlooking the river, for an extremely reasonable rate—through the generosity of the Comtesse de Narbonne's connections—the marquis chose these rooms for an important logistical reason. Through the many years when he had to vacate a place quickly, he found being near a river or a shoreline limited his options for escape routes. Not that he always needed them.

Jean-Marc had, however, always studied the various avenues of egress. And as a matter of best practice, he even placed in a secure and hidden location requisite resources—money, jewels and other essentials—in case he could not return to his *pied-à-terre*. He studied the routes across the rooftops and knew the dead-end alleys in the streets below like the back of his hand, and he had also worked out scenarios where hidden passageways afforded the opportunity to make it seem as though he had disappeared, leaving pursuers searching, using valuable time, until they found the way he might have taken or lost his trail altogether. This was how Jean-Marc thought and how he lived.

Tonight, however, he planned a more orderly departure from the city. And if all was well, he might even be leaving tomorrow with everything he had set his sights on. Napoleon's fast-moving initiative from the south, however, made this all the more urgent, since the new and highly uncertain political situation in the country had undoubtedly thrown much into flux. Those who he might have considered allies today could show new colors as a lethal enemy tomorrow.

"Once you complete this task, I will need you to close up the lab. Take the essentials and leave the rest."

"Yes, sire," Roger responded.

"And tomorrow, you must be posted below the window as we discussed. I cannot emphasize this enough. I don't know when I might arrive, but there can be no hesitation, no waiting and searching on my part. In a moment, it will all take place; and once achieved, you must retire immediately and with discretion. Understood?" Jean-Marc pressed his assistant.

"I understand completely, sire. And if I may say, I long for our return to Languedoc. I miss the lands there. This city life and airs people take on—especially the women—it's all a bit too affected for my taste. And everyone lives so close together, where they're continuously forced to contend with each other's odors; and yet they all seem to seek that hovering proximity here. City life is a form of insanity if you ask me. Give me the fresh air of the open road!"

Jean-Marc laughed lightly, then studied the work Roger labored over and frowned slightly with concern.

"I fear you'll be up all night with this, yet there's no other way."

"Have no fear, Master. A loss of sleep has little concern to me. The mission remains a great one, and I am honored to be at your service in its completion. And with its conclusion, the sooner we may depart this strange, admittedly stylish, yet very mean-spirited city, the better."

Roger smiled and returned to his work with diligence and purpose.

Environs of Soubise Palace
3rd Arrondissement, Paris, France
3 March, 1815 AD – Morning Hour

Riding alongside the Seine River and leading a small contingent of sword-wielding ruffians on horseback, the duc de St. Pré chose the most direct route from his palace to the address of the Marquis Jean-Marc Baptiste de Rennes's apartments, located less than ten minutes away now by his estimation.

The duke had aggressively sought information identifying the marquis's location. He finally attained it with some difficulty through one of his operatives, and not a small bribe, from one of the Comtesse de Narbonne's minor and newer servants. The duke's fury had not subsided; far from it. Indeed the rage only burned even hotter with the impatience of revenge pumping in his heart, demanding satisfaction. The duke had not yet paused to take stock, or completely weigh the impact of his humiliation, and with it the irreparable impairment to his standing within the King's circle.

The thought of effecting preemptive damage control—possibly some prudent defensive politicking, or a smart action to attempt gaining influence over the perception of how others might be seeing his position in the elite inner circle around the King—had not even remotely occurred to him. What he did know was he would kill this man who had so offended and dishonored him the preceding night, and of that fact no doubt existed. St. Pré remained steadfast in his determination to exterminate this man, and he had no foibles of pride that he might need the ruthless crew of lowlifes he had hired late last night—again at no small cost—who rode with him now, to achieve that merciless end to the nefarious marquis's life.

Ahead, on the narrow cobblestoned street, a lone bearded priest in long dark brown robes, wearing a broad-brimmed black hat popular with the more common class clergy in Rome, sat riding a mule at a slow pace and he was coated with dust from the road. Sighting the approaching group, and plodding unhurriedly in the opposite direction, the priest attempted to guide his mule out of the way of the hustling group. The priest's large stubborn creature, however, seemed determined to maintain its own path down the middle of the alley, causing the duke to pull back on his horse and yell at the clergyman in frustrated fury.

"Get your stupid beast out of the way and let us pass,

priest!" The duke shouted belligerently as he gestured impatiently. "Move! We have urgent business!"

Preoccupied with controlling his mule, the priest waved deferentially and called back to the duke in Italian. *"Sì, sì! Perdone mi, Signore molto Importante!"*

The priest struggled with the reins of his mule and finally gained mastery of his willful beast as the group surged by the cleric, close enough to brush aggressively against him. The mule continued to be somewhat unruly as it whinnied shrilly in protest, the priest's down-turned face remained obscured by the brim of his hat while he managed the reins. Completely preoccupied, the duke brusquely pushed passed and went on ahead to his targeted destination. The priest offered a good-natured wave while the group rode on, and gave them the sign of the cross as they picked up their pace and trotted on out of sight around the corner.

A few blocks on, with only ten more minutes of riding at his leisurely pace, the seemingly road-weary priest finally sighted the approach to his destination. Visibly glad to be ending whatever journey he had been on, the priest arrived at the gates of a grand palace, the *Hôtel de Soubise*. There, along with his modest minimum of belongings strapped to the beast's back in two weathered canvas bags, he presented himself to the two royal guards. With something of an officious manner, one guard checked his papers, which appeared in order; and he let the humble cleric pass. Studying the mule with a sense of imperious disdain as the priest rode by; the second guard instructed the new arrival.

"Go to the side entrance and tie up there. That's where the servants and deliveries are received."

"Grazie... Merci, monsieur," the pious priest replied, as he

and his mule quietly rode on.

The guard noticed one characteristic about the priest he had let pass into the inner courtyard of the palace—a curious facial detail: a white right eyebrow

At the service entrance to the palace, Father Giovanni Baptisti presented his travel documents, as well as Vatican assignment and transfer papers, to Padre Federico DiScotti. An elderly member of the Roman clergy, dressed in a Jesuit's cassock, DiScotti studied the papers with distraction as he also glanced at Father Baptisti's dusty robes of the Franciscan order. They spoke in Italian to each other.

"We had no notice you were coming, Father Baptisti," Padre DiScotti revealed.

"Oh, no? I was informed before my departure that the Vatican messenger would have reported here, possibly at least a week before my arrival. Notice of my assignment would come by a special arrangement through the ambassador's pouch, which offered the quickest and most reliable way to assure communication of this in a timely manner to you."

Father DiScotti nodded knowingly. "There have been problems with the road. And now with everything affected by Napoleon's march north, communications are apparently less reliable."

"Napoleon?" Father Baptisti inquired with concerned interest.

The elder Jesuit priest explained the news which came in late last night; and how now a growing sense of uncertainty pervaded the disposition of the Vatican Archives which had been seized from Rome by Napoleon in 1810 and stored now in the Soubise Palace.

Padre DiScotti lamented. "Napoleon, in his brusque authoritarian treatment of the Vatican, besmirched the Church's prestige, privilege and power. And, as you know, with all that, he also took one of their most invaluable possessions and a source of their power as well: all their records—the precious Vatican Library.

"It would appear Napoleon saw his own uses for that power," Father Baptisti observed.

"Indeed, and yet after Napoleon's fall, the Bourbon king, a loyal Catholic, promised to return the library to the Pope," DiScotti observed as he continued. "However, the logistics of the task have proven to be profoundly daunting. Well over three thousand large crates of books and papers had been taken from Rome. And complicating the challenge, Napoleonic scholars reorganized the inventory according to their own logic. So accounting for the contents of the archives from the Vatican's perspective, organizing the records, and cross-referencing them with their original inventory records remains an arduous task for our Vatican specialists, of which very few reside here in Paris."

"I have all the skills you require. I might be able to help," the new arrival offered.

Father DiScotti stated that, since Father Baptisti was not expected, he would have to go and meet with the senior cleric in charge of the Vatican Archives—Monsignor Gaetano Marini—to determine how the new arrival could be best put to use. Padre DiScotti observed with professional courtesy, however, and with some reflexive camaraderie for a fellow Italian, that with the daunting task the clergy faced with the archives, "It will be good to have another pair of Roman eyes and hands to do the Lord's work among so many of the godless, especially during these uncertain times in this pagan city."

Father Baptisti humbly volunteered that he was fluent in all of the ancient Biblical languages, Latin, Aramaic, Greek, Hebrew and Coptic, asking if that might be of any help to determine how he could best be of assistance in the archives.

Reflexively guarded against revealing how impressed he was, Father DiScotti nonetheless indicated such expertise in this array of languages may be useful since the breadth of volumes lay sprawled in a maddening state of disarray and complexity. "It is staggeringly vast, and in varying stages of re-organization. And based on what misguided work Napoleon's men already performed—and what the French failed to re-catalog from the original existing format of Vatican organization—I expect Monsignor Marini may very possibly welcome a new set of scholarly, learned and intelligent eyes with such polylingual skills. The cataloging schema stands in an infernal state of chaos. It's a labyrinth of confusion, and it must be put in order before the archives are shipped back to Rome. Critical missing documents are being sought out straightaway, and we must determine if they're lost on this side of the journey to aid in their possible provenance and immediate retrieval. I swear I've not had a sound night's sleep since I arrived," the Jesuit confessed.

"My prayer is that I may lighten your load, even in the smallest way. My sacred mandate is to assist in the mission of Yesu the Nazarene to the best of my abilities and to use whatever gifts I have to offer to that end," Father Baptisti replied with respectful modesty.

Inside Monsignor Gaetano Marini's office, the senior white-haired and wiry Jesuit clergy member studied the priest's Vatican travel documents very closely. As Prefect of the Vatican Archives, nothing transpired without Monsignor Marini's knowledge or approval.

"We were not informed of your coming, Father Baptisti," the monsignor stated with distraction as he continued to study the paperwork of the new arrival.

"Father DiScotti indicated the message which I understood should have preceded me to announce my arrival has apparently not come through with the Vatican messenger," Father Baptisti offered and then continued with his best assessment of the situation. "I can only guess the courier assigned to the Italian embassy was possibly detained by unforeseen circumstances. Father DiScotti explained the news of Napoleon's march north. I can't help but think the courier may have been on the same path and detained beyond his abilities to proceed."

The monsignor's slight nod indicated that Father Baptisti's assessment of the situation made sense; but the senior cleric was not a man easily sold on anything unless he accounted for all ambiguities. "This is highly irregular, Father. While we certainly could use help here... Even though their king ordered them to assist us in any way to facilitate transfer of the records back to Rome, these French archive administrators are very, very difficult. They seem to have an inherent attitude that we're stealing from them. And hence, everything requires repeating over and over again, because they feign misunderstanding, despite the fact that I and my holy companions speak French fluently—though it is admittedly with something of an Italian accent. They press that detail to their frustrating advantage, continually causing delay after delay."

"*Je pense qu'il serait possible que je puisse vous aider à résoudre ce problème,*" Father Baptisti offered with impeccable French, completely without accent.

The monsignor was impressed. "You are French then, Father Baptisti?"

"No, Your Reverence. With the grace of God, I have a gift of languages. Some say a good ear. I lived in the hills east of Nice and had dealings with the people of the city for some time before taking my holy vows. That was not far from my cousin's family across the frontier in San Remo. I think I picked up some of the 'music' of the French language there in Nice; and with the grace of God, I acquired other qualities of accent along the way on my travels. I listen closely to how people speak, their rhythms, their eccentricities, Your Reverence. I love the spoken word, in all of God's tongues."

The monsignor nodded absently, studying the travel papers yet again, regarding the Vatican seal nostalgically, running his finger over the red wax.

"I miss Rome, Padre. These people—these *Parisians*—are wanton libertines, with no sense of morality. So many have broken their relationship with God. It is a criminal tragedy."

"I hear at their salons they sometimes even glorify ancient gods of Egypt and who knows what other abominations," Father Baptisti observed with sincere concern.

The monsignor nodded, finally smiling at Baptisti. "I think you can be of assistance here, Father. Tomorrow we shall assign you to your tasks. I'll have one of our brothers show you a room where you can clean up, then dine and rest after your long journey. I'm sure you're weary from the road and glad for some respite from your travels, brother."

"Your Reverence, my duty to God is to work. I am here. I am ready. I'll have plenty of time to rest when the day is done. Please put me to work now, so I may fulfill your needs."

The monsignor smiled again and nodded with appreciation at the younger humble priest with the white eyebrow.

Set in the heart of Paris, the grand Soubise Palace was acquired by Napoleon's administration in 1808 and mandated as the location of the Central Imperial Archives of the Empire. When Napoleon conquered Italy, as well as the extensive Papal Estates—a large principality in its own right—he ordered that, along with the many art treasures there, the Vatican Archives from Rome would be shipped to France for study. Three thousand, two hundred and thirty-nine huge wooden chests were transported on a horse-led wagon train out of Italy, at first to Rheims, but ultimately to the Soubise Palace in Paris.

It had been Napoleon's intent to search for any records which might weaken the Pope's power, to fortify his own;

for example the policies and procedures for anointing of bishops. Information in any age was invaluable, and the loss of the archives inflicted a crippling blow to the entire bureaucracy of the Roman Church. With Napoleon's defeat, however, the new Bourbon king quickly granted permission for it to all be returned. Pope Augustus Pius IV immediately sent the Vatican archivists to Paris to facilitate a quick return of the precious records.

Securing the royal permission, however, was the easy part. The logistics of return revealed a nightmare for the Vatican archivists who had to cope with the new filing system created by Napoleon's people, as well as, the French royal archivists, who still considered the documents to be French property. And despite orders, they seemed quite reluctant to part with this treasure trove of historical information and potentially powerful political ammunition for the future.

Jean-Marc originally studied the organization of the archives as best he could at a distance, discreetly interviewing members of the French Imperial archivists during Napoleon's tenure. He even gained brief access on two occasions, under the guise of an administrative clerk, but he had not achieved his ultimate goal. He attained, however, a working knowledge of the filing system.

Jean-Marc knew, for example, that since arriving from Rome in 1810, the Vatican Archives had been re-organized by the French into an alphabetical arrangement of categories: A) *Chartes*; B) *Registres de Bulles, Brefs et Suppliques*; C) *Priviléges, Biens et Prétentions de la Cour de Rome*; D) *Nonciatures et légations*; E) *Secrétairierie d'État*; F) *Daterie*; G) *Chancellerie*; H) *Pénitencerie*; I) *Congrégation du Concile de Trente*;

K) *Congrégation de la Propagande*; L) *Congrégation du Saint Office*; M) *Congrégation des Évênques et des Réguliers*; N) *Congrégation des Rites*; O) *Archives Administratives*; P) *Archives Judiciaires*; Q) *Inventaires, Tables et Répertoires de tout ce qui précède.*

For all of the judicious organization that went into implementing this system, Jean-Marc never found the explanation for the missing letter in the classification list: *J*. He felt there must be material there which would be of great interest, if he could only discover the location and have the time to study whatever might be there.

Jean-Marc's main goal, however, was to access the locality of the *Q* category of archives. On his last day in the archives two years ago, he found by chance an inventory list of these documents, but he had never been able to regain entry to the archives since then. Setting up his admittance today took months of planning, which only finally came together the previous night with the receipt of the sample Vatican traveling papers which he replicated with Roger's help.

The snowy–haired Monsignor Gaetano Marini, Prefect of the Vatican Archives, escorted Father Baptisti down a long hall on the second floor to where his nephew Monsignor Marino Marini, coadjutor of the archives, pored over a list of files as he discussed the strategy for document evacuation with a cleric when his uncle and Baptisti arrived. The younger monsignor, also in Jesuit vestments, glanced up at his uncle, revealing a clear sense of stress, frustration and distraction.

"We've only been able to organize seven wagons and drivers on such short notice. We'll easily need forty, probably more, Uncle. If Napoleon succeeds in his bid for power, we could lose this all again. And *they* do everything possible to impede our progress."

The 'they' the younger monsignor referred to were French archivists, two of whom had just passed his doorway, glancing in with mild self-assured smiles.

"We must make do with what we have and be ready for the contingencies which stand before us, Marino," the elder monsignor intoned. He then gestured to Baptisti. "God has sent us some aid. Father Baptisti just arrived this morning on his journey from Rome, and he insists he's ready to work now, without rest. He is fluent in the classics, and even conversant in Aramaic. These are the kind of priests our Holy Church needs to rebuild the Faith, especially in such godless places as this cursed country."

Finally bringing his eyes to study the new arrival, frowning slightly, the younger monsignor stated: "We were not expecting any new support from Rome, Uncle."

The new arrival replied, "Cardinal Ribossi thought with the magnitude and urgency of the task at hand, having eyes and hands familiar with records and archives, as well as a facility with a broad range of languages, might be of assistance to your needs and requirements." Father Baptisti then inquired, "You mentioned something about Napoleon? Is there more news about this development that I am unaware of, Your Reverence?"

"I have no idea what you know, Father. However, Napoleon has escaped from Elba, and he's marching north, gathering an army on his way. When he landed near Cannes, he had eleven hundred. Now we hear he has thousands," the younger Marino reported, then continued. "So, you say you were sent by Cardinal Ribossi?"

Sensing deeper intent behind the questioning, Jean-Marc treaded carefully with his choice of words.

"That is correct, Your Reverence. Although, I confess I hardly know him. It seems I apparently caught his notice some weeks ago, and he thought my skills could be put to good use here," Jean-Marc explained in his persona as Father Baptisti.

Jean-Marc knew he needed to keep this part of his story vague and general. All he knew of Cardinal Ribossi was that his name appeared on other Vatican travel documents which he obtained the night before. Jean-Marc indeed remembered meeting a Father Carlo Ribossi many years ago in Naples, a squat pugnacious man, whom he hoped was not the cardinal in question. This ambitious Neapolitan cleric of the Dominican Order had been a man with a rude instinct for trouble and intruding his self-righteous judgments on anyone with whom he came in contact.

The younger monsignor gestured to his uncle and both went to a small room adjoining the younger monsignor's offices for private counsel, beyond the new arrival's hearing.

"Cardinal Ribossi sent him, Uncle. This cannot be good news."

"I know, Nephew. But we must deal with the situation with delicacy. As you know, Cardinal Ribossi sits in a position of great influence very close to the Holy Father. We cannot appear to offend him. We must strive to manage and contain Father Baptisti's presence here for as long as possible. With events moving as quickly as they are, delaying

Baptisti's impact may be our best plan," the elder Marini strategized.

His nephew weighed the advice with gravity, and finally gave a slight nod.

After leaving his belongings in the small room assigned to him, and then being ushered down two flights of narrow spiral stone stairs, Father Baptisti found himself in a large cellar room, without windows, one of the ad hoc archive chambers housing dozens of wooden trunks of archives. The younger Monsignor Marini escorted Jean-Marc to this location and gave his instructions: to look for any documents he thought could be important and which might warrant a quick evacuation, if the newly developing circumstances might warrant it. And with that, the monsignor left him with one last guideline.

"Listen for the supper bell. It will tell you when we break for the evening meal." The unsmiling cleric then left the unwelcome guest to his tedious work assignment in the bowels of the palace.

While some in this position might quickly sense they had been exiled or buried in this chamber, with the most uninteresting category of the Vatican Archives—*Inventaires, Tables et Répertoires de tout ce qui précède*—it was in fact precisely the place Jean-Marc needed to find: the location of the collection of files organized and known as Section *Q*.

Because of his unnaturally heightened sense of hearing, he also knew when the two monsignors spoke privately that they expressed concern about his unannounced appearance, and that Cardinal Ribossi's connection was obviously not welcome news. They sent him down here to work, obviously with the opinion that the least sensitive documents were here—it housed miscellaneous files—and assigning the new stranger from Rome to this station offered the smartest strategy to contain him in the short term.

He guessed there undoubtedly was a section *J*, conspicuously absent from all inventories he had been able to study—which they were most certainly jealously protecting—and Jean-Marc wondered exactly what secrets might be held there. His curiosity, however, was temporary, since he had a clear mission. Fortune placed him precisely where he needed to be. Jean-Marc had memorized what trunk he needed to locate and set about doing so in short order with the aid of the oil lantern issued to him by the younger monsignor.

Before long, and surprised at his good fortune, Jean-Marc found what he came for, stacked behind other cases and against the back wall. He climbed over the cases with his lantern to finally reach the one storage crate he sought: Section Q, Case 322.

First setting the bronze lantern onto a nearby crate, Jean-Marc opened the iron-hinged trunk made of Italian red oak, and then positioned the lantern high overhead to search in earnest for that which he had sought for centuries. He frowned in concentration while he flipped through the spines of various volumes—reading their title notations inscribed on small hand-written labels discolored with age— as he strived to discover the volume he had toiled so long to recover.

Having discovered only a notation on an inventory list which he acquired on his earlier visit to this facility over a year before, under a different guise of identity, and before the Marini monsignors were in residence, Jean-Marc realized he had invested a great deal of hope and anticipation over the expected fruit of his quest. So much counted on recovering this prize, after so much time had passed, because the contents of the volume were timeless, priceless.

Finally, after working through the various files stored in the crate, toward the end, he saw a gap, a distinct spacing in the files stored here; and he sensed against all hope he might be a breath away from his goal. And there in the space between the other volumes he found a thick book—narrower in width than the other bulky bound documents filed on either side—hidden in the shadows between the files.

He reached into the gap and carefully withdrew the tome. Jean-Marc brought the lantern closer to provide a better view of the cover, the gold-leaf letters worn with age, but still legible: *Pupillus et Omnimodus Compendium de Appendices.* Confirming the object of his quest, a rush of excitement coursed through his veins as he finally held the manuscript in his hands, and he confirmed it was indeed the volume he had been seeking, much worn by the centuries. He barely had a chance to open the cover, however, when a basso baritone voice called to him through the doorway directly behind him.

"Do you have it?" the impatient voice resonated from the entryway to the storage chamber.

Momentarily startled, Jean-Marc glanced back from where he had been perched on top of the archive trunks to see a short squat silhouette, dressed in clerical vestments, standing in the doorway—someone he did not recognize.

"Excuse me?" Jean-Marc replied respectfully, climbing down off the trunks and moving toward the figure, but at the same time sliding the treasured book out of the new arrival's line of sight. As he closed the distance with the squat man, lantern light provided more details of the stranger's appearance. His stark black and white vestments identified him as a member of the Dominican Order; and the details of his golden holy cross which he wore hanging on his chest suggested a much higher rank in the clergy than Father Baptisti.

"I have no time for coy games at ignorance, Padre. I checked your room, and it's not there, so I assume you have it with you," the imperious senior cleric declared impatiently.

Casting his mind back to the name which appeared on the Vatican documents that had been the source of his forgeries from the preceding night, and noting the religious order he hailed from, Jean-Marc ventured a guess: "Monsignor Falcone?"

"And who else would you be expecting?" the Dominican monsignor barked with brusque aggressiveness as he entered the cool subterranean room. "So give it to me now. With developments moving as quickly as they are, I cannot afford any more delays. Your arrival was well-timed, considering the circumstances. I don't expect Cardinal Ribossi had any way of anticipating Napoleon's move, but it is good news you're here, nonetheless."

Jean-Marc strived to get a better understanding of what exactly this discussion was about and improvised in reply.

"Indeed, your Very Reverend Monsignor, events are changing quickly; the circumstances appear to be fluid and subject to change at a moment's notice."

"All the more reason to hand over what I require without further delay," the Dominican snapped with impatient annoyance.

"Yes, Your Reverence. Any further delay is most certainly undesirable... Just tell me what you require and I shall endeavor to respond in as helpful a way as God makes it possible."

"Stop playing the idiot, priest! Give it to me now, damn it!"

"If I could, I would gladly do so, Your Reverence, without hesitation. There was a problem on my journey. I was at a river crossing, and the package I carried was washed away. I had no chance to retrieve it. With the grace of God, I hope you will understand and forgive me my failure to provide you what you need."

"Idiot! You dare to offer me this pitiful story? If you'd lost the document, you would have returned straight to Rome to report, otherwise there was absolutely no reason whatsoever for you to come to Paris. Cardinal Ribossi said the next cleric he sent would have the orders he wanted from the Pope to place the Vatican Archive under my authority, immediately relieving Monsignor Marini and his insipid nephew of their prattling interference!"

"Monsignor, I am so very sorry. It could not be avoided. The journey here was—"

The Dominican cut him off. "Silence! I'll make this inconvenience work to my advantage. By Cardinal Ribossi's order, you're now *my* man. No matter what, it remains my destiny to take command of these archives now, before any further compromising damage occurs to the precious files contained here. As the Pope's holy spearhead of the reconstituted Roman Inquisition here in France, I have been hampered by the Marinis's preoccupation with preserving the complete collection. And it is only with the grace of God that I have withstood the temptation to strike these two bookworms with a holy cudgel to silence them once and for all," the imperious Dominican cleric railed with a sense of holy and inflated self-importance.

"I'm so very sorry your intentions have not been achieved as smoothly as you planned or expected. You have my deepest apologies. I have, however, critical work to do here with the archives that—"

"Did you not just hear me, you dimwit? You're now under *my* direct command, by order of Cardinal Ribossi. First I will have you testify to the Marini Monsignors the content of the ratified orders issued with the Supreme Holy Father's authorization, which dictate that I am to be the new Preceptor of the Vatican Archives. From there, as head of the Paris Chapter of the French Inquisition, and armed with the extensive records contained in these vaults, I can more effectively press my cases against a number of the recalcitrant 'noble' French families who've been fundamentally paganist in their involvement with the new régime of Louis XVIII. And first on my list are the Comte and Comtesse de Narbonne."

"The Comtesse de... who?" Jean-Marc inquired innocently.

"La Comtesse de Narbonne. They are of the most ancient bloodlines in France, but their deistic proclivities lean obscenely toward the pagan. I understand last night the Comtesse even had the audacity to host a salon vaunting her enthusiastic embrace of ancient Egyptian gods—the infernal witch Isis to be specific. Influences from these older bloodlines must be crushed completely and quickly. As they're tolerated and have free reign of expression, they give a shameful example to other families, fundamentally indicating it's somehow acceptable and allowable to exhibit disgraceful pagan tendencies or behavior that remains the bane of Christ, the Church, and decent Christian society which is the very backbone of our European culture and history."

"Holy Father, I clearly see this is indeed a powerful concern for you," Jean-Marc concurred, positioning his body in the monsignor's line of sight as he placed the newly acquired and long-sought tome under his canvas shoulder bag which sat nearby. Jean-Marc chose his words carefully at this point, to assure his next actions, which he composed on the spot, were the right measures within the larger picture of his goals and objectives.

"I know of the de Narbonne family, Your Venerable Reverence. While their devotion to the Roman Church is clearly not exactly in line with the Pope's desires, they are *not* Roman Catholics. And these people have been supportive and generously contributing to the needs of the communities of their province, the majority of them good Christians. The family established a mission to care for the poor. With the realities of newer, yet equally devout Christian faiths, and equally devoted families contributing to the advance of civilization, I don't see how the Inquisition can take a stand to persecute a family which has already respectfully declared itself outside of the dominion and jurisdiction of the Roman Church. They profess a more Protestant form of Christianity, and their enthusiasm and fascination for ancient Egypt is not at all unusual in France these days. It reflects a curiosity for understanding cultures beyond and outside local perceptions and mores. It's what Renaissance thinking is all about, Your Reverence."

"That has been my challenge exactly, Father. People minimize their infernal acts as stylish tendencies with such self-serving excuses, while all the time Satan deepens his insidious grip on the hearts and souls of the populace. But my researches enabled me to find records of the predecessors of the de Narbonne line, who, with the right interpretation of secular jurists, could result in the complete disenfranchisement of this family. And I discovered a host of other lineages which I have also targeted. Ultimately the goal is for all their lands, rights and any titles to be stripped away, and with luck, have them all thrown into prison for the rest of their lives. Yet ensuring their summary execution, however, might prove more of a challenge. Burning at the stake, of course, would be what they deserve. We can but pray to the Lord for support and guidance on that. In the short term, attaining uncontested control of the archives enables me to accelerate a process already well underway in the gathering and organization of the needed documentation to exterminate these infernal bloodlines," the Dominican declared proudly.

"You have indeed been busy, Monsignor. I'm sure the exalted Holy Father in Rome would be very pleased with your progress," Jean-Marc observed respectfully and without a trace of irony.

"We must act now, to take advantage of the uncertainty, to take command of the situation with authority and to provide a sense of dynamic leadership, which these Marinis sorely lack," the ambitious inquisitor declared.

"Action should clearly take place, Monsignor, and indeed it *must* be conclusive action which addresses the problem decisively, effectively and quickly. Your mission demands unmistakable urgency and importance," Jean-Marc declared with conviction. "And if I may kiss your ring in the spirit of admiration and reverence, I would be honored." Jean-Marc extended his hand, seeking the senior cleric's touch.

The Dominican monsignor had a weakness for flattery, and he welcomed the first opportunity someone provided which appeared to affirm his elevated rank and point of view. The monsignor offered his hand with entitled anticipation.

Jean-Marc took the monsignor's hand, kissed it briefly, then swiftly and firmly shook his hand vigorously and yet ultimately would not let go. A look of unfamiliar discomfort overcame the monsignor as he stared into Jean-Marc's strangely compelling and powerful smiling eyes. The Dominican only now glanced down to see that a sturdy cotton cord had been rapidly wrapped around his wrist. As he brought his other hand to try to vainly disentangle it, Jean-Marc deftly ensnared his second hand with the cord, completely binding the cleric's hands with dexterous speed.

"You fool! What are you doing? How *dare* you! I command you to remove these restraints and release me at once! You have no idea what punishment I shall rain down upon you if you refuse!" the Dominican loudly threatened with indignation.

"I think, in point of fact, this action will better remedy the situation. I'm sure on some level you'll eventually agree, Monsignor Falcone. However, then again, possibly not," Jean-Marc remarked lightly as he retrieved a cotton kerchief from his shoulder pack, secured it to gag the cleric's mouth, then grabbed another piece of cord from his pack and tied it tightly around the monsignor's waist, and finally brought the rope around to bind the cleric's tied hands to the waist restraint with speed and seasoned expertise. Jean-Marc took one more piece of cord and tied off the monsignor's legs, leaving the cleric bound and gagged, sitting awkwardly on the floor.

With his quarry incapacitated, Jean-Marc went to his canvas shoulder bag, and from it extracted a small bottle, which he uncorked. He tapped the bottle until two small white pills fell into his palm, then he brought them to the Dominican.

"I can see you're extremely upset with my behavior, Monsignor. I'll remove the gag, if you agree to not speak. And if all goes well, I will also unbind you. You must give me your sacred oath that you'll not raise your voice again. You must pledge to the Holy Father and in Christ's name that you will not call out. And if you agree, I shall explain my behavior. If you nod, I'll take that as your sacred pledge."

Jean-Marc stared expectantly at the indignant and initially uncooperative Dominican, a man quite unaccustomed to being in a subservient role such as this one. Finally the overweight monsignor nodded, clearly displeased with the requirement and predicament. Jean-Marc undid the gag.

"Now unbind me, priest. Immediately," Falcone ordered.

"I cannot do that quite yet. But by my sacred pledge, I promise to unbind you, after you have taken these." And Jean-Marc showed the Dominican the two small pills.

"I'll do nothing of the sort! I demand you release me and explain yourself. In the name of Cardinal Ribossi, I demand it!"

Jean-Marc smiled slightly. "My presence here is dictated by a higher authority, Monsignor. I have given you my sacred promise to explain myself and release you, but only after you have taken these. I pledge to you they are in no way poisonous to your health or wellbeing," Jean-Marc promised.

"What are they then?" the monsignor demanded, eyeing the pills suspiciously.

"Natural herbs from China. Harmless. They sooth the spirit, and I need you to be calm for our discussion. You're clearly a very excitable individual, and I cannot have you acting out. You'll not be released without taking them. And if you do not, I shall replace the gag, since I have much work to do which cannot be interrupted by you in your current state of ignorance." Jean-Marc paused for effect. "Listen closely, Monsignor: my work is conducted by the will of the Holy Apostles themselves."

"You're here on the Pope's behalf?" The monsignor spoke with involuntary and restrained deference, clearly taken off-balance by the situation and this pronouncement. "Is there some new initiative afoot of which I am not yet aware?"

"The Pope's mandate is said to come directly from the Apostles, does it not? Are you suggesting there are other sources of authority any more important? Are you inclined to ask questions that reveal the level of your ignorance so casually?" Jean-Marc inquired with a veiled sense of unrestrained power. He held the pills up for the monsignor to take.

"You guarantee they're not poison?" the monsignor inquired hesitantly.

"If it was your destiny to die at my hands, I promise the process would have gone much more quickly and efficiently than this. This substance is not poison; and by my holy oath, I have solemnly pledged never to take a life, in any circumstance, nor will I ever speak an outright lie. Can you make the same claim to me?"

After a hesitant pause, the Dominican allowed the two pills to be placed into his mouth. Jean-Marc poured a glass of light watered wine from a decanter nearby and offered it to him.

"Drink it. I must assure they have been swallowed."

The monsignor followed Jean-Marc's instructions.

"Now unbind me," Falcone ordered with tentative and hesitant authority.

"I will follow my pledge shortly, Monsignor."

"You said you would unbind me after I took those infernal pills."

"Indeed, but I did not say I would do so immediately... You see Monsignor Falcone—and I openly confess I use this honorific title with some degree of irony—your work must be interrupted for just a short time while I arrange matters so your entitlement is adjusted in accordance with necessity."

"What're you talking about?" The Dominican revealed some irritation, but more so, the effects of the drug he took had begun to have a strong influence on him. His speech began to slur and he showed marked signs of drowsiness.

"This is *not* God's work you're performing, Monsignor. Your activities are an abomination inspired by the Evil One himself. And I must do my part to relieve you of your involvement and authority. I believe I have a plan that should work out well enough on such short notice. One must embrace the spirit of improvisation, yes?" Jean-Marc observed lightly with a knowing smile.

"I coooommand you to reeeeleeassse mmmeee!" the monsignor demanded, albeit groggily, as he now slid toward unconsciousness. Jean-Marc began to comply with the order, as the sluggish eyes watched, but Falcone could do nothing else.

"There. You can see I am a man of my word."

The monsignor nodded vaguely and then passed out unconscious on the floor. Jean-Marc then swiftly went about executing his newly devised plan.

Father Baptisti stood at an open window on the second floor of the older section of Soubise Palace, part of the original medieval residence from which this grand sprawling structure expanded with construction through the centuries.

Peering down on the modestly populated Paris side street—where a few street vendors set up their carts to sell vegetables, freshly slaughtered poultry, and rags—he watched the back of a man walk away across the narrow cobbled street directly below him. As the man slung a canvas bag over his shoulder and made his way to a small cart with a tethered workhorse, he then climbed aboard the cart. The priest with the white eyebrow studied the man a moment longer, then turned and strode down a hallway which led back to the main part of the palace.

A short time later, Father Baptisti appeared in the doorway of the younger Monsignor Marini. The monsignor glanced up from his desk, frowning at the appearance of the unwelcome arrival.

"Yes, Father? The supper bell has not yet sounded. What do you want?" the monsignor asked with the slightest glint of guarded wariness as he put down his pen.

"Your Reverence, it is about Monsignor Falcone…"

Monsignor Marini's suspicion amplified instantaneously at hearing the name. "What about Monsignor Falcone, Father Baptisti?"

"It appears he has fallen prey to unspeakable temptations which I care not to describe in detail, Your Reverence. While working with the archives in the cellar, I heard a sound, and then came upon the monsignor in a state of… grave compromise… I was not sure what should be done next, and I requested assistance from the King's archivists to assure the monsignor was in good health."

"What in heavens are you talking about, Father Baptisti?"

In the wine cellar of the Soubise Palace, located just two doorways down the basement hallway from the room containing the Q archives, Father Baptisti led the two Marini monsignors to a niche off the main cellar where two of the royal archivists stood over the unconscious and stark naked Monsignor Falcone—legs spread apart, creating an unflattering display of his corpulence and diminutive manhood. Empty open bottles of wine lay littered about, while nearby his Dominican robes were neatly folded in a corner. Spread out in front of him were numerous copies of works considered pornography by the Church of Rome, from the Kama Sutra of India, ancient Egyptian papyrus scrolls depicting forbidden carnal practices, old Japanese rice paper books portraying couples in graphic portrayals of coitus, as well as other historic sources of sexual knowledge explicitly prohibited by the Church.

Long outlawed by the Roman Catholic Church, they were nonetheless part of the Vatican Archives, which Jean-Marc recalled from his review of the inventory list, and they were included in the Q section of records. Finding them and displaying them, along with the Dominican monsignor in his compromised disposition took little more than twenty minutes. Following that, he beckoned the royal archivists to come to his assistance, officially, but more to bear witness to the Inquisitor's irreparable humiliation—guaranteeing a chain of rapidly spreading gossip—and thereby hopefully ensuring the cleric's inevitable downfall from his duties as the main Inquisitor for France. The archivists would also officially report this to their secular superior; and before the day was out, it would reach those in power who determined who would be allowed access and involvement in the management of the Vatican Archives from the royal French perspective.

The two Marinis stepped closer to survey the shocking

and disgusting tableau. As they did, they could smell the strong reek of wine and urine, and they both shook their heads in revulsion and disbelief. The French royal archivists displayed undisguised amusement at the grotesque display of this clergyman's downfall from impeccable respect and, most logically, from power as well.

Father Baptisti led the two monsignors into the hallway, away from the unpleasant scene. "As you may imagine, Most Reverent Fathers, I must report this matter to Cardinal Ribossi as soon as possible. While this was not my original understanding, I now interpret my sacred duties to return to Rome and report this in person. Anything in writing would not capture the gravity of Monsignor Falcone's alarming fall from grace. I plan to depart within the hour, Your Reverences. I expect a separate edict for the monsignor's departure will follow my report. But since Monsignor Falcone is far above my station, it is not my place to have him removed directly," Jean-Marc observed without irony.

"Indeed, Father Baptisti, your sense of holy duty is commendable. I support your instinct for correct action," the elder Monsignor Marini commented.

"I will return to my quarters and arrange my belongings for immediate departure," Jean-Marc announced.

"Of course, Father Baptisti. And as I am sure you would understand as part of our normal procedures, we will need to ask to inspect your belongings, as well as your mount, to assure nothing departs the archives by 'accident.' This is done with all visitors, and I am certain you recognize the need for this standard procedure for all those visiting the archives. Unfortunately, we have seen problems in the past," the younger monsignor declared pleasantly with a calm smile and a steady penetrating stare.

"Of course, Monsignor, I am heartened you take such prudent measures to guard against any unauthorized access to these invaluable records," Jean-Marc replied with sincerity and complete accommodation.

"Good. And to take full advantage of our rare opportunity for getting the latest news from Rome, I'll accompany our good and able Brother Salvatore as he conducts the search. We hardly got to know you during your brief time here," the young monsignor announced pleasantly, having gestured to a robed brother who stood nearby.

Jean-Marc observed that the Jesuit acolyte who would be conducting the search was an inordinately large, strong member of the Order, with something of a lack of light in the eyes. Revealed within the dullness of his gaze, however, Jean-Marc recognized something else: implicit threat. This large hulking man was their work ox and enforcer, when needed. For all the decorous and respectful politeness conveyed by the two monsignors, Jean-Marc suspected this final requirement of departure might include more than he planned or the monsignor promised. He sensed the distinct possibility of a trap. And from past experience, he had no intention of exposing himself to that risk.

"An excellent idea. I look forward to it, Monsignor. In my belongings, I also brought along modest mementos of Rome, from the Vatican, which I intended to offer as gifts to the brothers here. I have a rosary within which the cross bears earth from the Sacred Calvary itself. I also brought a prayer missal, personalized by hand, bearing the script of the Holy Father, Pope August Pius himself. I bear other modest offerings as well, and I shall place these in your good hands so you might determine the best way for them to be distributed," Jean-Marc proffered.

Both monsignors seemed pleased at this generous gesture and appeared to look forward to see what other gifts they might be assessing.

"In all the excitement, I have neglected to answer nature's urgent call. May I suggest I meet you and Brother Salvatore at my room shortly?" Jean-Marc suggested.

"But of course," the young monsignor agreed, "but for your convenience, since the layout of the palace is still quite unfamiliar to you, I am sure you will appreciate having Brother Salvatore accompany you. He'll wait for you until your private business is done."

The monsignor's manner clearly indicated he would not take 'no' for an answer.

Playing along and not wanting to alert them to any suspicions, Jean-Marc remained relaxed and completely in character as Father Baptisti. "I do confess taking a wrong turn here and there today while navigating my way back to your offices. And since I've only been to my quarters once, to drop off my things, your offer is most thoughtful, generous and very much appreciated. Thank you, Monsignor. I would hate for you to be kept waiting on the off chance I might become lost in the halls of this venerable and great palace."

"Very well then, I will meet you in your quarters shortly," the young monsignor announced. Before departing, however, Marini whispered something into Brother Salvatore's ear. Jean-Marc saw the monsignor's man glance at him as he nodded and his eyes narrowed slightly, while acquiring additional instructions. Jean-Marc could only guess the orders had something to do with the possibility of employing the use of physical force if deemed necessary. Brother Salvatore nodded with steely intent, and his dim sluggish eyes became fixed on 'Father Baptisti.'

Jean-Marc turned to his guardian, inquiring where the nearest place to relieve himself might be. The brother led him up the stairs, out of the cellar, to the first floor and finally to a door in a hallway behind the main entrance of the palace. Not far, further down this hall, Jean-Marc knew from his earlier visit to the palace, a stairway led to a hallway on the second floor which ultimately brought him back to the old section of the palace, to the same location he visited less than an hour ago. Jean-Marc entered the palace privy and closed the door behind him.

After a reasonable amount of time in measure with managing the answer of nature's call, Jean-Marc reappeared, and proceeded to walk along the hallway where Brother Salvatore waited for him a short distance away. Jean-Marc engaged his guardian in conversation, to gauge his receptiveness to distracting tactics.

"Have you been here in Paris long, Brother Salvatore?"

"I have been here as long as the Lord has seen fit to need me here," the brother replied somewhat robotically.

"I'm sure Monsignor Marini depends on your good services a great deal. I can tell you're a man of conviction, reliability and discipline in the Lord. In a world of uncertainty, having dependable people around them is critical."

This compliment touched Brother Salvatore's inner core of vitality, personal definition and validation. He smiled slowly to himself, pleased that his commitment to duty had been recognized by this newcomer to the Vatican Archives. The discussion all took place as they passed the stairway leading up to the second floor.

Jean-Marc stopped for a second, with a sense of personal embarrassment.

"In the midst of answering nature's call, and in the middle of so many distracting events, I did not assure I had all my possessions with me. I fear I left my bag of essentials in the relief room. I must go back to retrieve it," Jean-Marc said as he started back toward the doorway of the toilet, passing the entrance to the second floor stairway.

"Please wait here, and don't bother yourself with this, I shall return quickly and in due course."

Brother Salvatore paused uncertainly, peering at Jean-Marc, who glanced back at him, then pointed beyond the hulking man, further down the hall.

"Isn't that Monsignor Marini beckoning you, Brother Salvatore? Is he agitated and in urgent need of your support? Well, now he's gone. Did you see him, Brother?" Jean-Marc inquired sincerely.

Brother Salvatore turned to peer down the hallway, at a juncture not far away, and then glanced back at his charge doubtfully.

As Jean-Marc stepped toward the door to the toilet, he observed: "Maybe it's not important. I'm sure you'll determine that sooner than later. And if for any reason he is angry, I'll just tell him I told you, but you didn't see him, and you did not believe me." He then stopped at the door to the privy. "I'm sure whatever it was he might require can wait. I certainly won't be long, even though you can see the privy door the whole time from the hallway if you indeed went to the corner to look for yourself, allowing you to confirm the monsignor's need."

Brother Salvatore found himself caught between two conflicting senses of duty. As Jean-Marc opened the privy door, the brother finally decided. He turned his back and trod a few paces toward the hallway juncture Jean-Marc indicated, looked down it, and saw it was vacant. Troubled, he turned back, scrutinized the hallway where he had just been with Father Baptisti. It was also empty: he was gone, presumably back into the toilet. Brother Salvatore ran to check the privy, which he quickly discovered was unoccupied. Rushing back out, he returned to the hallway, and then headed up the stairway leading to the second floor. The brother concluded this could be the only direction Jean-Marc might have taken.

Reaching the top of the stairs on the second floor, Brother Salvatore looked both ways, made a decision, then ran down the hallway, and finally arrived at the older section of the palace.

The hallway split in two directions. One ran back into the depths of the palace; the other led to a juncture of the hall which turned to the right, leading back toward the front of the palace. At this point, he came to a double-paned window which overlooked the side street that ran alongside the palace.

The window was partly ajar and a soft breeze blew in. The Jesuit brother pushed it open, and leaned out over the street. His view on the second story overlooked two streets: one which ended directly at the palace and the other at a right angle to the first, which ran north and south. Scanning for the errant Italian priest, Salvatore saw no sign. All he observed were a few peasants selling their wares, fresh poultry, and a lone man with his horse-led rag cart wheeling away. The back of the cart was covered with an old canvas tarp, a common sight in Paris.

Salvatore moved on, searched the halls of this part of the palace a bit longer, cursing himself, since Monsignor Marini gave specific instructions not to let the priest out of his sight. Brother Salvatore finally ran back down the hall, continuing his search for the elusive Father Baptisti, dreading the bad news he would most likely need to deliver to the monsignor.

The Streets of Paris
3rd Arrondissement
3 March, 1815 AD – Late Morning

Beneath the tarpaulin in the back of the wagon, Jean-Marc had removed his theatrical beard, was changing out of his priestly wardrobe and back into his traditional clothes which his valet Roger had placed there for him. He felt a surge of relief and excitement that the book he sought for so long to retrieve was finally back in his possession. He had successfully dropped it down to Roger below the appointed window, though not without some initial confusion on Roger's part.

Instead of exiting out of the window after the book had been passed down, as was originally planned, Jean-Marc signaled he had one more priority to attend to, which was the Dominican inquisitor. That finally achieved, Jean-Marc returned as quickly as possible and concealed himself beneath the tarpaulin only an instant before Brother Salvatore came searching for him at the palace window overlooking the street.

The next order of business was their immediate departure from the city. With so much in flux including Napoleon's daring escape from Elba, as well as more recent personal developments, Jean-Marc looked forward to leaving the city at long last. He felt as though he might not return here for a very long time. Life in any city required a very different commitment to the management of an intricate fabric of high-maintenance social relationships which he found quite distracting and very wearying.

After the cart rounded a corner, Jean-Marc finally climbed out from under the canvas and joined Roger as the valet prodded the two horses leading the cart along one of the back streets of Paris.

"The retrieval of the book took much less time than I anticipated, Master. But I must confess I was surprised and concerned when you signaled you had to return back into the palace for other matters. What was it you needed to do?" Roger inquired.

"Unexpected business of the highest priority, Roger," Jean-Marc replied, glancing over his shoulder, down the narrow street, to assure no one followed in pursuit. Satisfied the coast was clear for now, he continued. "Indeed, this mission was not without its particular challenges," he observed as he then proceeded to fill Roger in on the events which involved finally taking possession of the book and his narrow escape from Soubise Palace.

"I would indeed still like to know where the *J* section is stored in the Vatican Archives and what exactly they're hiding there," Roger observed as he prodded the horses on, approaching another corner.

"Some other time, perhaps. Our goal, however, has been achieved at long last," Jean-Marc declared with a relieved smile.

Yet as they approached the corner, a phalanx of men on horseback rounded the edge of a building, blocking their approach. At their lead rode the duc de St. Pré. It took only a second for the disgraced nobleman to recognize his newly defined archenemy.

"That is the very man I seek! Seize him! Then beat him into utter submission before I decide what his final fate shall be!" the duke cried.

One of the gang quickly jumped down to seize one of the cart's horses by the bridle, cutting off any hope of escape. The rest of the duke's pack climbed down off their mounts with a relaxed quality to their menace, confident the cart was trapped and their quarry unable to flee.

Jean-Marc turned to Roger, handing him the canvas shoulder bag holding the precious book he worked so hard to retrieve from the Vatican Archives. He whispered so the approaching thugs could not hear. "Take the book and protect it. I'll meet you at our staging point outside the city."

Roger protested, grabbing an old short sword from under the canvas tarp, ready for battle. Jean-Marc glanced at the weapon with concern and disapproval and then compelled Roger to quickly push it back out of sight. "Where did you get that sword?"

"I bought in the market a few days ago, anticipating the needs of our travel. Master, I would be honored to fight at your side and defend you. This rabble doesn't deserve to face a person of your stature and importance."

"No. We shall not draw blood in anger, Roger. I am the only one they seek. Where I go, they will pursue. I'll end it here. The book is the thing. Protect it, Roger, and deliver it to safety. Do not fear for me. I have an advantage, as you know, that they do not," Jean-Marc reassured him.

Reluctantly, Jean-Marc's valet took the book, jumped off the cart and ran up the street away from the looming conflict. Still sitting in the cart, and reaching for his own sword which had been stowed beneath the canvas tarp behind him, Jean-Marc drew the blade as he stood in the cart and pointed it casually in the direction of his prospective assailants. He directed his words to the duc de St. Pré, who remained aloof and safely distant on horseback.

"My sacred and ancient pledge not to draw blood in anger or take a life is one I will not break, no matter the circumstances. However, the latitude of physical consequences between that and what stands before us now is frankly quite wide, sir. I can and will cripple someone who threatens my life. I hope your cohorts have been, or will be, well paid, because they'll need it to hire physicians to recover from their many injuries they are about to sustain on your behalf. For you, however, duc de St. Pré, no doctor has the knowledge or skill to heal the injuries I shall inflict upon you. I have offered you the opportunity to withdraw before. This is the last time this offer shall be extended."

While the hoodlums paused in momentary uncertainty at Jean-Marc's calm confidence, the duke immediately grew petulant and annoyed.

"Kill him if you must! But silence this knave!" the duke ordered imperiously.

As the thugs approached, drawing their swords, however, Jean-Marc leapt from the cart and displayed an agility and nimbleness which caught them off guard. There were five assailants, and one—the tallest in the group—was instantly neutralized as Jean-Marc landed from his jump off the cart and slapped him soundly across the eyes with the flat of his sword blade and he then spun quickly to face the other members of the duke's ruffian crew. As he did, the one who sustained the strike to the eyes dropped his sword and fell to the cobblestone pavement, screaming in pain as he clutched his face in panic and agony.

Jean-Marc confronted the other four with a businesslike manner. "Sirs, I am a very busy man and have much to do today. I would be grateful if you would commence your attack forthwith." His statement had an intentional mocking tone. The brute closest to him—a stocky man with a burly beard—took the bait and attacked with more bravado than skill, employing a forceful downward swing of his sabre and a loud shout.

Jean-Marc easily parried the strike, and then, in close proximity to his attacker, took advantage of the man's vulnerability and swiftly stamped down soundly on the top of the man's boot with extreme force, quickly crushing most of the comparatively thin delicate bones on the top of the foot. The aggressor fell to the ground in crippled agony.

"Kill him now!" the impatient duke shouted from the seeming security of his high horse.

After a short hesitation, glancing at his two brethren

already on the ground, the next assailant came at Jean-Marc with a brazen sword thrust, which was again deftly parried. Jean-Marc feigned another foot strike, which the ruffian anticipated, pulling his lead foot back, straightening his front leg and stance in the process. Fully expecting this move, and before the attacker could bring his sword around for a second attack, Jean-Marc raised his front leg, knee high, then swiftly brought the side of his boot down, just above the man's kneecap, in a sudden thrusting downward motion. A sharp sickening crack sounded as the man's knee was broken, and limp-legged, he collapsed to the ground, crying in startled pain.

"Both of you, attack him together, you cowards!" the duke nervously commanded, as he saw the odds swiftly narrowing away from his favor, and he drew his sabre.

The last two hired thugs stepped forward, tentatively at first, yet their resolve gained a sense of momentum as Jean-Marc seemed to show fear now, and he retreated toward the cart. And as Jean-Marc slipped one hand into the back of the cart out of sight, while the other hand kept them momentarily at bay with his waving sword. He called out anxiously. "Please! No more! There are two of you now! Please let this end before more harm comes to anyone!" Jean-Marc entreated them.

"Take him now, while his back is against the cart and he has no escape from you! Kill him! I order you! I'll pay you double!" the duke called out, directing their actions with his waving sword.

With the prodding from the duke, and the perception Jean-Marc's resolve might be faltering, the two surged at him from both sides at once. In a lightning instant, Jean-

Marc rapidly grabbed the tarp from the cart in a sweeping motion, effectively blocking the assault on one side from the first hoodlum, and came around to entangle the second assailant on the other side. Before the second attacker could recover, Jean-Marc took the rest of the tarp, and in a flashing motion completely entangled the first aggressor in it as well. A rope attached to the tarp was speedily deployed around them, to bind the pair securely, with their heads still exposed. As they gaped with startled confusion, Jean-Marc swiftly and soundly struck each on the skull with the dull backside of his sword blade, leaving both ensnared and slumped into unconsciousness.

In the aftermath, the team of five thugs laid in varying states of crippled infirmity on the cobblestones of the Paris street. And also by now a small crowd had gathered on the periphery of the action. Jean-Marc's gaze turned to the duke.

Suddenly uncomfortable in his originally commanding perch on his saddle, the duke was dumbfounded at witnessing his five hired hooligans so quickly and soundly neutralized with such a minimum of effort. Caught in a moment of indecision, he deliberated whether to attack from horseback himself, dismount and fight, or turn and retreat.

In this instant, he reflexively spurred his horse on to charge. At the same time, however, Jean-Marc swiftly came to the duke's horse, just as it reared in panic and defiance, grabbed the mare's reins, and yanked them to the side, causing the duke to tumble unceremoniously and painfully onto the ground, his sword scuttering onto the pavement. As Jean-Marc released the horse and it galloped off down the street, and the duke struggled to rise and regain his sword, Jean-Marc got there first, kicking the sword away.

"You are a coward! You're afraid to face me man-to-man with sword in hand," the duke declared venomously as he glanced at the gathering of onlookers.

The throng of spectators grew quickly for this exciting street action. Eager shouts brought more citizens to watch the event. While Jean-Marc remained quite cognizant this contest had already been won the night before, and the duke's humiliation assured, now with the conquest of the duke's gang, he saw that the story had very likely acquired the potential of ribald storytelling at taverns and other gathering places of the common folk. And he knew an accounting of what was yet to transpire, could travel in the most unusual and unexpected ways, to a much wider audience and take on legendary proportions.

While Jean-Marc might be eager to be on his way, he recognized the benefits of taking the time to assure this tale was well-finished. Jean-Marc composed his thoughts to facilitate the popular retelling of this encounter, among the masses, and its logically resounding effect in decisively concluding the story of duc de St. Pré. He turned to the gathering crowd.

"Good people of Paris! The man before me is known as duc Henri de St. Pré, allegedly one of the King's closest advisors. He has worked actively against your interests in more ways than I can describe at this moment; but he is a vigorous opponent of the hard-fought Rights of Man. He implies I am a coward and unwilling to face him with the sword, because of his claim to mastery in the art. My aim is to disprove this allegation and silence his lies against me and the people of France. My pledge is never to draw blood, nor take a life." He gestured at the duke's decommissioned minions and continued. "While he sends these five men to murder me, and with their failure, he wants to kill me himself! All of this because I exposed him as the fool that he is in Paris society. So please bear witness to the following contest for my honor, and for the welfare of the good people of France, with this in mind."

Jean-Marc then turned to the duke who had gotten to his feet, and he stared at the King's erstwhile cohort coolly, but without anger.

"Have you ever reflected on the Wrath of God, duc de St. Pré?"

The duke made a dismissive gesture. "I don't need to talk to the likes of you. A coward and an impostor," the haughty nobleman replied dismissively.

"You're about to experience the Wrath of God, sir. You'll be surprised at the variety of the ways the Lord works. Now pick up your sword and we shall finish this thing."

Duc de St. Pré stood hesitant at first, wary to turn his back on Jean-Marc to retrieve his blade. The duke backed down the street, facing his opponent, as the multitude grew closer with anticipation. Standing over his blade, the duke's only distraction was the occasional moan of his men, still semiconscious, crippled and in pain, unable to move without assistance. The duke frowned for just a moment glancing at his sword, which laid before him on the cobblestone.

"You could withdraw, sir, with an apology and a bow, and I would grant you leave without harm," Jean-Marc offered in a flat tone. "To do so would raise my estimation of your pathetic and depraved soul."

"I care not what you think!" the duke growled as he picked up his sword and eyed his opponent venomously.

"Then what happens next you have brought upon yourself, sir. It's your move, because I will not attack you," Jean-Marc replied casually, lowering his sword, creating an irresistible opening for the duke.

The duke hesitated, inching closer as Jean-Marc lowered his guard even more. Again the duke could not force himself to commit, as a flashing memory of last night's humiliation and defeat reverberated in his mind. St. Pré recognized what truly was at stake, no matter what sacred pledge his opponent supposedly claimed to have taken. It was life or death for one of them.

Jean-Marc studied the duke momentarily with icy calmness and a smile which the nobleman found unnerving. The duc de St. Pré still found himself unable to initiate his attack, being wracked with doubt. Jean-Marc saw this, lowered his sword so the point almost touched the cobblestone and he grasped the handle loosely in his hand as one might carry a jacket. He then turned to the nearest bystanders, offering his back to the duke.

"Good people of Paris, it appears this last act of the duc de St. Pré is '*Much Ado About Nothing*!' "

And with that the duke committed rashly to a fast attack with a feigned low jabbing thrust to cover the distance toward his opponent, immediately followed by a forceful overhead downward strike aimed at Jean-Marc's head. Witnesses would later recount the result as though the duke's opponent had rehearsed the counter move all of his life, so effortless and exacting was its execution, and so impressive in its impact and effect.

In one swirling motion, Jean-Marc spun around, anticipating exactly where the descending blade was headed, met it with his sword in a curving, hook-like motion, which succeeded in yanking the weapon from the duke's hand, casting it high into the air, and to clatter unceremoniously on the cobblestone pavement nearby. Before the duke could even glance toward the fate of his sword, Jean-Marc closed the distance so he stood directly in front of the nobleman and returned his sword to its scabbard at the same time.

Jean-Marc then quickly formed the fingers of his right hand into a clustered and concentrated striking-formation, positioning it reminiscent of a praying mantis. He rapidly struck two acupuncture pressure points on the nobleman: one on his chest, just below the collar bone on the left side, and the second strike to the high part of his temple on his right side. The duke was instantaneously stunned into paralysis, his eyes blinking with incredulity and fear. An observer could see by the expressiveness of the eyes that the duke was trying to move and to speak, but without success.

"I will release the paralysis of your body shortly, St. Pré," Jean-Marc quietly informed him.

The duke's eyes widened with rage and impotence, trying to make his body return to action, to attack his enemy, but to no avail.

"As I mentioned before, sir, you brought this on yourself. In my many years on this earth, I have learned the deeper arts of healing. And in the course of that education, I learned other skills as well. Your loss of speech is by no means permanent, but it can only be undone by someone who studied the same arts as deeply as I, and who has the same expertise and understanding. The 'Wrath of God' is due to the fact that you used your God-given gifts to speak to evil ends. And so, on the Lord's behalf, I have reclaimed this gift until further notice. A second gift you abused was the ability to see clearly and to act accordingly with that gift."

The duke's eyes widened in doubt and fear at the threat of what might come next. He struggled vainly to speak and defend himself, but this opportunity had passed. The citizens of Paris came closer to observe what had taken place with this now humbled nobleman.

"...And so, this is the second gift I must reclaim." And with that, Jean-Marc struck two additional acupuncture points simultaneously at the back of the duke's scalp, where the top of his spine met the skull and a point between the eyebrows. He then struck a point above the chest again and ran his palms down both of the duke's arms, slowly and firmly. The duke's paralysis was gone, but it remained clear that he could no longer see, and his power of speech was lost. He uttered guttural, animal-like sounds as he groped pathetically at his eyes, moaning in despair.

Jean-Marc firmly put his hand on the duke's shoulder. "Listen to me carefully, for I will not repeat myself. If you wish to be delivered from this crippling curse I sentenced you with, you must now devote your life to good deeds. If I come to learn you have sincerely worked to make amends, I shall come again and return God's gifts. In the meanwhile, I leave you with your pitiful life, which as all around will testify, could have so easily and justly been taken from you."

And with that, Jean-Marc turned to a horse belonging to one of his attackers, mounted it and rode off, leaving his wagon and the wounded assailants to their fates. The duc de St. Pré was left wandering aimlessly, muttering guttural sounds.

The people of Paris laughed at him and stood in wonder at the mysterious feats of Jean-Marc, as he rode off at a brisk pace and disappeared around a street corner.

Soubise Palace
3rd Arrondissement, Paris
3 March, 1815 AD – Mid-Day

"**D**escribe him to me," the newly arrived high-cleric of the Roman Catholic Church demanded of the recently disgraced Dominican Monsignor Falcone, who was back in the black and white wool robes of his order.

"Your Grace, he caught me completely unaware. He threatened my life, I swear! Despite his apparent deep familiarity with the Church and its procedures and holy scholarship, I'm convinced this man is in no way an ordained priest. There was something far too independent-spirited about him," the faltering Dominican cleric declared, trying to retrieve some sense of hope and respect in what he recognized was a highly compromised juncture in his religious career. Only this morning he perceived himself as destined for greatness, very possibly resulting years from now with a papal tiara and the throne of Rome. Now he scrambled for some bleak hope of survival, just to hold onto what he had.

Clasping his gold-jeweled crucifix with one hand, the young bishop brushed perceived dust off the otherwise pristine puffy white silk sleeves and the loose black satin vest accessory of his elegant vestments as he stared icily at his subordinate.

"I am unaccustomed to repeating myself, Monsignor Falcone," the clergyman exclaimed with an undisguised trace of impatience. "Do you require me to repeat my question, Monsignor? Was I unclear? Do you have a reluctance to answer?" The bishop's chilling, quiet tone held a telltale implicit threat. Monsignor Falcone got it and began to deliver the information demanded of him instead of making more excuses for his failures.

"I judge his age to be in the middle thirties. He was of medium height, bearded, raven-haired, and naturally tanned, suggesting, I suspect, a Mediterranean origin, Your Grace. Of a healthy disposition, he seemed very learned in his references to a broad range of writings, far outside the traditional body of knowledge even for a well-read man of the Church. No person of average learning could have been aware of, or located, those obscure yet obscene volumes in so quick a manner and displayed them with such incriminating cunning. His spirit is driven by Satan himself, of this I am certain."

The young bishop studied Falcone for a long moment,

his mind processing more than one channel of thought simultaneously.

"Did he have any distinguishing features?"

Nervousness clouded and delayed his response, as Falcone weighed with dread the possible consequences of how he had been discovered, naked and unconscious, amid a cache of historical pornography, with a host of almost a dozen empty or half-empty wine bottles strewn about him. His first instinct was defensive, and hence it distracted him once again from answering his superior clearly and decisively as required and expected.

"I don't know why he did it, but he staged that wretched ruse to make me look depraved, infernal. It all seemed as though he planned it, but, I was the one to approach him. I thought he was Cardinal Ribossi's messenger and emissary."

Despite his strikingly unique, and separate in hue, blue and green eyes, his slightly effeminate mouth, and fine feline features, the young bishop's tone was sharp and impatient, with a surprising vindictiveness and potent with threat. "Defending yourself is a meaningless exercise with me, Monsignor Falcone. The only hope you have to gain my favor or support is if you are in any way helpful to my requirements. If I must repeat myself, you're only indicating how useless you can be."

Monsignor Falcone began to perspire, trying to visualize his assailant, to grasp at something: "His right eyebrow."

The bishop's attention riveted completely on him now. "What about his right eyebrow?"

"It was white, Your Grace. His right eyebrow had mostly white hair, as though it was bleached by something or some process. I frankly thought it suggested some flamboyance or vanity."

The bishop—to all appearances in his mid-twenties—sat staring out the window for a long pause. Monsignor Falcone studied him with nervous hope.

"Was that helpful, Your Grace?"

"You must tell me all you can remember, everything he said, no matter how minor it might seem to you. I must know the entirety of your encounter with this man," the bishop decreed. "Even the smallest detail is critical."

Sitting restively in the anteroom outside the closed door of his own inner chambers, Monsignor Gaetano Marini shifted with discomfort, and he confessed only to himself, some irritation. The papal legate, Bishop Antonio del Julia y Sangresante, of the Dominican Order, and the highest-ranked cleric currently in Paris, representing the interests of the Holy Inquisition—and an imperious Spaniard—had peremptorily requisitioned his office to interview Monsignor Falcone without even paying the traditional courtesy of a request.

The two Dominicans had been in there for the better part of an hour, with the bishop's stern instructions that they not be interrupted. The elder Monsignor Marini had also been ordered to deliver all the personal articles the mysterious Father Baptisti abandoned in his quarters earlier in the day. Brother Salvatore had gathered these items and now sat with them gathered into a bed sheet, ready to deliver to the bishop at a moment's command.

Brother Salvatore anticipated this duty with dread, since

he was originally charged with the responsibility to escort Father Baptisti back to his quarters; and under his watch the errant priest had seemed to disappear so easily without a trace.

The door to the outer hallway flew open as though a gale force wind had blown in. A large, hulking hooded monk, dressed in coarse blackish-brown robes, entered the anteroom where the elder monsignor and his loyal attendant sat side by side. And without acknowledging either of the two Jesuits seated there, the monk proceeded toward the closed door leading to where the bishop's interview with Monsignor Falcone was taking place.

"Bishop Sangresante gave explicit instructions he was not to be disturbed," Monsignor Marini informed the new arrival.

The monk turned slowly, the shadows of his hood obscuring his face, as he studied the monsignor for an extended moment, and then peered at Brother Salvatore. A strange chill filled the room. The monk then slowly turned his head back to the doorway, pushed the door latch open and entered Monsignor Marini's inner sanctum without a word.

Revealing a hint of the rare, base animal fear he experienced in the presence of the massive mute monk, Brother Salvatore turned to Monsignor Marini. "I do not recognize the vestments of that monk's order. They're neither Cistercian, Benedictine, nor Franciscan. Do you know what order he belongs to, Monsignor?"

"Once, when I was in Rome some years ago, I saw such vestments, Brother Salvatore. They were from the Pachomean Order, a small group of monasteries in southern

Egypt, from the Orthodox Church. It is certainly not a common sight, especially here in Paris," the monsignor replied, striving to maintain a casual tone, while he too had felt the primal effect of the monk's intimidating presence.

Inside Monsignor Marini's offices, the hooded monk leaned over to whisper into the bishop's ear as the young pontiff stared coldly at Monsignor Falcone. A slight frown etched the bishop's brow as he turned to the monk and released the ornate crucifix at his chest from his grasp.

"You are sure it was the duc de St. Pré?" the bishop demanded.

The monk nodded. The bishop's lips pursed as his eyes narrowed. He gestured for the monk to sit on a bench nearby, just out of the now nervous Monsignor Falcone's sightline. The monk silently complied with the directive, and his shadowy disturbing gaze seemingly rested on the monsignor's flank.

Bishop Sangresante picked up papers in front of him, showing them to the skittish monsignor. "This is a complete list of the Albigensian heretic families whose property holdings and family lines have remained intact up until the present day?"

"Yes, Your Grace," the monsignor replied with an uncomfortable glance at the monk.

"And this list is associated with a collection of files you crated for immediate transport, correct?" the bishop continued.

"Yes, Your Grace. Having heard of Napoleon's brazen

escape from Elba, I took this to be an imperative initiative."

Falcone was relieved to have the opportunity to discuss a component of his responsibilities for which he could confidently claim some semblance of comparable competence. The bishop, it appeared, was already processing other priorities in his mind while dealing with the obligatory unpleasantness of the cleric sitting uncomfortably before him.

"Very well. You shall coordinate the shipment of these documents before the end of the day, and you'll accompany them yourself to Rome to assure they're properly attended to. You will do penance there while awaiting your orders."

"Yes, Your Grace," Falcone replied as he began to stand, seemingly relieved that his inquisition had concluded.

The monk tilted his head slightly at this action, subtly signaling that a clumsy presumption on the monsignor's part had been committed. The bishop glared sharply at Falcone.

"What are you doing?" the bishop demanded.

"I thought you wanted me to attend to the shipping…" the monsignor faltered.

"You have not been dismissed. I require you to remain here while I conclude my business." The bishop then turned to the monk and ordered him to bring in both Monsignor Marinis and Brother Salvatore.

Father Baptisti's meager belongings laid spread out on Monsignor Gaetano Marini's desk—with the elder and younger Jesuit monsignors and Brother Salvatore standing in attendance in the disposition of visitors to the room. The bishop stood over the articles, pushing through the fugitive priest's personal effects with a carved dark walnut walking cane he found in the office and conveniently appropriated. The property consisted of a spare cassock, a change of socks and underclothes in need of laundering, an old worn Bible, a leather wine flask, a rosary, sundry mementos from the Vatican and a small crucifix, all saturated with road dust suggesting extended exposure to a long journey. Distaining direct physical contact with these articles, the bishop flipped through the Bible with the tip of the cane, then peered intently at the elder Jesuit monsignor with an impatient frown and his wide alert predatory eyes—albeit mismatched in color—that reminded the monsignor of a hawk or falcon.

"There is nothing else? What about the saddlery of his mount? I said I needed to see everything the priest left behind. Is utter incompetence a tradition with you Jesuits?"

Intimidated and embarrassed, the older monsignor quickly turned to Brother Salvatore: "Brother Salvatore, go to the stables…"

"No, Brother Salvatore, I require your presence here. Go instruct someone else to bring these things and return immediately."

"Yes, Your Grace," Brother Salvatore replied without hesitation and left the room quickly, while giving an involuntary nervous glance at the mysterious and massive monk who remained hooded and mutely seated by the door. Monsignor Falcone stood nearby, yet remained silent, relieved for now that the focus of the bishop's annoyance was directed somewhere other than himself.

After Brother Salvatore exited, the bishop turned back to Monsignor Gaetano Marini. "It is true then, that this Father

Baptisti never had access to, or was shown the location of archives designated as the *J* section?"

"No, Your Grace," Monsignor Marini replied quickly.

"And no mention of this section was communicated in any way or suggestion?" the bishop continued.

"No, Your Grace. For all purposes, this section does not exist. It cannot be found in any official inventories. Brother Salvatore doesn't even know of it," Marini added.

"Nor should he," the bishop retorted.

"There has never been any confusion on that point, Your Grace. This section has always been regarded as the most sensitive, and only the most…"

The bishop waved the monsignor's defensive reply away as he would a nettlesome fly. He directed his focus on a new line of inquiry.

"The *Q* section…"

"Yes, Your Grace: *'Inventaires, Tables et Répertoires de tout ce qui précède,'*" the monsignor replied.

"What is that?"

"As you know, upon seizure of the Vatican Archives, the French archivists organized them in their own fashion. The *Q* section, Your Grace, is the category they deemed to contain miscellaneous documents which did not fit into the logical categories they created for all the others. It mostly contains inventories and lists of all manner of items which made their way into the archives of the Church of Rome through the centuries. Some represent holdings of relics and treasures of churches through different ages of Christendom. Some are even historical documents of inventories that simply no longer exist, but they represent records for posterity. Some are over a millennium in age and represent a resource for researchers to better understand the times they are studying."

"A millennium old? How far back might a document go, Monsignor?" the bishop inquired, lowering his imperious manner, which gave way to a sense of urgent curiosity.

"It's my understanding there are a few that date to before the Fifth Century, Your Grace," the elder Monsignor dutifully replied.

The bishop glanced at the taciturn monk, whose posture shifted slightly, now to one no longer sitting back, but instead sitting upright with expectancy. The Jesuit and Dominican monsignors noted this change of energy, but remained silent.

"The archive inventory for section Q: give it to me," the bishop commanded.

Monsignor Gaetano Marini crossed to a cabinet behind his desk, with a gesture excusing himself for coming into such close quarters with the bishop, who remained standing at Monsignor Marini's desk. After a moment's search in a pile of papers, Marini found what he sought and extracted a long paper list in fresh parchment from the papers, which he handed to the bishop.

Bishop Sangresante brusquely took the list and pored over it, showing a level of mental intensity he had not revealed before. The two Jesuit monsignors glanced at each other, striving to read in each other a possible hint to what the bishop was searching for. The list was quite long, with hundreds of entries. The room hung in silence as the high-ranking Dominican cleric studied the document with a severe and penetrating focus.

"Perhaps if you could tell me if there was something

specific you were looking for, then I might be able to assist you more effectively," the elder Monsignor Marini offered.

The bishop ignored him as he pored over the list, and the white-haired Monsignor Marini felt that silence from this point forward was the best policy. During this time Brother Salvatore returned, and at Marini's signal, quickly took a seat near him, and sat silently, watching Bishop Sangresante peruse the list with a hawk-like sense of predatory vigilance. And then the bishop abruptly stopped and let out an audible vexed and frustrated sigh, staring at an entry on the page: *Pupillus et Omnimodus Compendium de Appendices.*

The bishop looked up and glanced imperceptibly at the monk, giving a slight nod, at which point the monk stood and stepped over to the bishop. Sangresante leaned over to whisper into his ear through the hood, as his finger remained pointing at the entry, visible to no one else in the room.

"Crate 322," the bishop expressed in *sotto voce* to his faithful assistant as he then turned to Monsignor Falcone and gestured, indicating the mysterious monk. "You will show him to the location of the Q section immediately."

"Yes, Your Grace."

Without further hesitation, the monk and Monsignor Falcone exited, leaving the two Monsignor Marinis and Brother Salvatore alone with the Spanish cleric. Bishop Sangresante stared at Brother Salvatore for a long pause which resulted in a grave sense of discomfort for the humble acolyte who knew better not to speak until spoken to. And after a short time, that took place.

"Describe to me, Brother Salvatore, exactly how this

man was able to escape your notice while it was your one solitary responsibility to accompany him back to his room. Did he overpower you? Did he attack you?"

Deeply embarrassed at having failed Monsignor Marini in a way that apparently had such profound consequences, Brother Salvatore did his best to make amends. "Your Grace, I take all responsibility for what has occurred today. I have failed Monsignor Marini, who has been nothing but beneficial to me and to the duties of the Vatican Archives. I—"

A swift slam of the walking stick on the desk knocked over a lovely ceramic statue of the Virgin Mary, whose delicate arm snapped off, startling the two clerics and Brother Salvatore into wordless shock.

"The details, you moronic toad! I care not for your bumbling excuses! Give me information I can use. What did you see? What did he say? Did he touch you in any way?"

"I don't know. It was all so fast. Before I knew it, he distracted me, and then he apparently ran off up a flight of stairs which led to the old part of the palace. His speed was surprising, almost as though he moved like the wind. I ran down the hallway, and came to an open window…"

"Yes, and what did you see there?"

"I looked out and saw nothing, so I kept my search up inside the palace."

"What do you mean 'nothing'? You looked out the window and saw nothing? Tell me *exactly* what you did see. Were there people in the street?"

"Across the way, two venders were selling poultry and fish. A peasant was driving a cart down in the direction of the Seine. I think he was a rag vender."

"How far was the cart from the window?"

"Twenty yards, maybe less, Your Grace."

"And the back of the cart, what was in it?"

Brother Salvatore thought for a second, and then a pained look came to his face. "Your Grace, it was covered with a tarp. I could not see."

That detail nettled the bishop. "And was there anything near the window that might have facilitated an easier descent?"

This line of questioning created a deeper sense of dread for Brother Salvatore. "Yes, Your Grace. There is a small ledge below the window which leads to a drainage pipe. Someone could have used that to make their escape."

Incredulous at first, the elder Monsignor Marini frowned as he began to piece together a picture more graphically detailed and evolving into alignment with the one in the bishop's mind.

"Bishop, are you saying this Father Baptisti planned to gain entrance with the specific purpose of taking something from the Q section?"

Bishop Antonio del Julia y Sangresante merely stared at the inquiring Jesuit monsignor. The silence was deafening.

At this point, one of the livery boys from the Soubise Palace stables entered with the saddle and bridle from Father Baptisti's mule. The bishop gestured with the cane for the saddle to be placed on the desk as he brusquely swept all other articles off the surface with the cane to make room, taking the ceramic statue of the Virgin Mary with the broken arm in the process. It shattered into pieces on the floor. Glancing at his nephew, Monsignor Gaetano Marini held his tongue, sensing on the most primal level that their very survival was at stake here.

In the Soubise Palace cellar housing the Q section archives, the massive hooded monk deftly climbed over the crates to the location of the one marked '322'. He gestured for Monsignor Falcone to hand him the lantern, and the senior clergyman quickly did so, despite the monk's apparent lower station, not wanting to worsen his state of affairs any more than he could help it. The monk peered into the crate which he had just opened and examined the archives stored within.

His hood hampered his free view of the contents, and so the bishop's man casually pulled the cowl back, revealing a bald pate, with a particularly ugly scar running from the back of his skull down across the forehead. In many years past, some had described its similarity to the course of the Nile River. A thick muscular neck and meaty hands hinted at how powerful the man's body was. Cruel and intent eyes with a predatory assessment glanced at Falcone, who gave a shudder, which in turn produced a slight narrowing of the monk's eyes—a seeming satisfaction of how simple it was to intimidate some people. This was Brother Jerome.

Knowing exactly what he sought, Brother Jerome's search was quick and precise, ferreting through all the contents of the case. Nothing. The monk turned to the monsignor, who stood wide-eyed at the specter of the lantern-lit face which highlighted the more macabre and fierce animalistic features of the monk's visage.

"You had him here, with one of the most precious artifacts known to man, and you let him slip through your fingers. You'll surely burn in hell for this, you meaningless wart," the monk declared in casual accusation and damnation. And with that, the monk pulled the hood back over his face, then handed the lantern back to Falcone. As he climbed off the crates, he directed the monsignor with a sharp gesture to lead them back to where the bishop was located on the second floor of the vast palace complex.

Heading back to Monsignor Marini's offices, Brother Jerome allowed himself the luxury of knowing his presence next to Monsignor Falcone created the deepest sense of fear and dread within his temporary companion. This fear fed the monk as others might dine on a newly slaughtered roasted lamb or seafood fresh from the fisherman's net. This appetizer of a victim's primal fear invigorated him and whetted his appetite. Yet this was in no way comparable to the main course: a hunger which he and the bishop shared—a hunger to satisfy which remained one of his primary mandates for the bishop.

The execution of that charge also provided a source of fulfillment for him, since performing this duty was not a skill which could be performed by just anyone. And he had come to relish this particular duty over the years, since it also delivered that rare and delectable spice of primal fear, along with the main course.

But that was for later. Now he had to report his unfortunate news to the bishop.

Upon their return, and after Brother Jerome delivered the report, the bishop acknowledged the news which he had fully expected. The bishop was, however, more preoccupied with other revelations which he immediately communicated to his faithful assistant.

"Look: there."

The bishop directed Brother Jerome's attention to a small oval mark stamped into the leather—about an inch and a half long—located on the back of the seat of the saddle: a maker's mark. It had the saddler's name inside a border, with decorative flourishes surrounding the outside of the mark. Inside the border it read: *Les Frères Onzon Sellerie*', and in the center of the oval mark, the village from which the saddlemaker hailed: '*Mont Poq*'.

" 'Mont Poq' I *know* this place," Brother Jerome declared, his brow knit, revealing he still could not identify exactly how he knew it.

"Of course you do, Brother Jerome. But it is better known to the world by another name," the bishop observed wryly.

The recollection quickly returned to Brother Jerome. "Mont Poq… Yes, I remember now. It's been almost four hundred years…"

"Exactly. Make the appropriate preparations and send word ahead. We take the road south immediately. I want to be in Chartres before nightfall. We shall be in Languedoc within four days."

"Yes, Master."

Brother Jerome left in haste, knowing once the bishop was ready for action, any delay would not be tolerated.

Monsignor Marini had been studying the bishop's unusual eyes of mismatched color which were now pensively focused out the window. The bishop turned back to the two monsignors who awaited his next pronouncement.

"With the events of Napoleon's possible arrival here in Paris, we must get the selected Holy Inquisition files back to Rome with the greatest haste. We cannot allow even the remotest possibility that he might again take possession of these critical records." The bishop directed his next remark to the elder Monsignor Marini, "You will do everything to facilitate this action." And he then turned to Monsignor Falcone. "Go now and supervise the packing and organize the shipping. Commandeer anyone and anything you need to assure success. And after you accompany the shipment, you will await my orders in Rome. I shall follow in due course, after I have attended to other pressing business."

"Yes, Your Grace."

As Monsignor Falcone left, the bishop glared at the remaining Jesuit clerics as they stood flat-footed. Seeing they did not dare to move without clear permission to do so, Bishop Sangresante gave an irritated look and gestured impatiently for them to leave him. Brother Salvatore also departed immediately with the two Jesuit monsignors. Alone in Monsignor Marini's offices, the bishop again gazed out the window, into a gathering storm in the distance, he muttered quietly.

"At last I will have you, and all of your secrets."

Outside his own offices, Monsignor Gaetano Marini went with his nephew and Brother Salvatore to the younger Monsignor Marini's offices further down the hall. On their way, royal archivists conjectured and gossiped about the epochal events happening in the country. Speculations of the fragile state of France spread like wildfire. Now with Napoleon returning from Elba, confusion reigned. No one was quite sure whose orders should be followed now. Should the imperious officials of the Bourbon king be obeyed? Or should the lowly administrative assistants, earlier Napoleonic archive officials, who had been ordered to stay on site to facilitate the transition of power for the monarchy, now be in command as they stridently claimed?

Insulting arguments had already broken out over jurisdiction, and the monsignor knew he needed to address the most urgent of his responsibilities: the files of the Vatican Archives identified by Bishop Sangresante, and most important to him and his Jesuit Brotherhood: Section J.

The Village of La Beauce
Île de France, France
3 March, 1815 AD – Evening Hour

A small village, boasting its establishment long before the Medieval age, it stood on the northern edge of the rich fertile plain known also as La Beauce—the source of the town's name and the breadbasket for the region.

Just beyond the north side of the village, a narrow dirt lane crossed a small stone bridge spanning a wide rushing stream. Interrupting this bucolic setting, a rumbling of hooves pounding the earth resounded as it amplified to a cacophony. Shortly thereafter, a company of the King's Royal cavalry, two abreast, appeared trotting swiftly, north along the country track, with a clear sense of urgency. It took more than two minutes for the column of two hundred to pass and finally disappear up the narrow road to the north. They, along with military regiments across France, were being mustered to assemble in support against the threat of Napoleon's resurgence. This column was headed to Paris to reinforce the garrison there.

The dust created by their passing rose and drifted across an adjacent wheat field. Near this byway, a low stone wall edged the road and turned at a right angle meeting another lesser track—a somewhat overgrown pathway which defined the outer edge of this small quiet hamlet. From the shadows of the lane a rider emerged and he guided his horse out onto the road to gain a better view of the track to the north where the last royal horse soldiers had just disappeared from view. The rider—Roger—signaled another in the shaded lane, and Jean-Marc joined him. Both glanced ahead to their destination not far in the distance and visible down the narrow road to the south: the village. They rode on toward it.

La Beauce hosted an old stone church, two inns for travelers, and the traditional array of local craftsmen's establishments: a miller, blacksmith, saddlery shop, two bakers and stores supplying the general needs of the modest population. In the distance, further to the south, across the broad fertile fields of wheat, the top half of a striking medieval cathedral dominated the landscape with its powerful presence: Chartres Cathedral. The two riders approached the village along the road, the gait of their horses leisurely, as the two enjoyed the waning light of the day and the relaxation of their pastoral locale.

"I'm very glad to finally be free of the oppressive

confines of that city. Each time I go, I find the pressure of humanity in a constant state of agitation, all competing for their wants and desires, while all the time missing the essentials of their needs," Jean-Marc observed.

"But isn't that half the fun of being there, Master?" Roger inquired with his distinctive and refreshing sense of irreverence and readiness to adopt a counterpoint stance, which Jean-Marc dearly appreciated.

"I cannot argue against your point, Roger. And those of a younger spirit than my own might find it exciting to jump into the fray, if only for the entertainment value of it all. My view is, of course, everything in proper measure—with an eye on the consequences of all choices—as a small frog's jump might make ripples on the far side of a pool," Jean-Marc sagely observed.

"So the frog gets a little wet. He was destined to jump in anyway, right? It is his nature," Roger countered.

"You have a natural, native wisdom I've always found refreshing and often instructive, Roger. Though sometimes you might miss the mark. All in all, however, I'm grateful for your company and all of your invaluable assistance over these years," Jean-Marc said with an affectionate smile.

Roger returned the smile. "And I owe you in the greatest of measures, Master. I'm even more grateful for those opportunities you extended to me, considering our beginnings."

"Venice seems so long ago, doesn't it?" Jean-Marc remarked with a reflective smile. Then, as they cantered into the village, he pointed out the inns which stood further down the main road running through the village. He noted one in particular: *Le Coq Blanc*.

"If earlier travels through here bear any value, that inn caters more to the needs of travelers, while the first attracts a larger local crowd. I'd prefer for our passage here to be as inconspicuous as possible."

"Of course, Master," Roger replied as they reined their horses in front of the inn and dismounted. Jean-Marc then pointed out the livery barn where they could board their mounts—which he asked Roger to attend to—while he made arrangements for their lodgings inside the inn.

Right after Jean-Marc entered *Le Coq Blanc*, and as Roger walked the horses across the road to the livery stable, a well-appointed covered carriage came thundering through the village, forcing Roger to pull his horses back abruptly and calm them from spooking. As the carriage surged on in the direction of Chartres, Roger yelled after it, with angry frustration.

"Idiot! Be careful! You could kill someone!"

The carriage did not slow down. However, he did see a head thrust out, glaring back at him, and the sight of it gave Roger an involuntary shiver. The bald pate of an ugly and intense-looking man, with a scar running across the top of his skull, stared intensely at Roger with the eyes of some sort of hideous demon. An easy intent to exact cruel slaughter could be read on his ruthless features, and Roger got the message immediately, feigning to look after his nervous horses, rather than maintain eye contact with this strange, fiendish creature in the carriage.

Inside the carriage, Brother Jerome turned to Bishop

Sangresante. "We could stop here, Your Grace. There is an inn, and we could find the sustenance we need without the prying eyes of a larger city and then move on without consequence." Brother Jerome's teeth clenched with the desire to wreak unexpected and horrifying havoc on the individual who had just insulted their passage.

"We will find sustenance and lodging in Chartres. It is just thirty minutes further and I have additional business to conduct there. You must learn to control your urges more responsibly if you are to be of continuing use to me, Brother Jerome," the bishop chided him, knowing full well the true and vindictive motivation behind the monk's suggestion.

"Yes, Your Grace," Brother Jerome replied. But he did not like being chastened, despite the fact his benefactor had carried him through an impressive series of ascending accomplishments and garnering of influence, following a closely scrutinized strategy developed over the centuries of their long time together.

This comparatively mild rebuke caused Brother Jerome to sit back silently and reflect on the journey they had traveled together since their destinies first became linked so very long ago in that tumultuous Egyptian city on the Mediterranean—Alexandria, once the undisputed capitol of the Knowledge of Mankind.

After attending to the horses, and now inside the *Le Coq Blanc*, Roger found Jean-Marc waiting for him in the humble tavern section of the first floor, populated by over a dozen other travelers taking their repast and refreshment. The dominant discussion of the patrons focused on the disposition of Napoleon's movements and what might become of France. Roger joined his master at a table where a thick green bottle of local red wine, without a label, and two short, thick drinking vessels of crudely crafted glass were set out on a rough-hewn wood table well-worn with age and use. Jean-Marc poured both glasses to the brim, handed one to Roger, and raised his own.

"To new hopes and new beginnings, my friend," Jean-Marc warmly exclaimed as he drank. His companion stared at him with a meaningful smile.

"That's the first time you've called me that, Master," Roger observed in an unusually rare diffident manner.

"Friendship is a thing earned and cannot be taken for granted, Roger. You've earned my friendship and my trust over the years we've been together."

"Friends, as in: we are equals?" Roger inquired further, re-filling his glass and drinking deeply from it.

Jean-Marc studied Roger with an appreciative smile. "Friends as if we are brothers on the same path."

Roger studied the canvas shoulder bag, which sat on the broad bench, close beside Jean-Marc. Roger gestured at the thick oblong bulk of the book concealed by the canvas.

"So that's what this has been all about?"

"Yes, Roger. And I could not have achieved its retrieval without your help."

"While it remained briefly in my care, there was of course no opportunity to look at, so rapid have the events been unfolding. May I see it now, Jean-Marc?" Roger asked, addressing his master with surprising and familiar ease, which Jean-Marc privately noted.

"Of course, Roger." Jean-Marc replied, casually scrutinizing the tavern gathering, glancing at an old retired war veteran recounting his campaign with Napoleon in Russia. While no eyes were on them, Jean-Marc expressed caution regarding Roger's request.

"I'll let you see it in due course and in the right setting. We've worked a long time to recover this, and I don't want to risk anything by showing it now in the presence of people I don't know. Later tonight."

"Of course, Master," Roger replied, reverting to the more formal form of address, and with a trace of irritation and inner conflict within that he did not quite understand. Part of him, however, felt he had every right to see the book now, considering all he had done to make its return possible. He had forgone examining the object when he transported it from the city when it was in his care alone. And indeed now he believed, in some way, that this book was partly his because of his considerable efforts to regain it and protect it.

"...And the tide of war rises once again! With Napoleon on the march to reclaim his throne, the alliance to the Bourbon monarchy won't stand still for that! Mark my words, friends, the fresh blood of thousands will flow before the year is out!" The massive old veteran spoke loudly, as he swaggered along through the tavern with an empty glass in his hand. His uneven steps brought him alongside Jean-Marc's table, as he spied their bottle of wine. The old—well into his fifties—yet incredibly robust bearded man gestured at the bottle.

"Care to share some of that nectar of the gods with a humble veteran of the Russian Campaign? For one who survived the freezing retreat across hundreds of miles of hostile terrain, all the while loyally protecting his brothers-in-arms every inch of the way?" the man heartily inquired with a curious and admittedly overbearing vigorous charm.

Roger rose quickly, ready to fend off this unwelcome intrusion. Jean-Marc belayed this action, however, with a welcoming gesture and kind words. "Indeed, put your glass down, and join us, sir, but not before you have introduced yourself!"

The veteran smiled, bowed grandly and spoke with panache. "Master Sergeant Gaston Veilleux, infantry veteran of Egypt, Austerlitz, and of course the tragic, but historic, Russian Campaign, at your service, sir! I can tell you stories that'll make your heart soar, your skin crawl and your blood boil!" He sat down on the bench next to Roger as he spoke and slid his glass in front of Jean-Marc, who filled it to the brim with an accommodating smile. Roger, however, after being forced to move and make ample room on the bench for the hulking man, viewed this new disturbance with undisguised displeasure.

"Tell me of your experience in Egypt, Sergeant Veilleux," Jean-Marc requested respectfully as he gestured with his glass in a toast.

A spark of memory illumination lit the old veteran's eyes as he raised his glass, then emptied it quickly in one long quaff, and slid it back across the table to be refilled. Jean-Marc, in the meanwhile, gestured for the inn maiden to bring another bottle.

As the grizzled veteran began to recount his experience of the Battle of the Pyramids—of facing the Mameluks and their spirited armies, who fatally faced the powerful organization of Napoleon's army, along with their classic square fighting formation in the desert, and in the shadow of the pyramids—Roger noticed something very curious between his two companions at the table. While the veteran broadly told his tale, gesturing expressively with one hand, the fingers of his other hand danced lightly across a small square with letters carved into the wood, almost invisible and worn with age. And as the veteran paused with his fingers, Jean-Marc's fingers slid to the square, his index finger also tracked across the square, seemingly in reply. The square itself was somewhat difficult to read, but after adjusting his eyes to it, in the darkness of the inn, Roger could discern the pattern.

S	A	T	O	R
A	R	E	P	O
T	E	N	E	T
O	P	E	R	A
R	O	T	A	S

Roger came to realize they were 'speaking', quickly spelling out words in some pre-arranged coded system which did not directly correspond to the letters of the grid. Upon quick reflection, he surmised that with twenty-five squares, they most likely represented the first twenty-five letters of the alphabet. And he now studied the new overbearing arrival with a closer scrutiny and finally a revelation occurred.

"I *know* you! You came to our apartments in Paris some

months ago and delivered a bag of potatoes to my master," Roger declared.

The old veteran smiled, having originally wondered if Jean-Marc's valet was as astute as he should be. "And what a bag of potatoes it was, eh, Master?"

"Potatoes indeed, Gaston, potatoes indeed," Jean-Marc nodded with bemusement.

Roger, while pleased he had gained insight into some aspect of this previously unknown relationship between his master and this new arrival, found himself now on new ground trying to gauge exactly what his own relationship might exactly be with the Marquis de Rennes. Roger knew Jean-Marc had secrets, but he had not until now really paused to reflect on how truly labyrinthine and extensive they were, and how distinctly outside of that world of activity Roger may stand.

"So you were here waiting for the master, that's it, eh? And the discussion you had there?" Roger pointed to the Sator-Rotas square. "That's some kind of code. I'm guessing each square means a letter, except maybe the 'Z'?"

The wizened sergeant studied him with a sense of admiration and then nodded to Jean-Marc. "All correct, except for the 'Z'. He's a quick study, he is, Master, despite my reservations. I grant you may have chosen him well to be your loyal valet."

"He is indeed much more than that. I couldn't have achieved what we did without him," Jean-Marc admitted.

"We've got the book," Roger declared proudly, possibly much louder than was necessary.

Jean-Marc placed his hand on Roger's arm and with his eyes communicated a cautioning message, glancing around to the rest of the patrons of the inn, who apparently took no notice of their discussion. Jean-Marc leaned in closer so only his companions at the table might hear.

"While we enjoy success in the short term, we must remain vigilant to the unseen. My 'table' discussion with Gaston was for him to report his surveillance of the inn which produced no suspicious characters, and this information makes our stay here more comfortable... for now."

"But how did you know this table would have this letter grid, Master?" Roger asked quietly.

"I've been here before, Roger. I know the owner, Raymond Flesche. I helped his great grandfather open the inn some years ago. Raymond traditionally keeps this table reserved for special guests, friends from old times, as it were. You'll meet him soon enough. He's in the kitchen, tending to some sort of culinary surprise for us," Jean-Marc revealed with an expectant smile.

Sergeant Veilleux chortled. "I *like* Raymond's surprises! And I'm starving! I could eat a goat, a pig, and possibly that lovely woman over there!" He laughed heartily, having indicated the lovely barmaid who just served the adjoining table.

Jean-Marc chuckled generously, while Roger, smiling mildly, remained in reserve, still trying to gauge where he fit in the equation of this new tribal dynamic.

"What news of the road, Sergeant?" Jean-Marc queried.

Gaston Veilleux immediately turned all business, leaning in closer so only those at the table could hear. "Napoleon's brazen act has set the countryside abuzz, Master. Suddenly it's about whose side you're with. I've heard troops are being mustered to oppose him, *if* they can find him! Others I hear say they'd join his cause in a second! You know King Louis XVIII has made not a few enemies since Napoleon's abdication, what with all of his newly empowered proxies, stepping on all the throats of Napoleon's people. Now the wheel seems to be turning," Veilleux observed.

"And the road?" Jean-Marc repeated.

Sergeant Gaston Veilleux had just finished his glass of wine, once again filled it, emptying the bottle, which he picked up and gestured to the barmaid for a refill. "Ah yes, Master, of course—the road. It appears in the coming days there will be prodigious troop movements. The larger towns will be nerve centers of activity, and any strangers passing through might be challenged, or pressed into service. I recommend we take the back roads south. It's less direct, not as quick, but I think the safest option."

"This has been my thinking as well. I achieved my main objective today, and taking the route you suggest will allow me to catch up on some reading, as it were," Jean-Marc observed.

"And so that's the item in question?" Sergeant Veilleux asked, indicating with a slight nod the canvas pack which sat next to Jean-Marc on the bench.

"One and the same," Jean-Marc confirmed.

"It's settled then, except for one detail. We have one more companion on our trip south, Master."

Gaston gestured to someone across the room. Out of the gloom of the far corner, a raven-haired beautiful young woman appeared—dressed plainly, yet outshining her wardrobe—and strode toward them with fluid grace.

"My daughter: Solange."

Roger viewed this new arrival with an avid sense of interest and expectation. Solange, however, remained focused on Jean-Marc, as she bowed her head modestly and then offered a demure smile.

"Master, it's good to see you again," she declared with sincere reverence and affection.

"And you as well, Solange." Jean-Marc smiled as he stood to embrace her, and then both sat back down at the table, she at his side.

Solange now chanced a glance at Roger, who was eager to connect with her. When their eyes met, he smiled broadly, eyes glinting with practiced charm. She hazarded a brief shy smile in return, despite her protective father's watchful gaze. As final introductions concluded, Raymond, the innkeeper, arrived with a huge platter of food—roasted rabbit, chicken and lamb with cooked potatoes, carrots, turnips, two kinds of bread and more—placing it referentially in front of them as more wine was served.

Jean-Marc surveyed the sumptuous offerings with praise and gratitude and pressed a small object wrapped in silk into Raymond's hands, despite the proprietor's attempt to refuse payment, expressing extreme gratitude for past support. Nonetheless, Jean-Marc insisted; and the innkeeper took the gift with profound appreciation.

A short time later, just inside the kitchen, the entrance to which opened onto one end of the dining area, Raymond showed his wife the gift he had received as she stood in the doorway with him. The light of the kitchen lanterns caught the refracting properties of a clear precious jewel—a cut diamond of high quality. Raymond's wife held the gem with transfixed adoration and hugged her husband in quick celebration of their good fortune. She also bowed slightly with thanks to Jean-Marc who smiled and nodded in acknowledgment from across the room. As an afterthought, she glanced around to assure that this business had proceeded without prying eyes, and then the door to the kitchen closed again.

The only tavern patron who had the right line of sight to have witnessed this interaction was a lone man with an eye patch who had arrived after Gaston's earlier reconnaissance of the patrons in the room. To the innkeeper's wife's observation he appeared to be well into his cups and woozily called to the barmaid to refill his tankard.

As Raymond's wife returned to her duties in the kitchen and was out of sight, the man with the eye patch dropped some element of his seemingly drunken behavior, and brought his focus back to rest on Jean-Marc's company. They had caught his notice earlier, and now he studied them with keen interest, as a lion stalking unsuspecting prey.

Later that evening, in their room, Roger lay in bed, trying to sleep, his mind buzzing and body restless at all of the new developments which had taken place in the last few hours. That as well as the fact that the one room in the inn they had been given, which was the best lodgings in the establishment, was still not quite large enough for all four travelers.

The two modest wooden-framed beds had been pushed together to afford the most amount of sleeping surface possible, with Sergeant Veilleux and his daughter occupying the one on the left—theoretically, since Gaston's bulk pressed against him—while Roger tried to keep some space available for Jean-Marc, who sat reading at the lantern-lit small table by the lead-paned window overlooking the main road running through the village.

Exhausted from the day, Roger struggled to sleep, but Gaston's snoring and his massive restless girth, as well as the occasional explosive flatulence assaulted Roger leaving him in appalled irritation. Add to that the arrival of Gaston's daughter, whose lithe body, graceful movements, sensitive eyes and sensual mouth, to say nothing of the beautiful natural radiance she exuded, amplified Roger's stimulation in profound ways. And at the core of his inability to find rest in sleep was the presence of The Book.

Earlier, Jean-Marc allowed Roger to leaf through the thick and venerable tome. Its ancient velum pages, however, only served to agitate Roger's attention even further. Written in numerous languages he had no hope of understanding—such as Coptic, Egyptian hieroglyphs, Aramaic and Hebrew, add to that ancient Greek and Latin, as well as mysterious symbols, diagrams, schematics and mathematical equations—it all made Roger's head spin with what information might be included in there.

And it was all information he *could not know*, even if he wanted to, and even if he had The Book in his solitary possession. Roger knew he was a bright man. Jean-Marc had complimented him on it, and Roger even allowed himself the growth of a private personal mythology where Jean-Marc was helpless without him.

Yet now observing Jean-Marc pore over The Book, and make written notes in a small journal he kept, unfortunately eradicated that comforting old myth. In its wake came a vague feeling of jealousy and resentment, which Roger immediately swatted aside in his sour thoughts, reflections which had been inflamed by the large, farting bear of a man sleeping beside him.

To calm his mind, having just heard Solange sigh in her sleep, Roger found himself imagining being with her, alone in a quiet pine mountain meadow, running across a rushing stream together, barefoot, laughing and holding hands. As they reached the tall, soft grass, amid a sea of wild saffron flowers, they fell into each other's arms on the grass and made passionate love. As Roger found distracted comfort in this fantasy, some part of him insisted that he must possess Solange in reality, not just in his dreams.

Jean-Marc glanced over at the bed, teaming with companions, and allowed himself the luxury of a smile. He had not permitted himself to be in the company of so many people, for whom he had such strong affection, for a long time. Too often being in close proximity he had brought grave misfortune to those people who chose to be near him. But now, with The Book in hand, some part of Jean-Marc experienced a peace of mind and a robust hope for the future which he had not known for many, many years.

The sound of numerous horse hooves on the hard earth, riding fast, caught his attention, and he glanced out the window. A company of royalist cavalry, about eighty men strong, on the move, rode through the night to points north.

Their mission was obviously of high urgency, judging by the lateness of the hour and the speed of their forced canter through the tight confines of the village. He assumed correctly that these troops were on their way to Paris, to be in support of the King against any action by Napoleon's loyalists who were openly re-grouping themselves in anticipation of Bonaparte's triumphant return to Paris in the coming days.

Exactly when this arrival was, or precisely what route Napoleon might be taking north from the Mediterranean coast, remained unknown. That uncertainty had put the country's populace on edge, restless and suspicious. The detachment's passing served as a sober reminder for Jean-Marc that his work was far from done, and that he and his companions had many miles and days of travel before they achieved their ultimate destination.

After the horse soldiers passed, and the village returned to quiet—except for the flurry of barking dogs in the night—Jean-Marc refocused his studious attention again on The Book. He resumed his study of the tome which had not been in the hands of individuals with true understanding eyes for centuries.

Unlike his traveling companions, Jean-Marc's need for sleep was quite unlike other people. He could go days without it and not lose any advantage. He knew through the years how his metabolism had evolved into something very different from others, which would also mean that in the following winter, he might tuck himself away somewhere and sleep, more to hibernate, for over two months, and in doing so be refreshed and vital for seasons to come.

In the meanwhile, he returned to his detailed study of

The Book. The passage he was currently studying in ancient Coptic concerned a certain process he had been attempting to recreate without the benefit of this reference for years, and only with minimal success.

As he read further, he nodded with understanding, recognizing where his well-intentioned, yet slightly misguided work, had gone astray. And he wrote more notes.

In this state of deeply focused activity, he failed to notice Roger watching him from the bed, his valet's eyes barely open, but studying Jean-Marc with an otherwise expressionless face.

St. Paul's Chapel
Chartres, France
3 March, 1815 AD – Evening Hour

The Chartres Cathedral bell tolled the tenth hour as it echoed across the small city to this far more humble chapel on the western edge of the ancient town. The gathering inside, which had just reached a quorum, was no normal assembly of local parishioners. All were men of military bearing, with a rough, no-nonsense manner, and all were dressed for travel.

Bishop Antonio del Julia y Sangresante climbed into the narrow spiral staircase leading up to the high pulpit—festooned with ornate Christian gilt carvings of angels ascending to heaven—which overlooked the small meeting

139

of some twenty-five men. Standing nearby the base of the pulpit, in the shadows, Brother Jerome watched the proceedings in hooded silence.

After staring at the group for a long pause, the bishop spoke, his voice quiet at first, forcing those in attendance to lean forward to listen more intently.

"These are times which shall determine the course of history for the entire world, my brothers. As the Antichrist makes his infernal bid to reclaim unholy power, the armies of King Louis XVIII ride out from all corners of France to stop him. All of the crown heads of Europe, currently assembled in Vienna, are watching, weighing what their next action will require to assure that the balance of power, and God's righteous plan for mankind, is protected and maintained. We pray for their success on God's holy battlefield to crush this heretic Napoleon once and for all. What damage he inflicted on the state of the Holy Roman Empire—to Rome's sacred mission in the world, including the Holy Inquisition, and the humiliations he attempted to impress on the Holy Father, and the Vatican as a whole— will take years to heal. But I have faith God's will shall be done. I have faith that order and rightful leadership shall be restored permanently. And I have faith that those who supported the demon sent by Satan shall be punished severely, so that mankind shall not dare even to think of such reprehensible actions for untold generations to come. *This* is the will of God, my brothers."

The bishop stared down at the gathering for a pause, and then spoke with a rising sense of drama and volume. "But another grave threat to the Holy Universal Order exists which may very well pose the greatest danger of them all, my sons. Napoleon could not have achieved his evil goals without help. And one man in particular stands as the cornerstone of Bonaparte's malevolent designs. He is beyond evil incarnate. A necromancer, a rapist, a murderer, and a Philistine, he has eaten the flesh of new-born babies and drunken their blood. He has communed with the devil on a regular basis, and he has operated as a secret ringleader of spreading diabolical pagan and heretical beliefs among the innocent, by tempting them into licentious cabals where the worst abominations occur. *And* he has served as Bonaparte's personal emissary with Satan himself!"

The bishop displayed a wild, wide-eyed look, dramatically accentuated by his blue and green eyes, as he searched his audience to assess how successfully his message was reaching them. All were entranced. Confident he had their undivided attention, the bishop continued.

"But he made one fatal mistake. Adopting a disguise of a humble priest—he only today penetrated the confines of the Vatican Archives currently stored in Paris—a consequence of Napoleon's nefarious sacking of Rome. And this man stole an ancient pagan book of necromancy which had been secured and safely stored years ago by the Holy Vatican for study by our venerable fathers of the Holy Inquisition, so that they might be better armed to combat the infernal designs of Satan. And as I speak at this very moment, we now know this agent of Satan is not far from us. He is somewhere on the road traveling south."

The bishop gestured to Brother Jerome, who produced a sheet of paper from his robes with a drawing of a man's likeness on it: Jean-Marc. He held it up in front of the gathering for all to see.

"Study this likeness well. Note the right eyebrow is bleached white—the mark of the devil himself, laughing at all faithful who refuse to recognize his cursed signs."

As the sheet passed from one man to the next, all intently studied the graphic likeness, an albeit somewhat crude, portrait of Jean-Marc.

"You ride at first light. He must be taken alive, and the book he carries must be recovered intact." The bishop stared at the gathering. "Are there any questions?"

There were none. The bishop's gesture of dismissal brought about their silent departure from the chapel. By the time the bishop reached the bottom of the stairs to the pulpit, he was now alone in the chapel with Brother Jerome, at whom he glanced absently. "Now bring me sustenance," he commanded.

Brother Jerome nodded with a slight smile. "Yes, Your Grace... With pleasure."

The bell of Cathédrale Notre-Dame de Chartres chimed twelve times. A myriad of responsibilities lay before the determined cleric. Yet, with all things considered, he knew well of Rome's profound gratitude for his tireless work.

Had they truly known who, or rather *what* he was, he wondered if they would feel that same sense of indebtedness. There were times, however, when he reflected with bemusement that along the way of the various personas he manifested through the years that someone in the Vatican should have somehow had a hint or a clue of what he represented. Yet that question never came.

And over these years, he grew more accustomed to his age-old rhythm of cementing influence in the local clergy and then rising to a position of prominence, each time with a new name and a new personal history.

The older members, the ones who remembered him from their early years, and who found him again in front of them still in the prime of his youth, might sometimes present a problem, but rarely a serious and never an enduring one. Venerable older clergy members so often frail of health in their twilight age suffered heart attacks and other natural causes of death that were to be expected. They always had honorable funerals and were remembered for their loving service to the church. Exactly how they died, at that point in their lives, rarely became a topic of discussion. And Sangresante always made sure the deaths appeared as natural as possible, considering the circumstances.

He needed as well to restrain Brother Jerome at times from giving in to his baser desires, to commit ugly mayhem or enact a 'harvesting' on one of the old clergy. This management of the willful monk's actions remained critical to the bishop's maintenance of keeping his two conflicting worlds apart.

Bishop Sangresante studied papers, penned responses quickly and sealed them with crimson wax and his large gold and ruby signet ring. The core of his thoughts, however, remained totally occupied with the prospect of finally closing in on his prey. He believed his quarry made a fatal mistake by leaving the saddle behind at Soubise Palace.

While he sensed it gave him a critical advantage, experience told the cleric that he must not slip into over-confidence. The bishop needed to plan for all contingencies, to anticipate every unexpected event.

One of his first steps, upon arriving in Chartres, was to send a few loyal brothers south in advance of his movements, to arrive well ahead of him and to summon the rest of his Spanish cadre. His forerunners would also set up a beachhead of sorts, to provide for the bishop's arrival in as inconspicuous a manner as possible and to engage in an initial reconnaissance of the target city, while it lingered still in a state of blissful unawareness. The bishop was prepared, of course, to lay the entire *ville* to ruin in pursuit of his goal—which he had done in the past in Béziers in 1209. Yet he was also a fundamentally sensible man, feeling he would lay ruin to a place only if it helped him achieve his objectives.

Outside the priory, in the plaza overlooking the entrance to the Chartres Cathedral, the sound of horse hooves on cobblestone and the shouts of cavalry officers drew his attention to the window. There he observed a company preparing to ride north, undoubtedly on their way to support the royal troops mustering for the inevitable confrontation with Napoleon, wherever that might be.

Yet this activity, despite the fact it was the only subject on the lips of locals, whether pro or con, held little interest or concern for him. The looming contest of power for the control of the country had no significance whatsoever. His driving and primary goal endured as it had through the medieval Cathar Inquisition, through all the ensuing years. The quest remained to hunt down his quarry, and to regain possession of the knowledge contained in The Book, a tome which at one time had been his very own precious and forbidden treasure.

While his long-term goals remained clear, a sensation surged though him. A flash of something electric washed over him which left an emptiness and a fatigue that resembled a bottomless gnawing hunger. He knew it too well. The bishop also understood that a special nourishment was the solution for his craving. He glanced at the door impatiently, since he expected Brother Jerome by this hour, but he had not yet appeared.

The bishop again tried to focus on his administrative work of the Inquisition, but the lightness of his head, a slight dizziness, now distracted him and ate into his productiveness. With a sense of irritation, he knew the best thing to do was to lie down, but his driving persona demanded that he keep working and planning.

Brother Jerome finally arrived, after less than a quarter hour, and brought the bishop what he required and craved.

"Your *Sangria*, Your Grace," Brother Jerome announced, as he handed a large earthenware jug to his master.

The bishop took the vessel, poured some of the contents into a glass, and studied the red liquid intently.

"It is prepared exactly as required?" The bishop interrogated in a ritual exchange the two had performed through the centuries.

"Exactly to your specifications, Your Grace," Brother Jerome replied accommodatingly, sharing a rare smile. Quite familiar with the years-long tradition they went through, the monk knew well the bishop's need to assure the highest quality of product being presented to him.

"And it is fresh?" the bishop demanded as sniffed slightly at the contents and brought the glass to his lips.

"Yes, My Lord. This fruit was harvested hardly more than an hour ago," the monk replied, licking his lips slightly.

Bishop Sangresante took a tentative sip at first and swallowed. His eyes closed slightly as he seemed to sigh, then raised the glass again and consumed the contents of the glass in three thirsty gulps.

Brother Jerome looked on, pleased. "Good, eh?"

Ignoring the monk, the bishop frowned slightly at the large earthenware tankard, which he finally picked up with a hungry anticipation. He began to drink deeply, with an animal-like ravenous gusto. Finishing it, he handed the tankard back to Brother Jerome. "It was a special flavor, earthy and nutty in its own way." Somewhat sated, Bishop Sangresante finally released a small smile of satisfaction and licked his lips. "You have more?"

"Yes, Your Grace. I'll bring the remainder of the batch I prepared for you. I wanted to make sure it met with your satisfaction."

The bishop nodded and waved his hand absentmindedly, returning to the work at his desk, leaving Brother Jerome to exit and attend to fulfilling the cleric's requirement.

As he strode alone down the hallway, back to his quarters on the first floor, Brother Jerome experienced one of his temporary waves of irritation and resentment toward the man he served for so many years. Part of him wanted to brutally murder the bishop and step on his entrails which he had cut from the cleric's gut—an intimately familiar sentiment for him.

As always, however, he returned to the sensible

perspective that the bishop's intelligence and insights had consistently and reliably guided them through various pitfalls in the past. Sangresante always delivered them to a position of influence and privilege, to which in the long run, the monk had grown quite accustomed. Brother Jerome put up with the imperious manner of the bishop because it gave him advantages he could never have known based on his beginnings, along with his admittedly very basic instincts and tastes.

Indeed in some way they were a couple, married to their destiny. They had something of a symbiotic relationship, in that one could not really survive without the other. And indeed they shared one eternal passion: the capture of the one individual who had eluded them for centuries, but who now appeared to be tangibly within their grasp. To capture and take control of this elusive prey would be a crowning and empowering achievement, and it would transform their circumstances altogether.

Brother Jerome arrived at his quarters which had been set up to resemble a kitchen of sorts. A large urn filled with dark liquid sat on a table and jars of powdered substances laid about it, having been part of the bishop's 'sangria' recipe. Brother Jerome took a long drink of his own share of the brew, grunting with an animal satisfaction at the experience, before refilling the bishop's tankard and dutifully bringing it back for the pontiff's pleasure. The dark red liquid smeared his lips as he licked them, and a large drop of the crimson solution fell onto his chin unnoticed.

Some distance away from the priory, in a dark alley, where trash had been heaped by local shopkeepers, two pale white legs, haphazardly splayed on the cobblestone, laid partly visible in the dank light splashing from a lantern on the street at the end of the alley.

Closer examination of these remains would come in the morning with an ugly and horrifying discovery by a young shop apprentice depositing more refuse. The grisly finding would reveal the body of a dead young girl. What was most distinctive about her condition was that she had been completely drained of her precious bodily fluids: her blood.

The two small distinct marks on her neck would have been described as fang or bite marks to an objective observer. The circumstances of her demise were unlikely to be resolved or discovered any time soon, since no other clues to the cause of her gruesome death—except strange bruising on her ankles—could be found anywhere around. And following her discovery, supernatural explanations of bloodthirsty demons would seem to provide the only logical explanation.

The Village of La Beauce
Île de France, France
4 March, 1815 AD – Morning Hour

"**Y**es, Roger, I understand your concern, but after significant reflection, I believe this is the best plan for us. We'll meet up south of Vendome; Gaston knows the place. We've camped there before," Jean-Marc reassured Roger.

They were in the stable as the quartet finalized the arrangements of preparing their saddled horses for their journey.

"But I think it's best if I travel with you, My Lord. If anything should happen to you, and I was not there to be at your service, I wouldn't be able to live with myself," Roger insisted with urgent concern, hoping to change the traveling plan.

"I'd wager it'd be the honored marquis who'd be more active in saving your hide than the reverse, should urgent action be required, lad," Gaston laughed as he tightened the leather straps of a large satchel attached to his riding saddle.

"We'll ride as planned. As we progress, we'll consider our alternatives. For now, we must press on with this arrangement, Roger," Jean-Marc spoke with finality, yet with a reassuring smile.

Gaston slapped Roger on the back with good-natured robustness. "It's settled then. We ride now, and we'll prepare camp for the master."

With Gaston's compelling hand gesture toward Roger's horse, and no counterarguments remaining for the valet, he had no option but to climb onto his steed alongside Gaston. Mounted now, the unlikely pair faced Jean-Marc and Solange who both remained on the ground finalizing preparations for their own departure.

"The bivouac will be prepared for your comfort well before sunset, with a hot meal waiting for you, My Lord," Gaston promised as he turned to Roger and led his horse toward the stable's doorway opening out onto the main road of the village. "Let's give these mounts some exercise, eh?"

And with that, Gaston trotted out the door and cantered off at a quick clip. Roger glanced at the door, then at Jean-Marc with a look communicating some hope a change of plans might be forthcoming from his master. Jean-Marc smiled and waved, and Roger in turn was compelled to guide his mount out the doorway. Gazing south down the road, he called to Gaston whose horse was now well down the lane.

"Sergeant Veilleux, wait for me!"

The only reply came as a distant and taunting laughter. Roger spurred his horse into a quick gallop to catch up with his assigned companion and guide. Jean-Marc laughed, observing Roger's disconcerted state with amusement as he turned to his horse.

"So we're devout pilgrims on our way to Santiago de Compostella, My Lord?" Solange asked with studied shyness that revealed a spark of other charming liveliness behind her practiced demure manner.

Jean-Marc nodded and smiled in reply. "Gaston says you ride well. But for now, we'll travel in a manner indicating no urgency. As you can tell, the byways we chose are not the direct or main ones but will bring us to our destination in due course."

"Yes, Milord," Solange replied quietly.

"And I think it's best if you refer to me by my given name. I don't want to call any attention to what might be perceived as my rank or position," Jean-Marc advised with familial warmth.

"Very well… Jean-Marc," she responded, trying the sound of the name on her lips, a name her father would never dare articulate with such familiarity. She liked it. "Shall we ride, Jean-Marc?"

As they set off down the road, heading south out of the village, the shadows that hung between two nearby buildings shifted. A man's form could now be distinguished. He had been standing concealed for some time. And as the figure leaned out surreptitiously, further to track the couple's departure from the village, the broad brim of his battered straw hat shifted and his head turned; his eye patch came clearly into view.

It took Roger well over a half hour to catch up with Gaston. The old infantry sergeant enjoyed both being out on horseback on the open road and also providing a source of vigorous irritation for Roger by making the process of catching up with him quite challenging and difficult, especially since the sergeant's stallion was much larger, stronger and faster than Roger's mount.

Riding alongside the stone wall defining a broad wheat field showing the first nascent signs of green growth for the season, Roger had once again closed the distance with Gaston, coming within less than fifty yards, when without looking back, Gaston spurred his horse into a military light trot, widening the distance again from Roger and his tiring mare.

"Slow down, I say! Damn you!" Roger shouted with indignant anger.

Pulling his horse up, Gaston turned to look back at Roger with feigned surprise.

"Oh, it's you! I'd thought you'd planned to go it on your own, after what you said about me," Gaston remarked with casual distraction as he petted his horse's mane and let his mount drop into a slow walk, allowing Roger to catch up and finally pull alongside him.

"I merely said I thought we would best be served if I stayed at the marquis's side, to assure his security," Roger explained with a strained sense of entitlement meant to exert some influence on Gaston, which it clearly did not.

They arrived at a stand of trees, with a dip in the landscape which revealed a gushing stream running through the tract. At a nearby stone bridge spanning the brook, Gaston slipped easily off his horse, and gestured for Roger to do the same.

Their horses drank deeply—making audible sucking sounds, seeming almost to inhale the water. Holding the reins of his steed, Gaston glanced across at Roger, who gazed off into the distance as he held his horse's reins loosely.

"When speaking of the marquis earlier this morning in the stable, you referred to yourself and the master as 'us' and 'we' as though you were inseparable, lad, like you were equal parts in an equation," Gaston observed.

"Jean-Marc has spoken of the invaluable service I provided him, as though we were brothers. He used the word 'friend,' as well, Sergeant," Roger pointed out.

"Don't mistake sincere and humble gratitude for acknowledgment of equality, boy," Gaston stated brusquely. "You have no idea the depth of this man's story. You, like me, are but thin threads in the weave of his rich tapestry. I consider myself honored merely to be part of the process that helps shape the colors. I presume no more, lad. I recommend you do the same."

"I've been at his beck and call, providing for all of his needs; and in the bargain, I've learned the ins and outs of his method, and I dare say he considers me as his son. He has different plans for us all. I'm sure you'd agree. And with that, as a son, one expects to inherit something for his hard work, eh, Sergeant? We don't give everything away for free.

That's a fool's errand," Roger quipped.

"Then call me a fool, for I place no price on my service to this man," Gaston replied, eyeing him coolly. "I'd give my life for him in the blink of eye. Can you say the same, boy?"

Ignoring this point, Roger tried to turn the moment to a lighter mood and bantered in a tone which presumed a sense of undeniable agreement on the other party's part. "Does not he who has served loyally deserve his just rewards? Does the apprentice not become the master at some point?"

"The marquis always gives more than most people ask for. But listen closely: never take what is not offered. That would be the gravest of errors," Gaston counseled soberly.

"I know Jean-Marc plans the best for me. And I've earned it. Maybe you're jealous for what you see is coming to me and you wish you had it for yourself, Sergeant," Roger wagered, seeking the higher ground in this verbal contest.

"Presumption breeds tragedy, boy. I see you're a smart lad. But intelligent people, who are sometimes too smart to see themselves clearly, render themselves quite stupid. And I fear you fall into that category, lad. Too much attitude and not enough insight as I see it," Gaston observed bluntly.

Roger was indignant. "How dare you! Who're you to speak to me in this manner? I'm more than just his valet. He has no heirs, and I stand in the logical place to assume much, if not all of what he has, and to carry on his work."

Gaston studied him for a very long uncomfortable pause. "Are you saying you expect to inherit his legacy and wealth when he dies, is that it?"

"No one likes to think of the end, but I'm sure as Jean-

Marc reflects on the inevitable, that he must also think about passing on to the next generation, especially those who mean so much to him and have made his life so much more rewarding." Roger spoke sentiments he had never officially voiced outside his private thoughts before; but in this setting, it seemed only natural, and somehow cathartic, to stake his claim. He sincerely felt he deserved his due.

"You speak as though the marquis is privileged to have known you."

"He has said as much, Sergeant."

"No doubt he has, because he gives more than he can ever receive, and that's his gift to us all. I'm someone who's known the marquis since the time you were learning to use the privy, sprite. And I wager I've served in deeper measure, with much more at stake than a few quarts of midnight oil and brow sweat from a bit of hard work. But the way I see it, it's not his privilege that I happen to give him my services. No lad, it's my honor to serve him, as much as humanly possible," Gaston retorted. And then picking up steam, he pressed on. "This man is greater than Napoleon and any, king, emperor or Roman pope."

"We all see the world differently, don't we, Sergeant?" Roger chuckled dismissively as he turned to tend to his horse, tightening the saddle strap under the horse's belly.

"Don't think I don't know your beginnings, gnome. This has never been a secret to me," Gaston stated coolly, his eyes narrowing. "And if truth be told, I counseled the marquis against taking you in, but instead to send you off to a military academy to give you a proper new start."

Roger turned back, studying him with new eyes, frowning with disbelief. "You've not known Jean-Marc that long. It's impossible. I would've known. I've been by his side now for many years."

"The Palazzo San Marco in Venice, winter of 1799. A young boy steals the change purse of a well-dressed noble. His man chases him down just before trying to jump off a foot bridge into a passing cargo barge in the canal," Gaston recounted.

"That was you?" Roger remarked frowning in recognition.

"And more importantly, that was *you*: a petty thief, with nothing but quick talk and sob stories. But the marquis took pity on you and saw something I did not. So do not disappoint him, lad. He's given you far more than you can ever repay. Don't expect things that are not promised, nor are your due. Feel the privilege of who it is you serve. He *has* told you who he is, hasn't he? For it is not my place to tell you without his consent."

Agitated with the realization that the man before him knew so much of his history, Roger replied, only revealing a hint of his true irritation. "Of course he told me. Yet all men have their tall tales, don't they? I'm sure there are elements of truth in some of his story, but as for the body of it—well it simply defies all logic and understanding," Roger declared without embarrassment.

"Exactly. And so it appears you learned very little in the precious years you've been given with him. I pray you swiftly recognize the priceless gift offered to you and you honor the opportunity as it justifies."

With that, Gaston turned his back to Roger, checked the saddle on his horse, then jumped back onto his steed, prodded him on, leaving Roger to scramble and once again to ride much harder than he was accustomed to catch up with the old infantry sergeant.

Some miles behind them, traveling on the same road, Jean-Marc and Solange rode at a much slower pace. Jean-Marc enjoyed observing the countryside, amused by the birds flying overhead, hearing the buzz of insects, smelling the fresh growth blooming in the wheat fields. And as they progressed on their track, the road gradually rose to a crest of a hill which provided a more commanding view of the landscape around them.

"My father says you are an immortal," Solange declared with an attempt at being casual as she rode alongside him.

Jean-Marc did not react, but instead smiled as he observed a hawk soar in the distance ahead of them. Expecting to get more of a response from her companion, Solange frowned slightly, and then spoke again, with more conviction.

"I said: my father says you are an immortal. Did you hear me, Jean-Marc?"

"Yes of course, Solange. However, I didn't hear a question; hence I saw no need to reply. Besides, the luminous radiance of the day is at its peak, and the chances to enjoy such times are always so rare," Jean-Marc replied, now observing a flock of crows landing on a freshly tilled hillside field across the road from them.

"So?" Solange persisted.

"Now that would appear to be a question. But the subject preceding does not help me understand the specifics of your inquiry. What is it you want to know, Solange?"

"My father said you never lie. Is that true?" Solange inquired, taking a new tack.

"When asked a question directly, I cannot lie. Keep in mind, many people define this differently. But I hope your father will testify that I have always been true to my word and that I cannot and will not deceive through mendacity. And when people think I am perceived to be deceptive, I'm merely communicating on a deeper level than they're capable of understanding," Jean-Marc remarked as they approached the top of the knoll with the commanding view.

"Then what is it you say about being an immortal? Is it true?" Solange asked with a sense of empowerment.

"You state your father said this. If we're speaking truths, I must be clear what it is he said exactly: when and where," Jean-Marc declared evenly.

As they reached the top of the knoll, he gestured they should rest their horses and they slipped off their mounts. He withdrew a leather canteen from one of his saddlebags and handed it to her. She drank, a bit reluctant to proceed now, intuiting her rhetorical ground might not be quite so solid, as she considered her next move in the discussion. Now Jean-Marc continued the questioning.

"So, he said these exact words: 'The marquis is an immortal'? And if so, what did immortal mean to Gaston, and what does it mean to you, Solange?"

She finished her drink and handed the canteen back to Jean-Marc. "Well he didn't say that exactly," she hedged.

"I see. And what exactly did he say?" Jean-Marc continued, his eyes narrowing slightly as he also kept his attention focused on scanning the landscape around them.

"Nothing to me at all... And nothing directly. It's just that..." Solange hesitated, concerned now she might be violating a confidence.

"Yes?" Jean-Marc replied, his attention primarily engaged with her. Yet he did not, however, stop studying the terrain around them and the road behind them through which they had just passed.

"Sometimes, when he's quite exhausted, or he feels a sense of things being unsettled in his world... he speaks in his sleep," Solange confessed.

Jean-Marc seemed somewhat relieved at this revelation, but still in need of understanding more. "So what gave you this idea about me is based on your father's mutterings during his restless sleep?"

"It was over the course of a number of weeks. Things at first were spoken which made no sense. But there was a common theme. And once word of Napoleon's return reached him, he has never been the same. He says things."

"What kinds of things, Solange?" Jean-Marc asked mildly.

"Things like: 'The work of centuries must be completed'; or 'He sees across the eons.' I've even heard him say you were 'In the company of the Patriarchs.' My father said it more than once that he regards you as no other man on earth. He would die for you, if you asked him."

"I see," Jean-Marc responded thoughtfully as he gazed across the field behind them, frowning. His eyes narrowed slightly, seeming to focus on something in the distance.

Solange studied him closely. "So? How am I to make sense of all this? Is he going insane?"

"Far from it, Solange. Gaston is probably one of the

most stable and reliable men I've ever met. And I have known a host of reliable men in my time."

"You say you never lie, especially when a direct question in presented to you," Solange pressed. "How do you reply then to this direct question: are you an immortal?"

"That is indeed true," Jean-Marc replied, recognizing something of consequence would follow.

"Please tell me the year of your birth," Solange flatly challenged him.

Jean-Marc smiled at her directness and nodded. "I will indeed answer you, Solange. This is a sacred promise. But right now, I must ask *you* a crucial question."

"Yes, what is it?" she replied, taken off guard by the change of tactics in the conversation.

"Are you truly an experienced rider—without fear of galloping through unfamiliar terrain?" Jean-Marc followed, as he turned to his horse and began to casually mount it.

"While I am a woman, I am my father's daughter, and he would let no kin of his grow up and mature without a practical knowledge of many things in a man's world, which includes riding… and riding hard when required."

"Then a bit of galloping right now does not concern you?" Jean-Marc asked, as he gestured subtly for her to remount her horse.

"Not at all, I wager I might give you a run for your money," Solange replied with a mischievous and proud smile.

"There's a group of men—five by my count—hanging back in the stand of trees, across the field we just passed."

Jean-Marc gestured, and she frowned looking back, but could hardly perceive or confirm Jean-Marc's report. The distance Jean-Marc described was well over a mile away, and the men to her were nothing more than possibly a darker patch against the stand of trees which stood by a stone wall and the dirt road. He touched her lightly on the arm to guide her gaze back in front of them.

"Don't stare too long. The one with the eye patch is watching us with a telescope."

"How can you *see* that?" Solange asked with incredulous suspicion.

"The 'how' of it is a longer story than I can share with you right now, Solange. However, if your father told you anything about me, he would've likely disclosed to you I have faculties which exceed those of other men. Seeing across distances is one of them."

"He indeed observed you have powers which defy natural logic," Solange confirmed.

"After we ride casually down this hill, beyond their line of sight, we shall then race like the wind, until we reach that stand of trees ahead, where the road dips, leading to the bridge in the distance, before the road forks. We'll ride across it and then circle back, as rapidly as possible, until we're under the bridge. And don't look back, that'll be my job. If they breach this hilltop, giving them a line of sight before we reach the bridge, we must change our plan. But we must strive with all our effort to cross the bridge before they reach the hill's crest. Everything is at stake, I fear. Understood?"

Solange nodded warily, as they moved off slowly, maintaining the same pace they had before. Once they reached the drop in the road, however, where the line of sight for the group behind them was broken, Jean-Marc whipped his horse into action, and she quickly responded. They rode with an urgency she had never known, experiencing a deep gallop where the horses' stride extended so far in front and behind that their elevation in relation to the road lowered easily two feet, as the mad dash finally took them swiftly across the stonework bridge.

Upon crossing, Jean-Marc glanced back at the crest of the hill they had just been on. It remained clear. He gestured for Solange to follow him down the embankment, into the water and under the bridge where long dark shadows offered hopeful refuge. He and Solange dropped off their mounts, boots in the water, each taking their steed's bridles as they calmly petted and held the horses' muzzles to assure their silence. Staying mostly within the gloom, Jean-Marc peered out carefully from a vantage which gave him a view of the top of the hill.

Shortly thereafter, the group of five crested the hill. Their leader, the man with the eye patch, yelled in irritation.

"Let's go!" And they took off, galloping down the hill, finally crossing the bridge which lay before the fork in the road.

"You two, go that way. The rest come with me," their leader barked in clear irritation. And they rode off at a much faster clip down both roads which rose into two separate tracts of a hilly forest.

After a period, Jean-Marc remounted his horse and turned to Solange. "Both roads wind through different parts of these woods, climbing and falling, so it will be some time before they realize they've lost us. Thankfully it's rocky soil there, and both appear to have had recent riders on the trails, so tracking won't be as easy. We'll take a different route to our destination today."

Jean-Marc prodded his horse, and Solange followed, as they rode out from under the bridge along the stream—against the current—around a rock outcropping, and disappeared from sight.

Just before the pair slipped out of view, however, one of the highwaymen rounded a corner in the road up which they rode only moments earlier. He caught a parting glimpse of Jean-Marc as his horse followed Solange up the narrow river gorge and out of sight.

Glancing back up the road in the forest from which he just came, the horse raider made a hasty judgment. He knew his boss and compatriots were no longer in view and that calling out, or firing his pistol, would raise the alarm against their prey. Instead, he quickly determined what he thought to be a smart, expedient solution. He quietly rode his horse to the water's edge, near the stone ledge, and then carefully hung his hat on the branch of a tree which pointed directly to the outcropping and the running stream escape route Jean-Marc and Solange had just taken.

Confident his trail marker remained secure and clearly visible for when his companions returned, he guided his steed into the rushing stream and navigated toward the watery passageway in front of the rock formation. Leaning forward and listening carefully, to assure his advance was not conspicuous, he proceeded on. Quite pleased with his resourcefulness, the rider also anticipated he might successfully slay the man, take his loot, and have his way with the beauty before he had to share the booty with his cohorts.

Shortly after he rounded the corner of the ledge, however, a strong gust of wind surged through the steep rocky ravine, over the water, and picked up the robber's hat, so that it finally landed near the shore of the rushing stream. The current then caught the brim and pulled it into the water. There it was swept toward a rock and snagged in the currents. Within scant moments, the highwayman's headwear disappeared beneath the water's surface, as more rushing water saturated the hat, waterlogging it and finally sinking it in a swirling eddy of currents by the rock.

Further up the narrow rushing stream, Jean-Marc and Solange negotiated the route with caution while striving to maintain the best speed possible.

"Do you think we've lost them?" Solange asked quietly as she glanced back down the rocky stream.

"Too soon to tell." Jean-Marc studied the water route behind them which wound through a serpentine pass of steep rocky narrows, offering scant opportunity of a clear view on the course they just traversed. The sound of the rushing water through which their horses navigated made the prospect of hearing any attacker's approach doubtful at best. Nonetheless, as they pressed on, Jean-Marc remained vigilant.

Later, as the stream gradually rose higher in elevation and more shallow, they reached a break in the terrain where they guided their horses up an embankment to a wide open slope covered with conifer forest and blanketed with dry brown pine needles. Just as Jean-Marc pointed out the path which would lead them to a ridge above them, a shot rang out. An ugly red welt erupted on Jean-Marc's back, as he slumped and fell backwards off the right haunch of the horse onto the earth by the stream bank.

"Jean-Marc!" Solange cried out in alarm as she jumped off her horse to rush to his side. She pulled his upper body onto her lap, to see the ugly seeping wound: a gunshot to his back, just below the left shoulder blade. She frantically began to focus on any opportunity to treat Jean-Marc as harsh laughter abruptly seized her attention. Solange peered back to the brook and saw the unwashed bandit approaching her on foot from around the rocky cliff, a smoking brass stock flintlock pistol pointed at her in one hand, and leading his horse with the other. He quickly shoved the Greek miquelet ball-butt pistol—a trophy from a robbery earlier this year—into his belt and drew an old but freshly sharpened royalist cavalry sabre. He brandished it at her with threatening intent.

"You'll do as I tell you now, and you won't get hurt, wench."

His guttural and lascivious laughter negated any confidence in his verbal assurances. The highwayman licked his lips with anticipation of rich rewards for this afternoon's easy work. He assumed his gunshot would probably not have been heard by his compatriots, since the steep rocky landscape muted all sound, which was fine with him; it gave him more time to reap his private rewards. He knew they would pick up his trail soon enough, based on his hat as a trail marker.

"You killed him!" Solange screamed with passionate rage as she eyed her approaching thin and wiry assailant and his freshly honed killing blade.

"Aww, he had it coming, what with showing off his wealth at the tavern. It was an open invitation for enterprising individuals such as myself, who are of less fortunate circumstances, and must find ways to compensate for the injustices levied down upon us by people like him who feel superior to my kind of folk. It's all part of the nature and the risks of the traveler's road, girlie. He took his chances, and he lost. Simple as that."

And with these words, the grim-faced outlaw with long stringy hair stopped in front of Solange and the inert form of Jean-Marc, whose wound stained most of the back of his riding tunic with thick and spreading crimson lifeblood.

"It's a shame, the loss of any life. But one must make the best of circumstances. And I'm one who's equal to the task. You're a very beautiful woman, you are," the outlaw observed as he licked his lips in a savoring gesture, then smiled, revealing his stained, rotting teeth in the process.

"Stop it! You have no right!" Solange wept, her manner muted with the threat of imminent mayhem and death.

The ruthless brute dropped his horse's reins to the ground, and strode closer to Solange with an obscene sense of empowerment and invigoration. He stood over her now threateningly.

"A hero must claim his reward, lass. I've ridden hard and long for the bounty that is my due. It is *my* right of conquest. It would serve you best if you don't resist, because I *will* make it very unpleasant if you do."

The highwayman underscored his words with the point

of his sword, touching the jugular vein in her neck as she sat next to Jean-Marc's motionless form. Using the toe of his boot to wedge Jean-Marc's limp body away from Solange, he finished the motion with a rough shove from his heel. Jean-Marc rolled limply away from Solange. She fought fear and her tears.

Keeping the sword tip on her neck, the ruffian took hold of her wrist and compelled her to stand in front of him as he eyed her lovely body with undisguised lechery. He smiled revealing his repulsive rotten teeth again.

"So tell me your name, Mademoiselle," he commanded, feigning a tone of courtly flirtation.

Solange hesitated with clear repulsion, and he grew quickly impatient, moving the blade against her neck with imminent threat. "I said tell me your name, wench!"

"Solange," she replied reluctantly, her teeth bared with gritty resentment.

The cruel brigand very much enjoyed being in control and toying with her. He smiled again, with that false flirtation.

"I'm François. I'm charmed, Solange."

Maintaining his firm grip on her wrist, François dipped his head slightly in a lazy attempt at aping upper-class cordiality. His eyes widened as her ample chest heaved while she wiped a tear and revealed suppressed rage, her eyes glancing around for any glimpse of hope or escape. He straightened again, adopting a commanding and imperious attitude.

"Don't be rude, lass. Say: 'Hello François. I am very pleased to meet you, sir,' " the highwayman ordered her with lethal playfulness.

"Hello, François. I'm... pleased to meet you... *sir*," Solange muttered with obvious distaste and reluctant fear.

The brute ignored the revulsion she expressed, since she was repeating his words now, playing his game. After a moment, however—and still keeping a firm grip on her—he shook her wrist with impatience, pulled her down to push her neck more forcefully against his blade's point. A small pearl of crimson broke the skin, and the blood dripped down her neck onto her bodice.

"What do you want me to say?" Solange blurted out in frustrated alarm.

"Well, just say what you feel, girl. And I *know* what you want. Tell me I overwhelm you with my good looks. Tell me you can't help yourself. Tell me you want me to take you. ...Tell me that... you *love* me," François ordered her, his eyes smiling as he leaned in to smell her neck.

"I *love* you, François." The voice, however, came from behind the outlaw. And it was not female.

Startled, the brute spun around, trying to bring his short sword up into action, but it was too late. Jean-Marc was behind him, poised to attack with lightning speed, executing a series of hand strikes to François's eyes, chest, neck and temples. In an instant, Solange's assailant stood paralyzed— staring in helpless gawking awe at the man he thought he had murdered with a well-targeted shot centered in the victim's back.

In a rage, Solange struck François forcefully in the head with the butt of his own flintlock pistol which she had grabbed from his belt without hesitation. And as he collapsed to the ground unconscious, she seized his short sword, ready to slay the man, when Jean-Marc's faint words distracted her from exacting revenge.

"Solange…" Jean-Marc spoke weakly, as he fell to his knees, his strength quickly waning.

Solange leapt his side. "Jean-Marc, what do I do?"

"We don't have much time. You must act very quickly," Jean-Marc explained, wincing with unambiguous pain. "Go to my riding bags, the one on the right. You'll find a red leather satchel in it. Bring it here quickly."

Solange did as instructed and was soon back at her companion's side. He gestured for her to open it. "You'll find a small blue glass bottle with a silver cap. Pour the contents of it onto my wound after you have cleaned it with water and taken the bullet out of my back."

"Taken the bullet out?" Solange exclaimed with disbelief.

"Your father told me you studied the arts of healing, and that your spirit is true. There should be no problem, Solange. But time is of the essence. This man's companions can't be far behind. And riding will be hard enough with the wound. With the bullet in me, it will slow us down immeasurably. While I can withstand a great deal of pain, I am not immune to everything. If I pass out, we're lost. You must perform the surgery now. Please help me with this, Solange," Jean-Marc requested quietly wincing in pain.

Solange searched Jean-Marc's leather satchel and retrieved the bottle. As she went to her knees near Jean-Marc, she reached into the folds of her dress, revealed a previously concealed sheathed knife, and withdrew the blade. The scabbard itself had been sewn into the design of the dress near the waist, the leather part acting as a sheath out of sight behind the cloth.

Jean-Marc smiled at this. "No woman's mystery is

complete without a hidden blade in the story. I suspect this fellow is lucky to have been subdued when he was," he quipped as he winced in pain.

Solange gestured brusquely at the fallen bandit. "He stood a hair's breadth away from disembowelment and who knows what else. My father insisted I always carry it. I've been glad it was handy on more than one occasion." She directed her focus on the serious business at hand. "We have no alcohol to cleanse the blade to guard against infection, Jean-Marc. This is a very, very serious wound... Master," she observed while she assisted him as he laid face down on the hillside and she could have a clearer view of the work ahead of her.

"I believe as you come to know me better, Solange. You'll see that infection is not a great concern for me. My body has over the years developed unique defenses against that which concerns you. Go ahead and get started. Let's finish this thing," Jean-Marc said with a surprisingly casual air. He winced once again in pain as she probed the wound with her blade.

"The ball must have broken apart when it hit the buckle of your shoulder bag. The pieces did not penetrate as deeply as I feared. Still you should lie in bed for at least two weeks to heal properly from this," she diagnosed as her knife explored the wound. One by one, she coaxed out five pieces of shattered lead from the pistol and tossed them into the grass beside them.

"I think that's all of them," she announced with a concerned sigh.

"Now I need two things, Solange. First, get an ample amount of water and pour it over my injury, then pour the contents of the bottle directly on the wound," Jean-Marc told her.

Solange did as instructed and she marveled at how quickly the gushing laceration seemed to abate to a trickle. Finally, the bleeding stopped almost completely; only a small amount of his precious lifeblood seeped out.

"That's amazing, Jean-Marc! I've never seen anything like this," she declared with unabashed awe.

"There's one thing I would ask, but which I could never demand," Jean-Marc uttered, still lying on his stomach and in guarded pain.

"Just say the word," Solange pledged.

"I've lost a great deal of blood. If you could lend me some of yours, it will help me travel with a more effective and immediate strength."

"But how, Master?" Solange asked with urgent sincerity.

Jean-Marc described the process wherein she made a cut with her blade to the inside of her left palm and then placed the escaping blood against his wound.

Without hesitation, she did as requested. And as their wounds communed, she felt an overwhelming sense of well-being and calmness. Something indescribably deep and profound transferred and exchanged between the two in that moment. As her hand lay on his back, covering the wound, their gazes deepened. It was as though each viewed the other on a completely different and profound plane of existence. A few moments passed, concluding with Jean-Marc taking in an abrupt deep breath, after which he let out a long exhalation, and then began to sit up.

"Thank you, Solange. I think I can ride now." He slowly sat up, and then stood, drawing a look of awe from Solange.

Jean-Marc smiled and shrugged.

She stared down at their unconscious assailant with a disdainful frown. "What are we to do with him?"

The Countryside South of Vendome
Île de France, France
4 March, 1815 AD – Evening Hour

The sun was just setting in the west, across distant wheat fields rimmed by a thick dark forest. Gaston and Roger stood atop a grassy knoll, ringed with ancient oak trees and hosting large brooding dolmen—three huge stones supporting a massive horizontal table rock. A vestige of the ancient Gallo-Celtic civilization which once held sway over these lands—long before the Roman Empire staked its claim here—the megalithic structure exuded a sense of timeless mystery.

The pair arrived here as part of a process of reverse cat-and-mouse traveling, where Gaston briskly led the way, with

Roger forced to scramble and follow, since he did not know the exact route they journeyed. This, of course, brought about an extreme degree of irritation in Roger, now being so far out of control or influence of the overall plan with the marquis.

Roger had enjoyed the illusion of privilege back in Paris, where Jean-Marc allowed him great leeway to decide schedules and plan for the marquis's movements in society, with slight adjustments here and there by Jean-Marc. Now, however, an entirely different equation was in play. And out here, in the middle of nature, he found it was just not his element at all. Give him beautiful women, free-flowing champagne and he would consider it a good start to an evening.

Bivouacking in this manner was at best vexing and at worst a strange manner of torture, especially in the present flatulent company. In the past, Roger had been accustomed to traveling with the Marquis Jean-Marc Baptiste de Rennes in the finest of accommodations, in the best inns along the road. Now, however, he stood at the mercy of Gaston, a hale and hearty personality, who loved to yell at the wind and stand bare-chested at the sunset, which he was currently doing, slapping his face and body with a small oak branch routinely as he did.

"I'm still standing, Lord! Despite Your trials and tests! I'm still here to greet You as You conclude our day! Though Your trials continue, with this present company You've seen fit to place beside me, I complain not! I marvel at Your intricate designs! I praise Your good wisdom in providing us all with ample opportunities to make this a better world to live in—no matter how short a time we are given to walk this earth!" Gaston bellowed to the wafting breeze which accompanied the sun's lazy slide down over the distant hilly forested horizon.

Ignoring Gaston's behavior as best possible, Roger stared pensively up a nearby narrow dirt road which ran into the forest in the distance to the north. "Where do you think they are? They're long overdue," Roger declared as he now gazed across the road bisecting the field behind them.

"Concerned for your inheritance, eh?" Gaston goaded.

Ignoring Gaston's baiting remark, Roger challenged him. "Jean-Marc was clear in his urgency to make our way south to fulfill his charge. Are you entirely certain this is the right place? Too much is at stake to get this wrong."

Gaston glanced at him out the corner of his eye, refusing to honor Roger with his full gaze as he peered back out over the landscape. "We've camped here on more than a dozen occasions, more than I care to describe, lad. The master is a fine and experienced rider, and if he's not here, he has his reasons. Our job is to be here in his support. So why don't you go and gather plenty of dry wood before it's too dark, so we may have ample fuel for a fine beacon fire which we should have ready to welcome him, just in case he might be arriving after dark. It will aid in his navigation."

"And why am *I* the one to gather the wood?" Roger protested indignantly.

"You need the experience far more than I, Roger. Have you ever built a fire in the wilderness, lad? Do you even know how? Because, that's fine, if you're incapable of such a simple task, I can understand. After all, I suppose you're just a city boy with lovely soft hands. I'll just take care of it myself..." Gaston announced, in casual rebuttal, studying the younger man with bemused curiosity.

"I'll do it," Roger insisted in a resentful tone. He then proceeded to make his way to the edge of the clearing and began to gather firewood, grumbling to himself the whole way.

Meanwhile, unobserved by Roger, Gaston gazed into the distance, a frown of deep concern etched on his brow.

Peering beyond his eye patch with steely resolve as he rode, it was now a matter of professional pride, and a source of considerable irritation. He pressed his troupe further on, late into the day.

Robert O'Donnell, freelance predator, and an Irish expatriate in France, had been pleased in the past with the consistent success of his enterprises, moving from region to region, mostly in France, casing the various inns travelers frequented and sizing up the lucrative opportunities.

Today's operation seemed like easy pickings at first assessment. Roger and Gaston—the younger one and the bigger robust one, considered the greatest perceived threats to resistance, had gone off to travel separately, ahead of the woman and the well-dressed one—Solange and Jean-Marc. The well-dressed one, who passed the single, yet sizable, diamond as payment to the inn proprietor at *Le Coq Blanc*, was the main target: trouble-free plunder based on seasoned observation.

O'Donnell enlisted his ruthless hard-riding team of four to bring the prey to ground, as they had done successfully with efficient regularity in the past. But this time something went wrong. Somehow his quarry must have sensed their presence and their intent. Robert experienced this before, though rarely. In this case, however, he never saw where the hunted ones actually turned the tables on his pack of wolves.

Now he also pondered the fact that one of his team was missing. And while it took some time to finally pick up the trail again, an inner voice informed him he had not properly gauged the measure of his target as much as he should have. Something was different about this one, yet whatever pricked O'Donnell's subconscious failed to reach a conscious perception of how profoundly unique the prey was in this case.

After rejoining the other two members of his force, he sent one of his men ahead up the road to search; the highwayman returned later to confirm there was no sign of their missing compatriot—François—or the pair they hunted.

Much earlier, one member of his group discovered hoof marks by the water's edge, near the rock outcropping by the stone bridge. There they also found François's hat submerged in the current and came to understand that while the rushing water seemed forbidding as an escape route, it was actually shallow enough to navigate and proved that this indeed had been the route they took to evade O'Donnell's band.

Further up the stream, they came upon the site where the skirmish occurred and where they saw a copious amount of blood on the ground. From there, the tracks led up to the pine ridge above, and they followed the scent. There was, however, no sign of François. His fate remained unclear.

Now as the day grew long, the sun setting in the west, they still pressed on. Sometimes losing the trail, the seasoned hunter ordered his troupe to keep moving south, following the logical route, continuing on their track to where it might ultimately rejoin a point that converged with a main road which also headed south.

And at a crucial point, they found the scent again. It crossed the eastern fork of one of the two trails O'Donnell identified as their quarry's probable route of travel, and it led on to the western road heading south. One detail bothered the Irishman, however: they were following the tracks of three horses. And judging by the depth of the hoofprints each horse carried a rider.

Had François somehow been on the losing end of what the brigand leader guessed might have been a brash and failed attempt at a one-man ambush? If so, why had they not left the body behind and simply taken the spare horse? Had they dumped his body somewhere along the way, which he missed and his tracker Christophe was reading their trail wrong? This made no sense, since they were in the back country. Dropping the body almost anywhere was the simplest solution, and keeping it with them would only slow them down. Or, had François somehow actually succeeded? And in turn had he made some alliance with the woman, the man being the prize, and possibly a fine prospect for a ransom? If so, O'Donnell ground his teeth in jealous admiration at François's resourcefulness, and in irritation at the potential loss of a double-valued prize.

"We should set camp. We've almost lost all the light, Boss," Christophe, the rider leading the tracking announced with authority.

178

O'Donnell signaled for them to pull up as they arrived at a knoll overlooking fields and rolling hills in the distance. Indeed the sun had just set over the forests of the west, and the last glimmer of twilight would only afford them another half hour of riding time. The one-eyed Irishman stared intensely into the distance of the southwest in quiet and seething anger at the lost opportunity.

Something caught Christophe's attention, however. He frowned and squinted, gazing across the landscape, and then pulled out a telescope to peer further into the far distance. He laughed quietly.

"What is it?" O'Donnell demanded.

After he took the brass telescope from his eye and handed it to his leader, Christophe spoke. "There, on that hill, about two miles away: a camp fire. I think it's dinner time."

O'Donnell raised the eyepiece to view as he steadied his horse, and his sight finally came to rest on the subject of Christophe's discovery. Indeed it was a fire, and at this distance, his seasoned eye made out the dark silhouettes of at least two people. He snarled with satisfaction as he handed the telescope back to Christophe.

"Even if it's not those we originally sought, we shall dine on hot food tonight, and take our anger out on these naïve fools who trust the isolation of wilderness to protect them on their travels. If it is them, there shall be hell to pay. They'll not die slowly, nor quietly, for the trouble they've put us through."

With a sharp gesture from O'Donnell, they picked up the pace to cover as much ground at a gallop in the last bit of remaining light available to them, while the distance and the broad stand of trees behind and alongside them could still mask the sight and sound of their approach.

"We must set out to find them now," Roger insisted, peering out into the darkness for some sign of the other half of their traveling party.

"The only thing we would succeed in now is breaking our necks on some unseen rabbit hole, to say nothing of what it would do to our horses who need a well-deserved rest. We stay put. The master knows this place. And if we failed to be here when he arrived, he would question the state of our welfare, and that would concern him unnecessarily. Don't be so nervous, boy. I take it you've not traveled in the wilderness much. More accustomed to fine carriages and the most affluent of conveyances and accommodations, eh? Well, be aware your master is at ease and comfortable in every world he is placed. There's little need to worry about him."

"And I thank you, Gaston, for your vote of overwhelming confidence," came a voice from the darkness in the heart of the ancient stone dolmen alongside where their campfire had been set.

The lights of the campfire danced across the ancient and enigmatic megalithic granite structure, and from within its shadowed interior, Jean-Marc stepped into the light of the circle sporting a mysterious smile.

"Master, you're here! And all's well with you and Solange?" Gaston eagerly inquired, finally revealing his own nervousness with Jean-Marc and his daughter's late arrival.

"We are all well, my friend. I just needed to assure the camp and its perimeter was secure from uninvited visitors. We had an earlier encounter which required a change in our plan and our route."

Jean-Marc gestured into the darkness and Solange emerged from the line of trees in the near distance, leading three horses. On one, a struggling figure, bound at the wrists and ankles, François, was tied, belly down on the saddle.

Once in the light of the campfire, Solange described the saga to Gaston and Roger: of François's cowardly flintlock shot in Jean-Marc's back which concluded with the imminent threat of rape. She also showed the slight wound on her neck where the highwayman held his sword point. Gaston listened to this account with mounting and suppressed rage.

"Possibly I shall simply gash his throat in recompense for his dirty work, to give him something to ponder briefly whilst he slides into mortal oblivion," Gaston snarled to François as he roughly unloaded the captive from his saddle. As François's hands and ankles remained bound, the highwayman quailed in response to the tenuous nature of his destiny now in the hands of complete strangers, against whom he had committed the gravest of offenses. Gaston pulled a dagger from his belt and tested the blade and point for sharpness.

"It's like a razor. He might not even feel it if I cut him. Maybe I should fashion something from stone. Chip away a blunt edge, something crude and jagged, and then deliver the punishment. It'd be a more fitting deed, I'll wager. Certainly more satisfying: a slow agonizing cut with a dull stone blade."

"We certainly don't want to miss the opportunity to learn from our encounters, do we Gaston?" Jean-Marc observed mildly.

Suddenly humbled by his master's peaceful response, Gaston bowed in deference to Jean-Marc, backed off from his murderous ruminations, and busied himself with tending to the waning fire which needed more wood.

The evening wore on, and the five in Jean-Marc's troupe sat around the campfire at the foot of the massive dolmen. Flames from the fire danced light and shadows across the ancient stone structure as they had for centuries of travelers, and untold millennia.

Laughter erupted among the group as Gaston finished telling his tale of a misadventure in Egypt when he was part of Napoleon's army of occupation and he witnessed the artillery practice on the Sphinx, with the nose of the venerable stone figure being sacrificed in the process.

François watched with awkward awe, being first a prisoner, his ankles still being bound and soundly tied to a nearby tree to discourage the slightest notion of flight. For all he had transgressed against the travelers—intending to kill and rape—he found himself unsettled by Jean-Marc's leadership of the group's spirit, which dictated that he, the brazen highwayman, should be treated with respect and compassion and somehow a strange quality of acceptance.

Jean-Marc even gave François a diamond, indicating that if only his people had asked, they would have been given what they requested. As a result, despite the fact François remained tethered with ropes, he shared with the group his insight into the nature of his cohorts, whom he suspected might be somewhere nearby in the shadows. And privately fondling the diamond in his palm, he tried to compose how he might explain this freely given wealth, if rescued by O'Donnell, and he decided the prudent strategy was to conceal it and play the whole scenario by ear.

"You said you'd tell me when you were born, Master," Solange pressed Jean-Marc, finding a momentary silence around the campfire wherein to revive her line of earlier inquiry.

"Indeed, Solange. I am a man of my word," Jean-Marc replied ruefully. "Before I do so, however, I'll share with you a story which may give you insight into the answer to the question you've posed to me with such conviction and persistence."

"Thank you, Master," she responded with surprisingly awkward diffidence. She glanced involuntarily over at Roger, whose hungry eyes had never left her since her return to their circle—a detail which did not go unnoticed by Gaston, who frowned quietly.

"As you know, I met your father while we were both in Egypt on Napoleon's campaign. Your father was part of the *Armée d'Orient*, and I had been recruited to the *Commission des Sciences et des Arts*. At the time I joined as an expert with an understanding of the history of the ancient cultures which populated those lands in earlier times. As well, I enjoyed recognition for my facility with a host of foreign tongues, including reading Coptic, speaking various dialects of Egyptian, as well as other languages found in the general region of Napoleon's campaign. While I clearly provided value to the *Commission des Sciences et des Arts*, I traveled there with my own goals and objectives. Since I no longer possessed the book I commissioned so long ago in ancient Alexandria, I went in search of the place where I concealed the source scrolls for it, so that I might renew my work and fulfill my charge to my master and his family."

"When was this commitment to your master first promised, Master?" Solange asked.

"In another age, Solange. The burning of the great Library of Alexandria changed everything. I've been striving to recover from the loss ever since. My endeavors to retrieve the original source scrolls—which were hidden in a subterranean location beneath the surface of modern-day Alexandria—proved to be a failure. My fortunes, however, improved after Napoleon occupied Rome and he then transferred the Vatican Archives to Paris. Life—no, Fate— as you may have seen, nonetheless, has ways of making no path to desires and goals direct and certain. My course was complicated by various other commitments I had been required to honor, including providing personal and regular consultations with the man who ultimately became the Emperor of Europe."

"Napoleon himself?" Solange asked with dubious wonder and a sense of involuntary and deepening attraction to Jean-Marc.

Reflexively, Roger jumped in and picked up on this epic and intriguing story as he impulsively became determined to alter the focus of Jean-Marc's account into a new direction. For while he could not put words to it, if he looked clearly and deeply into his heart at this moment, he would have seen he was experiencing an intense jealousy relating to the reaction Jean-Marc received from the target of his own amorous, and likely lascivious, intentions. Affecting a jocular manner to his tone, Roger behaved as though it was his turn to pick up the heroic narrative.

"And before long, the marquis knew the requirements of his newly appointed responsibilities with the Emperor exceeded what he could handle alone. And Fate crossed our paths. Indeed the marquis found himself obliged to engage in missions of diplomacy among the various crown heads of Europe, and beyond. And so, he entrusted me as a worthy aide and steadfast compatriot. While my duties at first consisted of various administrative and arduous assignments of increasingly towering responsibilities, the marquis became ultimately impressed enough with my skills and knowledge that he sent me off on a mission of my own: to recover the Star of Burma. This sacred quest required me to travel afar, in exotic lands such as Tumbrinia and Kloubrushi. And thereafter gaining the trust of the crown prince of the latter domain, I procured a map which promised the location of untold treasures." Roger took a breath and mustered his wits for the next phase of his story. He was taken off guard, however, by the stern faces of his audience, especially Jean-Marc and Gaston. Solange regarded him with slight confusion.

" 'Tumbrinia' and 'Kloubrushi?' Such places don't exist, Roger. And what is this talk of a 'Star of Burma?' I've never heard of such a gem, nor did I send you on any journey to recover it," Jean-Marc spoke quietly, revealing a trace of disappointment.

Roger shifted uncomfortably, glancing at Solange, then back at Jean-Marc with a sense of insistence. "Jean-Marc, we all have our stories. I've never contradicted yours, and I'd be grateful if you'd show me the same courtesy." Roger spoke, trying to regain some dignity and composure.

"Roger, you're creating a tale, composing fiction. The context here at the fire was meant to share a story so Solange would have an understanding of what has brought us here and what our mission has been. There are appropriate times and places for tales of entertainment, and there are occasions where passing along information to provide understanding and insight into the purpose of things is needed. This is the latter. I thought there was no confusion on this matter."

"Jean-Marc, I've been with you for years, listened to your stories, and witnessed how rapt your listeners have been. Your experiences and encounters with all the great people of the age, and ages before, are wonderful entertainment. These are fine and remarkable stories, I readily admit. They have a powerful effect on people. And I feel now, having been in your service for as long as I have, that I too should be able to widen the effect of your pretense, and expand the legend of Marquis Jean-Marc Baptiste de Rennes—the Count de Saint Germain—or whatever other identity you chose to emulate in your peregrinations across the continent," Roger stated, mustering a newfound confidence.

" 'Pretense', you say? Are you implying the Master's stories are nothing but lies?" Gaston challenged quietly. The dangerous tone, however, was palpable and disturbing.

François, sitting bound at the wrists and with one ankle tied to a tree, watched mutely, trying to make himself as invisible as possible in his place around the campfire. Jean-Marc studied Roger with a slight sense of pain.

"Gaston's question has bearing on our progress here, Roger. Is it your view the information I've communicated through the years is based on nothing more than lies?" Jean-Marc asked softly, without threat.

Roger glanced around at the gathering, and mustered a sense of indignation, as though it was unjustified that he should be put through this line of inquiry. He dug in his heels.

"Jean-Marc, you say you do not lie, correct?"

"That is true, Roger," Jean-Marc replied.

"What do you have to say to the fact that you are known by more than one name here on the continent? Which one is really you? Where is the 'true' you, Jean-Marc?" Roger challenged.

"They're all true, Roger," Jean-Marc stated calmly.

"But how is this possible?" Roger demanded with impregnable doubt.

"In my long life, I've acquired a number of titles. The Comte de Saint Germain and Marquis de Rennes are merely two of them. The records and filings for them are all in order and available to those who inquire. Though some are quite old," Jean-Marc explained.

Frustrated with the readiness of Jean-Marc's explanation, however, Roger quickly latched onto what he thought to be another refuting point. "What about Father Giovanni Baptisti, whose papers I forged enabling you to gain entrance to the Soubise Palace, so you could steal the book?"

"One cannot steal something one originally

commissioned and rightfully owned and then recovered from the very body which seized it without legal cause and without consent, Roger. As for Father Giovanni Baptisti, I was indeed the padre of this name, some years ago. If the Monsignor Marini had the resources to check the records in Gaeta, Italy, he would learn that indeed a father Baptisti resided there in the years between 1743 and 1759. Most of my flock is gone now, but I suspect there would still be one or two alive, who would be shocked to see me in my current state of seeming youth. But you know all of this, Roger. You know I've been in other lives. This is not a revelation."

"Other lives, an endless trail of names and identities. You call this being truthful?" Roger pressed his challenge.

"Within each life of any man or woman, we experience different identities. When I am joyful, am I at the same time sorrowful and full of rage? This is unlikely. When you were an infant, are you now the same person as you were then? And when you are eighty, will you be the same as you are now? Who we are at any time in life bears witness to constant and drastic changes—it is the nature of life. Some changes are less discernable than others," Jean-Marc observed.

"But what of your march of names through the centuries you claim to have lived? Why not keep your one original name and live by it? What are you afraid of?" Roger pushed, now feeling indignant that none of his points had any effect in the argument.

"Through history, towns and cities change names for various reasons; but they are still the same place, and no lie is involved. A family moves from one region to another, from one culture or country to another, and in doing so, allows their family name to change to fit in with their newly chosen community. Am I not correct? Is this wrong?"

"Well, I don't think that applies," Roger insisted.

"Just because you think something with powerful conviction, does not mean you are right or that people agree with you, Roger," Jean-Marc observed lightly, then took a new tack. "A merchant purchases a trading vessel from a previous owner; he changes its name to that of his wife, to honor her. Does he not have the right to re-name that which is his?"

"Of course he does," Roger agreed reluctantly.

Jean-Marc pointed to his heart, "And who, Roger, owns this vessel in which my heart and soul travel? Do I not have the right to name it as I choose and require as I inhabit new cultures, travel through the world and the centuries, as my master has asked me to?"

Roger did not want to answer a question where he saw his advantage weakening, if not lost altogether. He remained, however, undeterred once he launched on his challenge, one that had apparently been simmering inside him for some time.

"We are men of confidence, are we not? We're individuals who through our words gain the confidence of others so we may do the things we do and achieve the goals we require. The ends justify the means. You say what you must to find the advantage in a situation, of a moment, or a story. If you expect me, Jean-Marc, to truly believe you've lived a life of centuries—it is frankly incredible—I dare say absurd, sir. Though I must concede that in the years I've known you, you've not aged a bit; and I've never seen you sick a day in your life. I suspect you've learned a thing or two of the apothecary's trade, possibly more than the average physician; and this has held you in good stead," Roger asserted, somehow relieved to get this off his chest and feeling a sense of empowerment in the process.

"Roger, he was *shot* in the back by this man!" Solange announced with indignant anger. François shrunk into the shadows of the dolmen, as best as possible, dreading his presence here, mutely agitated by the ropes restraining his wrists and ankle. He knew as well that Gaston maintained a steady eye on him should he try to free himself from the bonds.

"It was obviously a glancing wound from which Jean-Marc, with an admirable and robust constitution, recovered from more quickly than most. I see nothing refuting my original point," Roger declared stubbornly, especially rankled to have to argue now with a woman he originally intended to bed in as short a period of time as possible.

"How utterly contemptible," Solange declared as she studied Roger with cold disgust, and then after a long pause, she respectfully turned to Jean-Marc. "Master, would you stand, please?"

Jean-Marc did so at Solange's gesture of request, and he allowed her to then lift up his blood-stained riding tunic, revealing his bare back for Roger and the rest to see in the campfire's light. She pointed to the place on his back where the wound had been inflicted, and where now, there was only a scarred mark of what appeared to be a wound from weeks or months ago.

"The marksman's shot was right behind the heart, sir! Another man would've been dead in moments! He stood to disarm his assailant, and my potential rapist, before he collapsed. And indeed he guided me to use certain mendicants to aid in his healing, but from what I know of the healing arts—which my father will affirm is extensive—there is no treatment alone which could've healed him this quickly and completely from the grievous wound he sustained. His bleeding was profuse and the bullet targeted with deadly accuracy. And *you* call the Master a liar? You doubt his extremely unique longevity, sir? Just because it's your nature to lie with rash impunity, and because your weak intellect simply cannot comprehend something, does not mean it's proof others are lying as well." Solange glared at him with an undisguised distaste and dismissal.

Roger recognized at a very primal level his chances of winning this woman with any charm, or wile, had been defeated at the feet of his master. Yet he could not let go of stubbornness, rooted in an irrational jealousy, combined with a fundamental failing of his character: a quick yet shallow intelligence bonded with an incurious laziness.

"I was not there, woman. I didn't see what you describe. To me this is yet another story. Seeing the wound, I have to question was he actually shot at all? And I'm frankly curious what your angle in this story is, woman." Roger then turned to François, seeking some deflection for his argument. "You: what did you see? What's your story?"

"I was unconscious. I…" François began as Gaston cut off the reply of their captive with a menacing gesture.

"It doesn't matter what this lowlife says. My daughter has spoken, and I'll not have anyone impugn she is a liar. Certainly not you, runt! You've now insulted my master and my only child with your ugly suppositions and churlish vanities! Let's finish the set, lad. I invite you to insult me, and then we can have a *real* party." Gaston's murderous rage was barely unrestrained. Roger saw it, but remained tight-lipped, yet would not retract his words. He glanced nervously at Jean-Marc, who injected a calm voice.

"That's enough. There's nothing further to be said on this topic which will bring any benefit. I think we all need our rest. We must start early in the morning, before daybreak. I'll take the first watch. Gaston, you'll take the second and Roger the third. Good night to you all."

Jean-Marc climbed up along the thick branch of a large spreading oak tree whose lower limb extended up and out over the top of the dolmen's flat capstone. Here he had a commanding view of the clearing which opened out onto the distant moonlit landscape, as well as, the quiet meadow behind them, ringed by a stand of trees fronting a deep thick forest.

Below him, the fire's flames flickered against the ancient stone structure and the nearby venerable oaks. Jean-Marc listened as the sounds of the camp settled into silence. He suspected not everyone fell asleep right away, since such dramatic declarations of opposing positions had been revealed and expressed in such raw, unvarnished terms.

Jean-Marc had witnessed the shifting of alliances countless times in his past, and he reflected on the logical consequences of this revelation as he gazed out across the quiet moonlit landscape of central France. He knew from experience, part of his long path in life, that this deceptive calm too often concealed hidden and profound peril.

Recognizing the danger before it became an imminent threat, and taking the right action with all corollaries considered, weighed on his mind. He was especially concerned with the added sense of responsibility for his companions who traveled with him and on his behalf.

Not far away, crawling slowly through the underbrush near the edge of the dense forest—and taking full advantage of the moon shadows which mottled the wide meadow behind the dolmen—Robert O'Donnell and his men positioned themselves with seasoned stealth. A scout confirmed their prey's position. The band had tied off their horses far away, in a rocky cleft in the forest behind them, so even if they whinnied, they could not be heard and give any warning of their presence.

O'Donnell's men had lain patiently, watching for their opportunity, and it now appeared to have finally arrived. O'Donnell observed, as was usually the case, the first watch offered the least chance for surprise, since those attacking could not be certain of the slumber of those around the campfire.

The silhouette of the man on first watch atop the dolmen had regularly gotten up from his seated position, at various unpredictable intervals, to survey the landscape carefully. The second watch—sometimes the chance for an attack—had been without a perceived gap in his defensive vigilance. The large burly man, who O'Donnell remembered from the tavern being the boisterous teller of war stories, apparently was true to his tales. This man maintained an admirable military discipline. He never even sat, but kept a constant pacing motion, observing with a sharp eye for any perceived movement and he watched all possible attack routes to their campfire.

The third watch, however, offered the time of opportunity. Well into the night, the untended campfire had died out; the moon moved from its position directly overhead, further to the west in the sky, creating long shadows across the meadow: perfect conditions for a stealthy approach.

Best of all, however, the man charged with the third watch was not equal to the task. O'Donnell saw by the language of his body movements, that he was somehow agitated, possibly even resentful of his responsibilities? And during the time he looked out, performing his guard duty, O'Donnell could tell, even at a distance, that his manner failed to be attentive to the landscape around him, but instead he was distracted and preoccupied by thoughts within. Agitated gestures, silhouetted against his position atop the dolmen suggested his being engaged in an argument with someone, one where he finally won. O'Donnell's companions queried him with a quizzical look, to which he shook his head and maintained his focus on the camp, their target, their prey.

As O'Donnell expected, this man was the weak link. After this amateur sentinel paced in agitation for a while, he let himself sit and gaze in one direction, out over the landscape below, leaving the meadow to his back. And then after not a very long time, he began to slump, the fatigue of the trail and the night taking root in him.

Finally he allowed himself to lie down, ultimately

surrendering to sleep atop the dolmen. O'Donnell had his men wait a few moments longer before he signaled them to advance silently with their long knives drawn in lethal readiness. From the underbrush, they slunk through the protective long shadows of the meadow, patiently stalking and silently creeping up on their target.

Embers barely glowed in the last remnants of the campfire around which lay four reclining forms, each covered with a blanket. One stirred in his sleep; one was clearly larger than the rest; one distinctly smaller—likely the woman; the last was furthest away.

O'Donnell had already whispered the strategy, which was that the big one, the army veteran likely posed the greatest risk, and should be dispatched first. Any others, who stirred, suggesting a possible awakening and warning of the rest of the group, would be swiftly and ruthlessly neutralized. The first to achieve a silent kill by blade was to then produce their flintlock pistol and have it ready for the sentry atop the dolmen, who would likely awaken quickly once the deadly action had begun. The woman would be restrained with a blade and threat of death if she struggled. She would be reserved for other uses, O'Donnell assured his cohorts, who chuckled in anticipation of their carnal reward.

Closing in through the gloom, the four highwaymen approached from two directions, a pair on each side of the dolmen, the shadowy rock overhang concealing their final approach from the sleeping sentry above them. Now, as each assassin came into position above the inert forms, one of the figures lying by the embers stirred, aroused by a slight sound—a cracked twig—stepped on by one of the attackers getting into position.

But as the sleeping figure groggily began to sit up, all four went into swift motion. A long dagger plunged into the chest of the first victim, as a muffled cry went out. Razor-sharp steel blades stabbed into the other two larger unmoving figures lying before their attackers, as the fourth assailant stood positioned over the last, smaller one, ready to seize the woman and take her under control.

Suddenly all hell broke loose from the gloom around them. The encampment rapidly came alive with flashing sword action. Hurtling out from the shadows of the dolmen like a charging bull, Gaston held a cavalry sabre in one hand and a large wooden cudgel he had crafted in the other, and he fought through the group of brigands with brutal and devastating efficiency. To one assailant, Christophe, who raised his dagger in threatening counter attack, the French army veteran slashed downward, cutting forcefully through collarbone, chest and heart, leaving the attacker dead before he hit the ground. Gaston bellowed in rage as he charged his second opponent, who, after nervously jamming his blade into the figure below him, then brought his weapon up in uncertain defense to face the sergeant's assault.

"That would've been my daughter you slew without hesitation, you shit-ridden pig!" Gaston yelled, ready to exact his mayhem, sword held high ready to cleave the highwayman.

Having witnessed the fate of Gaston's previous opponent, the young outlaw fell to his knees and dropped his dagger, throwing his hands up in supplication.

"Please, sir! I surrender!" he yelled out.

In response, Gaston slammed him in the head with his club, splitting the ruffian's scalp, leaving a bloody gaping gash as the highwayman fell unconscious by the dying fire.

Emerging from the dolmen shadows as well, Solange, in the meanwhile, closed in on a third attacker. As he turned to see Gaston's brutality, she had already slid behind him, with her short sword held low, at knee level; and she thrust the blade powerfully into the back of the attacker's right thigh.

"And that would've been my honored master you sought to murder without conscience!" she hissed as she delivered the crippling wound.

This third assailant fell in agony, clasping at his leg injury. In disgust or distain, Gaston strode over to the wounded man and deftly, but soundly, clubbed him on the side of the skull, delivering him too into unconsciousness.

Robert O'Donnell found himself caught flat-footed in momentary confusion. With his one good eye, he watched helplessly as the lightning-fast turn of fortune for his ill-fated sortie, quickly unraveled into lethal chaos and a staggering defeat. O'Donnell spun around, looking for the quickest route of escape. Instead, he found Jean-Marc in his path, unarmed.

"You would be well advised to drop your sword, sir," Jean-Marc advised calmly. "You'll come to no harm if you surrender now. I cannot guarantee your safety if you remain armed."

O'Donnell weighed his options quickly, sized up his opponent and decided attacking the unarmed man in front of him was the most expedient course of action. Maybe he could turn the tables and take him prisoner and bargain his way out of the fiasco. He went for Jean-Marc full force. In doing so, the Irishman later reflected with profound regret that it had to have been the most ill-advised act of his wretched and depraved life.

With startling swiftness, in response to O'Donnell's sword thrust, Jean-Marc in turn delivered a rapid striking movement to his opponent's wrist, which paralyzed O'Donnell's control of his sword arm. Immediately thereafter, a forceful two-finger strike to the robber boss's one good eye blinded him permanently. The leader of the highwaymen fell to his knees, holding his savaged eye in agony. Jean-Marc surveyed his opponent with dispassion as he tied his wrists and ankles with a cord he took from his jacket pocket.

"You made an unwise choice, sir. This wound, I am afraid, will not heal. You'll have to find a new vocation," Jean-Marc observed quietly.

As it became finally clear all assailants were neutralized, a shout came from above, atop the dolmen.

"Master, are you all right?" Roger called down with excited concern.

In the scant time of the attack, and finally roused by the sounds of the clash, Roger later confessed with embarrassment—after he had climbed down and joined them—that at first the sounds of the fight were processed as part of his dream world. Only with the persistence and rigor of the battle sounds did he finally awaken. And only then did he see below him, around the campfire, the attackers had been neutralized and that he, in his role as sentinel and guardian, had failed the group. Roger apologized profusely to Jean-Marc.

"You are indeed a failure, lad. And so, what can you do now to redeem yourself, I wonder," Gaston said with a steely and unforgiving gaze.

"What with the rigors of travel, and the exhaustion we have all experienced from the events of the last two days, it could've happened to anyone," Roger blurted out defensively.

"In Russia, I marched day and night for fourteen days with Napoleon, braving Cossack marauders and savage guerilla fighters—with three day's rations of biscuits to do it on. We passed two or three nights at a time without sleep. So don't attempt to make excuses and sell me your tripe about the limits of human exhaustion. You're simply soft, and I daresay worthless," Gaston spat with disgust.

Roger studied the scene around him with evaporating hope. Solange would not even look him in the eye. Jean-Marc, however, broke the tension with a sense of purpose. He gestured to François, who died in his bivouac at the hands of his own brethren, and to Christophe's body as well. The unconscious forms of two others of the band lay nearby.

"We must give those men a decent burial and decide what we shall do with the survivors. We must be ready to ride at daybreak." Jean-Marc declared.

As Gaston gestured for Roger to help him haul off the bodies to bury nearby, Jean-Marc turned to O'Donnell, who held his wounded eye and moaned in pain. Jean-Marc placed his hand on the man's shoulder, demanding O'Donnell's attention.

"Your name?"

Reluctant at first to answer, the Irishman finally saw no

value in silence. "O'Donnell, Robert O'Donnell."

"So, Robert, how did you come upon targeting us for attack? Do you work alone? Did someone send you?" Jean-Marc asked quietly as Solange stayed nearby watching and binding the other assailants' hands and feet.

O'Donnell, however, was more preoccupied with the loss of sight in his last eye rather than responding to any of Jean-Marc's inquiries. Clutching his injury, he cried out in self-pity.

"My eye! I'm blinded, you bastard!"

Jean-Marc placed his hand on O'Donnell's arm, having the effect of calming the now retired freelance predator.

"While it's true I pledged never to take a life, and while it's also true that my valued companion accepts my guidance, I'm not in a position to control him completely. You've attempted to take both his and his daughter's life with no concern for the consequences. And while I'll do my best to advocate sustaining your life, I can't deliver any guarantees, sir. How you respond to my questions might very well determine your fate. Losing your sight is tragic indeed. Losing your life is, I am afraid, the end of the story... or I dare say something worse, since while the story ends in death, how one gets there and how long that process takes is open to question, isn't it? The choice is yours, Robert O'Donnell," Jean-Marc said casually. "I'll ask again, but not a third time: How did you come to target us, sir?"

Chastened by the prospect of his demise by torture in this remote location, O'Donnell chose disclosure over obstinacy and explained the circumstances of their encounter, complete with spying the diamond given in payment at the inn of La Beauce.

"I was indeed incautious. I must be more careful in the future," Jean-Marc observed as he frowned at his blind captive.

Dawn broke. Glimmers of the day's first light glowed atop the massive dolmen. Already mounted, ready to ride, the party was assembled into two groups. Gaston and Solange sat on their horses by a third steed, as Jean-Marc climbed on. Roger stood by his horse, along with his three surviving captives, each mounted and securely tied by the wrist to the pommel of each saddle, ankles bound under each horse's belly. Two other horses with empty saddles were also tied off, creating a train behind the last captive. Once again, the valet was not pleased with the riding arrangements.

"But, Master, would it not be more advisable for Gaston to ride in my place? He's far more qualified for this task than I," Roger protested.

Gaston replied in Jean-Marc's stead. "Your captives have been soundly bound, lad. Understand there's no stopping till you reach your destination. If they protest and claim they must relieve themselves, they know to do so in the saddle. If they're thirsty, they can beg and wail, but you'll not give them any opportunity to turn the tables on you. At the first sign of resistance, you must know your life is at stake, and you just thrash them into submission. You'll do fine," Gaston assured the reluctant valet with a loud intimidating voice more targeted at the two young brigands who still had the benefit of sight.

O'Donnell sat mutely on his saddle, turning his head

from time to time, listening to get oriented by the sound of things in his new world, but he remained otherwise withdrawn and taciturn. This was quite a contrast from just two days before while then the dynamic leader of the most profitable and lethal band of highwaymen in central France.

"So you're clear with the plan?" Jean-Marc inquired. "You will ride west for no more than thirty miles. Follow the way to the village of Saint Luc d' Espery. There at the livery, you'll find one Pasqual Onzon. He is part of our brotherhood. You'll give him my message. He'll assist you in conveying your charges to the authorities, for which I suspect there will be a generous reward. Pasqual will also give you a good price for all the horses. All of this is your fair reward for the task you must perform for us, Roger."

Gaston laughed. "And you're free to embellish any story you like on how you captured these pigs, *except* the truth. I trust you'll do well on that account. You might even start to develop a legend around yourself. It might do you some good! Something to live up to!"

"We'll meet you at our apartments in Venice. We should be there in a week or two. We'll keep our exact route a secret. I'm sure you understand. I look forward to seeing you there, Roger. And thank you for everything you're doing," Jean-Marc said with a quiet and warm smile as he embraced him.

With that, the two groups parted. Roger paused, watching Jean-Marc and his companions ride down off, over the low hills to the road south. Recognizing no more words could change his fate, despite his reluctance to deliver on his mandate, Roger mounted his horse. With the tether for the other horses in hand, he began to lead them off, heading west. His thinking was that the sooner he delivered on this unpleasant task, the sooner he could rejoin the marquis and return his life to privileged normalcy.

Wishes, however, are too often at odds with the stark realities of fate.

The Roadways of Central France
5 March, 1815 AD – Midday Hour

"**W**ater... Water! *Please*, sir. I'm dying of thirst! Your behavior is far worse than ours! Our actions were nothing personal. But yours are downright cruel and inhuman!" The complaining wail came from Bruno, one of the bound captives in Roger's charge.

"I think I'm going to faint from the lack of water!" the second captive, Nicco, chimed in dramatically.

"You are indeed a toady and a cad! You're clearly incapable of making your own decisions and doing the right action by us, sir!" O'Donnell added for effect as he struggled to maintain balance in his saddle, bound and blind. Vulnerable: yes, but helpless, not at all. He still had his wits, and he committed himself to establish some method to turn the tables on their hapless guardian.

Despite the fact Roger had been warned by Gaston and Jean-Marc of his captives' anticipated ploys to create and turn a situation to where they would try to convince him to stop and provide respite for relief of bodily needs, the strategy acted out over the last hour in the saddle had indeed exacted its effect on the inexperienced custodian of these ruthless criminals.

While Roger was determined not to give in to their whining demands, he found himself experiencing a growing resentment. It was not for his captives, but instead, for Jean-Marc and Gaston. Roger felt he had been displaced from his rightful station alongside the marquis, by unmerited circumstances, which amplified the festering and irrational agitation seething in his mind. A simmering and mounting rage resulted. He felt he had been unjustly treated. No. He *knew* he had been unjustly treated by Gaston and Jean-Marc.

For all the service he provided to the marquis, this was the disgraceful thanks he had been handed. Roger felt Gaston must have most certainly been working to regain a sense of advantage, access and proximity with Jean-Marc. Clearly the old, fat Army veteran was jealous of Roger's relationship with Jean-Marc and had worked at finding the best method to drive a wedge between the two.

Roger resolved to identify some means to counteract against this damage created by Gaston, and then ultimately, possibly gain access to Solange's fleshy treasures in the bargain. And in a strange way, he found himself identifying and sympathizing with his captives more now than he did with his original traveling companions.

Nonetheless, Roger remained steadfast in his determination not to be affected by his captives. He shouted back at the closest rider behind him, whose horse he guided with a rope. "Shut up, you sphincter of an ass, or you'll get the product of the same for your next meal!"

O'Donnell smiled slightly. His men were finally gaining control over Roger's temperamental willpower. Now it just meant a matter of time before the advantage turned.

The alpine route he chose, taking him near Grenoble, was less direct, yet more advisable. His intelligence sources informed him the regions of central France further west, specifically Provence—which lay in the direct path to Paris from his landing site near the small fishing village of Cannes on the French Mediterranean coast—held strong royalist loyalties.

On the march Napoleon Bonaparte saw his original force of eleven hundred loyal soldiers grow steadily, and now he pressed on in the company of well over three thousand. And the number grew with each village he passed through on his indirect route to Paris. Some had donned the Napoleonic uniform of servicemen from a rainbow of old regiments. Others simply volunteered wearing the civilian clothing they wore when they dropped their ploughs, pitchforks and hoes in the corn and wheat fields and abruptly decided to join the growing assemblage marching north to the French capital.

The column moved slowly down out of the winding alpine track to the more gentle rolling foothills of the region. With the snow-capped mountains, skirted with pine slopes behind him, and ahead of him the beginnings of spring showing buds on some of the trees, it offered a beautiful vista under normal circumstances.

A few minutes before, however, one of his cavalry scout patrols returned and reported the presence of a full royalist regiment deployed on the hills commanding the road leading out of the mountains.

But there could be no turning back at this point. To attempt an escape, climbing back up into the mountains, with a large body of fresh royalist troops attacking at their rear—and with his leading column whose front could not be organized and deployed effectively to reverse course in an orderly formation on this narrow trail—retreat was simply out of the question.

Besides, Napoleon came to march forward. And if a battle might be destined, he would take the initiative and attack decisively. The idea of retreat was anathema. He and his troops would press forward. Napoleon was known for this principle. Whatever their fate, victory or defeat, their fortune laid here on the road, fearlessly marching on to destiny.

Napoleon's column reached a bend in the road which now offered a wider and panoramic view of the rolling hills below spreading out to the west and north: the route to Paris. In the foreground, however, four squared battle formations of infantry troops stood in silent readiness, their regimental colors flying from standards flapping in the mountain breeze. Two thousand men at arms stood positioned on both sides of the road ahead, less than a mile away.

Their elegant embroidered flags identified them as the 5th Infantry Regiment, with the triple golden *fleur-de-lys* on a blue shield. Their standards clearly declared for whom they marched: they were King Louis XVIII's army. A ripple of tension and nervous muttering among Bonaparte's troops worked its way up the column so even those on the road high above—around the bend, who could not yet see the enemy regiment in their path—quickly understood the gravity of the situation.

As he calmly rode on, Napoleon studied the large force of royalist troops. He quickly assessed their numbers, strengths, potential weaknesses, and the terrain, with a sober reflection on logistics, timing, fate, destiny and the odds of turning the advantage. He knew this moment to be a fateful one, upon which the outcome of his entire enterprise might very well turn.

The narrow array in which his men marched placed him at a distinct military disadvantage, despite the fact he had numerical superiority and the high ground. His seasoned instincts relied on the flexibility of his trusted troops in the vanguard, along with lightning-fast responsiveness to threat and opportunity, which could very well win the day. All those behind him knew this as a hallmark of Napoleon's military campaigns. He would always take the initiative wherever and whenever possible, forcing his opponents into a decisive battle.

Napoleon played all the possible scenarios in his head as he led his horse on and the column continued to advance toward the royalist position. Now the majority of Napoleon's army had a clear view of the King's regiment arrayed below them.

Shouted orders and the blare of bugles reverberated through the columns on the low ground, and now the royalist troops moved with cold precision into the road to block Bonaparte's column.

The nervous ripple of charged tension which originally passed down with word of the royalist enemy, now stirred one man toward the back of Bonaparte's column to yell out: "*Vive le petit Caporal!*"

This cheer quickly shortened with others picking up their leader's name, repeating it louder, until it became a unified chant of pride, war and destiny, and defiant commitment. "*Napoleon! Napoleon! Napoleon!*"

And then the fateful moment occurred. The tipping point. Napoleon saw the first glimmer of reaction, which he did not entirely expect, but in the final result he could not say it surprised him.

The grenadier carrying the royal standard faltered with his grip on the regimental flag. It tilted to the side unsteadily; and as it did, a number of troops in the 5th Infantry Regiment pulled from their pockets small tricolor flags of blue, white and red, and they began to wave them over their heads.

Before long the royalist banner fell to the ground, out of sight among the infantry troops who now joined the echoing chant "*Napoleon! Napoleon! Napoleon!*" with growing ferocity. Troops from the 5th Infantry began to run toward Napoleon's column, with their rifles slung over their shoulders, their arms raised in welcome, tricolor flags waving, shouting the name of their beloved returning leader, the legendary Napoleon Bonaparte.

As the front of Napoleon's column advanced into the

area where the road opened to the grassy rolling hills, Napoleon's troops too ran to welcome their newly acknowledged brothers in arms.

The commander of the force, Colonel Armand de Fabray, rode over to Napoleon with his three aides-de-camp halting their horses in front of the returning emperor. With deference and respect, the royalist officers dismounted and approached Napoleon, who remained mounted. The colonel saluted smartly, took his sword from his belt and offered it to Napoleon.

"My Emperor, I offer you my sword in surrender of my troops to you," the proud officer declared with noble decorum.

"It is of no use to me, sir. If you would keep it and lead these men for me, this is a service for which I would be grateful and generous in showing my appreciation. Will you do that for me, Colonel?" Napoleon requested, with welcoming warmth and camaraderie.

"It would be my honor, Your Majesty!" he responded, adding another sharp salute. The colonel then turned to his troops, all poised to see the result of the interaction between their commander and their great leader. The colonel raised his sword, turning to face Napoleon and shouted the legendary name in salute: "*Vive Napoleon!*"

The combined troops yelled the name of their leader in unison, as laughter, and a sense of relief and brotherhood surged through the now unified force.

Napoleon gazed on the scene with a slight smile of satisfaction. One thought, however, persisted for him: the man who he could not do without if he was to be successful in his bid to retake power.

Since the campaign in Egypt, where he first met the mysterious but brilliant and prescient figure—almost a personal oracle—Napoleon privately credited him as being one of the most influential and decisive factors which consistently gave him a strategic edge and indispensable perspective over events as no other individual in Bonaparte's circle of valued advisors possessed. This man's guidance in decision making and developing strategy had been invaluable. And now that Napoleon was free from his imprisonment on the island of Elba, he wanted... no he *needed*, to have access to this man's gifts once again. And he needed him now.

Napoleon turned to one of his adjuncts and closest confidants mounted next to him. "The road should now be comparatively clear to Paris. Find me the Count de Saint Germain. As I have told you, he travels in the company of his valet, Roger Rosier. He keeps in his circle a veteran of the *Grande Armée*—who accompanied us on the Russian campaign—known as Gaston Veilleux... He was a sergeant. It is imperative I see the count with all urgency. It would be extremely advantageous if you could arrange for him to be in Paris waiting for me upon my arrival there. Find me the Count de Saint Germain... and this may not be the only name he travels by. I believe he is also known as the Marquis Jean-Marc Baptiste de Rennes. He has what I need. Find him with the utmost urgency. This is critical to my success, Lieutenant."

The confidant who rode beside Napoleon—one cavalry Lieutenant Jean-Luc Glastre—nodded acknowledgement of his master's command. Napoleon had spoken on more than one occasion of the critical and personal importance this enigmatic figure held in Bonaparte's perspective of the grand scheme of the ever-changing universal chess board of destiny.

The young handsome lieutenant, with long wavy chestnut hair which blew in the wind, reined his horse to pause alongside the column as a few rows of troops passed, and he then signaled three riders in the ranks. They pulled out of the formation to join him. After exchanging private words, the horse soldiers nodded their understanding and confirmation of their orders.

Lieutenant Glastre then led the trio quickly off through the celebrating troops, to the road leading to the northwest and ultimately to Paris. Once free of the celebrating soldiers, they picked up their pace to a cavalry trot, moving swiftly across the hilly green terrain. The riders finally disappeared around a bend in the alpine road ahead of the column.

During his exile in Elba, the deposed emperor strived to keep the most current information on the whereabouts of the count from a network of various informants. Napoleon knew of the apartments the count kept in Paris, under the name Marquis Jean-Marc Baptiste de Rennes, as well as two other locations in France and Venice.

Napoleon hoped this information, which he gave to Lieutenant Glastre a few days earlier, was current and helpful. In his mind, Napoleon felt the count—with his genius, resources and many invaluable international connections—held the secret which could mean the difference between success and failure. Victory or defeat. Finding the count meant everything to him.

Jean-Marc, Gaston and Solange rode hard all day, striving to put as much distance between themselves and their encounter at the dolmen as possible. Their path took them through the eastern-most environs of the Loire valley, what some said was the Garden of Eden of France. Lush noble estates—reinstated and rejuvenated by virtue of Napoleon's departure and the re-installation of the Bourbon line as king—were in evidence to the observant traveler.

Jean-Marc's inner focus attended not to the scenery, however, but to the concern that although his interrogation of O'Donnell revealed the highwayman's attack had been the act of an independent agent, the marquis still held doubts.

Despite the fact he had centuries of experience in looking into a man's soul through his eyes and detecting falsehood, with O'Donnell now being completely blind, his eyes did not allow the avenue of deeper insight Jean-Marc often relied on to see into the truth of men's words. A subtle spark, deep in the pool of the eyes occurred, that few could perceive, and which was an indicator of dissembling. Regretfully, since Jean-Marc had created the conditions in the heat of the skirmish the night before, that option of scrutiny no longer remained available to him.

This situation meant his traditional comprehensive techniques for affirming truth or identifying fabrication had been compromised and were fragmentary. Jean-Marc certainly knew how to read voices as well. He had listened intensely to O'Donnell's telling of his circumstances with acute sensitivity, assessing choice of phrasing, logic of message, syntax of unnatural pauses, any loose ends in his story, as well as tonal delivery to help detect possible falsehood.

Jean-Marc knew the man was a rogue and quite accustomed to lying. However, the marquis's experience with people like this—who had become ingrained in the habit of relying on lies—that instances of laziness or an inability to keep all the stories straight, where small details would finally come out, would reveal a hidden and defining truth. Jean-Marc saw no hint of this being the case with O'Donnell's story.

That acknowledged, Jean-Marc remained humbled by the thought that by giving the innkeeper the diamond—so others might see this action—was an error involving the gravest of consequences, and he soberly chided himself for it. He resolved he must forever maintain a heightened and fortified sense of vigilance. The marquis knew he had enemies. He knew his opponents had targeted him for longer than normal men's lives. And he knew these adversaries could, would and had enlisted people from various walks of life into their designs. And these new recruits posed the greatest threat because they were always new faces in new places.

Recently crossing a geological landmark in the terrain—a distinctive craggy mountain ridge—they had arrived at the northern-most reaches of the Dordogne region, the place Jean-Marc believed to be the very heart and soul of France. And crossing this threshold of sorts, he enjoyed a slight lightening in the sense of urgency in their passage south.

This felt more like home in a world where he had been forced to adopt so many different places as temporary dwellings. Here Jean-Marc and those he cared for had history—a story dating back centuries. The fact he was fighting a massive throbbing headache in the back of his skull, just above the spine—and a dull ache in his back—for the better part of the day, seemed of less concern to him now.

"…And what of the impetuous whelp, master?" Gaston inquired as they rode.

Riding alongside the pair, Solange glanced expectantly, since on a simpatico level, she had at first experienced an initial connection with Roger. She actually liked him in the beginning. He had found a way to make her smile with his own charming manner, that first night at the tavern. And it now appeared his ultimate fate was being discussed and possibly decided. As Solange understood from her father's stories of the past, fate for some individuals could be decided in the blink of an eye and not with pleasant results for some.

"I do have concerns," Jean-Marc replied, hedging on any definitive commitment.

"He does *not* believe you. He does not believe *in* you. He sees you as nothing more than a ticket to advantage. Once that's fully redeemed, he'll move on to whatever other offer might be available to him. He cannot be trusted, Master. He's a reed in the wind. He'll blow wherever the breeze takes him. Now, with so much at stake, we can't afford mistakes, as noble and well-intentioned as your original motivations might have been for him," Gaston observed without rancor but with unbridled frankness and urgency.

"Your judgment of character has always been accurate and reliable, Gaston. Your ready willingness to speak hard truths is something I rely on," Jean-Marc replied.

A silence extended through the trio as they rode on through the beautiful budding countryside where vineyards on the hills overlooked wheat and bright yellow flowering fields of mustard. Jean-Marc finally turned casually to Solange.

"What do you think, Solange? I saw you and he connected in a certain way."

"I confess, Master, he's rather handsome and charming. He makes a very strong first impression which is quite unforgettable. He seems very resourceful in his own way. There are advantages in having someone like that in your company," Solange ventured as she led her horse along the road. "But his words betray sobering and dangerous sentiments for which I fear there's no true hope of correction, for they appear to originate from the very core of his nature."

Jean-Marc nodded thoughtfully as they rode on for a while again in silence, he taking the lead. As he finally turned back to them, with the intention of sharing his decision on Roger, he winced slightly, revealing pain. Then, without warning, he lost consciousness and toppled off his mount, landing roughly in the dirt road.

Both Gaston and Solange jumped from their horses and dashed to Jean-Marc's side. Solange was the first to discover the red blotch on Jean-Marc's back, blood seeping through his tunic. She cradled his head in her lap as she gingerly opened the shirt to view his bare back. The bullet wound had re-opened and blood oozed out.

"Our hard riding must've undone much of the mending cure which took place," Solange observed with urgent concern. "I know a great deal of the healing arts, but this wound would've been a mortal one for anyone else. And if recovery had been possible, it would require weeks recuperating in bed," she observed and then expressed a sense of rare vulnerable anxiety. "I don't know what to do for him, Father, except clean the wound again and give him rest. He originally had a medicine I applied before, but that was all used treating the wound the first time."

Gaston gazed thoughtfully at Jean-Marc with equal concern. "I do know he has had periods of long sleep. He once slept for two weeks in Egypt. And with this wound, this may be what is required. But finding a secure location, and assuring the right treatment, must be performed without error. To do otherwise could bring ruin for us all."

Jean-Marc muttered unintelligibly. Gaston immediately fell to his knees, lowered his ear to hear better the marquis's words. After a moment Gaston raised his head, facing his daughter.

"He says for us to take him to Savigny, to the Curé of Boussac."

Satisfied the arrangements he required were set in motion, following a series of meetings in Chartres, Bishop Antonio del Julia y Sangresante felt content his carriage would not need to rush through the countryside to the south. All the hard riding would be performed by others as he believed it always should be in the grand scheme of things. If all worked as planned, he would likely arrive with his prospective captive in hand, and he would be left to harvest the long-sought reward of his ancient goals.

As his carriage neared the town of Saint Luc d' Espery, they passed a man on horseback, leading other horses, with three captives on their backs. The last one with a bandage around his face appeared to be blinded. Brother Jerome took note of this.

"That's Robert O'Donnell, the highwayman, and two of his henchmen. I've employed him in the past. And I've seen their captor somewhere before… Yes: in La Beauce, just before we arrived in Chartres, two days ago… If he succeeded in taking them prisoner, he must be a man of some consequence, Your Grace. Possibly he's someone we can use," Brother Jerome observed.

The bishop's eyes closed and lips pursed in pensive meditation on what this development might represent and the possible advantages it might deliver.

As he strode out of magistrate's office in Saint Luc d' Espery, Roger was glad to be finally rid of his prisoners. Having gone to the livery stable of Pasqual Onzon as instructed, he enlisted the quick and helpful assistance promised by Jean-Marc, especially after he mentioned the marquis's name.

Witnessing the large muscular stable keeper's instantaneous readiness to interrupt all his work, and to assist, by simple virtue of the mention of this name, affected Roger in a way he had not expected. In the past, Roger liked feeling the power when he mentioned Jean-Marc's name. Now, seeing the reaction of Jean-Marc's '*Tekton* brother,' it only filled him with a sense of resentment and irritation.

Roger, of course, knew very well he had been invited into membership of a lodge in the *Tekton* Brotherhood, under Jean-Marc's patronage. Roger demurred at the time with his traditional charm, indicating he did 'not feel ready for the honor, but would certainly embrace it in its due course.'

Jean-Marc accepted Roger's decision, as the marquis often did with his actions. Roger did, however, notice Jean-Marc's disappointment at his turning down this rare and significant offer. Roger, however, did not want to get trapped into the mysterious ritualistic mumbo jumbo he presumed they were involved with.

On another instinctual level, he avoided any society organized where he had to start at the bottom and where he knew Jean-Marc was highly regarded. As long as they had their one-on-one relationship, Roger deemed himself to be more in control of his own destiny.

However, in the last day, he sensed that entire dynamic with his master may have somehow changed irrevocably. And as he rode through the day with the prisoners, he ruminated vaguely on the possibility there might be some actual profound change he needed to recognize and respond to. But he would think about that later.

Now, with money in his pocket from the sale of the horses, and a tidy sum with the reward for the highwaymen paid out by the magistrate, he felt more the master of his own fortune, rather than beholden to Jean-Marc. Roger conveniently ignored that his bounty came to him by virtue of Jean-Marc's vast network of relationships in France, the extent of which he only had an inkling. Roger convinced himself he had received a duly-earned reward, and he actually enjoyed the praise he received from the magistrate and townsfolk for the feat of capturing the notorious O'Donnell and his highwaymen.

Enjoying the fruits of his labors and a well-deserved respite from the trials of the preceding day, Roger availed himself of the local offerings.

Now at the village inn, he flirted with the serving maiden as she brought him his second earthenware pitcher of local wine. He knew he would be expected to ultimately rejoin the party in Venice, but that wasn't for a week; and now he preferred to take care of his own worthy needs for a change.

Feeling the warm glow of the best of last year's wine harvest, Roger ordered roast pig; and as he generously tipped the nubile maiden serving him, he delivered a mischievous and suggestive smile, and he complimented her on her beautiful eyes. She liked that. If all went well, Roger reflected, he might be enjoying the comforts of the fairer sex tonight. And tomorrow he would worry himself about the suggestion of obligations and expectations of Jean-Marc and the long solitary sojourn south to Venice.

A handful of forty-franc gold coins dropped onto the table in front of him. The sound of their fall immediately pulled Roger's attention as he peered down at the tidy sum and frowned slightly as he glanced up at the hulking man who dropped the money there: shaved head, a scar across the skull, with an intense animal ferocity in the eyes and a broad smile on his lips. He gestured at the gold coins and for Roger to take them.

"You're a hero, my friend! You deserve this additional reward! Take it! It's yours by all rights! O'Donnell was the bane of the central provinces of France for some time, and till now no one succeeded in capturing him! The tale of your feats has already spread throughout the village! You're the Roland who tamed O'Donnell! You're the man who made traveling the byways of France safe at last! And, if I may, brother, I'd like to buy you a bottle of the house's best!"

The massive man with the clean-shaven head placed himself alongside Roger on the bench, blocking any exit from the inn.

In his current state of light inebriation Roger was quite receptive to flattery, spiced with more easy loot to add to his gains from earlier—and at this point in his robust drinking bout, everything sounded good. He especially liked the fact that the inn maiden heard the exchange with this new arrival, as forbidding a visage as he might have—which somehow looked vaguely familiar. Roger now became convinced this one factor heightened the chances of achieving carnal victory later in the evening with this delicious flaxen-haired servant girl bearing his beverages and revealing an ample bosom.

His earlier designs of expectant intimacy with Solange— along with the disappointment, frustrations and embarrassment that followed—evaporated in his present glow of self-satisfied, yet undeserved, glory. Roger heartened with the idea that his prospects were looking up and that other maidens, far fairer than Solange were destined to be his in the near future, along with other rich rewards. Yes, his time had finally come, he told himself as he drank deeply.

Brother Jerome grinned, pleased to see that with the least

effort he had accomplished his goal: to lull his prey into facile acceptance of his shallow compliments, with the mercenary lubrication of free libations and a few gold coins.

For someone who had allegedly conquered the formidable and legendary highwayman O'Donnell and his crew, this was easier than expected. The monk suspected an important part of this story was yet to be revealed. He smiled at his prey in fawning admiration, and Roger ate it up eagerly.

"I could use a man with your rare and unique talents, friend, and this gold is merely a small portion of what my master will supply to those who aid him with his worthy and sacred goals. Might you be interested, noble sir? Are you interested in becoming a very wealthy man, sir?" Brother Jerome spoke with the slightest touch of deference and a seductive spirit of enticement, something he had done with so many doomed souls through the many years he walked the earth.

"I'm interested in noble and sacred causes, especially if they're lucrative ones," Roger replied a little airily, somehow convincing himself he was the dominant one in this conversation.

"Ah, yours is the rarest breed in these times of upheaval, sir! A man of noble heart, with a sense of robust action and imaginative innovation, but who at the same time does not miss the reality of opportunity and commerce. If there were more men like you in the world, I daresay, sir, we'd not be in the situation we are today. The world would be at peace." Brother Jerome spoke with an admiring and intimate camaraderie as the fresh pitcher arrived and he filled Roger's glass. "We're searching for a man, sir. A man who's the basest form of outlaw. A man who must be apprehended at any expense. A man for whom we're in a position to pay for any costs, with handsome bonuses to boot. So important is the capture of this infamous criminal that the man who delivers him to us, or helps us apprehend him, will very possibly be set financially for the rest of his life."

Roger drank deep into his wine and listened eagerly to Brother Jerome as the fiction of his inflated worth accelerated and grew in his mind to Herculean proportions over the course of the next hour. Before his drinking bout was done, whether he knew it or not, his loyalties had been purchased. The devil, of course, would be in the details of honoring that to which he found himself committed on that fateful evening.

Sitting alone in his jail cell, the highwayman O'Donnell chewed on a stale heel of bread as he washed it down with water from a wooden cup. As he chewed, he listened to the sounds of prisoners in other cells: arguments brewed in one, in another a prisoner wept at the injustice handed to him, while in yet another, a prisoner sang a bawdy song to pass the time.

The blinded highwayman heard the sound of an outer door opening, footsteps approached, and finally the jingle of a key unlatching his cell. Someone entered.

"O'Donnell," the voice intoned with gravelly amusement.

"Who is it?" O'Donnell replied, somewhat defensively, but the seasoned experience of his life as a highwayman ultimately brought his attitude to a fatalistic businesslike sensibility. "So I have enemies here, do I?"

"Maybe just one who's employed you in the past," the voice replied, comfortable with the darkness of the lockup.

O'Donnell struggled to associate the resonance of the voice with memory. The shadowy figure allowed himself to be entertained by this. Finally O'Donnell smiled slightly, satisfied with his assessment.

"Ah, yes. The bishop's man," O'Donnell finally declared.

"Very good," Brother Jerome replied. "I have questions about the nature of your capture. I want to know all about the man who delivered you to the authorities. How you answer will very well determine your destiny, my friend."

The Dordogne Region
Central France
6 March, 1815 AD – Late Morning

They arrived at the medieval and formerly walled town of Boussac, situated on the borders of Berry-Champagne and La Marche and which overlooked the Petite Creuse River from a rocky promontory.

The aged brownstone castle of Jean de Brosse—which hosted the storied Unicorn tapestries—stood at the end of a stone outcropping commanding this part of the river. The local medieval-era church, a humble structure also of brownstone, had been easy to locate from there. However, upon inquiry, Solange learned that Savigny Souillac, the Curé of Boussac, was not in residence, nor expected back for some days. The young acolyte in the chapel disclosed he could likely be found at his secondary post: the church of Toulx-Saint-Croix, a small village roughly twelve miles south, further into the local high country.

"We're almost there, Father. I estimate another two hours, maybe less," Solange stated as she studied her father and the marquis who remained in the saddle together.

Gaston had fashioned a sling apparatus where Jean-Marc shared a saddle with him so he was seated facing the sergeant and tied with two crossed strips of cloth so that the unconscious marquis would not slip off.

They rode slowly the remainder of the previous day and as much into the night as possible to make headway, finally taking an exhausted respite in a moonlit meadow surrounded by quiet forestlands. Then, rising at dawn, they pressed on with the greatest urgency, yet riding with as smooth a gait as possible so as not to further harm or jostle Jean-Marc any more than necessary.

Seeing this tableau of the paired men in the saddle reminded Solange of the symbol of the Knights Templar: where two knights shared one horse, part of the vaunted and mystical symbolism of the long-dead chapter of chivalrous, legendary and yet mysterious knights.

Now faced with at least another two hours of riding before their destination, Gaston grumbled with frustration and concern as he nudged his heels into the tired horse's ribs a few times to rally his steed back into motion.

"I just hope the curé is where that lad said he'll be. The Master needs attention far beyond our capabilities. Without it, I dread the outcome. And who knows what skills this priest has? After all, he *is* a priest!" Gaston complained with a seasoned suspicion of the clergy.

"Everything will be fine, Father. Jean-Marc knows what is required for his needs, and we are fortunate to be so close to our destination."

Ignoring her father's worried attitude, and taking the reins to Jean-Marc's riderless horse, Solange climbed back onto her mount. She tapped her heels into her mount's sides, directing it on toward the southern exit of the town, and glanced back to assure Gaston and Jean-Marc were in stride as well.

While she studied her companions, she masked her own anxious concern with an encouraging smile as she led the third horse on behind her. And she had something else on her mind as well, as her brow knit in concentration, striving to recall something hiding out at the edges of her prodigious memory.

Sometime later, well after they left Boussac, and as their narrow road wound up through the rising high ground to pass by a curious mass of granite stone outcroppings, they could now enjoy a view out over the northern reaches of Berry and Bourbonnais, and to the south over the mountains of La Marche and Limousin. While gazing at the spectacular landscape, Solange finally remembered that which she had been searching for in her mind. She shared this with her father.

"Ah, yes, I remember now! I know why Toulx-Saint-Croix sounded so familiar. My mother referred to it as a source of many of the rare medicinal herbs she worked with in the healing arts. She said this part of the country— because of its unique climate, variegated lay of the land, profusion of floral varieties and the nature of its pristine state—was the source for a surprising number of rare and potent medicinal herbs. If we're unable to find the curé, we may be able to find someone knowledgeable in herbal preparation and curative applications."

Their slow ride finally brought them to an expansive wheat field which lay at the crest of a stony hilltop upon which stood the small village of Toulx-Saint-Croix. At the edge of the field, which gave way to a mountain forest, stood a small strange dolmen. A granite structure, looking much like a massive double-stalked mushroom—its broad capstone seemed balanced precariously on the supporting rocks of its foundation. One of the many vestiges of the Druidic Gallo-Celts, the culture thrived in this region long before the Roman Empire's dominion over these lands.

Indeed this place had been the center of an active medicinal herbal trade before the Empire's rule. However, when the Romans conquered the area, they enslaved many of the herb collectors. Much of the local knowledge had been lost, though not completely.

And as the riders rose higher on the road, approaching the village, they now saw that two standalone towers commanded the skyline of this modest settlement. The first, an old, cylindrical bastion with wide simple crenulations on top harkened back to late colonial Roman times—and the other, much taller, a more slender, medieval and skeletal-looking structure, with a circular parapet at the top, gave the impression of being a gray stone lighthouse looking out over the spectacular commanding panorama this curious village enjoyed.

After passing a formation of massive granite boulders at the outskirts of the village, which oddly resembled a small herd of large elephant backs, giving the location an added sense of strange and brooding mystery—accented by the gathering storm clouds overhead—Solange and Gaston finally reached the entry to the village itself. They found their way to the squat, ancient Romanesque church at its center: Saint Jean's Chapel.

Solange leapt off her horse and helped untether Jean-Marc from Gaston, who remained on his steed as the unconscious marquis slid into her strong and caring arms. Gaston then jumped off his stallion and took Jean-Marc into his arms to cradle him like a child as Solange ran to open the door to the church for her father.

Just inside the entryway of the chapel, they came upon a tall and ancient-looking bearded man in the cassock of a local priest: Curé Savigny Souillac. He had been chatting amiably with an old local woman, from whom he just took delivery of a large basket full of various herbs. The curé's eyes immediately widened with alert concern at the sight of Solange, her father, and their patient.

"Has your companion sustained an injury? Is he ill?" the priest inquired with immediate sincere and caring empathy as he approached them.

Gaston felt the need to establish his command of the situation and spoke with a challenging tone. "You're the Curé of Boussac, one Savigny Souillac? Is that correct, sir?"

"I am, my son. And I could ask for your identity as well, I suppose," the cleric countered delicately. "But more important: what is your man's ailment? I cannot help you unless I understand the nature of the affliction. Is it an injury? Some illness?" he queried as he came alongside them, but not yet to a position where he could see Jean-Marc's face clearly.

Solange took the lead on this exchange of information. "I dare say both, Father. His infirmity is beyond the scope of most doctors' abilities. Yet he specifically asked to be brought to you," Solange revealed as she gestured toward Jean-Marc.

The local herb collector knew her place was to depart now, and she did so as the priest moved into a line of sight where he finally saw the patient's face more clearly.

"Oh, my God," the elderly priest muttered under his breath through his snowy white beard with profound apprehension.

"I suspect it'll take more than some priest's version of the power of God to cure his ailment. Are you equal to the task, Father?" Gaston challenged.

"Whatever it takes, I'll serve his needs with all my heart and soul," the priest replied with passionate commitment. "Come. Follow me," he directed them as he led them out of the back of the chapel and to the small gray stone dwelling located behind the church: the priory.

Once inside, the priest cleared the large hardwood table in the main receiving room of the priory, which served as the modest dwelling the curé occupied during his extended visits to Toulx-Saint-Croix.

He found a pillow and as they laid Jean-Marc out on his

stomach on the table, they positioned his head carefully, facing to the side. The priest touched Jean-Marc's face with loving care, then delicately opened Jean-Marc's blood-stained shirt, and began to search for telltale signs or symptoms. As he did so, he quizzed Gaston and Solange.

"He sustained a wound? What was his condition before he became unconscious? Please give me all the details you can, no matter how inconsequential they may seem. Tell me everything you know about him and the injury."

Despite the fact Jean-Marc specifically requested he be brought to this man, Gaston balked at the concept of divulging Jean-Marc's inner secrets to a complete stranger, a member of the Church as well. "We had been riding after a very rigorous two days on the trail and he collapsed off his horse," Gaston disclosed stiffly.

The cleric opened the shirt wide enough to see the serious seeping wound in Jean-Marc's back. His gaze rose to meet Gaston's with doubt and concern, as his eyes narrowed with pensive concern, shifting to glance at Solange.

Solange impatiently jumped in and provided the critical essentials she knew were needed. "I assume, Father, you're familiar with Jean-Marc's unique background, and it's because of this you've been sought out. Our master suffered a mortal bullet wound in his back, which he survived with his unique vital energy. And following his recovery, he performed a number of feats which defy nature and logic. But nonetheless, when our urgent mission required us to ride hard, it must have been simply too much for him. As my father described, it was at this point on the road that he collapsed without warning off the back of his horse. With his last breath before succumbing to his current unconscious condition, he spoke your name as the one who might be able to balance the scales of hope for us all."

The aged priest studied her briefly with appreciative empathy. "I can see you care deeply for this man," he observed.

"He is the font of our knowledge and hope without which our lives are meaningless," Solange said without irony. She then proceeded to study the bullet wound with Curé Savigny. The profuse seeping of blood again seemed incapable of stopping. Tears welled in her eyes, as the priest took a bottle of brandy, poured it into a bowl, disinfected his hands and then skillfully studied and probed the wound.

"The bullet has been removed?" he inquired.

"Yes," Solange replied. "He directed me to do so. I took out five fragments. I believe I took them all."

The priest nodded and then, after a pause, he laid his hands on Jean-Marc's back, on either side of the wound, as he closed his eyes in intense concentration. Observing this, Gaston reacted with impatient irritation.

"What're you doing? Praying? You want to heal him with prayers?"

Father Souillac opened his eyes and regarded Gaston peacefully, without offence. "In this case I was checking for the heat of a deep infection and fever. But regarding prayers: they never hurt, my son."

Gaston's blood rose at this comment. "They may not hurt, but we need help, not platitudes, Priest! This man's very important to us, and his condition is…" Gaston struggled with the prospect of possibly divulging information he should not. Curé Savigny responded before

Gaston could continue.

"I know exactly who this man is, young man, undoubtedly much more so than you. My relationship with him goes back many, many years," the priest revealed.

Helpless to do otherwise, so taut were his emotions, Gaston responded to this statement as a challenge, and replied, "As I have, sir! Since the Egyptian Campaign! And I dare say we've endured gauntlets of life-threatening trials together you could not begin to imagine!"

"I have every reason to believe you're correct in that statement," the aged clergyman calmly replied. "But right now, I'm afraid that's completely irrelevant. I must get—"

Offended by the priest's remark, Gaston gathered steam. "Irrelevant? I'll have you know that the Master has given me—"

"Father!" Solange cried out loudly with forceful respect. "Please go outside and assure the horses have been positioned out of sight. This's the wrong place and the wrong time for this exchange, and you know it! I shall give the good curé the information he requires. And you know very well my extensive training with Mother in the healing arts will be offered in the measure they are needed," Solange stated firmly, allowing no room for disagreement or debate. Her steady, powerful eyes commanded her father to take his leave.

Surprised by his daughter's conviction and strength of character, Gaston muttered something unintelligible about Solange having exactly the same spirit as his dear wife—Solange's mother—as he left the room, glancing over his shoulder as he closed the door behind him.

The priest observed this action with a quiet

understanding nod and the slightest of compassionate smiles. "You would be Solange, I believe, accompanied by your brave and storied father, Gaston. Am I correct?"

"Yes," Solange responded with guarded suspicion.

"You have your mother's eyes," he observed with smiling affection.

Solange frowned with uncertainty. Curé Savigny Souillac briefly rested his hand on her shoulder, reassuringly with sincere affection. "Your mother was a student of mine many, many years ago, long before she met your father... So in a way, with you being your mother's student in the healing arts, you have by ancient tradition been my student as well," the priest revealed calmly.

"What? That's incredible. I never knew!" Solange replied with a sense of wonder, taken completely off guard by this disclosure.

Father Souillac briefly studied her surprise at this revelation. "I'm sure there's much for us to discuss, my child, after we've taken care of our precious patient."

The Curé of Boussac then proceeded to collect the complete detailed medical history of the wound: the extraction of the bullet; who fired what manner of weapon with lethal intent and from what range; the exchange of blood Solange shared with Jean-Marc; the desperate fight at the campsite, as well as the hard riding which ultimately resulted in Jean-Marc's collapse from the saddle.

The priest also questioned her pointedly if she had observed anywhere in her travels the presence of a massive bald man with a distinct striking scar across his head, possibly dressed in monk's robes, as well as a younger man, probably dressed in the vestments of high station, whose piercing separately colored singular blue and green eyes would be unforgettable.

"I have neither encountered nor seen anyone of this description in my entire life," Solange reported.

Father Savigny nodded soberly and only added, "Be ever watchful for them, for if they see you first, it could end with tragic results."

This disclosure gave Solange a shudder. Meanwhile she retrieved the bottle which held the medical substance Jean-Marc had in his saddle bags which was employed in the original treatment of the wound. The mendicant priest studied it by smell and tasted the last trace of powder still in the bottle.

"This is one of the treatments I prepared for him, yet more for general purposes in its utility. Acceptable in the short term, considering the circumstances, but not the right solution needed for the severity of this profoundly deep wound," he diagnosed. "We must be quick now, elsewise his body shall shut down into a long sleep from which he might not wake for weeks. Time is of critical essence, Solange. Your knowing hands will be of great assistance."

Over the next hour, Solange watched as Savigny Souillac, Curé of Boussac, went to work; and at different times he called her to assist. He moved around the kitchen area with the movements of someone in a trance, as though some strange form of ballet was being performed, so graceful and studied were his movements. Moving from cupboard to drawer, taking bottles, flasks, jars and boxes of different exotic liquids and powders, he put them into one of three different large copper pots which he set to flame on the stove. He instructed Solange to stir them in a specific manner at certain times, as well as adjust the flames once a boil had been established. One kettle stayed over a full fire until much of a solution boiled away to a thick sludge; another needed to be maintained at a steady simmer; the third had a complex series of boiling and simmering stages as different ingredients were added at precise times in the process.

As the priest engaged in these activities, he whistled a tune which Solange recalled her mother would whistle when she worked at the esoteric apothecary's trade, and for a moment, she found herself lost in the memory of her mother and the mystery of her disappearance years ago. The tune, however, also gave Solange a sense of deep spiritual calm, of wellness.

As she experienced this phenomenon, she realized the tune being whistled was for Jean-Marc, who lay unconscious on the table in the next room. With this strand of sound, the clergyman communicated to his patient, and in effect applied a preliminary treatment to whatever remedy the curé planned to implement for Jean-Marc.

And as she listened and felt the affecting sounds of the priest's melodic tune, she reflected on the lessons her mother taught her regarding the Music of the Spheres. Solange knew its importance in the complex performance of alchemy, and why her mother had compelled Solange to train for years in mastering the musical instrument which emulated the most heavenly sounds made from the hands of mankind: the violin.

During their hours-long preparations, and intending to quiet his agitated mood, Gaston ambled over to the lighthouse-like medieval tower of the village, and climbed to the top to take in the commanding view now dominated by a gray sprawl of storm clouds.

Having brought along the telescope he commandeered from Robert O'Donnell, he gazed down at different villages in the surrounding lower-lying areas and the roads which joined them.

He spied one thing that gave him pause and concern. About two miles away, by a mustard field at the fork of a byway, six horseback riders rode hard from the north and paused at this juncture in the highway to converse with each other. After a short time, two took the southern track, two the western route, and two the eastern road which would bring them in the general direction of Toulx-Saint-Croix.

Gaston's instincts for preparing to deal with unwanted guests were instantly alert. Yet as he studied the pair on their ride heading in the direction of the small village hosting the two towers, he was relieved to see that when they arrived at another fork in the byway, they chose the one taking them further on in a more southerly direction, rather than continuing due east toward their village.

While it appeared immediate contingency measures for potential intruders might not be needed, Gaston remained nonetheless unsettled by the knowledge that the land ahead of them from now on could very likely be populated by unseen enemies at any turn in the road.

After climbing down from the tower and checking the horses he stabled earlier in the small barn behind the priory, assuring their mounts were fed and wiped down, Gaston rejoined Solange and the curé in the priory.

"Ah, your timing could not have been more prescient, Sergeant Veilleux! We're now prepared for the next, most critical stage of the treatment, which we cannot perform without your hearty support."

Then, as Solange carried two earthenware urns in her arms, and as Gaston picked up and cradled Jean-Marc in his arms, the ancient priest slung the strap of a large brown canvas bag over his shoulder and led them to a door off the kitchen which opened into a walk-in cupboard with a number of wooden cabinets and shelves stocked with sacks of flour, dried goods, jars of preserves and other provisions.

The priest stepped to the rear of the storeroom where an old wood-paneled feature hosted banks of small square drawers with tarnished brass handles. The cleric opened one of the top drawers, reached into it and pulled an unseen lever. The left side of the panel of drawers shifted forward on a hinge, and the priest nodded silently as he opened it further revealing the panel's hidden function as a secret door.

"This door was built during the first Inquisition, in medieval times, but its utility is eternal," the cleric observed as he gestured for his guests to enter.

Once they passed through, he reached for a brass lantern which hung from a large wrought iron hook housed in the granite stone wall, retrieved a flint from a small niche and lit the lantern with deft ease. Father Souillac held the lantern high overhead, illuminating the secret chamber, revealing a steep narrow stairway, the stone steps dipped with ages of arcane use. Solange went down first, her lithe spirit ready for the challenge of the unknown. Gaston frowned reflexively as he turned back to the priest with Jean-Marc in his arms.

"The only reason I'm taking these steps into this infernal abyss is because my master willed it. Otherwise, I'd have taken my chances with fate," Gaston muttered with doubt and impotent protest.

"It's all for the greater good, my son," Father Souillac replied with quiet confidence. "Your daughter has been a knowledgeable and invaluable supporter of the vital requirements at hand."

The cleric closed the hidden door behind them. They made their way down the precipitous straight stairway into the inky darkness below, with the priest holding the lantern high to offer the best lighting possible for those ahead of him on the steps.

After slowly climbing down the equivalent of two stories, they reached an open subterranean grotto. Father Souillac took the lead as his lantern illuminated the impressive expansiveness of this cavernous realm.

"This was a place of worship for the Druids at the time preceding the Roman Empire and centuries before as well. The Romans tore down the Gallo-Celtic temple to Lug, god of light, and built one to Mercury, their messenger god. And when the Christian influence came, they tore down Mercury's temple and built St. Jean's Chapel from the original stone quarried by the Gauls and Romans. What the conquering Romans lost in the process, however, was the secret entrance to this cavern and the remarkable resources which exist here. The main reason the original temple had been first built on this site was because of the sacred waters of Mother Earth found here," the priest intoned without irony and a trace of reverence.

"So you're a priest who's secretly a heathen as well, are you?" Gaston challenged with a hint of amusement.

"I'm a realist who values history and the lessons it offers mankind," the curé answered. "The waters here are from a very rare source. They originate from deep in the heart and soul of the earth itself. Their properties are remarkable, as Jean-Marc well knows."

They arrived at a space where they saw and heard the robust bubbling of waters in a mineral pool. As the priest raised his lantern high, they could see more deeply into the dark subterranean chamber. The cavern's ceiling opened high overhead, at least a story and a half.

Spread out in front of them, a series of three pools laid out, connected by a narrow flowing stream. The first pool— the source—was closest to them and about ten yards across. Filled with steaming aqua-blue water, the mineral spring roiled with surging current and bubbles percolating from deep below the stone floor of the cavern.

A small channel of water, naturally formed over eons through the slanted granite rock floor, led to the next of two smaller pools: the middle, roughly ten feet wide; the last, smaller still, only six feet across. The stream supplied a constant flow of water to these pools located slightly downhill from the source reservoir.

The last basin, however, was not naturally formed. It seemed to have been cut from live stone; with round smooth edges clearly crafted for utility. Another stream on its lower side drained the cistern into a sluiceway on the grotto floor which disappeared into the darkness.

It was to this last, smaller pool, that the curé directed his companions. And having brought a thick blanket with him from his canvas bag, he spread it out on the stone floor by the cistern. He gestured for Gaston to place Jean-Marc on the blanket, and Solange helped ensure their master was laid out with care.

"The best I could gather from the local tradition, after I gained the confidence of the oldest families of the village—which took some time, and not without Jean-Marc's help—was that this particular pool had been crafted by the ancient Druids for sacred ceremonies. The hallowed observances in this place, however, consisted not just of symbolic rites of passage, but serious and profound curative procedures were conducted here as well."

Gaston glanced around the setting, not completely at ease with this environ. "I expect a ghost or two haunts this realm."

Assured Jean-Marc rested securely on the blanket, Father Souillac faced Gaston and Solange with a serious countenance. "What we must do next is something I'm certain you, Gaston, will believe is utter madness. But it's something that must be done, and it must be done *precisely* as I prescribe."

Solange searched the priest's face as he glanced at the cistern. She frowned with a troubled revelation and then glanced down at the surging effervescent pool next to them. She went to one knee and tested the water with the tip of her finger and withdrew it quickly, startled at the scalding heat of these primal waters. "This water's almost boiling! It's unbearable, Father!"

Gaston bent over and tested the waters himself and winced as he instantly pulled back his hand. "Are you mad? Do you mean to stew him alive, Priest!" he accused Souillac with agitated venom.

"I mean to give him back his vitality, Sergeant, and to provide him with exactly what he requested by asking to be brought here. Your requirement in this moment is to have faith."

Gaston's eyes widened, and then quickly narrowed, as if to hear an open challenge to mortal combat. Both men stared at each other with a conflicting and unrelenting sense of loyalty to what they felt was their cause: Jean-Marc. Solange placed her hand gently on Gaston's shoulder.

"I do have faith in this man, Father. Did you know he was Mother's teacher before you met her?"

This information hit Gaston like a lightning bolt. "You...?"

Savigny Souillac, Curé of Boussac merely lowered his eyes slightly in affirmation. "Mademoiselle Adella was an eloquent intellect, with a tireless curiosity and a boundless *joie de vivre*. You are a very lucky man to have had her as your partner in life, Gaston... And I am deeply sorry for your loss as well."

Compelled to experience an involuntary and poignant reflection of his wife before his gaze returned to Father Savigny, Gaston's shoulders relaxed, and he finally gestured with a sense of acceptance. "Tell us what we must do."

The priest directed Solange to take one urn to the second, middle pool, and pour the entire contents—a fine off-white powder—into the sluiceway from the first larger pool. She did so. He then directed Gaston to empty the contents of the second urn as close to the sluiceway of the middle pool feeding the waters of last pool.

As Gaston finished, the curé threw two handfuls of a reddish brown mineral dust into the last cistern. He then gestured for both Solange and Gaston to immediately join him by the blanket upon which Jean-Marc laid. As the waters from the middle pool merged with the last pool, a roiling effervescent chemical action ensued, and orange steam rose from it with a growing intensity.

"We must now act swiftly," the priest declared as he carefully supported Jean-Marc in his arms and removed his bloodstained shirt, while he instructed Gaston to cut a circle in the middle of the blanket, the size of a fist, with the sergeant's razor-sharp knife which he always kept close at hand.

Once achieved, the curé had Solange pull from his canvas bag a piece of gauze the size of a handkerchief which had been heavily smeared with a brown sticky substance. He instructed Solange to lay it out across the newly cut hole. Once completed, the priest laid Jean-Marc back on the blanket with great care, positioning the wound directly over the brown poultice on the gauze and the hole.

The aged priest then directed Solange to take firm hold of one corner of the coverlet. He took another, as he instructed Gaston to grasp the last two corners.

The trio carefully and smoothly raised Jean-Marc in unison and then, taking small shuffling side steps, positioned themselves so Gaston stood with his end of the coverlet over one side of the pool, while Father Souillac and Solange carefully side-stepped together so they were on the other side of the cistern. The curé nodded slightly, and together they all began to lower the mantle with Jean-Marc on it, until they went down on their knees, holding the blanket tightly. Finally Jean-Marc's legs, body and arms were totally immersed in the roiling waters of the scalding and potent mineral-rich pool.

"Gaston, make sure to keep his head well above the waters," Father Souillac directed.

Clutching the two corners of the blanket closest to Jean-Marc's head and shoulders, Gaston nodded with serious intent, gripping fast to his end of the blanket.

Solange saw the skin on Jean-Marc's chest quickly becoming a bright hue of red. So much blood rushed to the surface of Jean-Marc's skin, and with such force, it literally appeared as though he now wore a skin-tight crimson red shirt. And through it all, Jean-Marc laid completely still.

"How long must we do this, Father?" Solange inquired, battling her disturbed concern.

"We will know soon enough," Father Savigny replied, his eyes glued on Jean-Marc.

The thick orange steam of the waters continued to rise above them, enveloping the cavernous grotto. Jean-Marc lay completely still in the waters as they swirled around him with a torrid heat seeming to boil him.

Helplessly witnessing this strange, seemingly tortuous process, Gaston finally grew agitated. "We must remove him now! Elsewise we'll kill him!" Seeing no reaction from the cleric, Gaston pressed his point, speaking much louder now. "Priest, do you hear me?"

Solange glanced over at the Curé of Boussac with concern, doubt beginning to corrode her faith in the man who had been her mother's revered teacher. The priest ignored her glance, maintaining his complete focus on their patient and the roiling steam, which had now begun to gradually turn to an aqua-green hue.

The excruciating process continued for some time longer. Jean-Marc's skin had now become the brightest of crimson-blood red. Solange's faltering faith began to erode into despair, and she observed her father's eyes graduate from agitated concern to cold murderous rage.

She knew if this procedure did not succeed, that when they finally withdrew Jean-Marc from the pool, Gaston would just as swiftly throw the priest into it, to the horrifying agony of being boiled alive. A sickening nausea took hold of her as she watched her father gritting his teeth, eyes narrowing, setting firm now his lethal determination which Solange had no power to influence.

Instead of one possible death, she faced two: both of her mother's teachers, of whom she had spoken many times, but always studiously avoiding identifying them by name: Savigny and Jean-Marc.

"The deed is done, Priest! You failed! Have some heart, man. Let us withdraw him now so we may give him a decent burial with some dignity."

The priest kept his composed steady eyes on Jean-Marc. "Just a bit longer, my son," he replied calmly.

That last appellation pushed Gaston over the top, as he erupted into fury, while still holding the blanket firmly.

"I am *not* your son, Priest! And you're no doctor! I demand you withdraw him this—"

"Shut up, you stupid old fool! And hold tight to that blanket!" the priest bellowed with a powerful ferocity that shocked both Solange and Gaston. This old man had the force of power of a young warrior in his bearing and delivery. Yet strangely, he kept his eyes riveted on Jean-Marc as he continued his reply with equal force. "You have no idea what processes are at work and what is required! You would override your master's wishes and instructions, and risk his very life, based on your own belligerent, ill-mannered and uninformed gut instincts! It's impulsive stupidity like that which will get you and your daughter killed in the flash of a moment, to say nothing of the Master's fate!"

Wide-eyed with astonishment, Gaston became somewhat flustered at what his next action might be when a soft moan came from the blanket. All eyes instantly focused on Jean-Marc. Possibly roused by the shouting, he seemed to be awakening from a restful sleep. He moved and stretched his limbs as his eyes opened sleepily, only now taking note of the churning waters in which he had been immersed. Alertness came to his eyes quickly as he glanced at the curé.

"Now! Withdraw him now!" the priest called out. "Hold firm! Carefully!"

They immediately pulled Jean-Marc from the waters in careful unison and placed him back on the stone floor by the pool. Solange was startled to see how the flushed bright-red skin rapidly began to turn back to a normal hue, as a small lazy smile appeared on Jean-Marc's face.

"What were you arguing about? The waters were so close to my ears, and in my slumber, I thought it was a dream at first," his hand reached out to Savigny, who clasped it with loving affection and powerful support.

"We were just getting to know each other a little better, that's all," the priest replied with calm humor and a sparkle in his eye. He then slipped his other arm around Jean-Marc's shoulders and elevated him into a sitting position off the soaking wet blanket. The curé ran his aged hand over Jean-Marc's back and over where the wound had been. All trace of it was gone; it had healed over completely.

Solange studied it with reverent awe as Gaston frowned with a crippling self-doubt, and he turned to Jean-Marc, intent on confession. "Master, I almost undid us all. I almost—"

Curé Souillac, however, cut him off, disallowing the intended act of personal debasement and voluntary humiliation. "You brought your heart, your strength and best intentions, Sergeant. No one can fault or blame you for that. It's just at times those attributes must be directed a bit more productively," the priest offered with affectionate charm, and not the slightest trace of fire he exhibited only a moment earlier. "I, for one, am grateful for all your tireless commitment to this sacred man in our presence. Your service to him is stellar, without fault and deserving the highest praise."

Jean-Marc gazed at them all with a loving appreciation. His eyes rested last and longest on his savior, as he placed his fingertips on the priest's hand. "Thank you, my beloved son," Jean-Marc said quietly.

The ancient curé's eyes welled with emotion as Solange and Gaston glanced at each other, then back at the pair as the two men embraced each other tightly. When they disengaged, Jean-Marc glanced at the lantern which sat on the cavern floor with a far-off look as he shook his head slightly. All present noticed this, but Solange was the first to voice their common concern.

"Is everything all right, Master?" she asked.

"With the intensity of my wound, I fell into a deep trance while I was unconscious. This state was one where certain portals of greater perception opened, where connections were made that are impossible when the conscious mind is relentlessly active. When in this state, I many times experience visions—much as I do in dreams—but here with a more vivid and pressing clarity."

"What did you see, Master?" Solange asked.

"I saw many things, Solange," Jean-Marc continued to stare at the lantern's flame. "I fear for our young and absent traveling companion," he stated with a mysterious distant gaze, seeming to study the aquamarine mist of the pools with distraction.

"And he should fear for my version of God's wrath for the trouble he's put us through," Gaston added caustically.

Ignoring Gaston's comment, Jean-Marc turned to his companions, his focus on his present company regained. "The fear I have for him, Gaston, is linked to those who have pursued us for an eternity—who you have not yet encountered, my friend. And luckily so. We must stay on guard, at the highest level."

The Curé of Boussac studied Jean-Marc with prescient disquiet. "You mean the Parabolani and his master, Father?"

Jean-Marc nodded slowly. "It's always been just a matter of time until our paths cross again, and *again*, until a final reckoning. Hopefully we can finish our work before any of that must take place in the short term, and we can move on to new horizons. But I fear for Roger. His fate is fused to a destiny he can only partly understand and which he does not wholly deserve."

"Fate is too often unkind," the Curé Souillac remarked philosophically.

Jean-Marc nodded, and added: "And one of my jobs is to offer the hope of alternatives."

"And when alternatives run out, it's my job to be ready to offer the ultimate sacrifice," Gaston pledged valiantly.

Jean-Marc placed his hand on Gaston's forearm and smiled. "Hopefully it will not come to that, my dear friend. For these beings are like nothing you've ever encountered before. Where we strive to foster hope of new beginnings, they continually deliver cruelty and the ugliness of untimely and tragic ends. And they do it with a force and conviction you cannot imagine."

The elderly cleric added his observation with a distant gaze, as though reliving a nightmare. "While they were once born of a man and a woman, they have long since divested themselves of any and all bonds with humanity. Be warned: they are creatures of hell."

Southern Dordogne Region, France
9 March, 1815 AD – Mid Day

Riding alone, without his sabre or pistol at ready reach, indeed not even hidden away in his saddle bag, Gaston felt completely naked. Making matters worse, the ill-fitting priest's robes he wore, courtesy of Curé Savigny Souillac, drove him to irate distraction.

The thought that he was clad in the vestments of the church he so often criticized, clothed in the symbolic garments of the clergy representing Rome, frankly made his skin crawl with indignant revulsion—despite the fact he had found a genuinely warm spot in his heart for Father Souillac.

It had been decided by all, however, Gaston included, that this was the best strategy for their next stage of travel south. With the knowledge that unfriendly agents journeyed on the road ahead, with the likelihood their own entourage might by now be characterized in critical detail to those same agents, the decision meant that a different profile of travelers must take the road to help assure safe passage for all.

Priests of large girth were certainly not an unusual sight in these environs. Yet Gaston would pridefully note his own wide beam was a byproduct due to facing life-threatening challenges which produced hard muscle and seasoned grit; whereas those of the cloth, and of a seemingly similar silhouette, were much more of the softer, pampered class, unworthy of his ready respect.

Yet all of those sensibilities rapidly evaporated from his thoughts as he approached two travelers on the road ahead of him. They seemed to be taking a respite at a crossroad in the dirt track, relaxing in the grassy shade beneath a large spreading oak, their horses feeding in the dappled sunlight on the thick tufts of lush grass at the far side of the tree.

Having taken notice of Gaston's approach, both stood now—two young men with long black hair and beards, pistols tucked in their belts—ambling out into the roadway with their palms up, signaling him to stop. Their easy athletic manner communicated a relaxed presumption of superiority.

"Padre, pull up! We need your help! We have a few questions to pose," the first announced with a distinct Spanish accent and without expectation of disagreement.

As he approached, Gaston now spied a third, larger, jet black saddled stallion which grazed on the far side of the oak. He instantly intuited another man must be somewhere close at hand, probably lurking in the shadows of the nearby forest's edge. Gaston quickly weighed his options and measured them against the instructions given him by Jean-Marc: "Nothing must hint we're on this track headed south. Swallow your pride, Gaston. Belay your warrior instincts. Remember the robe you wear and play to its story without fail."

Gaston flashed the brightest and most empathetic smile he could muster as he complied with the young and arrogant Iberian rider's instructions.

"And what is you require, my son? Are you lost? Might you possibly need directions to make your way to where you want to be? I hear an accent which suggests you hail from south of the Pyrenees. Or could it be you've succumbed to some temptation, some indiscretion, for which I must hear your confession?"

The two riders laughed derisively as they glanced at each other in private amusement. "No, Priest, we require your report on what you've observed on the road: the travelers you've seen. We ride at the behest of Bishop Antonio del Julia y Sangresante, a gloried son of Spain and the newly appointed head of the French Inquisition—certainly your supreme superior in the scheme of things—and we seek a dangerous heretic of the most nefarious nature," the first young rider declared with a sense of entitled importance.

On the ground now, petting his horse, Gaston nodded with empathic understanding and exuded body language—an eager to please smile, his back slightly hunched, head a bit tilted—which communicated a subservient readiness to assist in any way possible.

"Bishop Antonio del Julia y Sangresante? I am sorry, sirs,

I do not know this name. But that being said, there are so many names I know not, of which I certainly should. I am just a lowly village priest. But please, young sirs, how may I assist you in your quest to seize heretics? For they're the bane of all righteous men who call themselves 'Good Christians'. "

"Well spoken, Padre. We seek a man who bears Satan's mark on his right eyebrow: bleached white by the infernal fires of Hell. He goes by many names, two include: Count de Saint Germain and the Marquis Jean-Marc Baptiste de Rennes. Have you encountered someone answering to these names or to this description?"

Mustering his best understated sincerity, Gaston slowly shook his head thoughtfully as he affectionately grasped the crucifix hanging from his neck. "I confess, with deepest concern, my sons, I've not seen nor encountered this infernal individual of whom you speak. Can you share any additional details which might help me support your quest, my son?"

"He's likely traveling with a young woman and an old fat man answering your general description," said the second rider, his Spanish accent even thicker than the first. "Everyone's a suspect as far as we're concerned," he spat out provocatively as he stepped over to check Gaston's old canvas bags strapped across the front of the saddle, behind the horse's neck.

Gaston maintained a peaceful look of concern as he addressed the second man, eyeing the search which was underway of his personal effects. "I must admit, I've certainly seen my share of old fat men meeting my general description, so you've got your work cut out for you, my son!" Gaston laughed heartily as he continued, "And there are indeed ample numbers of young woman all across these lands. But I've seen no groups traveling together like your description, that is, since I took the road this morning."

The second Spaniard had a Bible out in his hand, retrieved from Gaston's saddlebag, and leafed through it to assure nothing might be hidden in it. Gaston offered a compassionate smile. "Might you also be searching for some hidden truth in the Lord's good Gospels, my son? Might you need me to share some of their heaven-sent wisdom and glorious words with you? Do you even know how to read, my son?" Gaston inquired with seemingly innocence and a beneficent smile, but probing to find vulnerabilities that might help his cause later on.

The Spanish rider sneered and shoved the Bible back into the canvas bag with a trace of irritation. "*Madre de Dios*, I don't need your self-righteous pontifications, Priest!"

Both the young Spaniards seemed distracted now by another presence—and an influence of absolute authority— as Gaston finally observed the first rider glancing unconsciously into the shadows of the forest directly behind the large oak tree. Making no direct reference to this observation, Gaston nonetheless nodded to the third saddled horse.

"Now, in the eyes of God, I've been completely truthful with you, eager to assist you—especially if you ride at the behest of Bishop Sangresante, of whom I look forward to having the good fortune to meet. Yet I feel compelled to offer one humble observation: it appears a third rider may be in your company. Answering the call of nature, I suppose? Might introductions all around be appropriate? I am Father François Paunat and you fine men are…?"

The two riders became distracted at the shift in dynamics which took place in an instant. Instead of their intimidating this lone priest, he in turn was peacefully challenging them to reveal their full force and intentions without the slightest defense handy, except the will of God. Holding his crucifix in hand, Gaston stared at the two with innocent smiling expectation.

"I expect you saw the bread and wine in my other traveling pouch. I'm more than happy to share everything I have… with *all* your number. Might the third member of your party be shy or afraid? I assure you, I wouldn't hurt a flea!" Gaston laughed mirthfully at himself as his body language expressed the thought of him harming any living creature as the most extreme impossibility.

His smiling eyes, however, continued to scan the entire perimeter of the forest's edge, until one shadow expanded and lengthened, finally moving into the dappled sunlight on the grass. A tall hulk of a man, dressed in dark brown monk's robes, with the hood still up obscuring the face, stepped into view.

The man trod lazily across the grass with the lithe athletic ease of a lion; he pulled back his hood, revealing his fearsome visage. As he approached, the two riders clearly deferred to the man known as Brother Jerome. Upon locking eyes with him, Gaston felt an involuntary shudder like he had never experienced before, even amid the coldest nights of Napoleon's retreat from Russia with wolves and Cossack partisans lurking at every turn to ambush them. This man was different. He had strange and distant, otherworldly cruel eyes. Gaston gestured at his monk's robes with a curious smile.

"Ah, a fellow brother of the cloth! But I'm embarrassed to admit I do not recognize the order. While the closest I might estimate is something of similarity to the Franciscans, the color of brown is much, much darker, almost black, the cloth far more coarse, the belt and the cut of the robe are different in a number of ways. And you wear a Coptic cross around your neck. What order are you a member of, if I may inquire, Brother…?"

"You may not. I ask the questions; you answer them. What's your destination and where did you travel from?" the monk demanded brusquely.

"I began my day, at dawn, from the village of Beynac on the Dordogne River. My goal is to reach Cabrerets at the confluence of the Célé and Sagne rivers."

"And your business?"

"My ultimate destination lies much further south, Brother—almost to the Pyrénées themselves: Pamiers. My dear sister Camille, my sister in blood, and the last member of my humble family, is, I fear facing the stairway to heaven. I hope to be at her bedside to comfort her and deliver the last rites to her when needed. So if my unexceptional story is of no more interest to you, sirs, I'd like to be getting back on my way. I still have many miles to ride. And because of my generous girth, I fear I tire this horse out far more than it deserves." Gaston laughed as he petted the mare's neck and then turned back to the trio. "But it was a timely respite indeed to let my horse rest for a bit, and for me to see the robes of an order which is new to my experience. I'll need to keep my eye out for it in the future and learn more of their story—a venerable one I am sure."

Then Gaston became more upbeat and businesslike. "And if I see the travelers you seek, how would I get word to the noble men riding for the good Bishop Sangresante? I take it you're not the only ones seeking them?" Gaston inquired of the whole group.

The young pair hesitated, deferring to the monk for a reply. Brother Jerome studied Gaston closely, licking his lips slightly as his eyes narrowed; and he finally offered a small enigmatic appraising grin. "Leave word at any chapel or church, Brother. Indicate their direction and the essentials of when, what configuration of travel observed. Were they alone? Were they on horseback, or traveling by cart? I'm sure you understand, Brother. Though, I'd discourage trying to engage them yourself. They're quite dangerous—ruthless, very sly and tricky."

Gaston nodded and turned to climb back on his horse, feigning slightly awkward ineptitude in the process as he did, then faced them as he settled onto his saddle. "It sounds like minions Satan has taken close into his bosom. It would be my poor soul's greatest challenge, and it would likely threaten its complete undoing, should I have the abject misfortune to cross their paths. But I shall do as you directed, Brother. We can't have creatures like this spreading their infernal poison!"

And with that, Gaston gently spurred his horse onto the southern track of the crossroads as the two younger men were called into a quick private conference with the imposing monk. Both Spaniards glanced in Gaston's direction, which Gaston did not observe, since he remained focused on heading out onto the road before him. Both men nodded then jumped on their mounts. Brother Jerome observed for a moment as one man rode east on the crossroad, and the other south, behind Gaston.

Riding at a much faster clip—quickly overtaking and passing the disguised sergeant without a glance—the southern-bound rider soon disappeared around a distant bend in the road, beyond a stand of trees and a gently sloping forest-covered hill.

About a quarter mile further on the byway, before he too would round the same bend which the Spanish rider ahead of him had passed, and when Gaston felt it safe and logical to glance back to the crossroads of his encounter, he saw the junction was now deserted. No sign of the other two riders.

Gaston privately trembled in horror—a rare experience for him. The monk had the aura of a feral beast. He had no doubt this was the man Jean-Marc and the Curé of Boussac spoke of, and it left him gravely unsettled and concerned for his master and daughter who were on the same road some distance behind him. Gaston rode on, keeping his eyes open for any shift of a shadow that might speak of an unwanted intruder, wishing he could be at Jean-Marc and Solange's side.

Something about that fat priest bothered the monk as he rode his stallion west. If he was honest with himself, only an occasional experience, Brother Jerome would be forced to admit something about almost everyone he encountered in life bothered him and sparked the instinct to destroy reflexively.

He remained, however, under explicit orders from Bishop Sangresante to stay strictly within the parameters of the mission and not to act out in any way that might distract from the goal of getting their man. Nonetheless, the monk instructed Pedro—one of the two Spanish horsemen riding with him—to gallop well ahead of the priest, choose a hiding place to observe the road, and then follow the cleric for the rest of the day to assure he indeed told the truth regarding his travel plans.

Pedro was one of twenty mercenaries Sangresante requisitioned to be at his disposal from his base in Seville. They had been waiting only a couple of days ago in a small Spanish Pyrenees border town, ready to ride and prepared to do anything else the bishop required.

As the monk reflected on what it was about the priest that bothered him, he realized something in the man's eyes spoke to having witnessed and participated in lethal mayhem. Despite the soft peaceful words and jovial manner the priest communicated, the eyes revealed a vigilance and a readiness to face the cruel and ruthless storms of fate without hesitation. He showed *no* fear. And the man's size only amplified the sense of unanswered challenge Brother Jerome felt he left behind, along with the gnawing regret that he did not act on his primal instinct and call the man out.

As he felt the blood rush to his head, and his frustrated adrenaline pumped, he spied—ahead of him and to his right—a lone cart coming from the north on a small narrow track which crossed his road. It had just emerged from the shadows of a stand of trees, and with his greatly-enhanced eyesight, the monk observed an old bearded man—holding the reins of the two-horse team—accompanied by a young woman, on a cart which appeared to be hauling barrels, wine he guessed. Brother Jerome was not feeling especially magnanimous as he spurred his steed on to a cavalry trot and rode across the small field separating them, advancing directly on the slow-moving cart.

Dressed in drab peasant clothing of brown and gray earth tones, and a battered straw hat, Savigny Souillac held the reins of the two horses pulling the open cart hauling oaken wine caskets, with six barrels sitting upright, side-by-side in the front, and with two resting horizontally in the back.

The curé glanced over at Solange as he spoke quietly behind him. "It appears we have company. And I'm afraid he looks quite familiar. I remember him from a very long time ago—over a hundred and seventy years ago—while still in my youth."

Jean-Marc's voice emanated from somewhere among the barrels in the back of the cart, out of sight. "Stay with the plan, Savi."

Unaccustomed to his garments, the curé shifted uncomfortably as he smiled at the young woman. "Are you ready, my child?"

Solange nodded with stony resolve and then produced a smile with a charming glimmer in the eye. "We'll do what must be done, Father... I just hope he follows the behavior Jean-Marc predicts he will."

"Character is fate, and hence, some things are written, Solange," Jean-Marc declared from his hidden location on the cart. "I sincerely believe this to be one of them."

Brother Jerome approached the cart and halted his horse directly in front of it, forcing Savigny to pull up his team abruptly. Satisfied he had taken authoritarian command of the moment on this lonely spot along the byways of France, the monk dropped off his stallion with lithe ease and grabbed the bridle at the bit of the closest horse on the cart team.

"What's your business?" he demanded with a bored insistence as he leered at the woman with a brazen and unwholesome curiosity.

Savigny dutifully showed deference, fealty and subservience in his reflexive reply. "Kind sir, we're on our way to deliver the harvest to the market. The finest red wines our region can offer and at prices no sane man can argue," the covert priest replied with the tone of possibly interesting the monk in a sale of his goods.

Brother Jerome studied the pair as he released the bridle bit of the workhorse and approached the cart bench where Savigny and Solange sat in nervous expectation. The monk studied the large kegs loaded in the back of the open cart.

"Wine, you say." The monk licked his lips.

On cue, recognizing Brother Jerome's thirst, Savigny climbed off the cart, came alongside the monk and directed his attention to the back of the cart where two barrels laid positioned on their sides, secured from rolling by large wooden wedges, with their ends toward the open back end of the cart. One had a wooden tap housed in the casket, ready to pour. Two wooden cups sat in the hay nearby on the floor of the cart. Savigny picked one up and showed it to Brother Jerome, then brought it to the wine tap as he

261

spoke.

"The day is long, the road dusty, and a man's palate gets far too parched without proper refreshment. Please be my guest." Savigny finished pouring the cup to the brim and offered it to the monk. Brother Jerome grabbed it and chugged the contents thirstily. As he did, Solange dropped off the cart, and brought with her a small glass jug which she handed to Savigny.

" 'Tis indeed a fine time for a refreshment! Here, Grandfather, quench your noble thirst."

Brother Jerome eyed the bottle with covetous regard as it went into the old man's hands. "What's that?"

Seemingly oblivious of the monk's intrusive spirit, Solange spoke with pride. "In all harvests there's the wine we take pride in making for our customers—of the finest quality, of course—and there's also the private reserve, of which only a few bottles are possible. My grandfather always likes to have a taste of it during this ride every year. There's only just a little, and it's a family tradition that—"

Brother Jerome postured righteous indignation as he tossed the wooden cup onto the road. "You offer me the common swill and save the best for yourself? You pretend to be hospitable, when in reality you insult me!"

Showing a flash of profound fear, Savigny quickly handed the bottle to the hulking man. "No please, please! Be my guest! I would never want to offend a man of the cloth! I need God's graces in every way I can," he laughed uncomfortably. "Please have some! It is my pleasure to share and to please you."

"Have *some*? You would limit my sampling of this, while you give me a dirty wooden cup to begin with to drink your vile dregs?" Brother Jerome barked with amplified indignation as he stamped his foot down on the cup, splitting it to pieces. Solange and Savigny quaked in panic at this overtly threatening behavior.

"No, please, have *all* you want! The bottle's yours, Brother! It's an offering to you and to God! And if after that you want to drink from any of our other barrels, please be my guest!"

Satisfied he had sufficiently terrorized the couple, Brother Jerome brought the bottle to his lips and took a taste. He smiled and arched his eyebrow mimicking gourmet refinement as he wiped his lips with his index finger.

"Mmmmm. Now that's good. That's *very* good." Brother Jerome bared his teeth as though a wolf might when establishing dominance in a pack, then let his face graduate to a tolerant smile and put the mouth of the bottle back to his lips as he took a deep greedy quaff, and then continued to drink without pause, until he guzzled the entire contents of the vessel. And afterwards, he casually tossed the small empty jug onto the road. Turning to the pair with a glassy smile, he burped loudly without embarrassment.

"I want more of that," the monk stated simply.

Savigny cast Solange a nervous glance and offered a fearful accommodating smile to the demanding monk. "I am so sorry, noble sir, but that was the last of the private reserve which I set aside for this journey. I certainly have more back at home, but that's almost a full day's ride away. You're more than welcome to sample our other wines, kind sir. I could even recommend one barrel in particular which—"

"I have no patience for inferior products, swine! I have a

good mind to crush your skull for your impertinence! Trying to keep the best stock for yourself! ...And now, as I consider your actions, I realize that punishment *is* the right action! It *is* what you deserve, you offal-eating rodent!"

Brother Jerome stepped over to his mount, retrieved a large wooden cudgel from a sheath fashioned into the saddle and slapped the large knob end of the staff into the palm of his meaty right hand. "You deserve this, old man."

"No, please!" Solange pleaded with alarm.

Brother Jerome glanced at her with mild amusement as he raised the cudgel over his head, with both hands, gripping firmly now as he did. "It shall take more than a stupid wench's—"

And with that, the monk's eyes widened, as though momentarily distracted. He then frowned slightly, and without warning, collapsed onto the road into a jumbled heap. Solange stepped over to him, grabbed the cudgel quickly and nudged him with it. No breathing. No sign of life. Solange winced with distaste and concern as she tossed the cudgel aside on the grass.

"Have we killed him, Father?"

Jean-Marc came alongside her as Solange glanced back at the large wine barrel positioned directly behind the rider's bench of the cart where the top had now been removed. "He drank the entire jug, didn't he."

Savigny Souillac nodded soberly as he made the sign of the cross over the inert monk. "Indeed he did, Father."

"So he *is* dead?" Solange pressed, her brow furrowing more deeply with guilt. She only realized at this moment how odd it felt to look upon Jean-Marc's visage, now that he had colored his white eyebrow with black henna, camouflaging this distinctive feature from quick recognition.

"No, Solange. That wouldn't be possible for one such as him, at least not by this means. There is a creature of the African desert—a badger—who when bitten by the cobra merely falls into a deep sleep for a number of hours, then recovers as normal. Such would be the case with this man had a truly lethal poison been applied. But it was not. Although I do expect with this solution he shall sleep like the dead for some time and possibly have a considerable headache when he finally revives. One good drink would've done the job suitably. But we needed to make the taste irresistible to assure he'd take it in the first place. His gluttonous reaction is no surprise."

Less distracted with the karmic concern for taking another's life now, Solange continued to study the unconscious man—whose body odor was pungent and repugnant—with growing disgust. "He's more a beast than a man."

Jean-Marc nodded thoughtfully, then quickly directed his companions to help him drag the monk into the bushes. He then mounted Brother Jerome's stallion and led Savigny and Solange on the cart to a nearby ravine where they uncoupled the horses, took two saddles from a second wine casket, before pushing the cart out of sight, over into the small canyon choked with underbrush. The three then rode on to the south at a fast clip, putting as much distance between them and the site of the encounter with the monk as possible.

As 'Father' Gaston rode south, his seasoned instinct for searching for and finding the best place to lie in wait for an action against him stood at its highest state of alert. Finally, about an hour south along the road, he saw it: a rise through forested high country, between two open farming areas—where the trail grew twisted, underbrush thick, and rock outcroppings became common—there a small trail led up between the rocks and out of sight.

A drying puddle of water, leaving a fine silt of mud, had been marred by fresh hoofprints just up the side trail. So here the Spaniard had gone and hidden himself. What his stalker's next action would be remained unclear, but Gaston anticipated it would not be lethal. If he was being followed, it was because they suspected he might know something valuable to the searchers. He correctly deduced the plan was to find an opportunity to drop in behind and shadow him, to monitor his movements. If anything confirming suspicions was observed, the rider would be in a position to report back without crossing paths.

Satisfied he had identified the man's location, Gaston decided to alter the dynamics of the situation. Up to this point he had ridden at a pleasant ambling gait, not wanting to get too far ahead of the cart behind him on the trail carrying Jean-Marc. Now he decided was the time for him to stage his own cat and mouse game, with far more expertise than the Spanish recruit.

At the end of the hilly section, just as the downhill trail gave a glimpse through the forest to open fields and the straight track leading through them, Gaston discovered a cleft in a rock escarpment that faced the fields, which could not be seen until one rode much further along the road and looked backwards. Gaston used this location to tie off and conceal his mare. He gave it ample handfuls of grass to satisfy it and keep it quiet, while he scrambled up to the rocky high ground directly above the downhill path.

Soon enough, Pedro, the Spanish rider, came along at a cavalry trot, seeming by his actions in need of catching up with his prey, of whom he had now lost sight. Gaston even heard Pedro swearing at his misfortune, as he was compelled to slow his horse to walk on the steep downhill, rocky part of this trail, which led out through the trees to the fields. The old veteran listened to more angry grumbling, as Pedro, now having a clear line of sight on the straight track across the fields, could observe no sign of his quarry. Gaston knew this would be his opportunity: as the rider was forced to walk his Andalusian slowly and cautiously down the narrow rocky trail.

With a handful of stones in hand, the old Army veteran charged down the steep embankment, shouting and throwing the rocks, some hitting the proud mount, spooking it, one even hitting the rider on the shoulder. Startled, Pedro struggled to grab for his pistol as he grappled with his skittish, unruly mount.

At this point Gaston finally closed ranks, running full speed at both horse and rider. Like a juggernaut, he slammed his shoulder hard into the steed's ribs and rammed the horse with shocking impact. Gaston had chosen a highly-sensitive target on the horse and the spirited Andalusian stallion recoiled violently, whinnied in pain and alarm, reared, and stumbled on the declining part of the trail.

The rider, unable to control the powerful charger, fell hard, shoulder first on the stony trail. Spotting Gaston's' advance on him with an athletic and wary gait, not what he originally expected from this fat priest, Pedro feebly tried to grab his pistol which fell a short distance away from him, just off the trail. Gaston, however, reached it first, picked it up, handling it with ease, but forgoing the need to aim it at the fallen rider.

Maintaining the now flimsy yet entertaining pretext of his priestly calling, Gaston adopted a somewhat reverential tone. "Oh, *my* goodness, my son! Aren't you one of the fellows who questioned me at the crossroads? I'm so deeply sorry! I thought you were some highwayman coming to rob me! I mean, here you came at me from behind, when I thought you were somewhere far ahead of me on the road. Are you all right?"

Wincing in pain, Pedro attempted to regain a sense of dominance in the dialog. "You bastard! I think I've broken my shoulder! Give me my gun back," he insisted.

"Oh, no, my son! This is a tool of violence! And instead of identifying yourself to me as I approached, you tried to kill me! I'm sincerely afraid I don't trust you now. I think it's best if I keep this tool of Satan to help you resist the temptation of committing one of the gravest sins against God."

"But you attacked me first! Throwing stones! What was I supposed to do?"

Dropping any priestly pretense now, Gaston adopted his customary voice, edged with menace. "You shouldn't have been skulking in the first place like some mongrel dog, you toad. I'm afraid you haven't been keeping the right kind of company... I expect you'll thank me some day for this..."

And without warning, Gaston struck the man soundly on the head with the end of the pistol handle, knocking the Spaniard unconscious.

In a small village high in the hills, some distance south and west of their encounter on the road with Brother Jerome, Father Savigny concluded a transaction with the local stable keeper.

His snowy white beard and long hair now trimmed much shorter, and again dressed in his customary vestments of the church, he just finished the negotiations of trading Brother Jerome and Pedro's horses, for a single strong steed: a chestnut brown mare, with a tinge of gray—young and strong and a comparatively nondescript roan.

The curé knew he had been taken advantage of by the shrewd stable owner, since the two horses offered in trade were clearly superior in quality, but he feigned ignorance in the transaction. Recognizing both horses had distinctive markings—the monk's pure jet black stallion, and the Spaniard's Andalusian with its striking black coat and prominent white pattern on the face—Savigny's goal was to rid themselves of the two easily identifiable horses, despite their quality, and replace them with a single strong steed of extremely common looks. The negotiation was therefore a success for both parties.

Mounted now, Father Savigny paused in the center of the village by the fountain while a royalist horse garrison passed through, headed north at a cavalry trot, for some engagement, the specifics of which were far outside his realm of knowledge or curiosity. He and his companions purposely kept clear of any populated areas as much as possible, and in doing so, remained outside the current events of state.

Arriving at a small meadow beyond the south side of the village, the priest pulled his roan to a stop. Jean-Marc, Solange and Gaston sat in the grass by a babbling brook, eating bread, a bit of local cheese, and drinking the area's red wine as well. Gaston appraised the new mount with shrewd respect.

"You did not do half bad. It appears you know your horses, Father," Gaston conceded.

The curé dropped off the horse and let it graze on the lush grass surrounding them, crossed to the trio, and joined them sitting on the ground. Jean-Marc handed him a bottle of wine and a chunk of bread. Savigny accepted them, took a bite of the bread then washed it down with the wine.

Solange and Jean-Marc observed his pensive manner, while Gaston got up to inspect the horse more closely with his seasoned and discerning eye. Savigny nodded his appreciation of the repast, yet Solange would later privately note the poignant subtext between the two men in front of her. Savigny gestured at the offerings.

"A last supper of sorts, eh?" the cleric remarked philosophically.

"Would that it could be another way, my son. But we must keep our eye on the objective we all share," Jean-Marc observed cryptically.

Restoring himself with a sense of new resolve, Savigny stood, exuding a quality of refreshment and determination. "True, so very true. I shall take the road now. And by this time tomorrow, I'll have the appearance of another man altogether: clean-shaven and hair of another hue. My destination is, of course, Meganissi, where I shall prepare another laboratory for your needs, should that be required for the future. It is a good family there. I look forward to the warm climate, sea breezes and a safe haven."

Jean-Marc stood, and they held each other fiercely. Then their embrace loosened so their foreheads touched for an extended time in mutual and reflective meditation of each other. Gaston glanced over at the pair, then back at the horse, petting its flanks, in the spirit of respecting their privacy.

"I will join you when I can, Savi. I'm heartened by the progress we've achieved. Though hard won, I believe the effort will be well worth it, beyond measure."

Jean-Marc then reached for his canvas bag, which laid on the grass nearby, opened it and retrieved the Book stowed inside. He handed it to Savigny. The curé took it in his hands with reverential awe and immediately sat down on the thick grass. Savigny opened the ancient esoteric tome, and carefully turned the pages with hushed and avid curiosity.

To his observation, the Book was written in at least seven languages, as well as having a number of arcane symbolic systems, for which no references existed. This detail only intrigued him more.

"It appears some passages were written in the tongue of the Old Ones, before ancient Egypt."

Jean-Marc nodded with approval. "This is true, my son. This is now our only connection with the lost knowledge of the antediluvian wisdom tradition. I shall share with you my understandings and insights when we are reunited."

Savigny nodded with thoughtful respect, and then, against his keen desire to spend countless hours with the tome, he slowly closed the Book, stood and handed it back to Jean-Marc.

"I have so many questions. When you return to Meganissi, we shall have more of an opportunity to explore its mysteries together. And you could teach me more, as you have done over so many, many years, Father."

Jean-Marc placed the Book back in his shoulder bag and set it back down on the grass as he turned and nodded with a smile in reply to Savigny. "It's my duty and my honor … it will also be my joy to do so, my son." Jean-Marc placed both hands comfortably on Savigny's shoulders and gazed deeply into the curé's eyes. "Our solution is close at hand. But we must stay ahead of the hounds of chaos for just a few days more."

"It shall be so," Savigny replied soberly, as he raised his hands to place them on Jean-Marc's shoulders as well. After a moment of gazing into each other's eyes, they smiled at each other, nodded slightly, and then each went to their horses and mounted.

Solange and Gaston followed suit. Savigny prodded his roan on—as he set out due east across the meadow. Solange observed how fluidly the man rode. For someone who seemed so much older in years, he carried his body with a sense of youth and vigor which had been hidden from her observation up to this point. As the trio headed across the meadow, going due south, Solange turned to Jean-Marc, who had taken the lead.

"Master, the curé kept referring to you as 'Father' and you to him as 'Son.' Since the reverse is traditionally the manner of address to someone of the cloth I found that very curious."

Jean-Marc smiled slightly as he rode on. "Indeed. I suppose for some that would seem quite curious, Solange."

Region North of Toulouse
Languedoc, France
11 March, 1815 AD – Mid-Day

Riding alone down a narrow dirt track through a silent forest, with a sack of fresh provisions from a small village nearby for the long day's passage ahead of them—and dressed with a hat and clothing giving her the appearance of a young man—Solange had ample time to reflect on the events which occurred on their journey since the attack at the dolmen.

The violence was upsetting, yet she knew well the nature of her father's path in life. And while not a familiar experience, some part of her had prepared herself through the years for a rough road that might include this kind of encounter.

And just before this sojourn, her father warned her to be ready for unexpected dangers. She in turn had braced herself long ago for extreme physical trials which might require facing challenges with life and death stakes. However, what she learned about Curé Savigny's role as her mother's teacher, and Jean-Marc being Savigny's mentor—and possibly even the curé's father—were profound revelations.

Witnessing Jean-Marc's resurrection in the mineral pool of the caverns beneath St. Jean's chapel in Toulx-Saint-Croix endured as something completely outside her ken of experience and thinking, earthshaking to state it simply.

As she rode on to her companions' hiding place in a glen a short distance away, Solange continued to process all this, and she did not know if her mind was expansive enough to take it all in with the suitable level of comprehension.

Solange contemplated as well on the state of her life before the dolmen. Anything was better than what she had suffered through at the village she lived in, near Picardy in the north of France, after her mother disappeared.

Nothing remained there for Solange, except gossip, hatred and a local duke determined to have her as his plaything. And being rebuffed, the nobleman resolved to ruin her reputation with slander, despite the fact she had done nothing wrong, all the while helping care for sick people in her village. Her integrity had been gravely impugned.

The rage of feelings she felt when her father finally came to take her away—word having reached Gaston on his travels of her ugly situation—only grew with intensity over time. Picturing the duke, she could have easily killed any of her attackers that night at the dolmen and François as well. Her father had indeed trained her to take care of herself. And while she preferred to see herself in a feminine light, she knew if pushed the wrong way, that any one, man or woman, had better watch their back.

What occupied Solange's thoughts on the deepest level, however, were the sensations she had been experiencing in her body and the visions in her dreams. In moments as she rode these last few days, when her mind grew quiet, she gazed in the distance and strived to understand exactly what was happening to her. All very confusing and exciting somehow, it was as though she now received vivid glimpses of something beyond the veil of normal perception, something larger than life, something somehow sacred.

And on those days riding together since Jean-Marc's rebirth in the grotto, she observed the man's remarkable willpower and discipline balanced with such a pleasant and warm disposition.

She also ruminated over how Father Savigny took particular note of the details she shared with him, prior to the miraculous treatment, especially where she explained how Jean-Marc required some of her own life blood to recover enough to ride.

Only now did she realize that in that transference of primal essence, some of his life's spirit must have crossed over to her in the process. She could only now attune herself to the understanding that she stood at the threshold of an entirely new life from which no return was possible. That idea exhilarated her beyond measure.

Solange's excitement swelled further by the very thought of their destination at the end of today's riding. It was the city her mother had visited for an important part of her training, the city her mother had so often referred to as 'The Threshold': the rose city of Toulouse.

With the sun late in the western sky, and upon arriving at the northern entrance of the great medieval city of Toulouse—in the heart of Languedoc, the southwest region of France bordering the Pyrénées—Jean-Marc's spirits rose noticeably. He allowed himself to feel more at ease with the distance they had placed between themselves, Paris, the dolmen, and their encounter with the monk, as well as a calming sensation of being deeper in the heart of the adopted land he called home for what seemed countless decades.

Known as the 'Pink City' because of the extensive use of rose-colored stone, Toulouse hosted an ancient architectural tradition dating back to Roman times, during which it was known as the capitol of the province of Narbonensis. And later in history, following the fall of the Roman Empire, the city served as the capitol of the Visigoth nation.

As he, Gaston and Solange rode toward one of the oldest parts of the city, Jean-Marc and his companions passed ornate city palaces of governance, centuries-old-Romanesque churches, as well as the more recent buildings, which combined, made Toulouse a unique and beautiful city, situated on the bend of the placid and wide Garonne River, where a number of stone bridges connected both sides.

Finally on foot, and striding easily across a cobblestone

lane of the Old Town, Jean-Marc led his companions to a side street not far from a main square and marketplace of the city. They had brought their horses to a livery, assured their care, and then walked a short distance down the narrow back street, alive with talkative merchants heading home, many pushing cumbersome wooden carts, after a busy day in the marketplace.

The gossip, rumors and talk of the people, of course, focused on the latest news of Napoleon's advance through the Alps and his impending march on Paris. Talk also explored how a number of local office holders loyal to the Bourbon line who were thought to be facing uncertain fates regarding their positions, fortunes and welfare. Some of the royalists had made enemies with their privileged and vindictive policies against the members of the previous Napoleonic administration. They confiscated land from many and gave it to their favorites. Some grumbled that accounts would be balanced and settled when Napoleon rightfully retook his throne.

One swarthy and bearded merchant, rolling his cart of leather wares back to his shop, and having noticed the new arriving trio with their canvas and leather bags slung over their shoulders, road dust covering them, barked out to Jean-Marc.

"You there: you look like you're recently in from the road. Have you come from the north? Do you have news of Napoleon's progress, friend?" he asked with a presumptuous familiarity.

Jean-Marc smiled back with level friendliness. "I was going to ask you a similar question. I'm afraid we know nothing of Napoleon's movements. We've been in the back country and out of touch with the latest news," he said, revealing nothing further of his own or his companions' personal movements. "What can you tell us, friend?"

The leather merchant frowned slightly, "I only know what I hear in the market—that Napoleon crossed the Alps, met the 15th infantry regiment outside Grenoble and they joined his forces. That was about ten days ago. The news this afternoon is more royalist troops are moving north, but nothing concrete. No one knows if there will be a battle for Paris or not."

"Thank you, friend. I didn't know that," Jean-Marc replied as he led his companions on toward an inn which stood a short distance away, with a wrought iron sign reading: *Auberge des Pommes Bleues.*

As they moved on, and the leather merchant found another vendor to chat with, Solange gestured towards Jean-Marc's eyebrow, where his white hair was again a prominent feature of his face. "I'm afraid the sweat and toil of our journey has taken the henna from your brow. We'll need to reapply it soon."

The marquis smiled and nodded absently, seeming more focused on their approach to the inn ahead of them.

Inside the inn, Jean-Marc asked his companions to wait at a table with their traveling gear, as he presented himself to the innkeeper situated at a large dark wood counter in an alcove overlooking the main dining area. While one patron sang a bit too loudly and off key as he signaled for more wine, the innkeeper attending to his accounts ledger finally glanced up to frown in irritation at the singer and then turn to see who stood before him. His eyes widened momentarily in recognition as Jean-Marc's manner, in turn, communicated caution.

"Good sir, might you have lodgings for me and my companions? We are three. One room would be more than ample for all of us," Jean-Marc explained, yet as he did, his right hand rested on a slight carved design on the innkeeper's table.

Worn with age, it would be invisible to the casual onlooker; however the innkeeper keenly observed the message being communicated in code on the Sator/Rotas square by Jean-Marc's rapid index finger tapping different letters as he spoke. The innkeeper replied.

"I'm sorry, sir. But we're completely full. The local mushroom festival has many coming to Toulouse this season. I'm sure you should find something a little further away from the market. It may not be as nice, but I expect it will be adequate for your needs," the innkeeper replied, with his spoken words.

Another conversation, however, took place between the two, as once a coded message was conveyed, the other responded. During their verbal conversation, the hidden communication consisted of a separate and parallel silent exchange of 'dialog'.

"Well, I suppose we'll do our best to find something suitable. Can you recommend an inn, sir?" Jean-Marc asked politely.

"You might try the *Joyeux Mouton*; it's ten minutes on foot down the main lane. You'd go left when you hit the fountain square. Then ask. You'll almost be there at that point," the innkeeper advised conveying a manner of polite indifference and preoccupation with his ledger.

"Thank you, sir," Jean-Marc replied. With that, he got up, gestured to his companions. They left the inn and walked back out into the street.

"I'll be glad to finally be sitting still," Solange declared as they walked with their belongings. "But shouldn't we go back to the livery and remount? I expect there's a stable closer to this other establishment we could use."

"That won't be necessary, Solange," Jean-Marc said as they approached the corner of the building which gave way to a small dark alleyway.

At that moment the innkeeper came to the door with a slightly inebriated patron—the singer—and ushered him out into the street.

"I've told you I'll not tolerate your inability to hold your wine, Pierre! Come back tomorrow when you're sober and can behave yourself!"

As the eyes of the market men pushing their carts tracked on the minor street drama with Pierre and the innkeeper, Jean-Marc spoke with his eyes to Gaston, gesturing for him to go down the narrow alley. Gaston needed no more signal and took Solange by the elbow. Jean-Marc slipped into the shadows behind them as they made their way toward the back of the inn.

Not far away, the dark-bearded leather merchant who engaged Jean-Marc in conversation was busy picking up some of his rawhide samples which had fallen off his cluttered cart as the drunken patron lurched out of the inn. In doing so, he noticed Jean-Marc and his companions' actions as they slipped out of sight down the tight confines of the crooked and shadowy alley. He frowned, and then continued to pick up his wares, but not without peering down the alleyway once more to watch the travelers' progress as they disappeared around a bend in the confined cobblestone passageway, whose construction, along with most of the Old Town district in Toulouse, was medieval in age.

The alley reached a dead end. A minimum of light penetrated this area due to the lateness of the hour and the tight confines. Old red stone buildings two and three stories high surrounded them. Just to their right, at street level, a small thick wooden door housed in the wall and fortified by bolts and wrought iron reinforcements secured the back entrance to the *Auberge des Pommes Bleues*.

Before long, the door opened and the innkeeper appeared. His manner much different from the publicly cool indifference he conveyed to Jean-Marc in front of the other patrons of the inn, his warmth now exuded a welcoming spirit.

"Master! It is a blessing to see you in good health!" Turning to Gaston, he frowned slightly, striving to assure his memory was right, and extending his hand to shake in a subtle, coded ceremonial fashion familiar to their common brotherhood. "Gaston, is it not?"

"Indeed, and it has been years. It's good to see you again, Brother Loïc." Gaston gestured to the third member of their party. "My daughter, Solange."

Loïc bowed cordially and respectfully. "Mademoiselle, I am honored to meet you." He then turned back to Jean-Marc. "And, Master, I'll be honored to offer you and your party the best sustenance this humble inn has available.

Your wish is my command."

Loïc then reached for keys which hung on a leather cord around his neck and gestured for them to cross the alley to the small doorway of a building constructed in the same medieval era. Three stone steps below the cobblestone street level brought them down to a small low portal, seemingly the entrance to a cellar or storage area.

After unlocking the sturdy door, and once inside, Loïc found a lantern on a shelf in the entryway, then lit it before closing the door to the alley.

"This is the only traditional entrance into this dwelling," Loïc explained to Solange as he handed a set of keys to Jean-Marc.

"There's no front door?" she asked.

"It was never part of the original design, and purposely so," Loïc explained.

As they entered the dark dwelling, now illuminated by the innkeeper's lantern, Solange saw the interior space was a very narrow multi-story household, no more than twelve feet across where a short, slender stairway led up to a landing above.

The ground floor level was barely lit from the outside by pale light pouring into the front side of the residence through two tall, slender leaded glass windows, curtained and partially drawn.

Reaching the top of the landing to this first floor, the party now saw down the confined hallway a small furnished drawing room of sorts. Continuing on, Loïc led them up the narrow stairway to the next floor which gave way to a more open space dedicated to comfortable sleeping accommodations, with a simple kitchen arrangement, a large wooden table, and a privy.

In the far corner, toward the opposite side of the room and two slender windows overlooking the front street, a laddered stairway led up to a third floor. Jean-Marc nodded with satisfaction. "It's good to be back."

"You are certainly quite familiar with everything here, Master. I'll leave you to settle in. I shall serve you refreshments as soon as I'm able to organize them. Mine will be the only eyes that shall witness your presence here."

"Your family has been a reliable constant to me and my master, Loïc. You know I'll repay in kind."

"Master, you know there's never a charge for you or your party. It has always been an eternal honor and a privilege for my family to serve you... I'll leave you to your affairs, unless there might be anything particular you need that I can get for you? Any special request for your victuals?"

"Just a warm meal and a cool beverage, Loïc. Your hospitality and support are a much needed comfort after a long hard road."

And with that, Loïc departed down the stairway promising to return soon with hearty sustenance.

Gaston dropped his traveling gear on a bed as Solange followed suit. Jean-Marc crossed to one of the second story leaded glass windows overlooking the street, opened it slightly allowing him a clear view.

He observed the people of Toulouse as they went about their evening activities. A tavern not far down the block hosted patrons beginning to gather and celebrate the end of the day. Beyond, down the street, he caught a glimpse of the Garonne River which passed through the city in this district located in the very heart of the Old Town. Jean-Marc's eyes narrowed slightly as memories of the city welled inside him. A slight thoughtful frown touched his brow.

Loïc delivered a local delicacy, a delicious *cassoulet*—a soupy casserole with white beans, duck and sausage—along with local red wine, good fresh bread, cheese and goose pâté. They supped till they were filled, then Gaston announced he would go out in search of needed supplies. After taking the key Loïc provided, and after he departed, Solange finished her glass of wine and glanced at the laddered stairway to the top floor.

"Where does that lead, Master Jean-Marc?"

Jean-Marc smiled slightly, and picking up a lantern, his gesture invited her to explore with him. Leading the way, and reaching the top of the stair ladder, he pushed open a trap door and climbed through. Now on the top floor of the building, Jean-Marc crossed to a table in the chamber above, and then lit another lamp to fill the space more effectively with warm illumination. As Solange climbed through the opening onto the third floor, she gazed around in muted wonder.

Here an elegant study occupied the entire floor, three times as wide as the two floors below, with a windowed door leading out to a promontory overlooking the front street. The atelier boasted several large comfortable wood and leather chairs, a dark wood rolltop desk, and five massive bookcases with hundreds of volumes, many appearing quite old. A large table hosted a great atlas of the world, the book open for easy reference. Small masterpieces of bronze statuary from various eras, including the classic ages, festooned the desk and bookcases. A large bronze figure of Venus stood in a corner and a long couch along one of the walls could double as a bed. A number of French masters' paintings hung on the walls. At the opposite end of this chamber, a closed doorway led to a room which overlooked the alley and Loïc's inn.

Over the doorway Solange noticed a round, eight-leaf rose window, crafted in stained glass. It seemed to be a miniature of those found in Gothic churches she had seen, especially reminding her of Chartres. Solange found herself enchanted by the exotic details of everything she saw.

"This is *your* place, isn't it, Master?" Solange observed intuitively.

"In a manner of speaking, Solange. The property title is in Loïc's name. But I have paid for its upkeep and have funded improvements to his inn at various times through the years. And he's generously pledged, as his forefathers did, to keep the place with the appearance of being inhabited on a regular basis, lighting it at night a few days a week. The idea is that when I do come to use it, I don't want people to notice the new activity as an indication of my presence. This procedure is also conducted with the activities of the families and occupants on either side of this property taken into account. For all intents and purposes, the apartments we're occupying are invisible, since no front entrance exists, and these windows are matched exactly to those of the families on either side. I come here about twice a year, when I can. It's been a welcome refuge out of the storm from time to time," Jean-Marc observed, as Solange picked up and studied a bronze bust of Napoleon as First

Counsel, unadorned with hat or crown, crafted to make the emperor appear more from classic Roman or Greek times.

After returning the small bust to Jean-marc's desk, Solange crossed to the windowed door, unlatched it and stepped out onto the small balcony which offered an evocative sunset view across the city—the rose-colored stones of Toulouse now ruby-red with the waning sunlight. She leaned on the railing as Jean-Marc came to her side. The sun's amber rays highlighted a steeple slightly to the west of them; beyond, the Garonne River laid clearly in view and the venerable Pont Neuf, the medieval stone bridge which spanned it.

"It's beautiful. The light, the river, the rose-colored city, framed by that impressive church steeple. What's its name?" she asked with curious enthusiasm.

"Eglise des Jacobins," Jean-Marc replied neutrally.

"It appears to be centuries old," Solange remarked.

"Indeed, it is. First construction began in 1230 to be precise. This is your first time to Toulouse, is it, Solange?"

"Yes, it is, Master. Father told me about it, but not in great detail. Mother spoke of it as well, but with a quality of undetailed mystery. Possibly we might visit the church while we're here? It seems quite beautiful." Solange remarked, pleased to finally be relaxing from the stress of the road and looking forward to the possibility of a change of fortune for her happiness.

"Anything's possible. But I'd caution that, as you know, looks can be deceiving. And all places this old have a history. Some carry more weight of the human story than others... Sometimes that weight is measured with sorrows. This place, I'm afraid, is one of them."

"How is that so, Master?" Solange asked him with sincere curiosity.

"What do you know of the Cathars, Solange?"

"I know the Church of Rome branded them heretics and accused them of the most deplorable acts, Master."

"I note your careful choice of words, Solange. Most outside of this region would say they were heretics and that they were guilty of those deplorable acts and as many as their accusers' imaginations might furnish."

"If you know my family, Master, you know my mother's parents came from this region. Even though I was brought up in the north, my attitudes regarding the Cathars are possibly more informed by those who lived in these lands where some aspects of their beliefs survived… I know, too, that because their beliefs differed markedly with the Church of Rome, Pope Innocent II identified the Cathars as their mortal enemy and declared a crusade against them."

"Yes, the Albigensian Crusade, Latin Christians killing Latin Christians: a new precedent. Terrible and tragic times. The first and last crusade of its kind. It spread like a pestilence across Languedoc. This land was once the flower of European culture, tolerant of all beliefs, Muslim, Jewish and embracing a wider, deeper and humbler belief of Yesu the Nazarene than had ever been witnessed in this part of the world. People learned they could experience a direct relationship with God and that the hierarchy of the Church was unnecessary and misguided. And as the popularity of the Cathar version of Christian worship spread, the Pope perceived a deepening primal existential threat. As a result, his cardinals, his bishops, and he pressed his case with the king in Paris. The northern nobles of the Kingdom of

France with allegiance to King Philip II subsequently assembled for war, along with their vast train of loyal vassals and attendant combatant subjects. And on the Feast of Saint John the Baptist, they began their sprawling march south, a veritable medieval city of people in motion. The vanguard saw the warriors: the knights and men at arms. But behind, in the supply train, were the broad range of craftsmen needed to support such an extensive enterprise. The movable city also included the women, wives and whores, and whole families, who accompanied this long-term campaign of conquest and inhabitation."

Solange shook her head soberly as she gazed at the cathedral and the surrounding city as she listened to Jean-Marc's account continue.

"The first city these Crusaders besieged was Béziers, on the Feast of Mary Magdalene—a deeply symbolic day for the invaders who reviled the Magdalene tradition. Many took refuge in the Eglise de la Madeleine. They killed everyone: men, women and children, Cathar and Catholic alike. Twenty thousand died on that day. They attacked under the commanding abbot's merciless order: '*Caddite eos! Deus suos agnoscent.*' "

" 'Kill them all. God will know his own.' My mother told me the story, Master," Solange added.

Jean-Marc nodded thoughtfully, gazing as the bell of Eglise des Jacobins began to toll. "It took years to gain control, but the precious prize was the rich land itself, as King Philip doubled his dominion in the bargain, seizing the possessions of the Occitan nobles of the south. The native Occitans became a captive people with beliefs and sympathies that did not agree with the new rulers. And that sentiment has endured for centuries," Jean-Marc recounted.

Solange gestured to the church spire of Eglise des Jacobins, sonorously ringing out the seventh hour across the riverfront and the adjacent sector of the city. "And this church is part of that story, Master?"

"Oh, yes, Solange. But it was more part of the sad story which followed this tragic crusade. The Pope demanded that any vestige of resistant thought or contrary belief had to be completely destroyed and erased… And so a very robust and dedicated priest, many would say fanatical, who failing to convert Cathars with debate and persuasion, won the Pope's support for a different approach…"

"The Inquisition," Solange observed.

Jean-Marc nodded. "Indeed. And Padre Dominic Guzman, who founded the Dominican Order, as well as the Inquisition, built his headquarters there." Jean-Marc pointed to the church: Eglise des Jacobins.

"My God," Solange muttered with a shudder. She gazed at Jean-Marc for a long time, a frown of understanding deepening on her brow. "You were here when this all happened, Master, weren't you."

Jean-Marc nodded slightly. "I lost many friends on that day in Béziers. Some gave their lives so others might escape the carnage, the slaughter, the fires. After Béziers fell, most of the other walled cities lost hope. Carcassonne held out for a while. Here, the capitol of the region, Toulouse, fought as best it could. But once it finally fell, the city then became the strategic center from which to launch and administrate the abomination history knows as the Inquisition.

Solange turned to him with a searching look, weighed her words, then asked, "The unjust and untimely loss of loved ones is difficult to bear."

"The loss of one person pales in comparison to the loss of an entire community of loving and caring pious people, whose only transgression was to be devoted and humble in a way unacceptable to the power structure of Rome." Jean-Marc gazed back into her eyes, and took her hands. "While this history is indeed critical to understand, Solange, there are other things more pressing in the current flow of priorities that I must speak with you about. There is something I need to know… After you helped me recover from the bullet wound, when you shared your essence with me… And I thank you for it…"

"Yes, Master?" Solange replied, unsure where Jean-Marc's questioning was leading.

"While the nature of this kind of occurrence has been extremely rare in my life, experience has shown me that… a change occurs. I can only know for sure if… if you tell me your dreams since that night. Tell me the visions you've seen in your dreamscape, Solange. I need to know your oneiric world," Jean-Marc declared with a compelling conviction.

Solange gazed at him with a slight frown, not sure what words she would find next. "My mother also told me I should pay close attention to my dreams. But lately they've been very, *very* different, Master. More urgent, more colorful, frightening, and sometimes strange… But one in particular has left me with a sense of awe, because this one has recurred even in my waking hours. While I know I'm awake, but nonetheless it's as though this vivid dream is… I don't know a better word… it's flowing through me," Solange revealed.

"Tell me more," he encouraged.

"It's quite simple really. It is a dream, a vision as well. You know the experience where, when you look into the eye of a horse, or a dog, or a cat even, where you get the feeling of intelligence… somehow of connection? …But something deeper as well: an acknowledged and mutual knowing."

"Yes, Solange. I know the experience."

"Well this has that spirit, however, it's a continuous series of eyes, of people, from all different cultures and lands, blending one into another, with creatures, great and small—crows, eagles, dolphins and whales in the sea, lizards, even a spider. I've never seen anything like this before: small rodents, large bears, an elephant, even fish, and finally a man who is smiling with an overwhelming radiance. All of them have an intelligence, and all have a warmth, a feeling of connection and spirit, soul and heart. The images blend one into the other—these eyes—but they always end with this smiling man. And I am left with the impression that I'm gazing into the Eye of God… and I feel a deep sense of peace."

Jean-Marc studied her with a quiet compassion, frowned slightly as he nodded and then offered a small grin. "This is good, Solange. Very, *very* good. Now, tell me about your mother."

"Despite the fact you've been close to my father for years, I wasn't sure you'd ever met her. But now having met Father Savigny, and understanding his connection to you and her… I must suspect you knew her."

Jean-Marc smiled with a slight nod. "Tell me about how you knew her."

"She was a great practitioner of the healing arts." Solange

weighed these last words and then chose to re-phrase the statement. "She was a great physician."

Jean-Marc noted this with a nod. "She was both, wasn't she."

She nodded eagerly, pleased with Jean-Marc's acknowledgement of her mother's fullness of quality in the path of learning Solange too had taken and which her mother shared with her daughter. "She taught me so much, when she was in the house, though her travels took her away sometimes for months."

Jean-Marc nodded thoughtfully. "A peerless physician and a profound philosopher as well, would you agree, Solange?

"Yes, of course, Master."

Jean-Marc nodded. "She was a rare individual. Someone like this is educated in a different class of schooling far exceeding those scholars whose learning flows only from the ancient arts of healing, as well as a discipline that entails a comprehensive scope of knowledge including the ailments of the body, medicines and the study of anatomy and physiology. She was so much more than that… Did she teach you about the importance of the Four, the Seven, and the Twelve?" Jean-Marc inquired.

"You mean the mysteries associated with those who know cosmology, both macrocosm and microcosm? That which relates to the sciences and arts of the Moderns and Ancients alike?"

Jean-Marc nodded with satisfaction. "Very good, Solange. And tell me more about the Seven."

"I expect you refer first to the Seven Liberal Arts, which provide the very foundation of understanding the

Universe," Solange replied with erudition, gaining a deeper sense of investment and confidence in this dialog.

"And...?" Jean-Marc asked her lightly, requesting more detail.

Solange now intuited this was less a casual conversation and more an impromptu examination of her knowledge. She glowed with exhilaration as she shifted into her serious learned side to demonstrate what she knew—a trait her mother had always been proud of.

"The Seven Liberal Arts are always studied in order, climbing a ladder rung by rung. As one climbs, one has a higher perspective on the order of things in the Universe."

"And are you on this ladder, Solange?" Jean-Marc asked her.

Solange paused, expressing some concern. "The teaching of the traditional Church of Rome discourages this pathway of learning, Master. They say it leads innocent souls astray," she observed in a non-committal manner.

"I can assure you, as I suspect, and your mother did as well, that the study of the Seven Liberal Arts was very much in the original voice of the First Speaker of this faith. The centuries of men ruling the Church in Rome have added their own messages over time, which in effect changed far too much of the original message, and in doing so no longer accurately represents the True Word of God," Jean-Marc replied.

"How do you know this, Master?" Solange inquired.

"Personal experience, as well, an unbiased study of the historical records shows this as a simple fact. Through history the Popes have consistently discouraged this practice, of course, encouraging instead faith in traditions over recognition of facts as they stand. The culmination of this repressive practice over centuries resulted in an obedient and unquestioning flock. Doctrines of Faith: the manufactured tortured logic supporting the power and privilege agenda of a re-constructed history of The Word. The Cathars, however, embraced the study of the Seven Liberal Arts, and they were 'Good Christians.' Understandably, they were a profound threat to Rome, because they encouraged a direct relationship with God, whereas Rome insisted this was only possible through middlemen, such as themselves, but an experience which they were never able to deliver... So, Solange, returning to my question: have you stepped onto this ladder?" he asked her as the last glimpse of sunlight vanished beyond the hills to the west of the city.

"Yes, Master," Solange replied without hesitation.

"Tell me of your ascending steps on this venerable climb, and from what vantage point do you currently stand?" Jean-Marc inquired, ushering her back inside, into his atelier.

Feeling in a setting very much in the spirit her mother used to foster, Solange proceeded to explain her own rigorous journey of study through this sacred body of arcane knowledge.

"It began with *Grammatica*—where I immersed myself with the living word, both written and spoken; the structure of languages, etymology, philology and poetics. The second rung of the ladder—*Dialectica*—focused on strengthening logical thought, which embraced not just things of the material world, but the spiritual world as well. And Aristotle, of course, is considered a patron saint, of sorts, of this discipline," she added, then continued on without pause.

"The third of the Arts—*Rhetorica*—is blessed with the immortal spirit of Cicero, the legendary and greatest speaker of the ancient Roman senate. *Rhetorica* is concerned with the merging and amalgamation of the first two Arts, as it relates to developing the skill of powerful spontaneous and incisive oratory."

"If indeed you've completed this cycle of study, might your current measured and respectful manner of speech be a well-developed mask?" Jean-Marc asked wryly.

"I am a single woman in a man's world, traveling with new faces. My voice of knowledge presents itself when the time is appropriate, Jean-Marc," Solange stated evenly, meeting his eye as an equal.

Jean-Marc smiled at the strength behind her pride and confidence of expression. "And tell me of the next art on your climb, please, Solange."

She described the attributes of the fourth art. "*Musica* is the study of harmony, rhythm, melody and composition. Deeply embedded within this study is the development of singing skills and playing musical instruments. Considered a 'royal' art, and associated with the sun, its goal targets the ability to hear the music of the spheres, including the music of the sun itself."

"And what insight do you have about this music of the spheres?" Jean-Marc ventured.

"There is much that lies beneath the surface. The enjoyment of the sounds is fundamentally the smallest, most primal part. Its potential to create connections to different qualities of energy is something I'm only truly beginning to understand. My mother spoke on this principle quite often."

Jean-Marc nodded with appreciation. "And what

instruments do you play, Solange?"

"The violin is my favorite. My mother started me with it as a child. I also play the harpsichord, harp and flute, and I've sung in the church choir since I was seven."

"With your share of solos, I expect," Jean-Marc intuited with an appreciative smile.

Solange nodded with reflexive modesty, but revealing a pride at being recognized for her accomplishments in a world where a woman of her station was traditionally given credit for so little, if anything at all.

Jean-Marc studied her closely as he asked the next question. "And the double-stop of E-flat and G, this chord has meaning for you, Solange?"

Solange stared at him for an equally long pause. "Yes, Master. Known as the 'Devil's chord,' it is said by some, when played correctly, to deliver a mystical experience; some say it is a gateway to a higher plane of consciousness."

"And have you played this chord in any composition during your training, Solange?"

"My mother introduced me to Tartini and *The Devil's Trill*. I could never play it as well as her. And, indeed, listening to her affected me profoundly. It's very moving. Unforgettable."

Jean-Marc nodded slightly. "There are other important compositions as well that employ this chord." Then he moved on without pause. "Being as advanced as it sounds you are, making your mother and father very proud, I must assume you've climbed the next rung of *Arithmetica*?"

"And *Geometrica* as well, Master. I've been working on the Seventh Art of *Astronimica* for the last two years. Though I fear even another two years will bring me only slightly closer to mastering the body of knowledge I know resides in this level."

"And all of this as you also study the path of the physician and the arts of healing. It's a great deal of erudition for any man or woman," Jean-Marc observed respectfully. "What do you know of the study of electricity?"

Without missing a beat, Solange shifted gears effortlessly. "I've read papers by Alessandro Volta in the *Philosophical Magazine*, as well as the journal *Philosophical Transactions* on the findings of the devices he created, stacking disks with different kinds of metal which he called 'piles'. His recreation of an electric shock, similar to that produced by a Leyden jar, was very interesting. Humphrey Davis's advances in using acid instead of salt water are quite compelling, resulting in the flow of a more powerful electric fluid. I find the concept of *vitalism*: the study of life, death and electricity to be very promising. I think great discoveries are yet to be realized here," Solange's enthusiasm revealed her gratification of having someone to speak with who treated her as a colleague, or more.

Jean-Marc nodded with appreciation. "I know another woman who's quite intrigued by *vitalism*. She said she plans to write a book on it, possibly in the fiction framework. She's the companion of a dear friend, and a very promising poet, Percy Shelly: Mary. From what she told me of her potentially controversial work, I know it shall turn many heads. Her working title is *Frankenstein* which is the name of the alchemist-physician in her story who works with these principles to manifest them into reality: secondary life through the technique of *vitalism*. It's an intriguing concept."

"I shall endeavor to read it when it is complete, Master.

Her name is Mary…?" Solange inquired.

"Mary Wollstonecraft. Their love for each other seems like a force of nature and I suspect they'll marry before long," Jean-Marc observed. Then striving to further explore her range of knowledge, he casually shifted topics and continued his inquiry. "*Ni hao*! Have you traveled the world at all?"

Without hesitation Solange replied in fluent Mandarin, "*Dùibìqi. Wo shì siuxéushêng…* It is my dream to do so. My journeys have thus far been through books. And I remain fascinated by the journey of Chêng Ho's seventh Imperial Treasure Fleet to the Red Sea in 1432—where China's emissaries first reached Cairo and ultimately Italy. I believe this event to be one of the most critical points of our history, yet purposely obscured. Their maps of the world and books rich with technological innovations fueled the Renaissance. Despite how much their story is suppressed by the ruling powers of Europe this event remains critical to understanding our rise to awareness of things outside our sphere of knowledge."

Amused and intrigued, Jean-Marc inquired further. "You seem well versed on the widest range of subjects, Solange. To what influencing factor do you attribute that?"

Feeling more relaxed, Solange shared a piece of her personal life. "One night, years ago when I was sleeping, I awoke to realize my mother had been sitting by me, reading the lessons I had been working on earlier in the day. She somehow succeeded to speak to my inner mind while I dreamt. I think she created a space inside of me that enabled me to receive information deep in my mind in ways I never imagined possible. I learned seven languages. I was surprised at how I knew words I didn't even remember reading or hearing... I came to realize it was not just my own lessons she related, but others unique and original which I only later understood I learned... in my sleep. My mother was a remarkable woman."

"Yes, she was, Solange. And I am sorry for your loss," Jean-Marc replied with sincere compassion.

Something seemed to be confirmed to Solange by this reply. "You knew my mother, didn't you?"

"I did, Solange, quite well. I introduced your father and mother," Jean-Marc replied without fanfare.

The implications of this resounded more deeply than Solange anticipated. Her mind raced, making connections with this one piece of information.

"My mother told me I would soon be studying with a teacher after her. She never said the name, but spoke of this teacher with reverence and warmth... For a few days I thought it might have been Father Savigny, but I understood you were his teacher as well. Are you the teacher my mother spoke of... Master?"

Jean-Marc smiled. "I knew part of you, the part that would recognize me, would arrive at my door in its own manner." He led her to the closed door, above which the round, stained glass rose window was installed. "Your mother was an avid and resourceful student." After a pause, he chose his words carefully and delivered them with a quality of compassion. "I take it you might be ready for your next level of instruction?"

He opened the door; and inside, lit from an outside window by the last vestiges of light in the western sky, Solange saw three workbenches with various appliances and accoutrements of the chemist's trade. Also, above two windows, a larger version of the circular rose window dominated the upper part of the outside wall of this laboratory.

She noticed a particular detail at the center of the window, which was not part of the first window positioned over the door leading into the laboratory: it had a luminescent and faceted red jewel, a ruby, which seemed to pick up the slightest reflected light from outside the building and magnify it with a sense of life of its own. She stepped across the threshold with a sense of awe, and wonder.

"Yes, Master. I am ready," she replied.

The Byways of France
20 March, 1815 AD – Mid-Day

Another messenger had just arrived as Napoleon's swelling force continued their march northwest to Paris. Spurring his horse to pick up the pace, he led his troops in a long column which spread out on the road for over a mile behind them, and far out of sight into the wooded hills to the southeast.

Napoleon observed his horse-mounted security detail confirm the approaching courier's identity, then one of Napoleon's horse soldiers took the long shoulder strap of the courier's leather pouch and handed it over to one of Napoleon's aides-de-camp. While keeping his horse in pace with Napoleon and the column, the adjunct unbuckled the flap of the leather case and found the document intended for Napoleon. Studying every detail in the countryside around him, always wary of a surprise attack, Napoleon glanced over at his aide who just finished his quick perusal of the messenger's document.

"Well?" Napoleon inquired.

"It is confirmed, Your Majesty. Louis, the Bourbon usurper, has abandoned Paris. All our sources indicate he fled north, leaving the country and taking refuge in Ghent," the adjunct reported crisply.

"Ghent…" Napoleon responded thoughtfully. This single word masked a symphony of worlds and calculations which ran through the returning Emperor's mind. He recently learned that, seven days earlier, the Congress of Vienna, still in session with all the leaders of Europe, had declared him an outlaw. With Britain, Russia, Austria and Prussia all in one place, he assumed it was just a matter of time—if it had not taken place already—that they would form a new coalition against him, most likely led by the British.

While he knew another confrontation would be inevitable, Napoleon's gorge rose at the thought of the English stirring up problems. He pledged, however, that whatever engagement might take place, it would not be on French soil as before, which resulted in Czar Alexander and Russian troops marching through Paris. Napoleon knew that the British army, led by the commander who relentlessly harried his forces in Spain—Wellington—was concentrated in Brussels and Blucher's Prussian Army in Liège. No, he would take the battle out of France, somewhere to the north, with the intention of dividing his enemies and directly threatening Britain's presence on the

European continent as well.

Enough time had passed that thousands of prisoners from the Russian campaign had been returned to France, most ready to rejoin Napoleon's cause. Add to that the 46,000 battle-ready troops he inherited from Louis XVIII and Bonaparte in turn had a seasoned core of battle-ready soldiers at his command. Napoleon's march to Paris had also sparked the imagination of the nation, many bitter at the royalist's treatment of the citizenry and electrified by the charisma of a man who transformed an entire continent by his will indomitable and vision. They too joined the growing ranks.

As a result, where he began with 1,100 men when he landed near Cannes, and had 6,000 by the time he was in Lyon, he now had an army of 140,000 regular troops on the march to Paris and 200,000 volunteers in reserve. He knew he caught the crowns of Europe asleep, resting on their laurels. He knew if only he could face his enemies one at a time, he could defeat them all.

One critical component of Bonaparte's formula for success, however, still eluded him: locating the Count de Saint Germain. This man had provided the Emperor with prescient insights in the past and nuances of strategy which helped him turn the tide in a number of campaigns. And for his help, Napoleon had in turn exerted his powerful favor by ordering the end of the Inquisition as part of the right of his military control of Rome and the Vatican.

The agent of at least two French kings before him, and having relationships with other royals around Europe, yet completely free of their control, the count seemed to maintain an air of influence and mystery in continental affairs.

Identifying exactly where Saint Germain came from, and when he was born, however, had indeed proven to be elusive. Napoleon knew this about the man: aside from his uncanny insight in political and strategic initiatives, the count's skills in the arts of healing and medicine were without peer.

Napoleon had gratefully received certain medicines— elixirs—the supply of which he had long since exhausted. Their properties made him feel younger and remarkably energetic, delivering him a need for only four hours of sleep per night. These elixirs also provided him with a mental lucidity which astounded Napoleon with his ability to process complex layers of timely information, and with calmness and clarity.

Bonaparte knew that alone, he was a dynamic and brilliant leader. The count, however, provided him with a decisive and overpowering edge, the advantage of which he craved to have in his circle of influence once again. Indeed, in lighter and private moments, Napoleon referred to the count as 'my Merlin.' To this compliment the count had replied—which Napoleon remembered with much affectionate fondness—"No, *Mon Empereur*, I knew Merlin, but he did not have the sense of humor I have. He was a terribly serious man, but a brilliant student nonetheless."

A recent report from Lieutenant Jean-Luc Glastre, whom he sent ahead to Paris to find the count, was both curiously encouraging and worrying. Encouraging because the lieutenant had picked up a trace of the count's recent presence in Paris, under his name the Marquis Jean-Marc Baptiste de Rennes. This report included a rather public humiliation of the duc de St. Pré at the salon of the Comte de Narbonne, as well as the apparent masterful swordplay with the duc de St. Pré the following day in the streets of Paris, which left St. Pré blind.

From that point forward, however, the count's presence in Paris vanished. But the most worrying part of Lieutenant Glastre's report was that some altercation had taken place at Soubise Palace related to the Vatican Archives, allegations of a stolen book, and the names of Count de Saint Germain as well as Marquis de Rennes were somehow implicated. A group associated with the newly reinstated Holy Inquisition, whose exact identity and relationship with the Vatican remained unclear, was now in pursuit of the same man Napoleon sought, but for very different reasons.

Lieutenant Glastre had also activated his family's network of connections in Paris, and across France, to gain any insight into this group's movements or any sign of Napoleon's valued advisor. One report came in that an individual known as Brother Jerome used his emblem of office with the Inquisition to free two prisoners who had been in the employ of a notorious highwayman named Robert O'Donnell. This same Brother Jerome had also been reported to have passed word for the need for extra Inquisitional forces from Spain and with the instructions to make all haste to converge on Toulouse on March 20— which was today. For those who answered the call, great rewards were promised if the success of the enterprise was delivered.

Lieutenant Glastre sent this message by pigeon somewhere from the road south of Paris, with the detail that he too was assembling a force of his own to intervene if possible. It was certainly a much smaller unit, and details were sketchy. From where Napoleon sat, riding toward his destiny in Paris, he felt uneasy at not having this critical component of his future success secured and strategically in place.

Within elite circles, including the crown heads of Europe, the Count de Saint Germain's indispensable role as a close advisor to many, in various nations, at different times, had been quietly acknowledged by numerous important figures.

With these relationships, as well as the invaluable bonds the count maintained within the carefully guarded *Tekton* brotherhood—the extremely secretive pan-national organization, originally responsible for the founding of the Knights Templar, and subsequently the Freemasons— Napoleon knew the Count de Saint Germain could hold the very key to his success or failure.

And while many of the Freemason lodges had been drastically reduced in the Terror following the French Revolution, Napoleon knew the *Tekton* roots and networks ran much, much older and deeper. Indeed, while the Freemasons evolved into a collection of separate competing brotherhoods claiming a birthright to the same name, most represented and maintained only a light vestigial memory and knowledge of their roots relating to the original venerable *Tekton* tradition. And hence when the Freemason lodges underwent drastic reorganization, as well as infiltration by the ruthless and diabolical Illuminati late in the last century, the sub rosa underground stream of the *Tekton* brotherhood continued to flow across borders and seas maintaining a hidden sense of order and support to the worthy.

The count was woven into the very heart of this invaluable network of relationships. With a right word placed to the right people who were *Tekton* members—in the signal corps of either Blucher's Prussian Army, or Wellington's British force—marching orders could be changed, delayed or lost, keeping the forces allied against Napoleon separate for critical timing before a battle, which could be the tipping point of ultimate military success.

Also, with the count's support, Napoleon could possibly influence the balance of back channel negotiations in his favor among the European powers meeting at the Congress of Vienna.

The fact that the count had served as Napoleon's personal physician and had access to alchemical remedies no others possessed, only heightened Napoleon's urgent sense of need for this elusive figure. He *must* have the Count de Saint Germain at his side as soon as humanly possible. Bonaparte prayed for Lieutenant Glastre's success in this all-important undertaking.

Gazing into the distance ahead of them, on the road to Paris, Napoleon grew reflective. He had ignored the count's council once, and the consequences ultimately caused his earlier and historic downfall. Bonaparte insisted that invading Russia was his destiny, and it was meant for him to stand before his adoring masses in Moscow, whom he had liberated from their royal yoke of humiliating servitude. Napoleon had, of course, been gravely in error; and the cost of the Russian campaign was horrific.

One lesson the count taught him, and which Napoleon took to heart, derived from the man's extensive experience in the world of alchemy. The precept held the importance of a perspective on an issue that influenced all of mankind's endeavors in one way or another, the subject of *when* to begin any great work. In classical alchemical perspectives, beginning any essential endeavor was best implemented on a solstice event, and the most fortuitous was considered the Vernal Equinox. Napoleon had not observed that convention when launching the Russian campaign.

Looking north at the light of the late morning sky, Napoleon turned to his next in command and spoke with just a trace of distraction. "Tell the men to quicken the pace. We *must* be in the Tuileries by midnight tonight. I *must* be standing in Paris at sunrise on the first day of spring."

W ord arrived from the south. Reports came back to Brother Jerome, which he did not enjoy relaying to the bishop. The lead clue they had acquired from the markings on the saddlery left behind at the Soubise Palace by Jean-Marc, had not delivered results desired or expected. Agents of the monk indeed located and 'rigorously interviewed' the saddler who made the custom work. The torture and interrogation produced nothing substantive, however, and required the messy procedure of hiding the body of one more casualty on the seemingly endless trail of flushing out this damned and elusive quarry.

Ruminating over his options at a local inn located in the southern Dordogne region—*Auberge du Chasseur*—on the main road, with a day's ride further south to Toulouse, Brother Jerome recognized his reluctant compatriot, Roger, more than likely would be his best solution to achieve this centuries-old goal.

The monk quickly ascertained from Robert O'Donnell that Roger had not been the hero he represented himself to be. And, having some pull with local magistrates, by benefit of a royal governmental seal of authority the monk carried around for these occasions, he freed O'Donnell's two henchmen whom he judged to be most willing and beneficial to his cause. Brother Jerome left the blinded leader behind to rot in jail, his usefulness gone.

And when Brother Jerome presented the two highwaymen to Roger, as 'his men,' Jean-Marc's former valet blanched. Brother Jerome enjoyed this reaction, knowing many more details behind the story of Roger 'capturing' these men and delivering them to justice would be ferreted out in due course. He had heard as much from Bruno and Nicco, the two former associates in the employ of O'Donnell.

One detail of acute relevance, however, was that the leader of Roger's traveling party had a distinctive white eyebrow. And while Brother Jerome grandly announced Roger would command these men by the ancient right of conquest, the monk knew well that Roger would be their traveling captive and incapable of making a move without Brother Jerome's permission.

The recent imbroglio resulting in the monk being drugged on the road by the old man on the wine cart only intensified Brother Jerome's determination to seize his ultimate prey. The requirement to track down his missing man Pedro, and to rendezvous with his Spanish riders, originally thought to be an advantage by increasing his numbers, had instead resulted in his loss of almost a day on the hunt.

Once locating Pedro—who had indeed lost the fat priest's trail and his Andalusian mare in the bargain—the monk of course broke the Spaniard's neck for his abject failure, and in short order reunited with his main force of French riders. Still fuming over Pedro's incompetence, Brother Jerome knew, however, he must be closing the distance on his prey. Everything he had learned supported that view. But precisely where his quarry was at this moment remained the vital and unanswered question.

The challenge of locating Jean-Marc stood as the foremost consideration of Brother Jerome's priorities—now that the prime location originally identified and associated with the saddlery maker had been set aside as a prospect for the discovery of their prey's whereabouts. Prying the needed information from Roger would be the challenge.

Roger had no knowledge of what the monk learned from O'Donnell, Bruno and Nicco about his master's identity. The monk's reading of the young man was that, while he would not want to betray his erstwhile master, the self-important apprentice had issues that could possibly be exploited.

Finding the fine line of leverage for that fulcrum point was something Brother Jerome had managed time and again over the preceding centuries. It remained just a matter of waiting for the right opportunity before he found the key to turn the latch and gain access to what he needed from this young man.

And once the valet fulfilled his purpose in this manner, Brother Jerome had other uses planned for him, which would provide valuable nourishment for him and the bishop. The monk smiled pensively, licking his lips, as he meditated on the best strategies to paralyze and penetrate Roger's psychology.

"No, no, the proper block for such an attack would be first hit the arm with your wrist area, like so, and quickly thrust the dagger into the belly with your other hand, then yank the edge down, cutting the gut open. Then he's basically done."

Sitting on a well-worn hardwood bench in the eatery section of the *Auberge du Chasseur*, Bruno had just demonstrated his opinion of the most effective and lethal technique when fighting in close quarters to Nicco, in their present location sitting side-by-side in the crowded eatery. A few jugs of wine into the afternoon, neither felt too much pain.

"But to complete the action effectively, give a second thrust, then a twist, and yank down again. You want to do as much damage as quickly as possible to the gut," Nicco added, as he finished his glass and called to the inn maiden. "Another pitcher, woman. Our boss is paying."

Their 'boss,' Roger, was trapped at the wall end of the bench. And as Bruno and Nicco demonstrated their close quarters combat strategies to each other, Roger found himself retreating further still against the wall. The next pitcher of wine came and the pair ordered roasted lamb, potatoes and stew.

Roger paid for the round and nodded for the purchase

of the meal while he reflected on the lightening load of gold in his purse, since he now had the responsibility for the pair's room and board at the inn, as well as, the feed and keep of their horses. He knew, based on the recently liberated highwaymen's robust appetites, that in a few days' time, Roger would run through a good portion of the 'reward' money Brother Jerome gave him so freely. The expense of carrying these men would then eat into the bounty money he received as reward for their capture. And after that the money he had been paid for the horses, then… he would be without means in the company of men extremely hostile to his manner and station.

Roger dreaded this equation of inevitable consequence and kept his eye out for any opportunity to slip away and escape. Right now, of course, Bruno and Nicco sat hemming him in, blocking him from standing freely in the inn itself.

Even the slightest pretext of privacy was immediately neutralized by one of them. When Roger signaled his need to visit the privy, it always turned out one of them needed to go as well. He did not enjoy a room of his own, but instead, at Brother Jerome's insistence, the three of them roomed together.

While he had not yet realized the true depths of his dire situation, Roger clearly knew now he was trapped and needed to find some way to get free. But finding any opportunity of a certain getaway proved impossible so far. Indeed Bruno and Nicco always stayed at close quarters. Brother Jerome also traveled with four other highwaymen, so the circle of threatening company always seemed to surround him wherever he turned.

Roger had always been proud of his sly resourcefulness. Up to this point, however, he had not discovered an avenue which might provide him with a reliable hope of escape.

As Nicco and Bruno squabbled over the best combat techniques, Roger brooded over the many beneficial offers Jean-Marc extended to him over the years of their relationship. Most important had been the invitation into the *Tekton* brotherhood, a secret society—and over a millennium old—which endured hidden within a larger organization known to most by the name outsiders were familiar with: Freemasons. And indeed, the majority of Freemasons were not even aware of the deep ancient influence of the *Tekton* brotherhood.

The term *tekton* came from ancient Greek and its literal meaning of 'mason,' 'builder,' or sometimes 'carpenter,' also conveyed the designation of 'scholar' or 'man of knowledge.' Roger also had significant reason to regret his turning down the chance to learn the arts of fencing of both European and Asian styles to the degree they were made available to him by Jean-Marc. Indeed these were just a few of the opportunities he let pass him by.

In retrospect, Roger realized now that one or more of those lost opportunities might have given him an advantage somewhere in solving his current problem. But Roger regularly turned these offers down, always having some more selfish distraction related to satisfying his senses, which habitually took precedence.

He remembered once how Jean-Marc extricated both of them from a tight situation by knowing how to combine simple compounds so they made a powerful and quick-acting sleeping drug. Roger never bothered to learn it himself, always thinking he could get it from Jean-Marc if he ever wanted it.

Truly on his own now with this realization, Roger recognized how many critical opportunities he squandered which had been offered to him. And now he felt afraid, very afraid. Despite his hale-and-hearty mask of comradeship, Brother Jerome truly terrified him to the very core of his being.

Roger glanced out the leaded pane glass window of the inn to the front of the hostelry, where he observed Brother Jerome lead his saddled horse to the front of the tavern, followed by his group of four highwaymen with their horses. The monk handed his reins to one of his men as Roger watched him stride into the inn. Once there, the monk quickly located Roger and 'his men,' and frowned with menace.

"I gave the order to saddle up and be ready to ride! What're you doing here, laggard? Get moving!"

Nicco and Bruno got up in a flash, sprinting out the door, leaving Roger to fumble at covering the bill with the innkeeper, as he turned to Brother Jerome, making a gesture of apology.

"I heard nothing of the order to prepare to ride, Brother Jerome."

Brother Jerome waved Roger's reply away with an irritated gesture. "Excuses don't cut it with me, boy! You're not going to be a troublemaker now, are you? I've got no use for troublemakers!"

"I'll be ready to ride before you know it," Roger pledged as he rushed out to get his horse saddled.

Brother Jerome followed him out the door and cracked a

private mischievous smile at the psychological torture he inflicted on this man. He had actually never passed the word to these men on purpose and wanted to use it to further 'cultivate' Roger's subservience and fear.

The monk looked forward to applying more mental pain, with growing intensity. Anticipating the point when he needed this man to crack and open up, he felt he must nurture Roger's sense of paranoia and frailty as much as possible in advance to facilitate the process. Besides, with all the trouble the monk put up with on this frustrating quest, rife with unexpected scenarios requiring his stewardship, Brother Jerome had to find his pleasures somewhere.

As his carriage traveled south, having left the Dordognese inn shortly after Brother Jerome's party, Bishop Antonio del Julia y Sangresante reflected on the opportunity placed in his path by fortune. Originally not knowing if or when it would ever occur—that being the recovery of the Book and the possibility of having Jean-Marc under his complete control—he had, of course, laid the groundwork through the preceding decades for other opportunities to deepen and broaden his influence on the affairs of men on this continent, and elsewhere as well.

The bishop believed one of his crowning achievements to be the establishment of the Illuminati, through his proxy, Adam Weishaupt. While adopting one of Antonio's other identities, as a wealthy textile merchant from Romania, he had encountered Weishaupt during his studies in Jesuit training in southern Germany.

Born the son of a Jewish rabbi, Weishaupt converted to Catholicism after his father's death, purely out of survival motivations in the predominantly devout Christian region of Bavaria. The bishop exploited Weishaupt's abhorrence of the Church, and molded the brilliant man, providing him access to lower-level esoteric knowledge which few men of that age enjoyed.

Indeed, the bishop had no problem playing both sides of a philosophical and religious position, since whatever he did furthered his own agenda, whether with the Inquisition, the Illuminati, or any other institution he considered advantageous to his ultimate goals and desires. This was his practice in the past, and it would be so for centuries to come, until his ultimate sense of control had been achieved, at whatever the cost.

Able to present himself as a well-funded, dynamic and charismatic leader to Weishaupt, with kindred Jewish roots, Sangresante orchestrated a relationship with the newly formed banking family: the House of Rothschild.

Under the bishop's direction, Mayer Anselm Rothschild funded Weishaupt's founding of the secret Order of the Perfectibilists, whose name changed shortly thereafter, converted to the more familiar title known around the world: Order of the Illuminati—*the Enlightened Ones.*

Under the philosophical guise of liberalism, enlightenment, freedom and emancipation, Weishaupt rapidly attracted the brightest and some of the most influential and well-born men of Europe to this new elite secret society. All members were given classical names of great figures from antiquity—Cato, Pythagoras, Alexander—which catered to their sense of self-importance and place in the social structure.

Adhering to Sangresante's precise instructions, Weishaupt organized the Illuminati along the lines of the Freemasons and the Jesuit order. From their headquarters in Munich, the movement grew and targeted Freemason lodges, some of which they took over completely. Other lodges were infiltrated covertly to provide the bishop with insight into their activities and objectives.

Once members were in the Illuminati fold, Sangresante had Weishaupt use lucrative bribes—financed by the House of Rothschild—to blackmail, coerce and apply any threats necessary to control his minions absolutely, while keeping his own true identity and influence in the organization a complete secret. His goal targeted the entire dismantling of religion and the promotion of a single world government, ultimately and secretly led by himself.

In 1784, however, an Illuminati messenger detained by local authorities in Bavaria carried secret communiqués which revealed the true and covert agenda of the Illuminati. The Bavarian legislature acted swiftly, outlawing all secret societies; and Weishaupt fled Germany.

Yet, by 1786, Sangresante still surveyed his work with satisfaction. He had established lodges all over Europe, Africa and the lucrative and growing colonies in America. The lodges of Germany simply went underground, changed their names and by now enjoyed a sense of resurgent influence in the affairs of the new Prussia.

Indeed one of his darlings of the new German dialectical philosophy—Georg Wilhelm Friedrich Hegel—held great promise for the bishop and his plans for generations to come. One of his 'students,' the bishop guided Hegel to create a philosophical tract, employing an historical approach to the solution of human problems in society— with a persuasive perspective on the master-slave dynamic—which gained an impressive and growing popularity over recent years. Of course, it did not hurt that the bishop covertly commissioned various glowing reviews in sundry European philosophical journals. And even now Hegelism's institutionalization as the philosophical platform for Prussian schooling saw universal acceptance, to shepherd the masses in a way more conducive to unquestioning rule by his chosen elite.

Sangresante saw great promise in this initiative and his vision included a future where it extended across the oceans, ultimately to all the masses of the world. Yet experience told him all plans must be nurtured and supervised with ruthless and attentive care.

In the near term, the bishop tolerated the inconveniences of the accommodations at the local inns and the associated discomforts of rapid travel, to assure his interests were attended to exactly as he required.

While Brother Jerome generally followed his instructions to the letter, there were times when the monk took initiatives with sundry vexing consequences requiring extensive 'clean up,' often time-consuming and expensive. Too much was at stake now. With the widespread groundwork he laid out over the last few decades, along with acquiring the treasure of Jean-Marc, the bishop believed no one in history would stand next to him in towering achievement and unbridled power. He felt as well it was his right of destiny through the ages to possess this unrestrained entitlement.

Indeed, ever since he learned the secret of his birthright and true legacy, back in Alexandria in 391 AD—when he served as a low-ranking brother owing fealty to the imperious Pope Theophilus, Bishop of Alexandria—he had never been the same. Instead of being an orphan of some unfortunate house servant—the story told to him throughout his youth as a ward of the church, and for which he should be thankful for whatever meager benefits the church might give him—he instead discovered certain hidden archives, secret correspondence, which revealed a completely different story.

The young church brother came to learn he was a son of the Antonia clan, one of the most august and elite families in the history of the Roman Republic and Empire. Having the name Brother Antonius at the time, he discovered his lineage not only came from 'Antonia progeny,' but also from a bloodline of historic proportions. Finding correspondence thought long forgotten in the St. Athanasius church archives, he read letters written from the Antonia clan's secretary in Rome to the local representatives of the Alexandrian church. And in these letters Brother Antonius learned his father's legendary lineage came from the Julia-Ptolemaic line.

Apparently an unwanted pregnancy occurred when an unwed Antonia girl, a princess of rank in modern terms, and little more than thirteen, who was betrothed to another noble family, had been forcibly taken—raped—by the scion of Julia-Ptolemaic line—the bloodline of Julius Caesar and Cleopatra. While attempts were made to hide the birth of the child, by spiriting the infant away to Alexandria, some word eventually got out.

SUB ROSA – THE LOST FORMULA

The two families—the Antonia and the Julia-Ptolemy's—subsequently began to negotiate a possible retroactive betrothal, since the product of this union produced a male with the most elite qualities of noble blood. However, that was not to be.

The hierarchy of the St. Athanasius church, including the Bishop of Alexandria, had used the attractive young Brother Antonius—with the exotic and captivating twin-colored eyes—as something of a corporeal plaything for their private whims, since they considered the boy fundamentally abandoned and their rightful property. So instead of allowing the powerful Roman families to know the truth of his scandalous upbringing, they reported Brother Antonius had died in an unfortunate construction accident, closing all discussion of the noble heir and the youth's promising place in the elite hierarchy of the Roman Empire.

Yet years later, after Brother Antonius learned the true story of his legacy, and after having first acquired the Book—for a comparatively short period of time from Jean-Marc, then only known to him as 'The Stranger'—Brother Antonius made the best of his circumstances, especially as the longevity of his and Brother Jerome's lives was concerned.

With the benefit of his extensive education in ancient languages and private study of arcane knowledge—a byproduct of his rare native genius and his years of service as the bishop's personal secretary and scribe—Brother Antonius successfully replicated the procedure described in the tome and implemented the alchemical process which gave them the enduring lives they enjoyed.

One critical detail of the process, however, was that they

had benefited from a mysterious white powdery substance seized by Brother Jerome from the Stranger, a critical component in that procedure.

Antonius had been unable to re-create this compound despite repeated trials from the information in the Book. Before he could continue his experiments, however, the tome had been seized from him by the Bishop of Alexandria when this forbidden text was discovered in Brother Antonius's possession.

So much more hidden knowledge remained contained in the Book that he needed to possess and understand, including why this stranger apparently did not need to consume living blood to stay young as he and the monk did. The Book was the key to Antonius attaining the totality of his birthright, a claim centuries long overdue.

Bishop Antonio del Julia y Sangresante's face twitched with involuntary impatience at not having in his power that which he required now. He ground his teeth and flared his lips, revealing his incisors in a feral manner, an unconscious gesture of fierce animal aggression.

In his hand, a customary prop of his rank in the church—a bronze crucifix—had become crushed and disfigured with his superhuman strength, which he kept hidden from outsiders for centuries. He caught himself, glanced down at the misshapen and contorted crucifix, laughed lightly and then adopted the calm mask he used so often to hide the seething desire which lurked just beneath his surface. He casually tossed the crucifix out the window of the traveling carriage, onto the roadside.

After peering into his fine leather traveling bag for a replacement crucifix, which he hung over his shoulders, he smiled, thinking of some farm boy who might come upon the artifact which he had just discarded and this lad would logically become convinced that Satan himself wrought this horror upon the holy crucifix.

Were this misshapen artifact to come before his brethren in the Inquisition, and ultimately brought before him, the bishop would soberly recommend that the entire family of whoever claimed they had found the abomination would rightly need to be tortured until they confessed their crimes, so horrific was this offense against Christ the Savior.

The bishop chuckled as he pictured this fanciful travesty of justice while his carriage drove on swiftly to the south, headed for Toulouse.

Traveling south on a different road only a few miles to the east, through rich rolling hills with the fields of grazing cattle, yellow mustard, red poppies and wheat, broken by patches of forest and stone walls, Napoleon's man, Lieutenant Jean-Luc Glastre—accompanied by three other men—rode as fast as his horse could take him.

They had already lost two men to a riding accident. One man fell when his horse slipped while fording a stream. The result was a hobbled horse and a valuable man with a broken leg. Lieutenant Glastre winced at the change of fortune, since he needed every man possible, but his sense of humanity and duty to his men also prevailed. Quickly assigning one of his riders to stay with the wounded comrade and deliver him to local care, the cavalry officer had to make do with two less men.

As he rode, the lieutenant's mind flashed on an image of the Knights Templar's centuries-old symbol—which had two men sharing one horse—and he wondered briefly if there might be some relevant symbolism there. Napoleon had told him in the most general terms of the count's involvement with an element of the Freemasons, the widely acknowledged inheritors of the Templar tradition.

More pressing upon his concerns, however, was the fact that he started with five cavalrymen, including himself, and now he only rode with three. Making matters more concerning, Jacques, the man whose leg had been broken, was one of his best fighters. Jean-Luc sensed he would need everyone he could muster, and yet now his combined force was reduced by more than a third.

The lieutenant knew time was of the essence. He knew with the limited intelligence he acquired from his network of contacts, that he would probably have only one chance to engage with the elusive Count de Saint Germain, or the name Lt. Glastre came to learn was presently being used with more currency: Marquis Jean-Marc Baptiste de Rennes.

Indeed, while the loyal cavalry officer kept his life an open book with his beloved commander and Emperor, certain details of Jean-Luc's life simply did not need to be revealed to Napoleon, so seemingly minor and unrelated were the circumstances of his difficult and near tragic birth, twenty years before.

But one day, well before the Russian campaign, while he served Napoleon in his legendary residence at the Malmaison near Paris, an important personage came for a visit: the Count de Saint Germain. While the lieutenant knew of this name for some time, and was instructed to lead the man directly to Napoleon's study upon the count's arrival, Glastre was shocked to see the face attached to the name. Noticing this surprise with a mild smile, the Count de Saint Germain inquired warmly: "And your mother's health is well, I trust, Lieutenant Glastre?"

After quickly and respectfully answering in the affirmative, the young officer promptly led the count to his awaiting Emperor, without another word, leaving Lieutenant Glastre to sort out the story of this encounter and place it in proper perspective for himself.

Jean-Luc's father had told the story more than once to spellbound audiences. The infant Jean-Luc Felix Glastre's birth had been more than a month premature, during his mother and father's journey by carriage to their estate in Aquitaine from their small castle in Brittany. But the hope for a safe comfortable birth in their property in Aquitaine was not to be. Jean-Luc's mother, Angéle, went into a high fever and premature labor at a remote country inn. Fearing he might lose both his wife and child, Jean-Luc's father, Felix, was beside himself with concern, and against all hope asked the innkeeper if any medical assistance was possible.

Before long, a man seemingly on the younger side of middle age, with a distinct white eyebrow, and with a small leather bag, appeared at the duc du Glastre's door. The man's manner calm and reassuring, he spent over three hours with Angéle, and afterwards presented to Felix a new son: Jean-Luc. He gave Felix medicines with instructions for the new mother and the child's care to assure complete recovery and then left the new family to their privacy.

The following morning, the new father inquired about the man who had been there to save their lives. He wanted to pay him handsomely for his service. The innkeeper, however, revealed that the man had left at the crack of dawn, but that he had also left a gift for the child: a lovely emerald of exceptional luminance and clarity.

The message accompanying the gift was: *"The arrival of any child of an Angel must be properly acknowledged with a worthy observance of the miracle of life. Please accept this humble gift without sense of obligation, but only with the best wishes from a simple traveler on the eternal road of life."*

The innkeeper could not provide a name of the miracle-working physician, indicating the mysterious healer preferred to remain anonymous.

Fifteen years passed; and when Jean-Luc was a young man, just entering the military academy, a stranger came to call at their château in Brittany. Jean-Luc was surprised to see his father adopt so respectful and deferential manner with this unannounced arrival, who had introduced himself as Marquis Jean-Marc Baptiste de Rennes.

Duc Felix du Glastre normally a locally well-respected noble, was accustomed to reflexive deference among those who knew his station and his family's venerable noble legacy. Yet Jean-Luc quickly learned it was not due to this man's title that his father behaved so. This individual with the white right eyebrow had been the man who saved his mother's life and who brought Jean-Luc safely into the world.

When his father introduced him to the marquis, Jean-Marc displayed open pleasure at seeing the emerald on a chain around Jean-Luc's neck. The marquis observed he had owned the gem for a very long time, and it seemed a perfect occasion to make a gift of it to commemorate Jean-Luc's arrival in the world.

Jean-Luc's father and the marquis spoke in the study for some time. And as a young man—who was involved in his own pursuits of attention at the time—Jean-Luc realized the marquis departed before he returned from a ride in the country with a friend. Jean-Luc thought no more about the encounter at the time, until the meeting at Malmaison. He then reflected on certain remarks his father made, that this meeting the marquis had with his father may very well have resulted in this much-sought-after posting—a commission reporting to Napoleon himself.

As he pressed on to the south, Lieutenant Jean-Luc Glastre had become clearly aware that he rode not just to follow his emperor's orders. He was also on a mission to repay a debt to his family, for his mother's and his own survival. He knew like no other time in his life, that every resource he had in his command would be fully committed to protecting Marquis Jean-Marc Baptiste de Rennes at all costs... even if it meant his own demise.

Based on the intelligence he gathered, he knew he must be at the main market of Toulouse by the ringing of the ninth hour. This might be his only chance to be of any assistance to the man who had been so influential in his life.

As he and his men rode on swiftly, Jean-Luc felt the tap of the gold chain around his neck which held the emerald gem given by Jean-Marc at the time of his birth. Its steady light rhythm against his chest told him his heart was beating to a higher purpose.

Toulouse, Languedoc, France
20 March, 1815 AD – Evening Hour

They had been in Toulouse for nine days, and for much of that time, Jean-Marc slept in his atelier. Slept to heal. However, during Jean-Marc's waking hours, sometimes very late into the night, he took Solange under his tutelage. Gaston expected this for an apprentice-master relationship of this nature. It was with a flush of pride that he knew and understood this was a proper and honorable endeavor for his daughter, following her mother's path.

Long periods in Jean-Marc's small selective library, studying rare ancient books, and additional practical hours in Jean-Marc's laboratory, were part of the apprenticeship. It included such exotic practices as creating electric current in the ancient method used for electroplating, by employing a container of sulfuric acid into which a copper anode and zinc cathode was placed—a Parthenian battery. As the zinc dissolved in the acid, the process created a remarkable effect—when touching the copper cable extending from the urns containing the acid, a surprisingly strong and shocking current resulted. Solange laughed with surprise at the sensation she felt at the end of these copper wires. She had experienced nothing like it in her life.

"What the ancients captured, controlled and used over two thousand years ago, my dear friend Ben Franklin thought he discovered just three decades ago. I confess, I steered him in a few directions of scientific inquiry during our early discussions on one of my visits to what was then the American colonies," Jean-Marc revealed as Solange marveled at the phenomenon of electricity firsthand and for the first time.

Their topics of study and discussion ranged from the scientific description and makeup of the cosmos, to subjects more esoteric—the bridges between mythical and mystical—as well as the Gnostic system of belief. Spiritual forefather of the Cathars, the Gnostics were one of the main and original strains of Christian belief in early Christian times.

Solange's mind had become stimulated and empowered with new channels of thought which Jean-Marc encouraged her to explore. She experienced profound perceptions into the nature of body, soul and spirit. She shared one of her insights.

"I have often reflected on how, as tradition states, if mankind was created in the image of God—and if the mind of man exists in one manifestation as pure spirit—then the inner journey of discovery of the individual spirit and its direct correlation with mankind's essential and universal spirit, is therefore vital to ultimately enabling a relationship with the eternal divinity within us all."

"Very good, Solange. The inner journey is a key to understanding the pathway to the wider truth."

"I just question how this perspective is so markedly different from the teachings of the Church in Rome, and it concerns me," Solange confessed.

"While the long legacy of Christianity is filled with good people committing themselves to their fellow man and the greater good in very profoundly spiritual ways, this is more a reflection of the individual's good works and their devout and loving relationship with God. Unfortunately, the Church of Rome had other priorities over the centuries. They systematically suppressed knowledge and worked diligently at gaining complete and uncontested control of every aspect of humanity's mind and body, and everything mankind owned. Their actions defined them, not their teachings. They were less concerned with delivering the original pure message of Yesu, who so many now called the Christ. The Gnostics, and the Cathars long after them, strove to preserve the opportunity for achieving this direct experience with the divine, equally available to both men and women."

"So the Magdalene tradition and the Cathar tradition have a connection?" Solange asked.

"Without doubt. Magdalene delivered Yesu's message first to this region, long before France existed, and the Cathars incorporated these beliefs. And through the centuries, the Church Fathers of what became the established Roman Church grew threatened with this concept, promise, opportunity, and point of view, which they labeled as heresy. They did everything they could to destroy its existence and eradicate any vestige of this belief system, from the books carrying the knowledge, to the people who believed," Jean-Marc observed, then continued. "Then they sought to continually contort the Cathar story so traditional history viewed them as an abomination."

"It threatened their control of everything, didn't it. If a woman was equal to a man, and had a right to equal access to God, it endangered the very foundations of their institution," Solange observed.

"Indeed, and the process began long before the Magdalene tradition and the Cathars in Languedoc. From Saul of Tarsus, later known as St. Paul, the drastic changing of Yesu's message began. He told his flock to ignore logic and reason and live by faith alone, even at the expense of ignoring Yesu's original message itself, in favor of his own. Saul changed the message to the meaning of Yesu's death, not the meaning of Yesu's words and actions. And not one of Paul's gospels directly quotes Yesu's teachings from the original gospels of Matthew, Mark, Luke or John."

"Not one?" Solange asked with incredulity.

"No, not one. Though he seemed to vaguely refer to Yesu's teachings in one of his gospels. Otherwise it was all Paul's message, separate and independent of Yesu. And after Saul, Bishop Irenaeus, in 190 AD, continued Paul's work. The first one to codify the four gospels as being the cornerstone of the New Testament, he denounced all other gospels being preached at the time as cursed and heretical. A rabid antagonist of the Gnostics, whom he considered heretics, he also declared Yesu was himself a heretic for having preached outside the precepts taught by St. Paul after Yesu's death."

"Irenaeus declared Jesus a heretic? He was a Church Father," Solange observed somewhat disturbed by this revelation.

"Church Father, indeed. Think of what the Inquisition would have done with Yesu. Christian history is filled with Church Fathers who changed the original message and meaning of Yesu. In 212 AD, Origen of Alexandria—considered the greatest teacher of the age since the Apostles—promoted the idea of celibacy for the priesthood. That laid the groundwork for the demeaning and exclusion of women's engaged participation in the Church. This, of course, had nothing to do with Yesu's message. Origen also introduced the idea of martyrdom as being the supreme act of free will. Despite His death for what He believed in, Yesu would have been horrified to know His name was being used to compel so many to commit suicide in this manner."

"And to think, Yesu's teaching 'Seek and ye shall find,' and 'The truth will set you free,' were ultimately ignored to become this tragic horror," Solange remarked.

"Upon the shoulders of these 'giants' of theology, more followed with other traditions of enforced servitude. Around the same time, church chronicler and historian, Tertullian, taught that asking questions about faith and having curiosity in this regard were *evil*, the work of Satan, as he further encouraged the distrust and hatred of women."

"The battle against the Magdalene tradition goes back to the very roots of Christianity," Solange reflected.

Jean-Marc nodded and continued. "In 385 AD, Jerome—who translated the Vulgate Bible into Latin— purposely changed the message about women further and in turn traditionalized and profoundly cemented the disadvantaged position of women in society. Around the same time, St. Augustine invented the idea of Original Sin and predestination. Ignoring Yesu's hopeful and joyous message of mercy and forgiveness, Augustine injected the theme of cruelty and revenge, tolerating no disagreement. He was the first to support the idea of torture against those who disagreed with his interpretation of Christianity. His works were cited by the Dominicans to inspire and justify their cursed and murderous Inquisition. And centuries later, John Calvin used Augustine's vision to devastating effect in the formation of his harsh and unforgiving brand of Christianity, creating the first religious police state where death was the thoroughly reasonable response to disagreement with Christian belief…"

Solange followed the theme. "And through the centuries new innovators of domination would cite earlier Church Fathers to buttress and justify their positions, to further institutionalize their repressive traditions."

"Exactly. These 'Church Fathers' were all about control of the hearts, minds and bodies: the total possession of mankind. They worked to build and cement their power and privilege over the centuries at the direct expense of truth and justice… And, No, Solange, you need not fear what you're learning now goes in any way against the true and original teachings of Yesu. But it does indeed go against the rules set up by those who usurped Yesu's original message and his divine work," Jean-Marc confided with a compelling conviction, suggesting this subject had deep personal meaning, close to his own heart, and was one with which he seemed to have had some intimate and direct experience.

Later, in private, Solange confided to her father that there was so much to learn, so much to process; but the very thought of it excited her. Knowing she now studied with the teacher her mother had obliquely, yet reverentially referred to, from time to time, filled Solange with wonder and humility.

This apprenticeship also included a series of command recitals of her violin skills for Jean-Marc. Surprised at the importance Jean-Marc placed on this performance delivery, Solange found he compelled her to put her 'heart and soul'—every fiber of her being—into each passage she played, every nuance, every pause, and feel all the textures of the music.

"It should live in the listener's ears before it's heard," he would tell her.

Solange strived to deliver at the peak of her capabilities each time Jean-Marc obliged her to pick up the instrument and play. As she vied to perform with extreme excellence—especially on sections which involved the evocative double-stop of the E-flat and G chord—Jean-Marc queried her about her feelings as she played the instrument.

He needed to know the affect within her. Was it a highly skilled delivery of a prescribed set of actions with an interesting and evocative result? Or was it something else: something indescribable, but tangible, which touched her deep inner spirit? Was it possibly something that wove every fiber of her being into the moment of musical creation, which elicited the feeling of intense love, of exhilarating victory, of a different plane of existence for the player and maybe those experiencing it?

Reflecting on this line of questioning, Solange mused it did not seem so much that Jean-Marc expected answers to these queries, but instead they pointed to doorways which opened her to deeper reflection and insight. Jean-Marc's attitude toward this component of her study aligned itself in a way as committed and as serious as the chemical, philosophical and alchemical curricula she explored with him.

With this profound psychically stimulating experience, in the midst of all her other intense studies and activities, she found she could sleep only about four hours a night, so much was there she needed to absorb from this remarkable man. Yet she felt no fatigue, instead she found herself invigorated and excited.

Traditionally being a man of action, and not of books or academic study, Gaston understandably grew somewhat restless indoors. And so he availed himself of the local establishments while at the same time maintaining a close proximity to his master's abode; and he was careful not to drink too much.

Gaston had visited the *Auberge du Sanglier*—Inn of the Boar—on a few occasions through the years as his travels brought him to Toulouse, usually on the master's behalf; but before that, he first discovered the pub on his own. As he approached the tavern earlier in the evening, seeing the sign of the establishment's name, along with the wrought-iron and colorfully hand-painted icon of a boar, he breathed a sigh of comparative relief, glad to have some relaxation after the many trials of the road, as well as the close cramped confines in the lower floors of Jean-Marc's apartments.

The nights preceding their arrival in Toulouse, of course, consisted of mostly camping arrangements of sorts, with late arrival and early rising so they could reach Toulouse in the shortest time possible. Now on his free evenings in the city, he could reinvigorate himself and relax just a little. With a belly full of *cassoulet*, good bread and cheese, but not yet enough wine, it was now left to Gaston to fulfill the imperative of liquid refreshment.

The wood-paneled décor and wall paintings of hunting provided a calming environment for Gaston as he nursed the remains of his second flagon of wine—having just ordered his third—all still considered within the bounds of moderation from his worldly experience. A warm glow deepened in his body. He enjoyed the feminine sway of the young barmaid as she approached bringing him the next pitcher containing his 'nectar of the Gods.'

Yet now an irksome distraction intruded on his peace of mind. The dark-bearded leather seller—who interrogated Jean-Marc in front of the *Auberge des Pommes Bleues* on the evening of their arrival days ago—sat on a bench on the far side of the inn, well into his cups, argued with a serving maiden about the fact that his glass had not been filled to the brim when served, and hence insisted he had been cheated. Gaston did his best to ignore the man as the voice of a new arrival to the Inn of the Boar sounded from the doorway.

"I seek a traitor to France! An English spy! Ample rewards will be given! He goes by many names, two of which are the Count de Saint Germain and the Marquis Jean-Marc Baptiste de Rennes! His distinguishing feature is a white eyebrow over the right eye. His age is estimated to be in his middle thirties. His manner is well-appointed. Anyone who might know of fugitive, come to me now. I'll make it worth your while!" The man behind the voice, spry and in his mid-twenties, advanced further into the eatery with a self-righteous certitude.

Glancing over at the leather seller, who had not yet noticed Gaston's presence here, the old veteran saw for now that the bearded patron remained preoccupied with pressing his case of a shortchanged serving. So boisterous was the tavern as well that the new arrival's message may not have even been heard clearly all the way to the far side of the inn where the leather merchant sat. But Gaston did not take chances. As the new arrival advanced toward a seat at an open table, Gaston gestured for the new arrival to join him at his table. The younger man did so.

"You have seen this man, sir?" he inquired with something of an officious and self-important air.

"No, sir, I have not. But what is the nature of this fugitive's offence? And might I inquire if the enterprise you're involved with requires other participants? I am currently available for hire, sir."

The young man studied Gaston with a dubious frown. "I would judge you are somewhat *old* for the line of work I am engaged with, sir. Furthermore, I am also a veteran of the

Russian campaign, sir. My colleagues bring similar experience and reliability."

Mustering profound and dramatic indignation, Gaston spoke: "Russian campaign? *I*, sir, *I* marched with Napoleon to Borodino, and then back to Paris. I suffered the cold winter attacks of Cossacks in the dead of night. I stood at the bridge to wait my turn as the wolves of death gnawed at the perimeter while Napoleon's coach took him swiftly back to Paris, *sir*. What regiment were you with?"

"The Fourth Lancers, a first corporal. I am Lucien Bonard," the man replied dutifully, now reflecting a whisper of respect for an apparent brother-in-arms with experience seemingly comparable to his own.

"And I was with the 5th Legion of the *Grande Armée*, a master sergeant. We were in Borisov together."

The name produced a shudder on the corporal's face as he shook his head remembering the cold horrific nightmare of November, 1812.

Gaston continued his personal experience of the events. "General Chichagov with his Russian artillery batteries and infantry blocked our crossing of the Berezina River, as the bitter cold, snow and timber wolves picked off our brethren the cursed Russian guerrillas did not get. After Napoleon's engineers built the two trestle bridges over the river, your regiment was one of the first to traverse the bridge. Do you remember, Corporal?"

"I remember, Sergeant," the man admitted, not wanting to relive the experience.

"My battalion stayed and fought a rear-guard while your men went on ahead as part of the guard detachment who occupied Borisov... You remember that detail? While we stayed deep in Russia fighting the battles, you and your men were spared the horrors of ragged slaughter my brothers and I faced. We fought so you and others could pass across the bridge safely, *sir*. Thirteen thousand Frenchmen never crossed that river," Gaston declared with grave, stony emphasis. Gaston continued to speak, after staring at the corporal for a long uncomfortable pause as the barmaid filled his tankard. "So please spare me your pompous preaching about experience and reliability. *My* brothers-in-arms saved your hides, *sir*. The way I see it, you're in my debt."

After an uncomfortable pause, Gaston smiled and abruptly raised his cup to toast the now humbled bounty agent with a broad smile and a brisk slap on the back.

"To survival, sir! We're brothers in that, we are!" he declared with robust laughter.

Gaston invited the man to join him to drink to the campaigns they had both endured. And in time, the bounty agent—Lucien Bonard—revealed a bit more of his mission. He was a good cavalry veteran, hired by parties whose exact identity remained somewhat unclear, but whose cause for France was just—and they paid well, he insisted.

Bonard represented himself to be a man of decisive action; and if he found the party in question, he stood ready to take him into custody for a handsome bounty. Being an enemy of France only made the task more gratifying and rewarding to him.

The old veteran praised Lucien's good fortune. "Indeed young man you're lucky to have such lucrative employment in such uncertain times. With such a weighty responsibility, I have to assume you travel with others pursuing the same fugitive. One man hunting down this nefarious character simply does not seem like enough manpower."

"Indeed you are correct, sir. We travel in pairs. As we speak, another rider such as myself canvases the taverns, markets and public places on the western side of the city while I cover the east. We'll find this enemy of France, though I confess we're not even sure the spy is in Toulouse. Men of my talents and qualifications are spread out all across the southern reaches of this region."

Gaston raised his eyebrows and nodded respectfully. "This is obviously a very important and I dare say dangerous fugitive. What exactly is the spy guilty of, if I might inquire?"

Lucien busied himself with his drink, unable to provide a clear answer. "It is obvious to the more important people above my station to know. For me? I know my job," Bonard declared as he patted the cavalry saber on his belt, indicating his readiness for whatever trouble this character might respond with, should he ever encounter the man and be required to face the challenge.

Gaston plied the young man with more drink, and learned Lucien would meet his confederate at the fountain in the main market of the town, at the tolling of the ninth hour.

If for any reason one hunter located their quarry, the other would ride north to pass the word to the rest of their network, so they could assemble in the most effective manner to apprehend the fugitive. Failure to make the rendezvous would require the remaining man to ride north as well, reporting that possible trouble was afoot. Gaston then brought up the subject of possible employment again.

"With a fugitive so important, with bounty hunters everywhere, might there be a possibility for someone of my own background and qualifications to gain employment with these men in a cause so worthy and frankly lucrative?"

"I'm sorry, but I cannot encourage you, Sergeant. Everyone had to come recommended to the group, to assure a member's reliability."

"There we go with the reliability story again, lad! Was I not reliable enough to save your hide back at the Berezina River?" Gaston challenged the younger veteran. "I don't believe I even heard a 'thank you' from you, as a matter of fact."

"Your service was indeed noble, Sergeant. We all made sacrifices," Bonard countered.

"Then it would appear 'reliable' in this case might mean providing dependable and valuable assistance. Do you know the city, sir? Do you know the haunts spies such as the one you seek might be frequenting? Certainly not a place like this! It's far too public. I know of a couple of smaller, out of the way, establishments where particular undesirables feel safe from prying eyes to meet with certain international types to conduct their business in more of a secret setting. Would providing this kind of knowledge help establish someone as myself as possibly being worthy and reliable?"

"You know of such places, Sergeant?" Bonard inquired with feigned indifference, determined to mask his avid interest in this information.

"I know because I've been here through the years, and I admit not all of my endeavors have been completely above the board, so to speak," Gaston confessed with a light chuckle. "One man's import and export business is another man's smuggling operation. It's all a matter of perspective, I say. So do you want my help or not? You might be needing someone to watch your back as well." Gaston smiled conspiratorially as he poured out more wine while Bonard glanced around the room, feeling as though the quarry he sought was most likely not here.

"Well, I don't know…" Bonard replied doubtfully.

"I've been completely honest with you, lad. And I'm clearly interested in the possibly of gaining employment with your colleagues. But to do so, I must prove my worth to you. Am I correct? The only way I know how is to show you the best places to do the work you came here for. And I'd also give you some advice on how to do it," Gaston explained with an air of fatherly advice.

"What advice might that be?" Lucien replied, reluctantly taking the bait.

"First you don't go announcing it like some town crier. You must size a room up first. Find the right person to talk to, and be ready to grease a palm or two. It doesn't take much, especially with the potential rewards being so large."

Gaston saw Lucien nodding slightly, recognizing the value of the advice. At this moment Gaston began to stand, as he slapped coins down on the table, paying for their refreshment.

"I can see you're an important and busy man. I'll delay you no longer with the jabbering tongue of an old veteran. I wish you good fortune in your mission, sir." Gaston started to move off, but Lucien respectfully took him by the arm.

"No, please wait, Sergeant."

Gaston smiled back with warm accommodation as he glanced lightly over at the leather seller who just took a deep drink from his wine, glanced around the room, and met eyes with Gaston for a moment. If recognition registered in his distracted eyes, it was difficult to confirm. The bearded merchant's gaze moved on as he took another drink, ogled a pretty maiden passing and smiled lasciviously, muttering something to himself.

A short time later, Gaston guided Lucien to a corner leading into a narrow alley cast in shadows. The crooked passageway built in medieval times only allowed a clear view of the way for about twenty yards. Gaston gestured for Lucien to go first. Lucien hesitated, his instincts wiser than his conscious behavior.

"This is the place? It looks deserted to me," Lucien challenged his new companion.

"Indeed, as it should, Corporal. An establishment of this nature doesn't advertise itself. Patrons come only because they know of its location and its... personality." Gaston smiled and winked, his head tilting slightly. "Are we feeling afraid to go further, lad? That's fine. I'll let you go then, wish you the best of luck on your quest, and I'll resume my study of another jug of wine." Gaston began to turn and walk away.

"No. I'm not afraid," the corporal insisted, though his body language said otherwise. Out on the open battlefield, where enemies were visible, and one was on horseback, and shoulder to shoulder with his brothers-in-arms, was one thing. Standing at the gateway to some unknown underworld was another. An inner voice told him to walk away, but pride overruled him—as nerve signals flashed from the hackles at the back of his neck—and he stepped ahead of Gaston to lead the way.

Just after passing the crook in the alleyway, losing sight of the street they came from, Gaston gestured to an old greasy doorway two steps down off the alley. "Knock loudly once, with confidence, then three soft ones, lad. That's the code. And when the man answers, tell him: 'I come bearing a gift for the Huntsman.' Make sure your hands are in sight and empty."

Turning his back to Gaston, Lucien climbed down the two steps as instructed, knocked loudly, and then softly: No answer. After a pause he knocked again in the same sequence. It brought the same result. Before Lucien could knock again, Gaston spoke.

"I'm truly sorry to have led you here, lad. But I really had no choice."

Expecting the worst and immediately recognizing the disadvantage of his position, two steps down and hemmed in by the cramped entryway, Lucien turned quickly with alarm.

He saw Gaston standing in a relaxed manner, with a warm, yet regretful look on his face. Lucien's right hand instinctively reached for the handle of his sword. Gaston observed this with a perplexing lack of surprise. The very nature of his animal sense of ease unnerved Lucien, who spoke with tense indignation.

"What's your game, sir? I expect you see that only one of us is armed, which puts you at a severe disadvantage," Lucien insisted.

Gaston shook his head slightly with sincere sadness.

"This contest was lost almost an hour ago, lad. The rest is up to you."

"What are you speaking of?" Lucien demanded.

"The man you seek is my master. And I cannot allow you to proceed with your mission. There are two ways to do this. I'll escort you to your horse as the ninth hour rings, watch you ride over the Pont Neuf, and to the safety of your destiny. For you to do so, I would require you to pledge, on your honor as a fellow brother-in-arms, never to return to these environs and this mission again. The alternative, of course, is to risk an ugly end to your pitiful life story. Even if you accept, it puts me at a disadvantage, because you could return and raise an alarm. But I sense deep down you are a man of honor, despite the bad company you have allowed yourself to become entangled with. My master, on the other hand, is above reproach, and worthy of the ultimate loyalty. The choice is yours, lad."

"The man is a spy and a criminal and must be taken into custody," Lucien insisted, deliberating how he should draw his sword in the tight confines of the doorway.

"And who tells you this?" Gaston inquired, scratching his beard casually.

"Those who employ me! We cannot allow traitors in our midst who have designs on the fall of France," Lucien pronounced, as he glanced up and down the alley to see any hope of other witnesses or possible strategic advantage. None existed.

"We shall not haggle tonight, lad. I'll make the offer once again, otherwise we'll need to get on with it and end this ugly business," Gaston said with sincere regret.

"But you have no weapon! Surrender yourself to me,

take me to your master, and it will not lead to bloodshed," Lucien protested, as he quickly drew his sword, getting ready for battle, lowering his stance into a crouch.

"So you're challenging me then, Corporal?" Gaston said with mild amusement as a passionate fire in his eyes began to smolder. "Bad idea."

A moment of impasse occurred, where doubt deepened in Lucien's consciousness, exactly at the same time Gaston arrived at an even more animal state of relaxedness. Infuriatingly, the old war veteran let out a loud thundering belch just as Lucien deliberated his next move. It set the ex-cavalryman off on a desperately aggressive attack, as he charged up the stairs, with a rise of his blade intending a sharp downstroke of the sabre, targeted on the skull. Surprisingly, Gaston spun around, avoiding the strike, knocking Lucien's sword hand askew and slapping the corporal soundly across the face with his other hand as he did.

"Last chance, lad. Think of your mother," Gaston spoke as he stood facing his opponent in the narrow alley, now off to Lucien's left side, away from the bounty agent's sword arm.

Somewhat flustered but experiencing a proud, indignant anger, Lucien pivoted and renewed his attack, unfortunately more desperate and ill-considered. Gaston's response was agile and precise. Deftly blocking the sword attack once again, his open hands then rapidly thrust forward to either side of Lucien's face, roughly grasping the skull; and before his prey could react, Gaston robustly rotated his wrists in a quick snapping motion. The result was a single and sickening crack. Lucien fell to the ground, his neck broken.

"I do this for my daughter and my master, so they might continue their destinies in this world. I know I shall burn in hell for my sins… This is merely one more. …I will pray for you and your family, lad," Gaston declared with sincere regret at the dark deed he had just performed.

He dragged Lucien to a nearby sewer drain grate, which he had spied earlier, and opened it. With little difficulty, he lifted his fallen opponent into the opening and let him slide into it. As the corporal disappeared from view, Gaston closed the grate and looked at it.

"May you rest in peace, lad. I'm truly, truly sorry… But I *did* offer to let you go."

Sitting at the bottom of a small glazed earthenware bowl, a bead of molten metal the size of a pea had just cooled enough to display its traditional golden luster. Jean-Marc picked up the vessel and let the bead roll around in the bowl, promoting the cooling process even further, till he finally tilted the basin so the pearl of metal dropped into his palm. Satisfied it was cool enough, he picked it up with his index finger and thumb and passed it to Solange, who stared at it in awe.

"You have just made gold, Master. You created gold from a base metal," Solange declared with wonder as she stared at the precious yellow metal in her hand and also at a stone crucible the size and shape of a half-cantaloupe which sat on the worktable in front of them. It stood two-thirds full of red-hot molten gold, slowly cooling and congealing into its traditional solid metallic form.

Jean-Marc gazed at it with some distraction, unimpressed with the feat. "That's something which is no longer remarkable to me, Solange. I've been able to perform this transformation for countless decades now. I prefer to create gold from my own formula—one I developed from various esoteric sources through centuries of trial and error. The result is I am most assured of its purity for further utility in the greater process. That detail of purity is crucial. And the next step is the most critical one. This is where the Book has provided the missing piece of the puzzle, Solange."

"I stand ready to help in whatever manner possible, Master," Solange offered willingly.

Jean-Marc and Solange stood occupied in the rear chamber of the third floor where his chemist's laboratory was set up. Contrasting the front area, a library and study dedicated to books and art, and which held a sense of quiet order to it, this space pulsed with industry. Work benches lined the walls with dozens of shelves containing various ceramic and glass jars, wooden boxes and metal containers which held a vast array of compounds and elements. A blackboard stood on an easel in one corner of the room and bookcases in another. A large main worktable stood in the middle. In a third corner, against the outside wall, a large brick oven was mounted on a raised stone platform—a kiln. Also, in the middle of the room, not far from the work bench, stood a solid bronze oval cistern, the size of a small bathtub, set on bronze feet.

"Exact timing and correct application are now the keys to success, Solange."

Below the small elaborate stained-glass window, which paneled into two separate frames, and reminiscent of the work at Chartres cathedral, were two windows, both open, which allowed the fresh night air in to cool the room. The sizable kiln had a bellows to intensify the heat of the coals burning inside. Jean-Marc gestured to the bellows handles with a concentrated smile.

"Work the handles of the mechanism slowly and deliver a low steady heat to the enterprise at hand. I'll tell you when to stop."

He then took the crucible in a set of iron tongs, and moved to the center of the room. There on the worktable laid the ancient tome *Pupillus et Omnimodus Compendium de Appendices*. Jean-Marc set the crucible near the open book and consulted it, frowning slightly as he reviewed a passage, to reassure a clear reading. The marquis then reached sequentially to a number of glass jars and metal containers on different shelves, taking some orange powder from one, pale green powder from another, and poured an amber oily substance into the crucible. The still red-hot gold flared with flames as it received the new compounds.

This stage of the process complete, he carefully fit a matching cup-like stone cover on top the crucible, capping it. He then positioned metal clamps housed on the crucible over the cap, and then donned thick gloves to tighten the clamp screws to seal the molten gold in its small stone chamber.

The marquis smiled at Solange with a sparkle in his eyes and the spirit of a youth enjoying his favorite pastime. "We are almost there, Solange."

Jean-Marc then carried the vessel with large iron tongs, placed it carefully onto a stone pedestal in the kiln, and closed the metal door which was housed with a slab of light porous stone that insulated the heat. Wiping sweat from his brow, he turned to his companion, offering a gentle touch on her arm as he gazed deep into her eyes.

"We stand at the moment of truth, Solange. For, if my hopes are realized, I shall finally be able to produce the *m'f kazet* which has eluded my achievement for more years than I care to count," Jean-Marc revealed with an eager smile of anticipatory expectation.

" '*M'f kazet*': I don't know this word, Master," Solange replied.

"Ah yes. *M'f kazet* is how it was known in ancient Egypt. More recently, yet still in the not-so-distant past, it has been referred to as the *lapis philosophorum*."

Solange's confident command of Latin was due to the studies of the healing arts her mother involved her in during the last ten years of her life. "*Lapis philosophorum...* You mean the Philosopher's Stone, Master? This has been the myth of alchemists. Despite my teachings, I always thought it an impossibility and considered it really more of a teaching metaphor. I understood it to actually represent the inner journey for refinement of the individual in the quest for ultimate knowledge. That was the real Philosopher's Stone. But as an actual physical object, such a thing never really existed... However, after all that I've seen in the last few days, I can no longer be so convinced of that view."

Jean-Marc revealed a degree of enjoyment with the discussion. "Well observed, Solange. We must not discount the element of the inner journey and its importance. But at the same time, can any of us, with any certainty, know what did not or does not exist?"

"It's well known alchemists sought this for centuries, but

no one ever produced it… that we know of," she observed, then built her statement on a new thought: "But if anyone ever did achieve it… I suppose they wouldn't want to announce their news widely. 'Knowledge is power' Francis Bacon teaches us," Solange observed reflectively.

"Yes!" Jean-Marc affirmed, enjoying the exchange as he continued. "And who bore witness to the actions of all these seekers over the centuries? You only hear the stories of failure. But if ever someone succeeded, would the news be spread across the countryside with joyous acclaim? Or once achieved, would it not be an accomplishment which in the wrong hands could possibly mean unwanted consequences for innocents? Once achieved, might not some see a critical value at keeping it secret at all costs to maintain the supremacy of its advantages? …Beyond the teaching metaphor, what does the *lapis philosophorum* mean to you, Solange?"

"It is the ultimate quest of the alchemist, with an esoteric tradition dating back to Hermes Trismegistus. It's linked to the Egyptian god Thoth, the God of Knowledge… But weren't these details all the things of myth?" she inquired, revealing a hint of confusion in how her learning had been classified in her mind.

"A very honest response, especially for the modern times we live in. Good, Solange. To me, myths are the great stories of long-past events, which more recent men have been at a loss to place in proper context, and so they turn these accounts into something else, to help the mind process and digest. But even in myth, the spark of enduring and immutable truth remains. The trick is finding it and recognizing it… And what is one of the primary properties of the *lapis philosophorum*?" Jean-Marc queried further.

"Eternal life... Master," Solange answered, her eyes narrowing, processing new thoughts.

"And if this is myth, what are the stories of the Bible? Are they myth too?" Jean-Marc asked her gently.

"My father always said the Bible is just an assemblage of stories made to keep the underlings subjugated by the privileged," Solange observed, digressing from the question.

Jean-Marc laughed. "Gaston's statement may not be in complete error. But the roots of the stories—do you believe they're based in some element of truth?"

"I suppose some may be," Solange granted him.

"And what of Methuselah, son of Enoch, who lived 969 years? Or Jared, who lived 962 years? Noah, 950 years? Were these myths, Solange? Or did they know something the men of today do not?"

Solange was intrigued by this line of questioning. It opened a new window of perception in her mind as she recognized all the power of what she thought were myths for so long was alive all around her. It brought a heady feeling, one which made adrenaline surge through her body. Also, the atmosphere of this alchemist's workshop had its effect on her. The smells of the different brewing potions made her light-headed.

"How long have you lived, Master?" she asked tentatively.

"Many, many centuries, Solange."

"It all seems so incredible."

Jean-Marc laughed for a moment, then gestured for her to continue pumping the bellows of the kiln. "You know, the image culture has of alchemy—like that of the

Cathars—has been formed by tales which distort a true understanding of alchemy's gift to mankind. Leonardo da Vinci once told me of a ruse a supposed alchemist—a man named Galeotto—would employ to create the illusion of creating gold. With impressive industry Galeotto would utilize all his alchemist's implements—one of which was a very thick iron rod. And as wealthy investors watched him closely, he would stir his final concoction of a viscous and fiery organic paste which slowly burned away a hidden wooden plug in the end of his iron stirring baton. When the process was done, the paste had burned off, and what remained was the molten gold which ultimately melted out of the hollow iron rod and into the bowl. Galeotto's investors were ecstatic at seeing the creation of gold before their eyes and especially pleased at being given the small piece of gold to take home as proof. But what they left with the alchemist, however, were the funds to keep him busy for months or even years. Yet in the end bargain, he always gave them something of much less monetary value than they gave to him. He was more a showman, a confidence man and a charlatan, not an alchemist. And men like Galeotto damaged the perception of the legitimate and valuable work of others following the true path in the great alchemical pursuit."

Returning his focus to the work before them Jean-Marc studiously referred to a few sections of the Book, then opened the kiln door and adjusted the position of the pedestal holding the crucible with long iron tongs and closed the door again.

Solange's head spun with the sea of information Jean-Marc had shared with her. If she had not witnessed what she did over the last few days, she wondered if she would truly be able to believe in the work being performed in front of her now.

Solange reflected on the thought of the rare privilege she felt with a slight wave of sadness on Roger's behalf, because he had clearly been incapable of believing. At the same time, while Roger spent years with Jean-Marc, none of their shared time brought him in touch with the reality she had experienced firsthand merely in days. The first part, of course, began when she witnessed Jean-Marc initially recover from a certainly fatal gunshot wound to the back, and then again after his collapse off the horse, being reborn in the mineral pools with the aid of the Curé of Boussac.

But other developments made her believe on a much deeper and intuitive level. Because when Jean-Marc had asked her to share her lifeblood with him, to aid in his initial conditional healing, it had not been a one-way affair. Something profound occurred in transference from Jean-Marc to Solange. She sensed it as soon as it happened; but originally she dismissed it, due to the intensified excitement and peril of the moments they faced together. As the day wore on, however, and they finally reached the camp at the dolmen—joining her father and Roger—the distinct feeling of a unique and powerful connection on so many levels did not expire. It grew. At times she even knew what he would say before he said it.

The sensations and the phenomena she experienced as a result of her exceptional and seemingly supernatural connection to Jean-Marc represented a combination of manifestations.

One gave a persistent tingling in her nerves,

accompanied by the slightest itchiness on her skin. Her energy seemed bottomless. For all the hard riding they did on the first few days after the attack by O'Donnell's men, she would normally have been sore and exhausted. Instead she felt she could have gone on for hours.

The self-inflicted wound in the palm of her hand, which she incised to honor Jean-Marc's request, healed completely within a day, with barely a scar remaining. Her need for sleep became significantly diminished. When she slept, she dropped into the deepest sleep and experienced the most powerful dreams.

Solange's dreams became unlike anything she knew in her years up to this point. Instead her dreams—more like visions—were intensely graphic and at times otherworldly. At times she even had the sensation she actually saw events, distant in time or place, as they happened. And these were the dreams Jean-Marc had inquired about.

One recurring dream in particular, which first manifested itself the night of the dolmen, made Jean-Marc take pause. She described it as coming to her at first in shards, broken images out of order, but over time she could piece together a rough narrative for Jean-Marc. She described two men— one always stayed in the shadows, but seemed to wear the vestments of someone high in church office. In front of the cleric stood a bald hulking man, in a monk's dark robes, with a distinctive and wide scar across his skull. His burning eyes exuded a potent malevolence as he stared straight at her; and he raised a thick wooden club, threatening to attack without mercy. Before he did, however, the shadowy bishop spoke inaudibly and gestured something with his hand; and the bald monk desisted, but still maintained his menacing stare. From this recurring dream she always awoke pale with a fright.

Suffice it to say, when she finally saw Brother Jerome in person, blocking their cart's passage on the road, she knew a potent agency she could not explain made these dreams possible. And she had other dreams too. A particularly vivid one depicted the burning of what she surmised to be the Library of Alexandria in ancient Roman times; and these same frightful figures inhabited this world as well.

When first hearing these disturbing dreams described a few days ago, Jean-Marc calmed her more with his comforting and reassuring manner than with his words.

"Ours is a unique chemical wedding, Solange. We're bonded in a way I can only now begin to explain. But the dreams you experience are akin to mine. The fact that you had seen the monk in your dreamscape before you ever encountered him in person is of great significance. These are warnings of a sort and we must remain vigilant. Much of what will come to pass in the days ahead will change your view of reality and the world even further. It's the quote from *Hamlet* that comes to mind—which I once suggested William include in his play: 'There are more things in heaven and earth, Horatio, than are dreamt of in your philosophy.' "

Solange gazed at him in wonder as she pumped the bellows of the furnace. "You knew Ben Franklin, William Shakespeare *and* Leonardo da Vinci?"

"I've known many, many men and women, Solange. But it's not who you know, but what you do with a relationship that defines the meaning of life and our role in it. Do you make the world a better place—even in the smallest seemingly inconsequential way—or do you only pursue your own desires, and in doing so degrade humanity?"

Jean-Marc signaled that her efforts at the bellows could end as he opened the iron door to the furnace, and with long iron tongs placed a second large stone cup into the heat and onto the pedestal. He then closed the door, took over with the bellows and worked them with gusto and an accelerated cadence to the pumping action.

"I now need the fire's temperature to peak for ten minutes," Jean-Marc explained as he worked the bellows more vigorously than Solange had done earlier, maintaining the furnace at a lower level of heat.

As he remained focused on this robust duty, Solange crossed to the ancient tome which laid open on the nearby worktable. Jean-Marc watched her attentively, but without concern. She touched the pages of the book with gentle care, knowing its importance to Jean-Marc.

"And this is what they're after, a simple book?" she asked ingenuously.

"A simple book that contains more precious learning and wisdom than many libraries, Solange. A simple book containing erudition which has not existed in any repository of knowledge since the great Library of Alexandria burned. And this knowledge in the wrong hands could deliver pain for too many innocents. In the right hands, it remains a profound responsibility which cannot be taken lightly."

"And yours are the right hands, Master?"

"At present they are. All things pass with time. At some point, this will go to another. But for now, I have work I must complete. And I fear our time in this place as well is very limited. Your dreams of the monk and the bishop echo my own. I feel they are both drawing very near."

"And does Roger know of this place?" Solange asked.

Pausing momentarily at the bellows, the question compelled Jean-Marc into a manner of sober reflection and concern. "He's never been here, although he's been to many other of my holdings. However, I have received correspondence from Loïc in the past. If Roger had been observant of particular details in my communications, he might very well be aware this general location is part of my story. As you know, our current plans for a rendezvous with Roger in Venice were made with a spirit of flexibility, so in all likelihood he would be required to wait for us further east, in Italy, and encouraging a perception that our general location might be closer to that region. His manner on the night preceding the attack at the dolmen, however, deeply troubled me. I readily admit that. As always, and despite my many years walking this earth, I'm grateful for your father's seasoned instincts. From the beginning, Gaston counseled against allowing Roger to come too close to my affairs. I could not disagree with him. But I also saw so much hope and raw potential in Roger, that I thought, I wished, my influence might help him turn the corner of his destiny. Some people are given gifts, but are too blind to understand their value until after the gifts can no longer be useful. I fear this may be the case with Roger."

With that, Jean-Marc returned his attention to the furnace, turning an hour glass on a shelf nearby, and writing short notes in a notebook on the workbench next to the ancient book.

"May I?" Solange asked. She indicated a request to examine more closely the pages of the book which traveled so far and so long to arrive at its current location. This was the first occasion she felt comfortable to make this request. Up to this point Jean-Marc had kept the tome for his exclusive reference.

Jean-Marc glanced at her as he returned to pump the bellows of the furnace, smiled slightly and nodded.

Knowing that extreme care was a critical consideration in handling the codex, she turned the ancient parchment leaves of the book with cautious respect, growing fascination and reverent wonder. What she discovered staggered her with a recognition of how much she did not know—how, despite her learning in a vast curriculum of scholarship, it could only be considered the beginning of a very long path.

Originally, only weeks ago, she prided herself on the deep understanding and expertise she had acquired in the art of healing and medicine, mentored by her mother. This rigorous learning tradition came with a perspective dating back to the works of Galen, the Roman physician whose writings defined medical practice for over a thousand years. And Solange's education included the rich historical context of this knowledge, which gave her a unique and profound perspective on the known collective wisdom of mankind which was rare for men of learning in her age, and unheard of among most women.

In addition, she researched extensively the works of Philippus Aureolus Theophrastus Bombastus von Hohenheim—better known as Paracelsus—who led a revolution in modern medicinal thought based on his pioneering alchemical discoveries. As well, Solange studied history and many other great figures of the world's wisdom, including sages of Asia, which in her mind at least, gave her a sophisticated grounding in the erudition of the mankind.

Up to this point, when she encountered a piece of information she did not know, she at least knew what shelf in her mind to put the new knowledge. Solange had a very orderly method of classifying topics of learning and understanding of the world and the cosmos. But this ancient book changed all the rules of information correlation she had constructed in her mind, even with the aid of her mother's guidance. Quite accustomed to seeing ancient tomes, and attacking new systems of thought, this book simply astounded her.

Written in seven languages, three of which were dead tongues (hieroglyphic Egyptian, Latin and Aramaic)—and one she could simply not identify at all—it included a collection of different symbol systems which were not familiar to her. The book was, from what she could surmise, a compendium of extensive arcane knowledge. Included too were exotic renderings of symbols, some of which she recognized as part of the alchemist's world. The highly organized and conventional side of her mind strived to make sense of it all, with minor success.

Yet as she relaxed and allowed her intuitive mind to view the book, she sensed the messages therein were conveyed in many layers and platforms of communication, including both literal and symbolic. Solange glanced up from the *Pupillus et Omnimodus Compendium de Appendices* and peered over at her 'chemical wedding' husband in a new light—with a sense of astonished admiration and some concern.

Through the open casements, beneath the round blue stained glass window of Jean-Marc's laboratory, the bell of the Eglise des Jacobins began to ring the hour.

At the tolling of the ninth hour, the marketplace of Toulouse was deserted—a wide, empty space paved with cobblestone. A lone man sat at the public fountain, glancing here and there somewhat impatiently, seeming to expect someone's arrival.

Gaston chose his approach with care, from the figure's right blind side. To a casual observer, however, the old veteran appeared as a man deep into his cups, feeling no pain. Gaston loudly sang a bawdy old ditty from the Army, while interrupting himself with mirthful commentary to no one in particular, as he made his way, with the occasional misstep and stagger, across the market square, not necessarily in the direction of the fountain, but closing the general range and bearing covertly with deadly intent. As he approached, Gaston feigned discovery of his target.

"Ah! I spy one who appreciates the finer privileges of life," he laughed with a slur, then continued. "...And possibly a patron of the arts! I too am a lover of the fine arts! But alas, I am lacking a patron," Gaston laughed again. "But Providence provides for those who are humble and thankful!"

The lone figure at the fountain craned his neck to observe the approaching miscreant behind him, and his manner plainly vexed at this unexpected drunkard's approach. Shaking his head, the man at the fountain attempted to communicate through a dismissive hand gesture and body language to the approaching denizen his disapproval and non-intention to engage. Seemingly encouraged, however, Gaston approached now with the manner of one discovering a long lost friend.

"Kind, sir! It's divine fate that God has placed you here to assist this poor humble soul in dire need of spiritual sustenance! I only require one franc, noble sir, and I'll be on my way!" Gaston pledged, with an encouraging and assuring manner. As he spoke, he continued to close the distance with his target from behind.

"Be gone, drunkard!" the man barked, attempting to display a ferocity of intent, which Gaston ignored completely with a besotted grin and a hale and hearty manner of comradeship.

"...And gone I *shall* be, honoring your sacred and esteemed wishes, my *good* lord! But hast thou forgotten your implicit, albeit silent pledge to support the art of living? Hast thou lost thine honor, sir? A simple tithe of eternal brotherhood would render this sacred transaction complete. Without it, I am a ship adrift, sir! I'm a man lost on the jagged and rocky shoreline of a cruel destiny! A thespian without a stage! I shall be honored to render any Molière soliloquy upon request, if only for a small tithe to keep me going, to honor the timeless thespianic pantheon which dates back to Sophocles, Euripides and Aristophanes!"

Gaston bowed as he spoke with flowery elegance and rising passion, again somewhat slurred by seeming drunkenness. And with this last action, he brought himself almost within arm's reach of this as yet unsuspecting prey. Gaston's hand slid toward the handle of his newly acquired short cutlass, which remained hidden under his loose coat, as he chose his angle of advance representing the most awkward one for his opponent to draw his own sword in defense.

"Just a franc coin, for a fellow artist of life, or possibly a fellow Army veteran, a comrade-in-arms, kind sir?" Gaston requested with a sickly sweetness, mixed with teetering inebriation, composed to irritate and distract his target.

As Gaston closed a bit more distance, his quarry reacted as expected. "Be gone, you pathetic wine-sodden leech! You disgust me! I have no money for you! Now go crawl into the gutter where you belong and die, you scum!" the man at the fountain shouted, making a brusque dismissing gesture, standing and turning his back to Gaston.

Gaston smiled slightly, pleased his subterfuge produced the reaction he hoped and planned.

"But I have something for you in return, sir. Greetings from the underworld, from a dearly departed friend, one Lucien Bonard?"

Always striving to be the honorable man, even in the most treacherous business, Gaston could not kill this man without confirming his association with the bounty hunter and giving him a chance to defend himself. From that point forward, all was fair.

The man spun around in shocked surprise, fumbling to draw his blade from a bad angle, which Gaston had been orchestrating during his advance. Swords were now drawn on both sides. Gaston's opponent frowned for a moment, trying to make sense of his newly identified assailant.

"Who *are* you?" the man demanded of Gaston.

A complete surprise to both combatants, a deep thunderous voice, from the northern far end of the marketplace square, echoed across the medieval plaza.

"What ho? Thibaut and Lucien! What tomfoolery are you engaged in? We're involved with God's work! There's no place or time for idle gaming now!"

Apparently the tableau between Gaston and Thibaut, based on the former's casual stance, and the latter's seemingly comical grappling, had not yet defined itself to the observer at the north end of the square just how serious the business might be between the pair.

Both tentative combatants quickly glanced in the direction of the voice. There on horseback seven riders approached from some fifty meters away. The voice came from the lead rider, a muscular bald man in monk's robes with an ugly scar running the length of his skull. Behind him, even at this distance, Gaston also recognized another member of the party on horseback: Roger.

Both participants by the fountain knew the next instant would be critical for survival, and Gaston had the edge by virtue of his position and intent, one which still forced his opponent to adjust his stance in relation to his challenger.

As Thibaut turned to attack, intending that if he was at worst able to engage his opponent in a contest of strikes and parries, he hoped he might at least delay his attacker and have an advantage with the imminent arrival of superior reinforcements. Thibaut yelled out as he opened his assault.

"To arms! Lucien has been slain!" the man shouted as he pressed his charge against Gaston.

The effort of shouting and opening his attack, while well-reasoned, divided Thibaut's vital focus and energy at this most critical of moments. Easily blocking a downward head strike from Thibaut, Gaston immediately let his short sword follow the motion to a downward sweep to the back of Thibaut's left knee, slicing the outer tendons—a move Gaston had employed with lethal efficiency from Egypt to

Russia.

Crippled and stunned with excruciating pain, Thibaut stumbled, then feebly raised his sword in an uncertain strike, which Gaston swept aside with a kick, then finished his business with a robust thrust straight to the heart. Thibaut crumbled to the cobblestone in a lethal sprawl, his lifeblood oozing from his chest.

"I'm sorry, mate. But I'm afraid, like your friend Lucien, you've kept the wrong company," Gaston muttered, glancing at the rapidly advancing horsemen, now his main priority.

"Attack him! Do not let the spawn of Satan escape!" Brother Jerome roared at his subordinates. His rage intensified, however, as he at this instance recognized Gaston as the fat priest he encountered on the road days earlier.

"Seize that man! He's mine!" the monk bellowed.

The seven horsemen galloped as quickly as possible across the market square, Roger following, with Bruno and Nicco bringing up the rear. Roger rode with a spirit of distinctly less fervor. He gravely wondered what he got himself into, while at the same time, he failed to recognize the target of his group's attack.

Gaston, meanwhile, knew he needed to widen the gap between the attacking company in any way possible. Quickly glancing around the otherwise deserted square, he chose his escape route in direct opposition to the location of Jean-Marc's secret abode.

Gaston's advantage was his familiarity with the medieval, narrow and irregular back streets of Toulouse based on numerous visits to the city with Jean-Marc. Another advantage came from the hunting party's sound. Brother Jerome yelled continuously, and his men shouted back their positions and their status. Even when they were not calling out, their horses' hoof falls on the cobblestone also gave their position on the otherwise silent streets. Residents of the neighborhoods closed their shutters, not wanting to invite attention or involvement.

The struggle for survival was nothing new to Gaston. However, the setting of scrambling like a rat in a large trap contrasted with his earlier life experiences. Gaston knew patience was his secret to success. While they chased him with a wild and hot-blooded lust to avenge the death of their comrade, Gaston choose his shadows and nooks with care, as he pushed himself into a seemly infinitesimal crease in a gap between two buildings, in a narrow passageway shrouded in gloom, allowing his pursuers to ride past him without detection.

It ultimately took him well over forty minutes of valuable time to bait and evade his pursuers to a point far enough away to consider a return to Jean-Marc and his daughter.

Listening carefully to the location of the hunters' distant shouts, Gaston finally felt confident to jog down an alleyway at full tilt, to put as much distance between him and his trackers as possible. He headed south, toward the location of Jean-Marc's refuge. In doing so, he instinctively sensed this refuge was secure only for a small matter of time.

The continuously changing factors of the unexpected taught him over the years that comfort was always temporary. He thought of his daughter Solange's welfare, and this gave him a steely sense of heightened purpose and resolve.

Toulouse, Languedoc, France
21 March, 1815 AD – Midnight Hour

Solange's thoughts swirled. Jean-Marc completed the last of his preparations with the tolling of the midnight hour. He made her an offer which, a week before, she would have thought absolutely impossible. But due to her experiences in the last few days, her certainty of what might be impossible had eroded decisively.

While the preparations Jean-Marc had staged were quite Byzantine, or more correctly, beyond ancient and resolutely esoteric, he patiently explained the purpose of each component step and of the procedure: the metal cylinders with bare copper wires connecting to the bronze basin large enough for her to be immersed completely; the makeup of the chalky-looking water into which he proposed she would enter; and the process of what would ultimately take place. The outcome of the procedure, however, is what made her take serious pause: immortality... eternal life itself.

"It's just about complete, Solange. You feel that in no way you're being pressured or forced, am I correct? This is an invitation which very few in the Ages of Mankind have been offered with a certainty of successful and permanent results. Your life will change entirely. And with this change comes a profound responsibility. Do not enter the basin unless you understand what this means and you accept it," Jean-Marc counseled her with emphatic concern.

"I understand this could be my only opportunity and the rarest of gifts. It's just so much to process, Jean-Marc. So much to think about, so much to reflect on," Solange observed, feeling the events of the evening had sped far beyond her wildest dreams. Her brow furrowed more deeply with concentration and deliberation.

"I know, Solange. When the invitation was extended to me, by my master, it required a leap of faith. And like you, I had only a short amount of time to decide. However, I've had centuries to reflect on the consequences of my decision. At times, I severely regretted it—especially seeing ones you love grow old and pass beyond to their next station. But I feel I've contributed in the way my master needed me to. I feel I've helped to make a difference, for the better of mankind, at certain times... I feel I made the *right* decision... That was the right decision for me, at my time and place. That doesn't mean it is an easy one, Solange. Some of the greatest actions that determined a turning point in the fate of the world were decided in the singular flash of a moment.

While I now have the Book, and I have the materials to repeat this process described in it, I know nothing is certain except what we have now. As we speak, you know people search for me, hunt me. I have what they want. They won't stop. But here and now, we enjoy a rare moment of protection and respite, *and* a very important detail: a celestial convergence—we stand on the threshold of the Vernal Equinox, the first day of spring. This unique opportunity has not presented itself for far too many centuries. Right now, I can invite you to this baptism, as I underwent almost eighteen hundred years ago." Jean-Marc gazed on her with a loving, platonic smile.

"I don't know, Jean-Marc. It's all so strange," Solange confessed with hesitation, feeling both excitement and an intense fear of the unknown.

"That's fine, Solange, maybe some other time. There's an element of somehow *knowing* this is right for you." He regarded her without disappointment, with an understanding and penetrating look, and then continued. "Your father loves you very much. And it would not have been without his permission that I extend this invitation. We've spoken of you for some time; and I have observed you from time to time, without your knowledge, on my various travels. When you were initiated into the *Tekton* Brotherhood ten years ago, a special allowance was made for you, because of the unique strengths you showed to the brethren. The teaching and extraordinary knowledge you've been given were tailored for one with your exclusive endowments. Whether you knew it or not, we all, including your mother, prepared for this exact moment. And I know you're ready… But the decision is yours."

"But what about Roger? Was he not your protégé? Was this not meant for him?" Solange needed to know.

"Roger was always bright and quick-witted, a fast study at almost anything he applied himself to. That was the problem. He *chose* the things to apply himself to, not what I put in his path. He ignored the opportunities to see and interact with the ways of life in a more meaningful way. While I always hoped he might grow in the right way, he never had the depth—the *soul*—to carry this gift. I knew some time ago, that if offered, he'd have used it in the wrong way. He would use it for gain, for advantage. His choices and actions took him away from us. And based on the dreams both you and I had, I fear he's found himself on a very dangerous path, not just for himself, but for all of us. But most of all, he was not anointed as you are. This is why I must offer you this gift here and now, while I know it's still in my control to deliver... Besides, Solange, it is your inheritance and your right."

"My inheritance? What do you mean?" Solange asked, confused.

"Sadly your mother's disappearance occurred before you came of age. And your father felt unqualified to explain it."

"What exactly are you talking about, Jean-Marc?" Solange expressed with a flush of keen bewilderment.

"Through your mother, your legacy stems from the most noble and ancient bloodline. It dates back to when Narbonne was the capital of the Jewish princedom of Septimania, long before the broader region that contained it became commonly referred to as Languedoc. The royal line there cited their lineage directly to the House of David. And it is from this bloodline that the royal houses of France and

England have staked their most ancient and deep foundational roots," he revealed.

Jean-Marc gestured and he led her back to the front part of his third floor abode, to the library, where he took out an old genealogical tome. After a moment's search, he found the notation he sought. He opened the book in front of her, handing it to her, and pointed to a name at the bottom of the list. "Do you recognize the name?" Jean-Marc inquired quietly.

As she studied the book, a frown deepened on Solange's face, then the light of discovery and incredulity appeared. "That's my grandfather's name. And he's linked to Childeric III, the last Merovingian king?"

Jean-Marc nodded. "In the times the great revolution raged across France, any claim to royal blood was too often a liability and dangerous baggage. Your mother never carried royal airs; and when I introduced her to Gaston…" Jean-Marc smiled with fond remembrance, "It seemed a match made in heaven. They were perfect for each other. She understood his work and accepted it; and completely devoted to her, he honored and supported her path which included a prime motivation in life to bring you to your current state of refinement."

"My mother… a royal?" The information overpowered Solange.

"A royal in direct line to the oldest and most venerable bloodlines, Solange. Yet she was also a spiritual leader in influential circles of some consequence. Her presence in the world brought something which made a difference. And she once said, if ever offered, she would accept the invitation I extended to you in an instant. She believed it would give her more time to carry out the work she felt destined to perform. Sadly, Fate had another plan for her."

Solange reflected on her mother as she ran her finger over the entry in the book listing of her grandfather's name.

"I confess I fear the process you described, Master. I accepted the immersion, but opening myself so completely in the way you described… it would kill me, would it not? I can't get it out of my mind."

Jean-Marc smiled slightly. "Do you trust me, Solange?"

"I do, Master, but it's a question of understanding. I don't understand how this occurs, how it can be done." Solange responded, avid to get insight.

"Then I shall show you first. It may not help you understand the 'how' of it, but it will help you understand the 'what' of it."

She gazed at him, eyes widening in wonder and disbelief as she followed him back into the laboratory.

Their search went down too many dead ends in the labyrinthine back streets of Toulouse. Brother Jerome declared the trail of their quarry was cold and that they now wasted valuable time. Rubbing his chin while sitting in the saddle, gazing pensively at the empty streets, he turned to Roger, whose horse stood just a bit behind him.

"Have you been to this city with him in the past, Roger my boy? …And don't hold out on me, because I *will* know."

Brother Jerome's intense quality of questioning Roger over the last few days had revealed an insistent intensity which discouraged silence and hesitation. Traditionally a fast thinker and a charmer in tight situations, Roger now felt intensely uncomfortable with the direction and spirit taken by the group he had become involved with. He struggled to devise an escape plan when Jerome questioned him. Roger hesitated, reluctant to answer, fearing what consequences might lay in his reply. Irked at Roger's lack of responsiveness, Brother Jerome glared at him with unveiled disgust and menace.

"You saw what vile treachery his people unleashed. He surrounds himself with murderers. And if he's not stopped, more innocent Frenchmen and women will die. So whose side are *you* on? Because if you're not with us, you make my job quick and easy." Brother Jerome sneered as he slipped his cudgel out of its long leather sheath lashed onto the front of his saddle. The monk turned the weapon in his hand expectantly—slapping the thick handle in his palm—positioning it more in readiness to use as a lethal club. With his eyebrows raised he gave Roger an open questioning look. "Well, what'll it be, runt? Fresh meat for the stray dogs of Toulouse? Or have you got something to offer me?"

Roger blanched with anticipation, grasping for some memory that might give him a moment's respite from Brother Jerome's imminent threat.

"I've actually never been here, I'm sorry... And that's the truth."

Brother Jerome scowled, and a cold, hooded look manifested itself in his eyes as he glanced over at his fellow henchmen. The monk shrugged while Nicco and Bruno smiled with amused anticipation, awaiting what mayhem might transpire next. Nervous, Roger quickly offered the first thing that came to mind.

"I remember he received correspondence from an inn here, from time to time… but not frequently."

Brother Jerome smiled thinly, still holding the cudgel with threatening readiness. "The name of the place, boy," the bald monk insisted.

"It was a long time ago, I don't know if I can remember," Roger offered weakly.

Brother Jerome's grip on the cudgel tightened as he hit the thick end of the club again into his meaty and muscular palm, making a sickening slapping thud sound. The action took place too close to Roger's skull.

"Maybe you need some help to recall more clearly… something to jar your memory a bit?" Brother Jerome laughed lightly with a sense of amused anticipation of carefree injury to another.

Roger glanced at the part of the cudgel handle facing away from the monk's palm. It had two short sharp, slightly curved, iron spikes facing out of it which looked like claws or fangs. He gave a shudder of dread as he caught his breath involuntarily.

" 'Apples.' The name of the place had something to do with apples," Roger blurted out nervously, trying to remember as he glanced askance at the club which Brother Jerome swung far too close to his face for comfort. "Blue Apples… *Auberge des Pommes Bleues*—Inn of the Blue Apples. That's it. I remember now. A strange name."

"Well done, lad. You're proving to be worthwhile after all, although I admit I had my doubts."

And as Brother Jerome instructed his group to redirect their actions in response to this new intelligence, Roger felt physically ill, wondering for a moment if accepting his own death in the earlier moment, when Brother Jerome's threat was implicit, might have been better for all involved, including himself.

A horse-drawn carriage slid unobtrusively into the city of Toulouse from the north. Having been contacted by Brother Jerome's messenger, the bishop rode alone in the back of his coach, quietly pleased and frankly excited.

With the Book and Jean-Marc both finally in his virtual control, he would have complete mastery of the knowledge of the Book's secrets and the freedom to study it at his own leisure. When it had been in his possession in Alexandria, Egypt centuries ago—while he served as Bishop Theophilus's scribe and then known as Brother Antonius— he capitalized on its ownership as best as possible. With Theophilus's failing eyesight, it had not been entirely difficult to conceal the fact that Brother Antonius had not, as ordered, destroyed the Book originally confiscated from the fugitive the day of their first encounter on a Roman galley just off shore from Alexandria. Instead he had concealed the Book and took it to study in private.

Brother Jerome—then known as Brother Hieronymus— held a blue flask of a mysterious alchemical substance—also part of the possessions carried by the stranger with the white eyebrow and surreptitiously seized by the monk. And as Brother Antonius diligently studied the Book, he came to understand what Brother Hieronymus secretly appropriated was an alchemical compound of astonishing properties— *M'f kazet.*

Ultimately, the scribe had pieced together, as best he could, the process of enacting the gift of immortality elucidated in one section of the Book's pages incorporating the key component of *M'f kazet*. As a result of this revelation, Brother Antonius had no choice but to make a pact with the barbarous monk and forged an alliance of sorts to gain access to the critical and unique substance Brother Jerome retained in his possession.

Antonius's efforts to decode the exact process by which the substance—a strangely benign and innocent-looking fine white powder—was actually created had eluded him, despite his scholarly background in five languages of the Mediterranean. Written in seven languages, the Book also employed a number of arcane symbolic systems for which no references existed. They had all been destroyed in the fires that consumed the great Library of Alexandria on the day Antonius acquired the Book.

Ultimately, aided by his knowledge of different languages, and relying on other occult texts he had stolen before the fire, Brother Antonius pieced the process together, as well as discovered the specifications for and construction of the equipment required to enable the entire alchemical procedure. Brother Jerome and he had agreed to pool their pieces of the process and formula to share in its outcome. They secretly set up his lab in a small storage room hidden in a building not far from the St. Athanasius Church where both brothers were based.

The pair finally underwent the alien procedure, a truly strange experience. And it soon became apparent to both of them that the process they underwent had an unmistakable and lasting effect on their metabolisms. Indeed all their senses intensified drastically, their physical strength multiplied, they became immune to sickness, and their healing properties were shockingly rapid. A test wound of a sword cut on Brother Hieronymus's arm proved it: the incision healed within minutes.

Something else, however, went awry in the alchemical covenant. Three months after their re-birth into immortality, both men underwent a strange, gnawing and fervent hunger neither could explain, which drove them to a state of dysfunctional and desperate distraction. Especially intense— indeed debilitating during the full moon—so powerful was the effect that both Brothers Antonius and Hieronymus were forced to bed for at least five days during the full moon's peak in its cycle.

Studying all the books he could find, which were very few because of the Library's destruction, Brother Antonius's frantic search for understanding ultimately led him to an ancient desert Egyptian sage who lived by himself in a cave overlooking the distant Lower Nile.

This seemingly decrepit old wise man was said to be one of the last who possessed true antediluvian knowledge. Brother Antonius presented himself to the antique mystic, where he tried to conceal the true nature of his visit, asking elliptically about legends Antonius had heard, and what would happen if someone had achieved this immortality, but found themselves cursed with a hunger that could never be properly fed.

The wizened sage stared at him for some time, as though peering through him, and back through the ages. And he then explained that whoever this person might be had been cursed by the 'Full-moon Hunger of Osiris.' When questioned further, the old man became distant and uncooperative. Sensing the mystic knew the cure to his ailment, Brother Antonius pressed him.

The aged savant would not reply, but only spoke of the scourge this curse would bring to the innocents of the land. Where 'no one whose blood ran freely through their veins remained safe' from such an entity… The elder refused to refer to the individual Brother Antonius described as an actual person, a human.

Gazing out into the desert vastness, the mystic observed whoever this might be had become so completely transformed by the process they underwent that they could no longer truly be considered a human. 'Whoever this was would now be both much *more* and very much *less* than a man,' the sage intoned with cryptic obscurity.

Following extensive reflection of the desert mystic's sometimes incoherent ramblings, Brother Antonius came to understand that the blood—human blood—was the key. Yet at the same time, Antonius surrendered to private fears that the alchemical process he underwent might have not been performed precisely as originally designed. A misstep anywhere could have been responsible for his condition. And since he stood quite early on his path of knowledge, he could not be sure. What he did know was he needed to address the maddening and insatiable appetite: the Full-moon Hunger of Osiris.

After sharing his insight into the possible solution with Brother Hieronymus, the ruthless bald monk volunteered to try out the theory. He then found a victim in the back streets of Alexandria, subdued her, took her to an abandoned shed in the desert outside the city walls, slaughtered her, and captured her blood, which he brought back to Brother Antonius in leather wine sacks.

They both drank tentatively at first—but ultimately realized it silenced their gnawing hunger. They subsequently drank more enthusiastically. From that point on, their bond became locked in blood and guilt for centuries to come.

Shortly thereafter, Bishop Theophilus of Alexandria, the scribe's master, discovered the Book in Brother Antonius's quarters. Enraged, he confiscated the tome and decreed that Brother Antonius should be exiled to the most distant and remote church post possible in the Roman Empire— Northern Dacia.

Alone on the ship en route to his new posting, Brother Antonius regretfully accepted the fate of the Book which he assumed had been destroyed soon after its discovery—the fires delivering oblivion, being the originally designated fate for this arcane and forbidden knowledge. So many pages of the tome remained untranslated, despite his diligent, yet covert, efforts on that task.

Onboard the Roman galley taking him to his new posting, as he gazed out to sea and reflected on his new life in exile, he heard that a stowaway had been discovered on board: Brother Hieronymus, his new partner on their unholy path through an uncharted providence.

Their new life in the Roman province of Dacia—a region known in later centuries as Transylvania—they built together and this area provided their base, to which they would always return to regroup in fallow years of activity during their long tenure on this earth. Brother Hieronymus's technique of harvesting their nourishment became more refined over the years, with a macabre sense of enjoyment.

Inspired by night bats who feasted on the blood of cattle, he set upon his own method to harvest, which left a similar signature, a two-fanged mark, but obviously with very different logistics.

After targeting his prey, he would bring them to a solitary location. After punching two holes in the jugular from his cudgel, he would hang them upside down, then drain their blood completely into a large wine amphora, the most suitable vessel for transport. He would wipe the wounds clean and leave his victims in an open field, or elsewhere, where they would ultimately be discovered.

These victims, pale and lifeless, with no trace of where their blood had gone, logically left the imaginations of locals to soar on who or what creature might be responsible. The monk was not shy about adding to the rumors and fervor at local inns, which helped amplify the frantic imaginations at work among the more simple local folk. Such was Brother Hieronymus's monstrous view of entertainment.

Through the following centuries, Brother Antonius's names changed as he gathered wealth and positions, but always maintained one driving goal: to find the fugitive who had escaped them on the galley that day.

While he did not know the man's exact identity—Antonius—now Antonio, had his thoughts on who he might be. He knew: in current times one name that recurred with distinct frequency was the Count de Saint Germain, and more recently the Marquis Jean-Marc Baptiste de Rennes.

Bishop Antonio del Julia y Sangresante suspected these were but two of numerous, likely many, names he had used in recent years. Both these names, especially the former, had been associated with a personal legend of longevity and work involved with some aspect of chemistry—Saint Germain was also famous for his formulas for unique paints and dyes. The tradition of a connection with the ancient practice of alchemy was just a small step behind the veil of this man's life.

Beyond this speculation, the bishop remained certain that if all else failed, at the very least, drinking this man's blood would provide the ultimate nourishment, and possibly the solution to his eternal and age-old hunger. And yet now, knowing the Book had *not* been destroyed fourteen hundred years ago, renewed visions of exploiting all its secrets. Excitement surged back into his reinvigorated and passionate view of the world and how much of it should be rightfully subject to his desires and will.

As the carriage wound through the streets of the city, slowing to take a corner, the bishop could not help but laugh lightly, so pleased at long last to feel as though he would finally possess it all.

Inside the laboratory, and dressed only in a soaking-wet long off-white cotton nightshirt, Jean-Marc sat up from the bronze tub in which the special chalky broth was held.

Solange had been astounded by the fact Jean-Marc had remained submerged in the liquid for well over ten minutes, after exhaling all the air in his lungs and allowing them to fill with the watery solution from the bath.

After exiting the basin, he concluded his demonstration, somewhat indecorously, by gently coughing the contents of his lungs into a bronze urn, and disposing it—not wanting to contaminate the contents of the bath. He turned to Solange with a slight smile.

"Now do you trust me, Solange?"

"I always trusted you, Master… I shall save my questions of how this is possible until later, but I must know: *Who* are you? Please tell me the original name you were known by in this world? And who is the master you speak of? Is he also… like you?"

Jean-Marc looked at her with a beneficent smile as he dried himself off, leaned over to kiss her forehead, and then whispered something in her ear.

Listening avidly, her eyes widened with wonder, mouth slightly agape. She spontaneously dropped to her knees, and then kissed his feet instinctively. He patiently touched her shoulders and beckoned her to stand.

"I take it you now have a better understanding of what the meaning of all this is, Solange?"

At that moment, Gaston entered from the outside room, his manner deeply concerned. "Master, I fear there may be little time left. The bald monk has arrived in the city with six men. More will follow in short order… And Roger rides with them. Only trouble can follow. It's just a question of how long before it breaks upon our doorstep."

Jean-Marc nodded calmly, then turned to Solange. "Well, Solange, it's up to you. The timing is perfect. And this may be our only chance for the foreseeable future. Assembling the equipment and materials I have here this evening took some time to bring together, construct and prepare. I'll be happy to do it again, but as fate too often commands our destinies, I cannot guarantee the future. I can only offer you the 'now' of this opportunity."

After a moment's reflection, Solange replied. "Thank you, Master. I'm ready. Just tell me what to do."

Gaston stood in respectful awe as Jean-Marc instructed her to undress and then slide into the bronze tub so that her feet would be positioned facing the stained glass window. Both he and Gaston stepped into Jean-Marc's atelier to afford her privacy. Just before she disrobed, she glanced back out the doorway where she saw her father gaze at her with a look that reminded her of her childhood: one of affectionate wonder and glowing pride. He then quietly closed the door to the laboratory.

As her garments fell to the floor, she picked them up and placed them on a nearby bench. She stepped over to the tub and felt the water first with her finger. It was warm, virtually the same temperature as her own body, pleasant and welcoming.

She carefully slipped into the bath, her modesty somewhat relieved to see the chalkiness of the water obscured her intimate features. Settling in, she realized her buoyancy in the tub stayed virtually neutral. As she breathed, she felt herself rise slightly to the surface, and as she exhaled, she sank to the bottom. When Solange experienced the smooth surface of the bronze tub, its gentle contours supported her comfortably, and she knew she could spend hours here in this feeling of a protective womb. The design seemed form-fit for her shape. It felt heavenly, and she allowed herself to relax.

"I'm ready," Solange called out to Jean-Marc and her father, who awaited her word on the other side of the doorway.

The door opened. Jean-Marc had, in the meanwhile, changed back into dry clothes. He crossed to her with a sense of compassionate concern for her wellbeing.

"Are you comfortable, Solange?" he inquired.

"Yes, Master," she replied.

"I have a feeling you'll soon no longer feel the need to address me in that way, Solange," Jean-Marc confided.

Jean-Marc attended to last-minute adjustments with his array of equipment as Gaston went to Solange's side at the bronze tub and squeezed her hand briefly with a reassuring nod and smile.

The old warrior then gazed at Jean-Marc's activities, revealing a trace of apprehension. Solange, however, had found a trusting and peaceful place inside herself; and letting her ears slip beneath the water, she listened to her breathing as she shut her eyes in relaxation.

The bell of Eglise des Jacobins had tolled the fourth hour some time ago. The city laid shrouded in silence—at rest—all except for Brother Jerome and his band of mercenaries.

The group of men had grown, with word spreading quickly to the confederates nearby, to assemble at the marketplace fountain at the fourth hour, just as the bishop's carriage also arrived. Some were Spaniards, having been called from the south, across the nearby Pyrenees, and who were part of the bishop's Inquisition private police force. Many had been already stationed forming a perimeter at intersections of the surrounding city blocks, to cut off any hope of escape. Brother Jerome stepped over to the carriage and leaned in.

"Preparations are nearly complete, Master. I've planned to assure there's no possibility of escape. I've also informed all of them the importance of preserving the Book, as well as the fugitive. No bloodshed for him. Anyone else in his company is fair game."

Bishop Antonio del Julia y Sangresante nodded his approval. "Good. And have you made arrangements for where we will take him directly following this? We will require seclusion and privacy."

"I have secured a large estate, to the south, outside the city. It's ours for a month. We can extend our stay if we require," Brother Jerome reported.

"And do we know exactly how many he travels with?" the bishop continued.

Brother Jerome gestured toward Roger, who sat on the fountain studying the group with veiled discomfort. "That one traveled with them only a few days ago and gave their circumstances and location up for a handful of silver. Looks like two. One's a woman, and should be no problem whatsoever. She might even be a bit of a prize for the boys. The other we'll have to watch out for. He's an old war horse and used to seeing action. Good in a mix, it appears, but nothing for me to worry about. A tap or two with my cane, and he'll rest easy with the worms."

"I've warned you of this in the past, Hieronymus: your overconfidence is your weakness. Our man has shown himself ever-resourceful through the years. You know that well. We must always assume he has a surprise or two in store somewhere. Besides his ingenuity, he's quite dangerous. We just saw that in Paris—with duc de St. Pré who's now a pathetic whining stump of a man. Useless to me. And don't forget O'Donnell and his men. This single guard of his is certainly only part of the challenge before you," the bishop warned.

"I remember him like it was yesterday. He was no challenge then, and whatever tricks he's learned in the meanwhile, I've learned a hundred to match and surpass each one, Master. Besides on those occasions, he had the element of surprise working for him. Now it's our advantage," Brother Jerome reassured him.

The bishop only stared at him for a moment, then revealed a momentary flash of impatience. "This is the work of centuries, Hieronymus. Do not fail me. We may never have a chance like this again," he chided the monk. Then with stony finality and command, he intoned, "Bring him to me."

Brother Jerome nodded with an easy smile, then turned and crossed to his band of combatants and huddled with them for one last talk as Roger hung on the outer edge of the throng. His last details imparted, Brother Jerome then pivoted and began to lead the group out of the market, toward the *Auberge des Pommes Bleues.*

Roger followed in dread, weakly wondering what he could do next to undo whatever evil he felt certain would unfold in the following hour. And of this evil he could not deny he now played an integral part, whether he liked it or not.

His normally nimble mind, ever alert for opportunity, had become choked and frozen with gloomy images of death—either his own—or his former master's. He could simply see no way to make this thing right.

As he trailed the deadly squad, Roger's mind continued to race, desperately seeking some chance, any chance for hope. Glancing over his shoulder, he spied Nicco and Bruno, always at his back, always cutting off any opportunity for escape.

Solange lost track of time. The bells of the Eglise des Jacobins rang the fifth hour of the morning, which she heard on the periphery of her perceptions; and they reminded her fleetingly of the world from which she came.

The systematic and phased low-level electric current Jean-Marc applied to the solution she was immersed in seemed to touch every cell of her, inside and out. Closer to her in distance and heart—and as a result more emotionally engaged to her body, soul and spirit—the violin music Jean-Marc performed with masterful skill carried her to places she had forgotten, and places she had never imagined.

So this was how she spent the dawning hours of her 'birthday,' on the first day of spring. Floating just at the surface, in neutral buoyancy, suspended in the bronze tub— her eyes, nose and mouth the only part of her breaking the surface. From her position in the tub, facing the dull dark-blue glow of the stained glass window, she reflected on the overwhelming amount of detail Jean-Marc had shared about the logistics of her alchemical initiation.

The water she laid in had been composed from morning dew collected over years from various parts of Europe and finally assembled here. Along with the last of the ingredients which she helped Jean-Marc prepare in the furnace, additional components of the solution came from primal alchemical elements such as salt, sulfur and mercury. Other substances, prepared in an arcane and ancient formula, included frankincense, the juice of pomegranate, purified petals of a unique rose from Jerusalem, the venom of two different rare African vipers (the two originally appearing on the winged staff of Caduceus), the powderized abdomens of Egyptian scarab beetles, a number of exotic vegetable and animal oils, as well as various scarce herbs and unusual mineral compounds.

Solange smiled privately, picturing herself as a stew for some cannibal feast. She found her emotions rose and fell in the course of this experience, seemingly guided by the strains of the early Baroque music being played—an operatic composition of an Italian master of the seventeenth century—*Lamento d'Arianna* by Claudio Monteverdi.

Solange came to realize, on an unconscious level at first, that the music itself represented an integral part of building the alchemical process designed to synchronize the body, soul and spirit of the individual within the universal cycles at work—to 'hear the spheres of the Universe, and then dance with them' as her mentor observed.

This new reality, new awareness, new sense of being, generated its own electricity inside her which began to migrate to places in her mind, but also her spirit. It all made perfect sense, somehow; and she had, in a way, known it all along.

The heavenly violin music paused for a moment. Jean-Marc came to her side at the tub, as she remained immersed in the primal solution. He quietly explained to her they were approaching the final stage of the procedure.

Jean-Marc poured a new powdered substance into the tub—the *m'f kazet* which they had worked on earlier. It suddenly made the water become more enlivened with an extraordinary effervescence. Next he adjusted the two thick copper wires positioned on either side of the tub which led to two large metal cylinders—Parthian batteries. Jean-Marc described earlier to Solange how these provided a gentle current of lightning. The wires had first been located adjacent to her feet and knees, then moved up and positioned at different stages by her lower abdomen, belly, solar plexus, heart, and throat—covering the five lower chakras. The last position set closely aligned between her eyes and the crown of her head.

Solange could indeed feel now that the water seemed to come alive, creating an animated ferment everywhere. It invigorated and excited her in ways she never imagined possible. She sensed somehow she had *become* the effervescence. In her mind's eye, she remembered her dream of seeing the eyes of all creatures in nature, and how they beheld her with a knowing familiarity, a kinship... and that she was, again, now gazing into the Eye of God.

As this took place, Jean-Marc bowed down gracefully and quietly told her that in this, the final phase, she would need to open herself completely, as he had instructed her: to open herself in 'Body, Mind and Spirit.'

A day ago, she would have imagined this act to be utterly impossible. However, the time Jean-Marc took to explain the unorthodox process, and having her father there in support, as well as the mysterious and remarkable calm energy the substance made her feel, told a deeper, and a somehow higher and simultaneously primal-self inside her, that this was a natural thing to do.

As a flash of survival panic quickly passed, she sank deeper under the surface of the water and proceeded to exhale completely any and all air in her lungs. She then, very tentatively at first, continued to 'breathe' in and out the liquid solution in which she laid immersed.

Bronze handles on either side of her helped her maintain her position submerged beneath the surface as she allowed first a little, then more, liquid into her lungs.

Finally in one spasm and leap of faith, she filled her lungs with the oxygen-rich liquid formula. As she opened her eyes as wide as possible in the chalky solution—also part of Jean-Marc's very specific instructions—Solange had a strange sensation of being in another world, far away in time, dimension and universe.

Amber lights from the room filtered into her field of perception, as powerfully stirring violin music resumed, seeming to galvanize her body and soul to the universal cosmos itself.

He instructed her that when the music concluded its next passage, she should resurface again, with her eyes cast directly into the center of stained glass window, but not before. The substance and the electricity animated every atom of her being and she felt an overwhelming and exhilarating sensation—as though in flight, soaring through the air.

Gaston witnessed all this with a continued sense of reverence and awe. He knew of some wonders which occurred in the realm of alchemy, having observed his wife perform her healing craft in the early years, but nothing compared to this. And the old veteran also knew there certainly was more to heaven and earth than he would ever be capable of dreaming.

Yet now, as he witnessed the last ingredient—the *m'f kazet*—being added to the solution his daughter remained immersed in, he saw the water begin to transform. It turned vibrant, colorful and luminescent and seemed to come to life with the current of power emanating from the wires of the Parthian battery. Gaston stood in profound wonderment.

And as this took place, Jean-Marc calmly peered through a clear pane of glass below in the stained glass window, gauging the timing of the coming sunrise, then took up his violin and resumed playing.

In the solution, the electricity now pulsing near her head, the violin music immediately re-engaged Solange and the currents of her transcendent oversoul.

Jean-Marc had detailed to her the progressions in *Lamento d'Arianna*, the operatic composition he played, and how they would align with her inner journey.

First she would intimately experience the mythic and ardent story of lost love between Theseus and Ariadne. The intensity of that poignancy helped initiate the progression of a successive building of powerful emotions which were integrated into the overall binding of the alchemical formula.

These emotions were a key component that drove the process: from *molle* (the soft beseeching loving force), to *concitat* (the passionate powerful animal force laced with anger and rage), to *moderato* (the reconciliation of fate, acceptance and commitment to move on to destiny). All stages of the music elicited, wrapped and bound her spirit to the purpose and goal of the Great Work.

By experiencing the range of powerful feelings the music evoked, combined with the influence of all the elements of the process Jean-Marc had orchestrated, the final step remained hers, he told her. It could not solely be a journey she was carried on. No, it must be her own chosen horizon—something *she* sought—as the body, soul and spirit became bound into one singular purpose and function—a conscious choice to cross the threshold into the realm of immortality. Solange had to see it, and to believe at the very core of her soul, in her totality, that it was her right and legacy to experience. The last distance laid ahead as hers alone to travel.

The music assisted her on this journey as she felt her deepest emotions usher forth, a combination of something akin to joy, love, victory, and the sensation she had in her dreams when she had the exhilarating experience of flying.

Spontaneously, tears welled up inside her. As she shed them involuntarily into the bath solution, an electro-chemical process occurred, where every fiber of her body tingled with amplified life and receptivity to the strange magical energy which coursed through the solution—a solution she had become one with through her tears.

In this moment she also understood she was One with the Earth as well. Solange knew by virtue of the fact from Jean-Marc's explanation days earlier that the base of the bronze tub she laid in was connected directly to the Earth by a long bronze rod, which passed through the three stories of the building, through the bedrock below it, and joined a seam of iron ore which ran under the city of Toulouse, the location of a very powerful and major magnetic current line. Her energy had been wedded directly to the core of the Earth, and she felt it profoundly.

As Solange underwent this sacred process, she vividly pictured events in her mind's eye, this grand, yet secret, project as though it happened before her in a succession of live moving images—the construction of this building, almost four-hundred and fifty years ago, built by members of the *Tekton* Brotherhood, to the exacting specifications of Jean-Marc. It had all been designed to house his small apartment and this alchemist's chamber with its remarkable properties, all virtually unnoticeable to the outside world, constructed only two windows wide, with no traditional entry to the front street. The building of apartments had all been built for this one, single purpose, to be able to complete this profound sacred procedure. Her tears continued to well, amplifying and intensifying the tingling, electrifying reaction of the solution in which she laid immersed.

Time ceased for Solange. She sensed some spiritual entity in her core being, rising from the bath, floating in air, able to look down on herself, barely visible in the cloudy liquid. Solange knew from her mother, and others, that this was, for some, very much like a near-death experience, yet she had no fear. She took this ethereal opportunity to study the surroundings, as well as her mentor, Jean-Marc, who continued to play the violin.

Solange noticed too that her father stood awestruck and concerned, glancing nervously between Jean-Marc and his daughter submerged in the bronze tub. In the middle of his violin playing, Jean-Marc glanced up and seemed to look directly at her ethereal being, despite the fact she knew she must be invisible, and her physical body completely submerged beneath the opaque solution. She found herself smiling back. He nodded with satisfaction and continued to play with an intensity creating sensations she never knew before.

As the Sun rose, its first light gleamed through the bottom of the round stained glass rose window, specifically designed for this procedure. Around the edges of this circular design sat the symbols of the Zodiac. The majority of the window's center 'canvas' depicted a lovingly crafted representation of Yesu and Mary Magdalene, holding hands across the very center of the window. At their feet three young children embraced them: one girl and two boys. Yesu and Mary's hands joined just above the heart of the window's design which had a small symbol of an Egyptian ankh. The 'eye' of the ankh held a large faceted ruby.

As the Sun's light rose, it engaged the ruby, which began to glow with a forceful luminescent power, and a beam of brilliant crimson light cast itself across the gloom of the chamber. As it did, Jean-Marc stopped the music and spoke softly in Aramaic.

" *'Tailitha cum!'* " he spoke, and then repeated it with much more conviction. " *'Tailitha cum!'* "

Taking her cue, Solange rose from the water, her eyes wide open, and the Sun's ruby ray met these open eyes for an extended and magical moment. She knew to blink now would be to lose some of the transference of power, and she strove to keep her eyes open the entire time... until the sunlight cycled higher, and the beam of ruby light dimmed.

Sustaining this position for some time, Solange was finally overcome by the power of the moment; and she almost fainted, slipping back into the solution in the bronze tub. Gaston quickly helped his daughter out of the alchemical bath and into a robe he had waiting for her.

Jean-Marc gently helped her cough the liquid in her lungs back into the tub. She gazed into his eyes with a faint smile as she breathed in the morning air.

"I felt my spirit fly overhead, Jean-Marc. It was wonderful."

But she was clearly exhausted and needed to close her eyes, as she relaxed, supine, into her father's powerful and loving arms.

"She'll require a great deal of rest. She may very well sleep for days," Jean-Marc observed knowledgably.

Gaston nodded and carried her out of the workshop through Jean-Marc's study and down the steep ladder-stairs to a waiting bed on the second floor.

As he delivered her to the mattress, Gaston felt a sensation something like a series of light static electric shocks emanating from the tips of her fingers and different parts of her body. Solange was like a highly charged battery giving off sparks. She was sound asleep by the time her father laid her down in bed.

A short time before this long-sought alchemical culmination for Solange took place, Brother Jerome's band of rogues arrived at the entrance to *Auberge des Pommes Bleues*, just after the Eglise des Jacobins rang the fifth hour and dawn began to glow on the eastern horizon.

The bald monk motioned for his confederates to hide

out of sight in the nearby shadows. He glanced down the street where the bishop's carriage stood some forty yards away, at a corner. The monk knew the bishop observed intently from his perch in the darkness, eager to finally possess what they sought for so long. Before he knocked at the inn's front door, a thought occurred to the bishop's ruthless red-toothed task master. He turned to two of his men and also gestured to Roger.

"You three—go down that alley and see if there's a back entrance to this place. If so, stand ready for any who might try to escape. You know what's at stake, and you know the orders. The book must be protected. Anyone defending the fugitive is expendable. The quarry must be taken *without* drawing blood."

Already accustomed to commanding secondary squads, Bruno gestured for Roger and Nicco to follow him. Bruno made no effort now to play at the earlier charade that Roger might be their leader. Roger followed somewhat sheepishly, glancing back at Brother Jerome, wondering if he had really sold out his old master so easily and without the true intention to do so. With each step forward, his dread deepened.

With eight men hiding in the gloom, Brother Jerome turned and knocked at the door with respectful restraint. After some moments passed, he knocked again in the same manner. Again, after a reasonable interlude, he knocked once more with the same sense of persistent but considerate moderation. Finally, a voice from within could be heard. It was Loïc.

"I'm coming, I'm coming!"

First, a small security portal on the door protected by a

grill of weathered wrought-iron bars opened, and Loïc peered out. "Yes, what is it you seek?"

Brother Jerome chose his spot in the muted street lighting wisely, assuring that his face and the top of his skull, with its disturbing scar, stayed veiled in the shadows. Hunching just slightly and tilting his head sideways in supplication, he adopted the most helpless and self-effacing manner he could, as he spoke in the softest, apologetic tones possible, making it hard for Loïc to hear clearly.

Brother Jerome showed Loïc a metallic scallop shell emblem sewn onto his robe: the well-known symbol of the 'Shell Pilgrimage' indicating someone on a sacred religious journey, always on foot—to Santiago del Compostella on the far side of the Pyrenees Mountains in nearby Spain.

This sort of traveler had been a common sight in Toulouse for centuries, a main route many took to get to their holy destination on the Iberian Peninsula. Brother Jerome spoke with humility, warmth and charm.

"Kind sir, I've been journeying on foot all night to make up for lost time from an injury I sustained on the road north of here. By the Grace of God—and Jesus our Savior—I ask only a half-day's lodging. I need only to rest for a few hours, and to clean up. I shall be on my way to continue my sacred pilgrimage to Santiago del Compostella before the mid-day meal has begun. I can pay full price for my stay, but I do not want to inconvenience you. If you only had a wooden bench to rest on, that would be sufficient for this sinner's unworthy body, kind sir."

Originally on guard, Loïc's face flashed a warm empathy, and his nod followed a slight smile as he closed the security portal. Unlatching of the lock sounded; the thick oak door opened, revealing Loïc in the dimly lit entry way of the inn. The trusting innkeeper glanced instinctively out into the pre-dawn gloom. Perceiving nothing of concern, he gave a smile and gestured welcome to the large monk.

"The Saint James Path is a sacred pilgrimage, and those who walk it are among the richest in Christendom. Where do you hail from, Brother?"

"My master's travels take me so many places, but I suppose I must consider the lands north of Bucharest, near the city of Sighisorha, my home." And with this last statement, Brother Jerome crossed the threshold into *Auberge des Pommes Bleues*.

Loïc's hospitality was heartfelt. "I see you're far from home, Pilgrim. I have a small room and a hot bath. They will do you wonders."

Having gained deeper entry into the building, Brother Jerome casually slid the handle of his cudgel from its position as a walking aid, to one that facilitated offensive combat. "Thank you, Brother. Your establishment comes highly recommended to me, by an old acquaintance."

"Oh, and who might that be, sir?" Loïc asked amiably.

"He goes by more than one name, but I suspect you might know him as Marquis Jean-Marc Baptiste de Rennes," Brother Jerome replied with an intent and penetrating gaze, very different from the self-effacing persona he adopted only moments earlier.

The flash of alarm would have been imperceptible to most, but it was exactly what Brother Jerome sought to confirm the value of this location and the currency of it as well. He was now certain his quarry laid somewhere near at hand and he smiled slightly.

"You know the man I speak of, yes?"

Loïc covered smoothly, observing thoughtfully, "Hmmm. Marquis de Rennes… I'm sure I'd remember such a figure. You mentioned he had other names?" Loïc angled toward an open cabinet by the door. Before he could reach it, however, Brother Jerome swung his cudgel with surgical precision, striking the innkeeper swiftly and hard in the shoulder, crippling him in stunning pain and leaving two small penetration marks of his twin-pronged 'fangs.' Brother Jerome then roughly took hold of Loïc's neck with forceful command.

"You wouldn't want to be inhospitable to a weary traveler you invited into your lodgings, would you, Brother?" Brother Jerome inquired mockingly. He kept his hand clamped on Loïc's neck and opened the cabinet Jean-Marc's defender had reached for with his free hand, revealing an unsheathed sword, ready for business.

Brother Jerome took it, studied the blade and then casually pushed it slowly into Loïc's lower ribs on his right side, crossing the boundary of flesh, but in a tortuously slow entry. As Loïc cringed in silent pain, the rest of Brother Jerome's shock troops poured in through the doorway, their swords drawn, ready for deadly action.

The monk smiled at their arrival, then turned to the innkeeper, whose primal agony deepened toward despair before the inevitable. Brother Jerome laughed heartily at his prey's misery.

"Oh, I forgot to mention I have a few traveling companions and they'll need to break a few bones. I hope you'll be able to accommodate them."

In the alley behind the *Auberge des Pommes Bleues*, outside the back entrance, two of the three members of Brother Jerome's detachment waited impatiently, frustrated they might be missing out on the action their leader conducted inside.

Nonetheless, they knew better than to act on their own—for example, to try entering from the back door they deduced was the rear entrance to the inn. The bald monk's instructions were explicit. Only be ready for any fugitives trying to exit, to escape, through the door. And for that scenario, the element of surprise remained decisively on their side.

"I just think we played our cards wrong before. We should've volunteered earlier for the all-night duty yesterday. Then we would've been part of the lead party going in with Brother Jerome," Nicco complained.

"Well, maybe you'll look at your lazy habit of wanting to get your sleep a bit differently, eh, Nicco? If we lose out on our fair share of any rewards, I shall blame it all on you," barked Bruno, his more-brash-than-bright sidekick.

Both fretfully practiced drawing their short swords in case of action and re-sheathing them. Bruno studied Nicco's technique with imperious bravado. "Your draw is too weak. Any drunken sot could overtake you. You must cut *as* you draw and then thrust, like this!" Bruno executed a move which demonstrated somewhat less impressive results than his bluster intended. Still, Bruno commanded the alpha position of the pair and he ordered "Nicco, Try it again! Your life may depend on it!"

The duo fundamentally ignored Roger; however, their orders were also clear—keep him close, and don't allow him to run away. Roger observed them with guarded apprehension, idly wondering if he had any chance at all against them, considering the fact he was completely unarmed—Brother Jerome had made sure of that.

While somewhat athletic, Roger was by no means trained in the martial arts, despite Jean-Marc's attempts to give him lessons through the numerous years he spent with the marquis. No, Roger always did things on his terms and kept it comfortable, focused on the leisure his privileged position as the marquis's valet provided. Too much exertion, or work, were pursuits that frankly never interested Roger. Since he was very quick and quite bright, with a sharp memory, Roger felt he had proven his worth a number of times to Jean-Marc. Now he painfully regretted that he never took more advantage of the opportunities Jean-Marc generously offered him through the years of their relationship.

Through the impromptu sword drawing exercises Bruno and Nicco performed in the alley, strains of violin music—muffled from their point of origin some three floors above them—filtered into the alley emanating down from the building across the narrow alley from the inn.

The sword duelists ignored the melody, of course; but after a very short time, Roger realized he recognized this particular composition of music—and the one playing it on the violin as well.

Trying to cover his actions from the distracted pair, Roger casually glanced up to the window which he surmised was the point of origin for the harmonic chords. He spied as well the stained glass window, just as the beams of sunlight hit the ruby center of the glass rose in the design. Roger's eyes widened and his mouth opened slightly in wonder as a realization came to him.

Inside the inn, Brother Jerome had forgone the formalities of interrogating Loïc about the whereabouts of Jean-Marc and opted instead for pummeling the innkeeper with his massive fists first.

Experience told the veteran *Parabolani*—of 'the reckless ones' from ancient Alexandria—that this practice offered a far more productive motivator. Bloodied, Loïc collapsed on the floor without complaint or protest, wincing quietly in pain, bleeding slowly from the sword and cudgel-fang wounds the monk had inflicted earlier out of pure malevolence. The monk was privately impressed by this victim's fortitude and lack of fear when it came to facing his beating.

"Please, sir. What do you want from me?" Loïc asked respectfully.

Brother Jerome licked the blood from his knuckles with savor as he responded with gusto. "I *like* it when a man asks the right questions! Well done! …So then, down to business. Where is he?"

"Who, sir?" Loïc asked plaintively.

This response drew Brother Jerome's ire; but on some level, he sensed the innkeeper might be sacrificing his life to create a delay, and he glanced at his confederates with evaporating patience.

"I try to give a man a chance to do the right thing, and he toys with me, stalls for time." And with that, Brother Jerome seized Loïc by the front of his shirt and roughly hauled him back up to a very uncomfortable eye level, forcefully pulling the collar tight against the back of Loïc's neck in a potentially crippling way. A quick and robust yank would snap his neck.

"I'll ask this question but once. Where is the man known as Count de Saint Germain, also answering to Father Giovanni Baptisti, or Counts Bellamare, Tsagrogy or Surmount, Lord Weldon, General Soltikov, the Marquis de Monteferrat, Chevalier Schöning... or possibly the Marquis Jean-Marc Baptiste de Rennes?"

For years, in his heart and mind, Loïc suspected at some point that his family's good fortune through a number of generations in service to Jean-Marc might come to this. Having reflected on this eventuality more than once in the past, he had also weighed his response, and not without considerable reflection or sober meditation, as he knew his forefathers had done in the past.

"I am sorry, sir. I know not of whom you speak," Loïc replied stoically with a flat fatalism.

Brother Jerome expected this reply; and his response was a thundering downward strike of his cudgel, with the spikes in it pointed forward. Striking Loïc in the neck, the brutal blow was powerful and quick. Loïc's knees buckled in shock as he collapsed to the floor and feebly grabbed at his neck to staunch the flow of oozing blood.

Brother Jerome briefly reflected on his unquenchable passion for delivering death, as another part of him would have enjoyed torturing his victim more. The monk sucked the blood from his cudgel spikes and glanced at his shock troops with an intimidating and searching look. He saw no challengers. The monk occupied himself with rifling through Loïc's effects, the innkeeper helpless to resist. The monk finally found a ring with keys tied to his belt.

"I don't want you wandering off now," Brother Jerome quipped as he stomped on Loïc's knee, breaking it. The wounded man passed out in pain.

"Onward! Our search begins in earnest! No one leaves this establishment alive without my approval!"

And with that, the group headed to the stairway leading to the lodgers' chambers. The search did not take long, since the establishment only had ten rooms. Once inside a second floor room, however, Brother Jerome found himself at a window overlooking the alley.

He peered down to assure Bruno and Nicco were in place and Roger's freedom properly restricted. Then something just above his eye level, across the alleyway, caught his attention.

On the floor above him Brother Jerome noticed that lights were lit behind two narrow windows, where the rest of the building remained dark. The monk's eyes narrowed as he sensed something here was important. He opened the window, giving himself a better vantage; and when he did, he heard, as Roger did, the violin music.

Studying the windows across the way, another detail caught his eye. Multi-colored light emanated through a third smaller window, which stood above and between the others. While the frame for it on the exterior was rectangular—comparatively inconspicuous—like the rest of the windows in the building, he saw that inside the casing and exterior glass a second window behind it was framed by another portal. This inner concealed window was round, and comprised of colorful stained glass which glowed from the inside—a small rose window matching the style of the great Gothic cathedrals. Morning sunlight had just finished hitting the small window, and the red jewel in the center ceased glowing.

Below in the alley, as Nicco and Bruno continued their martial arts training, Roger peered up to see Brother Jerome open the window as his attention was directed to the location Roger *knew* was where his master was. The monk glanced at him and then disappeared back inside the inn.

The monk stormed back down the stairs and went to where Loïc remained unconscious on the floor. He shook the innkeeper till he roused the man.

"Give me *all* the keys! I want access to the property across the alley!" the monk demanded.

Getting no response, Brother Jerome roughly searched Loïc, tearing open his shirt, and found a smaller, separate set of keys hanging from a leather strap around his bloody neck. As the monk ripped it off, he shouted, "Show me which one opens the door across the alley!"

Loïc's expression blanched and Brother Jerome knew for certain that one of the keys in his hand opened the door to his unsuspecting quarry.

The *Parabolani* monk swung his spiked cudgel swiftly, striking Loïc with sickening force on his temple, causing an ugly double-gash to slash open on the side of his head. The innkeeper toppled over onto the floor, shuddering involuntarily in the last spasms before death.

Brother Jerome again casually licked the blood off his

spikes and then headed through the tavern section of the inn, calling his men to muster. Once all his forces rejoined him, he quickly and quietly led them to the back of the inn where he finally located the back door opening out onto the alleyway.

Roger noticed the violin playing above him had just ended as he heard the latch on the alley door being manipulated from inside. Nicco and Bruno heard it too; and they crouched in readiness, their swords drawn toward the opening of the back door.

With their backs fully turned to Roger, this gave him just a moment to step further away, toward the small door leading into Jean-Marc's apartments. As he moved as silently as possible, he reached into his pocket, searching desperately for something, anything that might prove helpful in the moment. He found the key to the Paris apartment, which he had neglected to return to the landlord before their hasty departure many days earlier. His eyes widened with inspiration.

As Brother Jerome passed through the doorway, he sneered at Nicco and Bruno. "Stand down. Has anyone passed through this door?"

"No, sir!" Nicco replied dutifully.

Brother Jerome peered over at Roger, who had by now repositioned himself more to the center of the narrow alley, away from the door. The bald commander gestured to one of his men. "Report our location to the bishop. Now."

The mercenary ran up the alley and out of sight. With the keys in hand, the monk crossed to the small doorway, nearly invisible in the deep shadows of the early morning light.

"Bring me a lamp. Now," the monk commanded quietly,

but with seething impatience and vehemence.

One of the men ran back into the inn. When he returned with a lantern, Brother Jerome studied the small ring of keys, looking for the one which most closely matched the lock aperture on the small thick wooden door. Yet as he tried the likely key it failed to gain entrance to the key hole. Gesturing for the light to be brought closer, Brother Jerome pulled a dagger from his robes and probed the opening to the lock with mounting frustration.

"There's a key in this lock, broken off. The lock's useless."

Suspicion immediately penetrated the monk's wary mind. He turned his ruthless gaze to Roger, then to Nicco and Bruno, and then gestured impatiently toward Roger when he spoke to the pair.

"Was he ever out of your sight? Was he over here at any time? Speak!" Brother Jerome demanded.

Both Nicco and Bruno were at a loss for words, recognizing that ugly consequences could result for the wrong answer. Brother Jerome quickly became impatient.

"Come now. Out with it, you idiots!"

Bruno ventured his assessment: "I did not see him go there, sir. And we kept him close to us at all times."

"Did you ever turn your back on him for the shortest time?" the monk demanded.

Nicco ventured his reply. "Not for a second, sir!" Then a thought occurred to him and Brother Jerome saw it.

"What? And be quick, fool!" the bald monk spat impatiently.

"When you came through the door, sir. We heard you first and prepared for action. We didn't know who it was.

Both of us stood ready to seize whoever came through. All our attention was on the door, sir."

Bruno added his point of view. "Yes, sir. It's remotely possible he could've been out of our sight for a short instance, sir. But certainly not long enough to escape."

Brother Jerome had the evidence he needed and stepped over to Roger, swinging his cudgel in a threatening manner.

"I'm beginning to think your usefulness has run out, toad. I don't even care about confirming you've done this. I'll just finish it here, and let my lads empty your pockets of the gold you're still carrying."

Roger soberly considered his next move, recognizing any hope of escape was fundamentally lost. He noticed Brother Jerome's men salivating at the prospect of inheriting his portable wealth.

"Ah, maybe these lads have just the solution to our problems!" an unfamiliar, yet jovial, and somewhat inebriated, voice came with a laugh from down the alley.

Roger, Brother Jerome and his troops peered up the narrow passageway where the silhouettes of three men, their arms around each other, staggering in laughter and apparent drunkenness, made their way toward them. The middle one, who had called out, raised his hand welcoming them. It was Lieutenant Jean-Luc Glastre.

Having reached the city market on the tolling of the ninth hour, from yet another approach than Brother Jerome's force, he witnessed Gaston's attack on the agent waiting to rendezvous. Then shadowing Brother Jerome and his men in response, Napoleon's officer determined now was the time for decisive action.

The lieutenant had been sizing up his opposition the

whole time, soberly assessing the fighting power of the monk and his men, and left lacking the assurance of his small team's prospects for success. He and his two men faced a force of seven, though one seemed reluctant, possibly a captive. That left a ratio of almost two to one.

The opposition, from Glastre's military perspective, all seemed to have a rough-and-ready manner, the type whose body language communicated an animal readiness to fight and kill. And the strange monk represented a different evaluation altogether. Despite his religious garb, the way he carried himself spoke nothing of humility or service to humanity. And now, seeing his clear manner of intimidation to his subordinates, and the threat he conveyed to the seventh member of the party, Roger, Lt. Glastre knew this was not a character to take lightly in any way.

The lieutenant's best strategy was to get his men bunched together in a tight formation and feign an all-night drinking bout. Their close proximity also helped conceal their weaponry.

"Hail to my brothers in the eternal celebration of Dionysus and wine! We seek continued and divine refreshment! We've been turned out of the last establishment, even though we have good money to pay," Jean-Luc announced loudly, pulling out a leather pouch from his belt, and shaking it, allowing some of the gold coins to fall onto the pavement, which he did not even seem to notice. "So is this the back entrance to the inn? Is this where we can pick up where we left off? We're already getting very thirsty for an eleventh round!" Glastre declared with jovial expectation.

The clattering coins immediately took Brother Jerome's

men off guard—reflexively distracting them—causing them to anticipate the opportunity of easy prey coming their way. Bruno and Nicco edged toward the shortest line of approach to the fallen money as Jean-Luc and his men staggered closer.

"Nothing here for you, boys! No wine. Now off with you!" Brother Jerome barked brusquely, making a rude gesture for them to leave immediately.

At these close quarters, the monk's visage was even more fearsome than Jean-Luc glimpsed in the muted light of the streets of Toulouse while he had earlier shadowed him. But the lieutenant had served in Russia with Napoleon. He had endured the fearsome nightmares of that ill-fated campaign. He survived his share of harrowing gauntlets there. On this mission in particular, he stood prepared to go the ultimate distance because of the sacred debt he owed. He believed with certainty that the marquis was close at hand and these men blocked any hope of access to him.

Glastre also noticed that Roger glanced at him hopefully with this momentary distraction from the grave business at hand. Noting he had successfully split some of the monk's forces with the fallen money ploy, Lieutenant Glastre's jovial manner dropped; and his two compatriots stood widening their stances, as their commander stepped forward facing Brother Jerome. As he did, his two men revealed they were both armed with two pistols. One faced Bruno and Nicco, covering them with one gun, his other pistol was pointed in support of restraining the larger group standing with the monk which Jean-Luc's second man covered with his two weapons. Brother Jerome sneered at this new development.

"Looks like some form of illegal activity. What's going on, Citizen?" Lieutenant Glastre's manner adopted a completely official and professional bearing, and showed not the slightest trace of intimidation by the larger numbers his group faced. Having drawn pistols first, the advantage was with Napoleon's man.

An instinctive chameleon with centuries of experience, Brother Jerome adopted a friendly, accommodating manner.

"I was thinking to myself, I might need some extra help! I'll pay you and your lads five gold *soldi* each for the time well spent. Shall we shake on it?" Brother Jerome stepped toward the lieutenant.

The lieutenant drew his pistol, leveling it with lethal accuracy, targeting it in the monk's direction. "Stand your ground, Pilgrim. I have further inquiries to make." The lieutenant studied Roger for a moment, and then gestured to him. "You, what's your story? You don't look like you're with them. Is that true?"

Roger weighed his alternatives, uncertain which way the winds of fate might blow for him. As Roger faltered in providing a reply, the monk interjected, still trying the camaraderie angle.

"Brother, we're all just trying to make a living, and it seems like you three could maybe use the employment. My master pays well and handsomely rewards those loyal to him. There's plenty of opportunity for you beyond tonight."

Unsure exactly who Lt. Glastre was, Roger's hesitation held until the sound of horse hooves on pavement echoed down the alley. Jean-Luc gestured for his men to stay calm and hold their ground as the bishop's carriage edged into view.

The horses were led by the man Brother Jerome sent off earlier. The carriage came to a halt. After a moment, the door to the carriage opened. The bishop stepped out, wearing his pontifical cap, and shedding his outer garment of warmth which had originally obscured his rank of office in the church. Lt. Glastre and his men frowned with uncertainty at this development, but still maintained their armed readiness.

Accustomed to taking the command and initiative in all instances, the bishop spoke directly to Lt. Glastre with compelling authority. "What is the nature of your business here, young man?"

Unintimidated, Jean-Luc maintained his steady stare and displayed his vigilance and readiness to respond with force if necessary. "And I can rightly ask you the same question, Your Grace. With all due respect, what are *you* doing here?"

Showing impatience at being challenged in this way, or any way for that matter, the bishop replied with a manner he often used in the past, suggesting his empowered tolerance was thinning by the second.

"These men are here on my business. We've been tracking down a smuggler, a dealer in stolen goods. And in this case, some of the goods he's trafficking belong to the Church—rare books and religious relics, stolen from holy places and being sold for unholy profit. I have absolute authority to pursue these felons to the full extent of the law of the land."

Unimpressed, Jean-Luc continued his testy exchange with the bishop. "And the name of this supposed smuggler, Your Grace?"

Growing increasingly impatient and indignant, the

bishop replied, "I do not have time for your nettlesome interference, young man. I represent the Church of Rome, and I have the complete support and empowerment of King Louis XVIII. I demand you stand aside and mind your own affairs or there shall certainly be very severe and costly consequences to pay for you and your cohorts."

Maintaining his respectful yet firm manner, the lieutenant was in no way cowed by the bishop's threats. "Your Bourbon usurper has fled to Ghent. And as I speak, the Emperor Napoleon has returned to power in Paris. I am Lt. Jean-Luc Glastre, a direct and personal representative of the Emperor."

The lieutenant pulled out a silver medallion of office and showed it to the bishop and the monk's men, then continued speaking. "And so your claims of authority here are null and void. You can either answer my questions or respectfully withdraw yourself, Your Grace." Continuing his pronouncement of Napoleonic authority, Lt. Glastre, addressed his remarks to the rest of the group. "And any of you who stand opposed to us are duly warned that you will face the full measure of the law for your actions."

Lt. Glastre now stood face-to-face with Brother Jerome and showed no fear. The rest of Brother Jerome's men stood momentarily uncertain, but watching for any signal to act.

Jean-Luc turned to Roger. "You. What's the name of this supposed smuggler? Answer me now and I will know what your will is in all of this."

Roger hardly hesitated. "The name of the man is Marquis Jean-Marc Baptiste de Rennes, and he's no smuggler or thief!"

Brother Jerome's eyes widened in lethal fury, but the bishop was the first to act decisively. Ignoring the cavalry lieutenant, he spoke to Brother Jerome, while also gesturing to the foot soldier who guided the carriage down the alley.

"Enough of this delay. Your man here says there is no front entrance to the dwelling. This is the only access. I order you to proceed."

Brother Jerome's response was immediate. He shouted as he swung his cudgel into action against Lt. Glastre. "Attack!"

Roger, however, quickly swept his boot in front of the monk's advancing step and caused Brother Jerome to stumble, throwing off the focus and force of the monk's full assault. That was enough for Jean-Luc Glastre to fire his pistol at another of Brother Jerome's men—who charged at Roger from behind with his sword drawn—hitting the attacker in the chest. In an instant, the lieutenant drew his sword against Brother Jerome, who renewed his aggressive attack.

With the first report of gunfire, Roger looked up to the third floor window and yelled at the top of his lungs. "Master, it's Roger! You're in danger! The door here is blocked for escape! It's not safe!"

Brother Jerome swung around in rage, intending to slay Roger quickly with his cudgel; but as he raised it overhead for a downward strike, Jean-Luc swung his blade up swiftly in Roger's defense, hewing the wooden weapon in two with his razor-sharp cavalry sword.

Lt. Glastre's two men, meanwhile, were good shots. They either crippled or disabled half of Brother Jerome's force with their four pistols before they cast their firearms aside, drew their swords, and dealt with the remaining enemy in close quarters combat.

As Roger grabbed a sword from one of Brother Jerome's disabled men, he glanced up to the third floor window and saw a silhouette briefly peer down from the portal, then disappear from view. Roger was relieved that his message had been heard and that he could warn his master, offering some chance of escape. Though what that chance was, he could not know if this was indeed the only entrance into the building.

Lt. Glastre was surprised to see the bishop pick up a sword, as the cleric attacked one of Jean-Luc's men with rapid and ruthless ferocity, overcoming the man and slaying him with quick and deft work. Now the bishop turned his potent aggression on the lieutenant, as Roger came to his savior's side and defense.

Freed of attackers, and with a more critical goal in mind, Brother Jerome quickly led the horses of the carriage over so that the coach came alongside the wall of the building opposite the inn.

Lt. Glastre instantly surmised the monk's plan and struggled to break free of the bishop's attack, but too late. With surprising agility and strength, the monk had scrambled up onto the roof of the carriage, used it as a platform to spring to the first floor windows, which were barred. He then climbed to the lower sill of the second floor window, where he pulled himself up with lithe ease. Breaking the window, he quickly clambered into the dwelling as the first rays of the morning light beamed into the shadowy alley.

At the instant of this momentary distraction, the bishop

used it to his advantage. Quickly overpowering Roger with a block, parry and lunge to the chest, he dealt Jean-Marc's apprentice a lethal blow in one ruthless thrust. Just as Lt. Glastre turned in response, the bishop was on him. He bodily threw Jean-Luc across the alley with the power of a raging bull, so that Jean-Luc's head slammed and cracked on the stone wall with crippling force and he fell limp to the floor of the alley. The last of Napoleon's men was swiftly subdued by the two remaining members of Brother Jerome's force as the bishop surveyed the aftermath with impatient irritation. He gave orders to have the carriage turned around for a quick departure.

Inside his atelier, Jean-Marc had just peered out the window, having heard Roger's clarion call. As he witnessed the skirmish below, and with his enhanced quality of sight in the dimness of the alley, he saw as well that Lieutenant Glastre was part of the action.

He grew instantly cold, however, sighting the distinctive forms of both the bishop and Brother Jerome. Jean-Marc turned and called down to Gaston, who remained on the floor below with his daughter.

"Gaston, you must bring Solange up here to the workshop, immediately! There's danger! We're under attack!"

"I heard the call, Master. We're on our way," Gaston called back from the room below, as he carefully picked up his daughter, striving to carry her in a way which allowed her, as best as possible, to remain in repose. But the shouting and the energy of the moment roused Solange. Being borne in her father's massively strong arms, she looked up at him wearily.

"Father, is there a problem? Is something wrong?"

Gaston smiled reassuringly, but with a distracted look, as he replied. "Everything's fine, my little pear blossom. We just want to make sure you have a bit more sunlight now, and the best place is up here."

Deep in total exhaustion, Solange smiled trustingly, and nuzzled her face against her father's chest while he brought her up the narrow steps to the third floor. As he conveyed her upward, Gaston again felt the light staccato static electric shocks emanating from his daughter's body and into his, though now they had become somehow stronger. And while this occurred he experienced a remarkable set of vivid flashes in his mind's eye.

In quick succession he witnessed scenes from the distant past, in the Holy Land, he then viewed strange images of a city with tall rising buildings made of mirrored glass and steel, and finally, he gazed into the unblinking knowing eyes of all living creatures, which he sensed was the Eye of God.

And as his focus quickly returned to the urgency at hand, and he carried his daughter swiftly up the steps, he felt a rare surge of wondrous and loving joy.

Brother Jerome's entry into the second floor was effortless. After breaking the window with the head of his now half-cleaved cudgel, he climbed to the sill, leapt over the jagged broken edges of glass in the window frame and landed on the floor ready for any opposing action.

Silence met him. The monk drew a long-bladed dagger from under his robe and held it out in readiness. Like a feral animal, he relied on his primal senses as he proceeded, smelling the air, listening for the smallest sound, sensing the slightest draft on his cheeks to indicate another open window or door in the dwelling.

The monk quickly scanned the second floor, where he discovered a disheveled bed. He crouched over it, smelled it, and drew in the scent of a woman, a fragrance he memorized and briefly savored considering the possibility of future sustenance, to say nothing of her potential as a vessel for his unbridled and violent recreation. He allowed himself no further distraction, recognizing the bishop's clearly established priorities—the marquis and the Book.

A slight sound caught his highly sensitive ears, and the light draft he felt on his cheek upon entering had just stopped. He cursed himself silently, thinking this might mean the closing of some escape portal, very likely a hidden one, through which the marquis may already have exited—possibly a trapdoor to the roof, across which escape could easily be facilitated.

Brother Jerome focused on the narrow stairway leading to the third and top floor. Fear had nothing to do with the senses he experienced, only hunger for action. His only concern was he might have to kill the female as a requirement to get to the marquis, which meant his final reward and pleasure, might be diminished.

He understood the marquis also traveled with a man of robust description whom he remained certain was the same man he encountered days before at the crossroads, and who more recently killed one of his men at the marketplace fountain.

Yet experience through the many years gave the monk a certainty and an invincible confidence that no mortal man could be his match. No matter how big and strong and skilled they might be, Jerome would always be better, always stronger—stronger than ten men.

And while he knew he could certainly die, only two certain ways this could happen existed; he had successfully evaded both of those alternatives with studied determination and comparative ease through the years. He fully expected the same to be true here as he hunted down his prey for the bishop on this dawning morning of the Vernal Equinox.

The predator monk climbed the stairs, lightly as a cat, with the burning killing desire and the bloodlust of a famished lion.

Gaston knew from what Jean-Marc told him about the monk, that he would very likely have only one slim chance, one opportunity to make a difference. He understood very well the power and properties of this ruthless marauder who climbed the steps toward him. And as he heard the almost imperceptible padding up the stairs, Gaston knew, despite all of the actions he had seen in battle with Napoleon, where he had faced vastly superior numbers and survived, that this was to be the battle of his life, where the likelihood of survival was essentially nil.

And yet, never before did he have greater passion for victory—and need to prevail—for he stood to defend both his daughter and his master, who had introduced him to the love of his life. Gaston accepted this as his destiny to fight this battle no matter what the outcome, even if it only bought the couple a few moments to widen their margin of escape from the ruthless beast approaching.

The old veteran had no second thoughts about his personal welfare. He made peace with that some time ago and Gaston knew he had plenty of sins to pay for, including taking two lives earlier this very evening.

He only wanted his actions here and now to make a difference. Gaston knew from Jean-Marc this enemy had many of the same properties of strength, resilience and invulnerability—if not all—that his master had. Hence Gaston's strategies focused entirely on producing an effective delay of Brother Jerome, not expecting to slay him.

The seasoned warrior stayed absolutely still, crouched in his hiding place until the opportunity presented itself for an attack that could produce the right results. One last battle.

As Brother Jerome topped the stairs to Jean-Marc's atelier, all his senses reached their peak of alertness. On this floor, however, the strong smells of the alchemy lab, intermingled with the still air, impaired his ability to pick up Gaston's scent as effectively as he might normally expect in a more conventional setting.

Brother Jerome's hearing was acute. As he crossed the study section of the third floor, he had his dagger ready, assuming the marquis's guard dog would be the gate keeper the monk would need to slaughter quickly before he could take possession of his ultimate prey.

Forewarned of Brother Jerome's heightened sensory powers, Gaston successfully remained dead still, holding his breath until the monk neared the threshold of the laboratory workshop. Staring intently at a small reflection on one of the flat-sided bottles crowding a nearby shelf, which had a direct angle that gave him a small mirrored view of the doorway, Gaston spied the instant Brother Jerome leaned in and peered warily through the portal.

Gaston saw his moment; and mustering all his energy, he committed fully to his assault from behind the nearby worktable in the center of the room—a direct lunge aimed at striking the monk squarely in the eye with the thrust of his sword. Seasoned in combat, Gaston realized his attack was fundamentally on target, requiring only the slightest correction mid-lunge.

Brother Jerome's reactions, however, were shockingly swift. He parried the full penetrating force of the attack, but was unsuccessful in defending the strike completely. As a consequence, his forceful blocking motion resulted in unintentionally raking the point of Gaston's sword in a slashing cut across his right eye and the bridge of his nose. Brother Jerome bellowed with pain and rage as Gaston committed himself to a full body charge knocking over lab implements as he did.

Trying to see as he warded off the attack, the powerful monk threw Gaston aside like a dog tossing a rag doll. As Gaston struggled to get up and renew his assault, he paused momentarily to assess his adversary.

Gaston had already rubbed grease and a powdery poisonous compound—from Jean-Marc's chemical inventory—onto his blade. It appeared that his additional last-second inspiration to dip his sword in the solution pool his daughter had been in, with its rich brew of rare and powerful alchemical compounds, had an additional effect which was to facilitate the infliction of a more serious wound on the monk, more severe and lasting than would otherwise have been possible in normal circumstances.

The monk brusquely shook off his disorientation and renewed his attack, but now only with the benefit of his left eye. His useless right eye bled profusely.

Gaston braced himself as he attempted to strike the attacking monk with his sword. The monk easily blocked it with his forearm, and with lightning rapidity, slammed his dagger deep up into Gaston's gut—yanking it down as he withdrew it—then quickly slashed Gaston across the neck before the veteran could react. As Gaston sunk to his knees, Brother Jerome glared down at him through his one good eye with vehement distain.

"You meaningless dog. Where have they gone?"

Still on his knees, Gaston struggled with his last iota of energy. Unable to speak, he groaned and raised his arm, seeming to make a feeble pointing gesture at the door to Jean-Marc's library. Amused, Brother Jerome watched his prey's last death throes with curiosity.

However, in one last unexpected lunge away from the monk, Gaston's arm reached to the nearby workbench where a lantern stood. Before Brother Jerome could stop him, Gaston succeeded in knocking the lamp over as he collapsed on the floor. When he fell, the lamp fell too, spilling lamp oil and spreading flames all around him. Brother Jerome cursed him, seeing his exit blocked with the rising flames, which quickly caught onto other inflammable objects nearby and an inferno rapidly grew in force.

Glancing at the window nearby, the monk saw the last

passing of a silhouette's shadow outside, and dropping below the sill, out of sight. He lunged away from the flames toward the windowsill. Then using his power of smell, he caught a scent of Solange; and he moved to open the right casement below the stained glass window.

Roger knew, as his lifeblood seeped out of his midsection, that the last moments were at hand. He could hear the bishop nearby directing Brother Jerome's men to reposition the carriage so the horses were headed toward the alley's only exit. He managed to open his eyes, instinctively struggling to crawl away from the carriage which wheeled near his virtually helpless form. In doing so, however, his gaze took him up to the window of his master's workshop, which he now saw had been opened.

Roger's eyes widened in surprise as he saw Jean-Marc, with Solange unconscious over his shoulder, climbing out the window, closing it and struggling with some difficulty to make his way along a narrow ledge, to a far corner of the building which would take him out of sight. The progress for the pair, however, appeared excruciatingly slow. As the focus of action in the alley seemed to be shifting—the repositioning of the carriage was almost complete—the bishop began to look distracted.

"What's happening up there?" the bishop demanded to know with marked irritation and impatience, to no one in particular.

Roger knew the bishop's next action—conscious or not—would be for him to look up at the building's upper floor, immediately putting his master in danger where Jean-Marc remained in plain sight. Mustering what he knew was the last spark of his vital life-force, Roger yelled out as he struggled to stand, having grabbed a sabre which lay nearby on the cobblestones. Holding it in a threatening, albeit feeble, manner, he yelled out with all his heart and soul.

"I'll kill you all!"

And as he struggled painfully to lunge at the bishop, who was closest to him, another of Brother Jerome's men jumped in and cut him deeply in the stomach, with a decisive killing blow. As he fell to his knees, he glanced up to the sky. Out the corner of his eye, he thought he saw his master smile and nod at him, just before he disappeared around the ledge corner with Solange.

Just around the corner of the building—on the slender third floor ledge—Jean-Marc struggled to assure Solange's weakened form remained safe and secure as he carefully set her down in a small shadowy alcove located there—a declivity in the wall behind the quoin, the vertical cornerstone feature.

The view of this space from the alley was masked by the wide corbelled ledge as well as the thick decorative cornerstone feature which extended over a foot from the wall of the building and which ran vertically the height of the entire structure.

Solange secure, and with his hands now free, Jean-Marc first located an old bronze ring attached to a round copper plate housed nearby on the red stone wall, and he rotated it briskly. A hidden waist-high narrow doorway in the side of the cornerstone feature opened inward. This small door was situated so it too was invisible either from the alley below or any other buildings nearby.

Next, Jean-Marc yanked the bronze ring forcefully, and he heard the sound of metal sliding through stone in response to this action. He nodded with confirmation— recalling instructions from the master builder who created this edifice centuries ago—as he listened carefully for the sound of Brother Jerome, who just now reopened the window of his laboratory around the corner overlooking the alleyway.

Calm and unperturbed, Jean-Marc assisted Solange through the low doorway and followed her inside. There, within the stone entryway niche was a dark and cramped floorless space, which had one curious feature: a smooth bronze pole leading straight down into the darkness.

A series of small slits in the wall, not visible from the outside because of their inspired design, allowed touches of light to pour into the vertical shaft. The slivers of light on the pole made it evident that it descended past all three floors, and further, down deeper into the darkness below.

With soothing words, Jean-Marc carefully helped Solange to the pole, then placed his arms protectively around her, so both would slide down the pole together. They disappeared into the subterranean darkness below.

His opponent inert on the floor, and the laboratory raging in growing flames, Brother Jerome quickly peered out the window, and to his compatriots below, with a rare sense of urgency. He scanned the ledge which skirted the building below the windows, both to the right and to the left. A curious feature of this building was that the face of the building extended a few feet deeper into the alley than the adjoining buildings on either side.

This meant the monk could not see precisely which way along the ledge they went. His prey had obviously gone around the corner on one side, since there was no sign of anyone at all. He climbed out the window, sliding down onto the ledge. Searching for any indication of Jean-Marc's passage, and seeing none, he called down to the bishop and his men.

"Did you see them out here on the ledge? Which way did they go?"

The responses he received in return indicated they knew nothing. Brother Jerome therefore relied on his intuition and let his nose touch the stone surface on either side of the window. Sniffing, he nodded, smiled slightly, and then started along to the left, which was toward the river, and indeed the route Jean-Marc had taken.

Comfortable with most environments, he judged this setting held no great challenge for him. Despite his loss of sight to his right eye, the monk assumed it would return to full health and functionality after a proper period of healing. As a result, he remained unconcerned and pressed on with his predator's sense of primal purpose. He now focused on the valuable prey and his prize: the Book.

As he carefully advanced on the ledge, he sniffed the air around the red stone wall, and his eye narrowed with further confirmation he was on the right trail. Moving along the ledge, he kept his weight low and relaxed and angled toward the building, with one palm dragging along the wall to maintain a steady balance.

Brother Jerome made his way about halfway to the corner when his highly tuned senses told him the ledge he stood on had just shifted slightly, as though something supporting the cement cornice had weakened in some way.

Pausing for a second, he considered the options of continuing toward his target and around the corner, or retreating back to the window where the flames began to lick the exterior of the building. Quickly considering his alternatives, he had no doubt of his goal. And if he returned without what he sought, there would be a raging fire to face in the lab and there would be hell to pay with the bishop.

His mind remained clear and direction confirmed. The instant he moved forward, however, a sharp cracking resounded in the horizontal stone ledge cornice below him. Before Brother Jerome could react, the ledge collapsed under his feet. As he plummeted downward, he noticed a hole in the ledge work housed on the side of the building where a short metal rod hung by a chain.

As he fell the three stories without panic, the monk had just enough time to surmise that this metal component was part of some sort of locking mechanism which had been disengaged after Jean-Marc's passage across it, hence making anyone following fall into a certain trap.

The monk hit the cobblestones of the alley below with a resounding and sickening thud as the bishop quickly crossed to him and appraised his unconscious fallen comrade with anger and disgust.

The Foothills
The Southern Pyrenees, France
21 March, 1815 AD – Late Morning

Having left the southern reaches of the city of Toulouse, and finally gaining the solitude of a forested country road some distance south of one of the city's nearby villages, Jean-Marc began to feel some semblance of temporary safety.

The cost for this sense of comparative security, however, had been dear. It was with painful reflection that Jean-Marc privately acknowledged Gaston's sacrifice for their wellbeing. Even Roger had redeemed himself, shouting his warning and sacrificing his last moments on this earth by creating a distraction for his passage on the ledge with

Solange.

Jean-Marc knew too, that the bishop and Brother Jerome would not have been at their doorstep had it not been for a moment of weakness on Roger's part resulting in his remembering and divulging the existence of the *Auberge des Pommes Bleues*, which certainly meant Loïc had likely paid the ultimate price as well. So much sacrifice, for so many years, he pondered soberly. Would it finally be over?

Jean-Marc and Solange had reached this place due to advanced planning that he and Gaston always maintained as a contingency during their stays in Toulouse. Gaston assured fresh horses were stabled at a livery a short distance from the entrance to the tunnel which ran more than a mile south under the city streets of Toulouse, the Garonne River, and finally to the entrance's location at an old well house. The narrow tunnel had been designed and constructed three hundred and fifty years before, at the same time Jean-Marc's atelier was built, again under his supervision, and with the invaluable aid of the *Tekton* brothers—one of whom had been Loïc's distant ancestor and forefather.

While their escape had been successful, the going had not been easy. Solange's frail condition would be compared to someone ill with the worst influenza. The alchemical process she underwent—while ultimately resulting in a transformation which would afford her immortality—had in the short term left her completely weak, helpless, and barely able to stay conscious.

Allowing her to sleep for at least a full day and night, before even considering any travel, would have been ideal. Even more bed rest than that would promote the final and successful transformation taking place inside her body that much more quickly and effectively. Despite that fact, as Jean-Marc assisted her along their way in the subterranean passageway, she revived somewhat and insisted on walking herself.

Once they climbed the narrow and hidden stone spiral stairway which led to the old water house, and finally made their way to the stable, Solange had been adamant about riding alone, assuring Jean-Marc she would be fine in the saddle.

Admiring her determination and her seeming resilience, he permitted her to ride. And for the first mile from the stable, he actually thought they might be fine, as he kept her riding ahead of him, so he could keep watch on her. After a short time, however, she began to slump on her horse and allow it to slow to a plodding, wandering walk. Jean-Marc pulled alongside her, just as she would have otherwise fallen out of her saddle unconscious.

Jean-Marc put her on his horse, positioned her in front of him, holding her steady as he held his roan's reins, and they pressed on with their journey.

Solange's original mount stayed tethered behind them, carrying provisions Gaston set aside for this eventuality. Jean-Marc knew they would need this horse as a fresh mount since his horse now carried the weight of two riders. A third horse, Gaston's, remained in the stable overlooking the river. Jean-Marc told the stable keeper it was his to sell if Gaston did not come to pick it up, or get word to him, before a week had passed. Jean-Marc still held out a remote hope for his old comrade.

Before leaving the stable, however, Jean-Marc sent off two carrier pigeons which he kept at this location for this very purpose, with the hope they would get through to their two critical destinations. He knew from past experience, however, wherever the bishop traveled, the cleric had sporting falcons which specifically hunted pigeons of this sort, with the purpose of gaining any insight to messages traveling in the skies.

The marquis employed a cypher code which he had used for some time, since the broad network he worked in could not be issued new replacement codes on any regular basis. Jean-Marc could only hope the bishop had not already broken the code, should he succeed in intercepting one of his carrier pigeons.

As he rode on, Jean-Marc refocused his mind, knowing that to fret about issues which were out of one's control was a fruitless exercise. He remained determined to concentrate on what he could influence as the best expenditure of his mental efforts.

The bishop seethed with agitation at this failure. The closeness of the seeming success of his enterprise, only to have his rightful prize ripped away from him, made his torment that much more intense. Bishop Antonio del Julia y Sangresante remained emphatically determined this would be only a temporary condition.

Brother Jerome, he reluctantly acknowledged, would unfortunately be out of commission for the next few days at least. The bishop left the monk at the Eglise des Jacobins with one of his men, along with the instructions Brother Jerome should not to be disturbed and that he be allowed to sleep for three days straight, if need be. To disturb him would only lengthen the healing cycle and make him useless to the bishop for that much longer.

Having examined the injuries Brother Jerome sustained—including the slashed and disfigured eye—the mendicant nun at the cathedral asked the bishop if he should not also be getting a traditional doctor to look after his wounds.

It appeared as well that Brother Jerome had broken his right arm and leg in his fall from the ledge at the marquis's laboratory. The bishop, however, straightened the bones himself, with surprising ease and expertise, and assured the nun that "God would heal his own, and it is in his hands."

As his carriage continued south, with a column of eight riders ahead and eight behind him, the bishop reflected with grave concern, however, over the monk's eye wound. Unlike lesions in the past, which would heal quickly, even before his eyes, this wound distinguished itself as being something quite different. Where his and the monk's living tissue would bind quickly in healing action, this injury did not react in the same way, being very slow to bind and its properties stood clearly unique and disquieting.

The bishop also succeeded in getting a disjointed description of what Jean-Marc's laboratory looked like from the somewhat delirious monk—while setting his bones— and how it was equipped before Gaston set it on fire, thereby destroying everything and rendering it useless for the bishop's investigation and study. One particular detail kept reverberating in his mind: the description of the large bronze tub full of liquid and of a shape and size large enough to hold a human.

He correctly suspected this basin held the millennia-old solution he sought to reanimate himself. He wondered if Gaston, before his attack on Brother Jerome, had possibly dipped the blade of his weapon into the solution—combined with some poisonous substance—thereby giving the sword a power to wound which Brother Jerome had never encountered before—except prior to his transformation centuries ago.

These reflections only made the bishop's frustrated anger burn hotter, thinking he had been so close to possessing what he needed, only to have it wrested from his grasp in such an infuriating way. It remained *his* destiny and birthright to own this knowledge completely, no one else's. Nothing must stop him.

With no other information of the whereabouts of his quarry available, his instinct told him the marquis would head south, either to travel over the Pyrenees mountains into Spain, or make for the Mediterranean and find passage out by sea. The crossroads a few miles ahead would require the bishop to make a decision. He instinctively felt that somehow he would know which way Jean-Marc would choose.

The thought of the article of saddlery, which Jean-Marc left behind at the Soubise Palace in Paris, haunted him. He felt, despite the fact his men already checked this line of inquiry before his arrival in Toulouse, that it still held the possible key to Jean-Marc's future movements. And if this was indeed the case, the bishop would be waiting for him.

In the high foothills of the Midi-Pyrénées, the Shepherd sat on his favorite rock overlooking the steep grassy slope where his flock grazed amid the early spring flowers. The blooms, mostly purple hues, peeked out from the young green grass. Off in the distance, to the north, he could see the strikingly distinctive peak—Montségur—which held such painful generations-old history for so many locals, and for him as well.

Part of him appreciated being able to see it, since it had been the last place he saw her, before the horror ravaged these lands. And yet here in the meadow, life went on. Indeed, he felt less a visitor—since he had not been born here; and one is always seen as visitor no matter how long one lives in a place—but instead he actually felt as much a part of the terrain as the trees, wildflowers and mountain streams.

An unusual flurry of dragonflies flitted here and there as his gaze took them in; but his view included his sheep, the mountains beyond, and the sky as well. He smiled faintly as a waft of breeze crossed the wildflowers, somehow stimulating the sheep to move a little closer toward him as they refocused their grazing on a new patch of grass. He nodded slightly, then seemingly spoke to no one in particular.

"Yes, his attempt will fail. Yet he will again draw so many into his web of ambitions and so much more blood will spill. He simply does not know it yet, but his real work on this earth has already been performed. He'll finally come to learn this at a place called St. Helena, I suppose."

The Shepherd casually glanced to his side where a hedge

of wild honeysuckle attracted a flurry of dozens of hummingbird hawk-moths—their similarity to traditional hummingbirds not native to these lands was striking. Some of the flight took off and darted over with the dragonflies, manifesting an abstract ballet in the air, creating swirling, colorful designs which flashed wildly in the sunlight. This amused the Shepherd. He then nodded, looking off in another direction in the sky, seeming to answer an unheard voice.

"It is my wish to help nurture and sustain the changes. We know I cannot do this alone, and Johan—capable as he is—is simply not enough. And so many refuse to listen, and yet insist they carry Your message, Your blessing... and mine. A change approaches though. This we know. It is inexorable."

Something caught his attention in the sky to his right, well over two hundred yards away from him—a bird in flight. It winged across the line of forest below him and headed toward a lonely stone hut located at the bottom of the pasture over a hundred yards from him. His eyes narrowed slightly, focusing more acutely on the bird. The Shepherd observed it was a pigeon; and with his remarkably potent sense of sight, he also saw it carried a small leather tube tied to its foot.

Something else caught his attention from his rock promontory on the meadow. Much higher above, behind the pigeon, a falcon had targeted this new prey; and it just now pulled its wings back to initiate its attacking dive. The Shepherd frowned, and in this instance he shook his head and raised his index finger in seeming disapproval. In that exact same moment, the falcon seemed startled by something, broke its attack and flew off in another direction over the trees, out of sight.

The Shepherd smiled slightly and then let out a light whistle in a single note, hardly loud enough for the sheep grazing in front of him to hear. At the instant of the whistle, however, the pigeon immediately changed its course, executing a wide change of direction to achieve a ninety degree turn and proceeded to fly directly toward the Shepard. He casually extended his right hand, flat, palm open to the sky. The pigeon landed on it, and he quietly petted the avian messenger affectionately.

Noticeable now, a ragged somewhat circular and faded scar laid just below the wrist of the Shepherd's right hand. And as he turned his hand, to pet the bird gently, the scar mirrored on the backside of his wrist as well. Another scar matching the first also sat on his left wrist, a detail of the Shepherd's appearance to which he paid absolutely no attention.

"We know what news you would bring from Johan, my beloved. But it's always nice to see you or your friends," he said gently as he carefully untied the leather tube and extracted a thin paper roll contained within it. He did not bother to read it, but instead turned his distant gaze across the sky, nodded, then got up and began to stroll down through the verdant mountain grassland, passing his flock of sheep, petting a few as he did, and approached the small stone hut which sat at the edge of the forest and this remote pasture.

Once inside, the Shepherd quickly began to pack a few possessions in a simple canvas shoulder bag. He paused at an object wrapped in a small cloth, sitting on the table of the hut. He opened it and gazed at it for a short time. It was a large emerald, uncut except for a smooth face on either side, allowing the light to pass through it, resulting in a magical illumination. In earlier centuries he recalled it was dubbed the "Eye of God."

"Possibly this shall purchase my passage back to the land of the Nephites," he reflected to himself.

"Are you leaving us, Master?" the voice of a child questioned from the doorway of the hut.

The Shepherd turned and saw a young girl he knew well, and he smiled warmly.

"Ah, Christine. Is your mother feeling better?" he inquired with sincere empathy.

"Yes, Master. Your attentions to her brought an immediate betterment of her condition," the girl replied dutifully. But more serious matters clearly weighted on her mind. "I did not mean to eavesdrop, Master, but I heard you speaking about returning somewhere. Are you planning to depart our mountains sometime soon?" Christine was clearly crestfallen at this prospect and seemingly on the verge of tears.

The Shepherd's gesture welcomed her to approach; and as he sat at his modest rough-hewn wooden table, she joined him on the stool next to him. He put his arm around her gently and lovingly.

"Christine, while I truly love this place, it's time for me to move on once again. I expect I shall return in due course, because I love these lands so dearly, and consider them to be my home," the Shepherd assured her.

"But when? In a week? In a month?" she asked, fearing a far graver and imminent reality.

"It will be soon. And I will be gone much longer than a month, Christine. But I will always be with you, even though I visit distant lands."

"But you're everything to us, Master! You can't leave us! Life is *right* with you here." The girl began to cry. The Shepherd took her in his arms to comfort her, and then brightened the moment by showing her the emerald jewel which he placed into in her hands with affection and purpose. She was awestruck by the luster of the large precious gem.

"Do you like it, Christine?" he asked.

"Yes, Master. It is a thing of great beauty. I've never seen anything like it. The green is so deep and clear," Christine marveled.

"Yes indeed." He guided her hands so she held the jewel as though it were a thick lens of some sort, one flat side facing her eye and the other directed toward him. "Can you see me through it?" he asked her with kindly warmth.

"Why, yes, Master, very clearly," the girl observed.

"I want you to keep it. I think you need this more than I. When you want to see me, you shall look through it. If you believe with all of your heart and soul, you'll see me. And I'll know it, and I'll wave to you when you look for me. I want you to have this, because you, like these mountains and this land, are very dear to me, Christine."

The girl was in awe of this invaluable gift. "But Master, I heard you say just a moment ago that you might use this to buy passage to your destination far away."

"That's true, Christine. But I can always find payment for that which I seek. I can't always give you something which calms your soul and puts your heart at rest. The decision is really quite simple." And he clasped her hands so they closed around the emerald. "Tell your mother and father 'thank you,' and that I will return when I can."

The Shepherd kissed her on the forehead, and then turned and walked out the door. The girl sat at the table for a moment, looked out the empty doorway, and then gazed into her palm at the limpid green jewel. She closed her eyes for a moment concentrating, then held it up to the light of the doorway and peered intently. After a moment, a big smile spread across her face.

Due to Solange's condition, Jean-Marc could ride at only a fraction of the pace he originally thought possible. As a result, he decided to take an entirely different route—one which took them to their destination by way of the back trails through the foothills—rather than the main tracks which ran at the floor of the valleys of this mountainous region.

And so, as they shared his horse, with Solange riding in front of him on the saddle, and as she slipped in and out of consciousness, Jean-Marc decided to adopt the technique of teaching Solange's mother employed in past years.

Despite the fact Solange seemed unconscious for much of the time, Jean-Marc took it upon himself to chronicle for her the rich story of this locale, which had been his home for so long, in this southerly region of Languedoc. He felt strongly the critical nature of assuring her understanding on a deeper level, because the story of this land was also part of her story, by way of her mother.

The people of Languedoc were different, Jean-Marc told her. They were more innately spiritual in his view, in a profound way, far more than people in the north of France. Here the natives maintained a connection with the eternal truths of their deeper hidden history of the ancient land— the Cathars, the Visigoths, as well as the early settlers of Septimania—the unique Jewish Principality of the Late Roman Empire.

Jean-Marc shared reflections on the chronicles of the people here as they rode, and how on the very trail they traveled, he had witnessed what horrors of history mankind brutally forced on others whose pure spiritual intent sought the freedom of body and soul to have a direct and loving relationship with God.

Jean-Marc recounted the era when Toulouse was the capital of the Cathar domain of Occitania, a land uniquely separate from France, not just in administrative jurisdiction, but in a culturally profound and very different way. Aside from the fact that traditional French was not the native language of the region—*langue d'oc* (the language of 'Oc', of Occitania)—their belief in Christ, and their devout and faithful practice of worship, stood uniquely separate from the rigid and dogmatic teachings dictated from Rome.

Jean-Marc explained how the Cathar teachings reached back to the ancient roots of the original teachings of Yesu— the Aramaic name Jesus had been known by at the time of His Teachings—and how they faithfully followed His original model in spirit and practice.

The Cathar's position on the Church of Rome was quite simple and clear, and was expressed without aggression or hate. These 'Good Christians' held the perspective that all the centuries-old maneuvering for expanding control and power over land, people and resources, too often through the most ruthless means necessary, did not reflect the True Belief—Yesu's teachings—or God's will.

These actions were instead the will of the Lower God— the creator of the material world—but not the Greater God who ultimately gave this lower deity his power. Indeed, the Cathars' interpretation of the Roman Church's draconian actions through history was that the enforcement of their beliefs resulted in making this physical world a hell on Earth.

The Cathars' position simply expressed that a man or a woman could—and *should*—have an equal and direct relationship with God. Rome, meanwhile, insisted this was impossible without going through the incommodious hierarchy of the male-dominated Church, which claimed its right of legitimacy from a direct and apostolic succession.

They claimed their uninterrupted line, from Saint Peter to the present, gave them the sole guardianship and access to the Grace of God. Anyone else, as demonstrated through the ages, had been branded a heretic and under the unequivocal evil influence of Satan.

The consequences of any disagreement with this view were profound and traditionally fatal. Yet the Cathars had an equally opposite point of view, peacefully expressed— which was the supporters of the Church of Rome, worshiping their god as the one supreme god, were themselves guilty of their own grave error and heresy.

And despite their tortured logic to the contrary, the Roman clerics could not escape the fact that Church Fathers ages before them had inadvertently validated Satan as a second god in the New Testament, undermining the legitimacy of monotheism. And in early debates with representatives of the Roman Church, citing the Bible passage in question, the Cathars observed this was indeed the Lower God Rome was ruled by. Their logic was irrefutable and infuriating.

Through the early years, the people of Occitania welcomed the Cathar tradition. Yet at the same time, in the spirit of universal tolerance and acceptance, they respectfully acknowledged the traditional Roman faith, many members of whom were their esteemed neighbors. They coexisted and accepted those people who wanted to worship God in the way that they saw fit. So many of these traditional Christians at the local level shared a similar spirit and will, being good, devout and God-fearing people, sincerely wanting to do God's will through their peaceful yet varied worship of Christ.

Indeed, so profound was the Occitanian sensibility toward welcoming faiths outside their own, that the city of Narbonne, which had been a Jewish center of learning for centuries—originally the capital city of the princedom of Semptimania—maintained peaceful relations with their Muslim neighbors across the Pyrenees and their inclusive spirit remained admired all around the Mediterranean.

Over the decades, however, the number of converts to the Cathar faith continued to grow impressively. Their belief in Christ—from the revolutionary Cathar perspective—grew in influence as well.

Numerous cities throughout the region became openly Cathar. A renaissance of arts and cultural harmony resulted. The mathematics of reduction in the numbers of *their* faithful in this region was noted by the Church of Rome with grave and growing concern.

The Cathar belief expanded across the land, by virtue of their traveling adepts—known as *perfecti*—who continued to spread the word to a wider geographical audience. Observed with ominous and sobering concern by the Roman Church, Pope Innocent III recognized the Catholic Church faced serious competition. A compelling message of what many felt to be a purer form of the Original Christianity continued to spread, and this could only be labeled indignantly by Rome as a heresy of the gravest order.

The Cathar *perfecti*, who traditionally traveled in pairs—a man and a woman—were renowned for their exemplary life style of humility, chastity, simplicity and poverty—so much like Yesu. They only placed themselves in a setting where they asked for nothing in return, no alms nor obedience; but only to be heard—like Yesu. The effect of the message spread organically, naturally.

And over time, the feudal aristocracy of the region—the noble families ruling Toulouse, Narbonne, Carcassonne, Béziers, including their knights, fortified castles, as well as lower nobles and a vast populace of the region—either openly, or privately followed or supported the growing Cathar faith.

The Cathar movement reached growing numbers by virtue of the *message* conveyed—the 'Good News,' not a forced compliance with the strict uncompromising orthodoxy of dogma which demanded unquestioning obedience. Here the true 'Good News'—the original meaning of the word 'gospels'—purported to communicate the *original* gospels of Yesu's faith, before St. Paul. Here then was the heart, soul and spirit of the unadulterated teachings of the man known as Jesus the Nazarene.

This grass-roots style of Christianity stood much in contrast with the prevailing alternative found in the Vatican, rife with greed, corruption, privilege and the continuing consolidation of great wealth benefitting a very select few in the hierarchy of the Church. Most bishops indeed acted as feudal landlords, enjoying lives of shameless, ostentatious and outrageous luxury, indifferent to the privations of the poor.

In time, Catharism grew strong in fertile ground, with no end in sight of it stopping. Over half of the population of Occitania converted.

In 1208, however, sparked by an ugly incident which the Church of Rome instigated, Pope Innocent III declared that this heretical movement must no longer be allowed to continue unabated. Named after Albi—a main city within northern Occitania—the Albigensian Crusade became the first time that a crusade had been declared against Latin-speaking Christians by Latin-speaking Christians.

A plan was drawn, and support sought from Philippe II, Philippe Augustus, king of Île-de-France, the region primarily around Paris, well north of Occitania, Languedoc. The people of this northern dominion spoke a language that would later be known as traditional French—*langue d'oil*—Langueoil—the language of 'oui', the declaration of 'yes' in English. The king and his nobles openly coveted the rich lands of Occitania and seized the opportunity to bring it under their control. Philippe II would became the first to declare himself king of France.

Also coming to the aid of the Pope's cause, a new militant religious sect within the Catholic Church had been formed—the Dominicans: 'the dogs of God.' Their critical mission in their early years of this crusade was to ferret out heretics by whatever means they deemed suitable. The notorious tradition of the Inquisition began with these passionate, and in Jean-Marc's view, gravely misguided warriors for Christ. Indeed, anyone who considered themselves 'Warriors for Christ' had missed the point of Christ's message, and with tragic results for the innocent and faithful victims in these rich lands.

Those subjected to the Dominicans' highly efficient and ruthless methods of suppressing anyone whose philosophy lived outside the canon of the Church—and intimidation of all who sympathized with them—were attacked mercilessly and without constraint.

Indeed, as Jean-Marc advanced toward the Pyrenees on horseback, through the bucolic beauty of the countryside south of the small medieval city of Foix, he could not help but share with Solange—who continued to drift in and out of consciousness—his experiences centuries ago, striving to stay one step ahead of the rabid priests, eager for the head of anyone they thought might have heretical leanings. And in their view at that time, Jean-Marc would have been a prize catch and destined for torture and execution.

The present rumors of a new war, with the nations of royal bloodline interrelationships across nations allying once again to oppose Napoleon's un-flagging talent for the prospect of revolutionary governance, created an undeniable imbalance—infuriating for the royals—in the scheme of how the succession of power might be conducted in Europe's future. Jean-Marc also observed to Solange—how, with the prospect of troops moving north across the border from Spain to join forces against Napoleon—it gave rise to his own reflections of the Cathar movement—which was ultimately brutally suppressed. These new movements of armed forces in the area reminded him of what he saw and experienced at that fractious, volatile and tragic time.

The imperious perspective from Rome was that this threatening 'evil' must not be allowed to continue. It was really all about eliminating competition in the only way the Church knew how. As a result, cities burned and citizenry slaughtered, the lands callously wrested from their rightful owners and awarded to ambitious nobles from the north.

Over the course of a decades-long battle of attrition, the Cathars ultimately lost. Faced with overwhelming superior numbers, they systematically retreated to refuges which were more and more remote. The Roman-sanctioned crusaders remained relentless in their pursuit to annihilate any last vestige of the Cathar's brand of compassionate Christianity, which so compellingly, and without effort, made the Church's own hypocrisy a tell-tale fact.

Rome's extermination drive included one target in particular—a *perfecti* known simply as 'The Shepherd.' The inquisitors interrogated everyone they tortured to discover if they knew who and where he was as well as the identity of his companion.

Most resisted, especially those who had personal encounters with him. But some, after extreme torture, and a complete breakdown of their sanity, would call out to the Shepherd, "My Lord Yesu's Voice and Hand."

Some rumors even claimed that the Shepherd was a direct descendant of Jesus himself, one of the *Desposyni*. This infuriated the Inquisitors even more, which they responded with accusations of demon possession. The punishment for uttering any of these revelations brought an ugly and deadly nightmare to whoever spoke them.

Finally, the Vatican Inquisition directed the crusaders to where the Cathars appeared to have taken their last stand, where Rome thought they finally cornered their quarry, and they would be able to place this 'Shepherd' in their clutches, to force him to confess to the worst of sins.

While the Cathar faith claimed no central leadership, nor any city as a headquarters, the Vatican Inquisitors latched onto this particular *perfecti*, simply because of the name he acquired, and the similarity of his title to that of Jesus Christ. They held him responsible for so many of the Cathars of this region being led astray by his tempting and infernal words, promising salvation and a direct relationship with the Lord God.

The location of this last stand was the solitary mountain fortress of Montségur, at the foot of the Pyrenees in southern Languedoc—a place from which there was no escape. And to this mountaintop refuge the majority of the surviving faithful Cathar flocked and the last of their *perfecti* retreated. The Shepherd was rumored to be there as well, with his wife Marie, his *perfecti* partner in carrying the sacred Word.

A siege encircled the mount, all contact with the outside world cut off. And for Solange, this was critical to understand, Jean-Marc explained, since the Shepherd, Joshua, and his wife Marie were Solange's ancestors through her mother's bloodline.

The horrifying and climactic moment of Montségur occurred after the defense against the months-long siege failed—the 'heretics' were burned en masse. The sacred wife of Joshua, Marie, was part of the inferno of the Cathar faithful. Joshua had actually not been present during the siege of Montségur—instead traveling across the far sea in a place known then as the land of Nephites, sharing the Word.

Upon his return, he remained forever wounded with the knowledge he had not been by her side at the crucial time. Jean-Marc only barely escaped the night before, climbing down the remote cliff on the end of a precarious rope, along with a sacred text of the Cathars. Marie refused the offer to accompany Jean-Marc, so committed was she to those who staked their fates with the community. She also insisted Jean-Marc could not stay because of his duty to preserve the text and carry the word of their story on Montségur.

While that Cathar sacred text of Gnostic teachings over a thousand years old had been critical to save, the tome he carried now was possibly the most important for the faithful of the present and for the future. For the Book he carried now—which for years he thought lost for good—had knowledge much older, profoundly ancient, and a bounty of arcane wisdom and erudition.

Jean-Marc reflected on the promising opportunities the future held for them. With the return of Napoleon, the hope of fortifying the governmental changes he promoted in law and policy that supported the rights of mankind held the possibility of being profoundly encouraging to Jean-Marc.

He remained concerned, however, that Napoleon's good work on earth may now have concluded. The seeds of change he had already planted actively grew in the hearts and minds of men and women. But further change was now unlikely with so many powerful forces stacked against him. And as was the case with so many men who gained absolute power, this condition affected Napoleon in unfortunate ways. Jean-Marc observed this classic and yet ill-fated change over the years.

Lt. Glastre rode as quickly as he could under the circumstances. His man, Sergeant Sauveur Auzac, whom he originally left behind on the road north of Toulouse two days before—to attend to his fallen rider compatriot—had rejoined the lieutenant in Toulouse.

Jean-Luc had been taken—half-unconscious to a military barracks—after he identified himself in the alley where the local gendarmerie arrived and tried to make sense of the mayhem they found, with over a half-dozen bodies.

Jean-Luc was the only survivor. While he had suffered no sword or gunshot wounds, he remained in critically grave condition. Being thrown against the alley wall with such force as he experienced, which also included his head slamming against the solid stoneworks, had left him in a state of shock from the severe concussion he sustained. He constantly fought persistent nausea. He also had an intermittent nose bleed and yet he assured his man Sauveur there was nothing to worry about.

Now back in the saddle, but still riding somewhat slower—and more than a half-day behind the man he had solemnly pledged to protect—Glastre had sent Sauveur ahead on the road for reconnaissance.

Jean-Luc understood, based on reports from farmers and villagers along the way, that the bishop in his coach and mounted escort had taken the route south. He ordered Sauveur to track the bishop and his followers and leave markers at any road junction, so Jean-Luc could navigate effectively in pursuit with whatever superior forces he might muster in this short amount of time, which had been the better part of the morning.

The young cavalry officer indeed succeeded in commandeering three men from the local detachment of horse soldiers, but not without much argument, coercion and threat. With the political situation in Paris in such a state of flux, the local cavalry commander initially dismissed Napoleon's lieutenant out of hand. But despite his lower rank, Lt. Glastre was not a man to be dismissed so easily. In addition, he was immensely more intelligent than the officer with whom he had this debate.

Finally, after the threat of dire consequences for resisting Napoleon's command began to gnaw at the local captain's will, the lieutenant lubricated the proposition with the promise of a promotion in rank, and a handful of 40 franc gold coins—a small fortune.

While Lt. Glastre stated he needed the captain's best riders and fighters, he could only take their talents on faith, though the three men riding behind him seemed skilled enough horsemen. The moment of truth, sure to come, would reveal their strengths in combat soon enough. And

Napoleon's lieutenant assured before riding that each were armed with their swords, as well as two pistols, loaded and ready to fire on short notice.

Glastre repeatedly went over in his mind the experience of the alley, and the shocking force with which this mysterious bishop had so easily thrown him against the wall. It was as if the smallish cleric had the power of a raging bull. Jean-Luc could not understand how this might be physically possible. But what he did know was that when he faced this man a second time, no hesitation must exist when responding to him with conviction and attacking him with full force. The church vestments made the lieutenant hesitate and think twice before. Never again.

Jean-Luc also briefed his newly acquired men on the bishop's robust and lethal nature, composing a story that the man in the cleric's robes was an imposter and hence shooting him, if required, would not mean facing consequences from Rome, but it would instead result in the Church's hearty gratitude.

As he rode, and fought off the symptoms of shock and nausea from the action at dawn, Glastre tried to think through all of the contingencies possible in this strange mission. But with conditions so fluid, all he could rely on at the moment was traveling as quickly as possible and helping the Marquis Jean-Marc Baptiste de Rennes in any way he could. He viewed this objective now as his highest duty.

A fork in the road lay ahead; and in the shade of the tree by a stream, a formation of stones stood by the left fork. Having battled his intense queasiness up to this point, Jean-Luc used this opportunity for a respite, after he slid off his horse to inspect the stone markings configured to signal a left turn at the fork.

Boots on the ground now, Jean-Luc turned aside, away from his riding party and surrendered to a violent and explosive release to the intense churning in the pit of his stomach. He vomited, feeling a full vacating of what scant contents remained in his gut, and he continued to dry retch until the heaving spasms passed. As he glanced up, he noticed his men staring at him with frowns, distaste and concern. He took a tentative sip from his canteen as he met their dubious looks.

"Tighten your saddles and water your horses in the stream. We'll be underway in a minute, and we'll ride hard from here on," Jean-Luc declared with crisp authority, despite his acute discomfort.

He felt intensely dizzy, however, and was not even sure he would be able to climb back in the saddle again. He had suffered two wounds in the various campaigns with Napoleon, but nothing as debilitating as this. Jean-Luc mustered all his discipline as he tightened his own horse's cinch, almost in a robotic manner, just to do something positive. He then drank from his canteen again, more deeply, and struggled to suppress the reflex to vomit once more as he did.

"Are you not well, Brother?"

Despite the calm tone and quiet volume of the voice, it startled Lieutenant Glastre to his core, having come at him from behind on his blind side. As he turned, he was surprised to see the clean-shaven man, in local peasant garb standing before him with a peaceful smile. The stranger had a canvas sack slung over his shoulder and carried a shepherd's crook, which he seemed use as a walking stick, though only earlier in the morning it had been a tool of his vocation in a meadow not far from here.

"I am well enough, sir. I thank you for your concern," Lieutenant Glastre responded a little stiffly, feeling a bit humiliated that his traditionally well-honed senses failed to tell him of someone who got so close to him without his detecting it in the least. He even glanced at his men with a look of annoyance that they had done nothing to warn him. Their response indicated they did not see the man until it was too late as well.

"What were you doing there? Hiding? Hiding from whom?" the lieutenant challenged the Shepherd somewhat impatiently, working at salvaging a sense of authority from this unguarded moment.

"I am on the pilgrim's path to Santiago de Compostella and points beyond, sir. But all on the road do not travel with the same destination and spirit I do. The approach of so many men—your men—clearly armed, gave me concern that I might be an unnecessary distraction from their ultimate destination somewhere further down the highway, hence I remained out of sight until I was able to determine your spirit," the man replied calmly. Studying the young lieutenant as Jean-Luc wiped blood from his nose, the Shepherd continued his expression of concern for Lt. Glastre.

"Your state of wellness, Brother, concerns me. I *can* help you."

Yet as the Shepherd extended his hand toward the lieutenant, the young officer put his arm up in a reflexive blocking motion and gestured toward his horse. "I have an urgent mission and I cannot waste time on another's good intentions, which experience tells me will likely result in nothing more than some temporary relief at best, and which I must pay for with precious time and ultimately disappointing results. I thank you, sir, for your offer, but I must press on."

The Shepherd studied Lt. Glastre's eyes closely, as a light arrived in his own luminous green eyes, seeming to have gained a deeper revelation, an understanding of something relating to the lieutenant. He smiled faintly and nodded. This action clearly made Jean-Luc uncomfortable and amplified his impatience to get back on the road.

However, he found himself silently thankful, at least, that the distraction had succeeded in diminishing his nausea enough so the prospect of getting back on his horse was no longer so completely repellant. As he took his horse's reins, and began to raise his left foot into the stirrup to climb back into the saddle, the Shepherd spoke calmly and pointed to the stone marker which stood at the fork in the road.

"If it is Marquis Jean-Marc Baptiste de Rennes you seek, you will only encounter the bishop and his men by following the path to the left. They do not yet know Jean-Marc's whereabouts."

Startled at this revelation, Lt. Glastre turned to the man standing calmly beside him. "How do you know this? Who are you?"

"Jean-Marc is my friend. I sometimes see things which others fail to perceive. It is my way."

"Have you seen the marquis?" Lt. Glastre queried with heightened urgency.

"Today I have not. But I know his path. And I know yours, Jean-Luc du Glastre. And I see your intentions are true. That is why I have told you," the Shepherd quietly revealed.

"But how do you know all this? How do you know my name, my *full* name, which I have not used for years?" the lieutenant pressed, unsettled by this man's powerful yet peaceful presence.

"Repeating myself will not provide you with any better an understanding of the matter, Brother." The Shepherd then stepped closer to the young officer, again raising his hand gently toward Glastre's face. "But I can help you with this…"

His soul distracted, Jean-Luc somehow accepted the man's action. The Shepherd gently touched the sides of Glastre's head at the temples with his palms.

Lt. Glastre's eyes widened at first, startled. "The heat… Your hands are so…" Overwhelmed by the effect of the Shepherd's touch, the young officer's eyes closed involuntarily, as he found himself taking a deep involuntary breath. And when he opened his eyes, they widened with a sense of grateful shock and wonder. He felt his head, then touched his nose, looking for blood and found none. Placing his hand on his stomach, pushing slightly at it to test for nausea again, he found none. Jean-Luc turned to the Shepherd.

"What have you done?"

"I have helped you, Brother, because without it, you would have been unable to go much further, despite your commendable and strong determination. Do you see this now, Jean-Luc?" the Shepherd responded with a patient and knowing smile.

"Yes, the pain is gone. But how…?" The lieutenant

regarded him with new eyes of wonder and understandable confusion.

The Shepherd raised his finger encouraging momentary silence. "One more thing," he stated simply as he then placed his left palm on Jean-Luc's solar plexus and his right palm on top of the lieutenant's head. He closed his eyes and breathed slowly and deeply five times.

Jean-Luc's eyes widened in amazement. "The heat… It is like a liquid fire passing through me."

The Shepherd then opened his eyes, smiled and let his hands fall to his sides, releasing Jean-Luc. "Your vitality has been restored as well. You can ride now. But you must take the northern path here to properly reach your destination, Brother. A half hour's brisk trot will bring you to a large oak on the right of the trail, by a rocky stream. Follow the stream higher up until you find a small hut and Raymond the gamekeeper. He will guide you from there," the Shepherd advised.

Lt. Glastre turned to his men with a look of bewilderment, which they too shared. And as he turned back to the Shepherd to thank him, he saw the man had gone from view.

Turning back to his men, he gestured. "Where did he go?"

"He stepped around the tree," one of them offered.

But when the lieutenant went to the nearby large oak tree to investigate, no sign of the Shepherd could be found. While thick underbrush behind abounded, it seemed impossible for anyone to navigate the dense growth without making some sound. But this much was clear: the Shepherd had disappeared.

After looking around once again, Jean-Luc's sense of duty returned with renewed urgency. Fortified by his restored health and feeling a vitality far in excess than he usually enjoyed, he ordered his men to head up the route the Shepherd indicated. They rode with greater speed now that Lt. Glastre had been healed by this mysterious stranger— this Good Samaritan on the road.

A narrow rocky trail led up a tortuous winding track through the mountain forest. All was quiet, except for a loon calling for her mate, unseen in the mottled, lengthening wooded shadows of the early afternoon. Jean-Marc listened to the footfalls of his horse and the spare mount following them on a lead as he guided them on to his ultimate destination, a journey which had been centuries in completion.

The marquis thought of the many faces, the many masks, he had been required to adopt to finally regain possession of the precious tome safely stored in the satchel slung over his shoulder. He did not even want to trust the Book to a pack on his horse, on the chance he might be thrown and separated from his mount. No, he finally had the Book, and with it the transformation of Solange, the only living descendant of his master. He had at long last achieved the completion of a sacred plan, the fulfillment of a hallowed pact.

Jean-Marc reflected, too, on the young woman nestled in his arms and the long journey to bring her this far. He thought of the many selfless sacrifices of those who helped him through the ages, and he considered the cost to his own happiness and dreams of whatever semblance of a normal life he could have enjoyed.

But long ago, he pledged his path to that of the greater good of man. And he was, if nothing else, a man of commitment. It would not be much further till they reached their destination. Just around the bend ahead he expected the trail to come alongside a peaceful meadow, where a stream ran alongside it, pointing his way to the gamekeeper's hut.

As Jean-Marc rode on, however, arriving at the bend, he smelled something which piqued his awareness. A light rain had fallen the night before; the damp grounds gave off a distinct, pleasant and evocative scent as the smell of wood burning in a fireplace touched his senses. He smiled in appreciation and anticipation of reaching safe haven.

Jean-Marc picked up the pace, encouraging his horse to a gentle trot, attending to Solange's secure comfort, as he finally came in sight of the meadow. Up ahead, where he expected to see the small cabin and a barn overlooking the meadow, he also observed a solitary child, amid a rash of yellow and purple wildflowers, chasing butterflies in the golden sunbeams of the day. The young girl spotted the riders and immediately ran toward the cabin at full speed, without uttering a word, only glancing back once at Jean-Marc.

As Jean-Marc and Solange arrived, an older massive man appeared at the doorway, with a large hunting rifle in hand and a deep furrow in his brow. However, as Jean-Marc and Solange emerged from the shadows of a nearby stand of trees—allowing a beam of sunlight to illuminate their features, giving the gamekeeper an opportunity to perceive their identities—his face brightened. He handed his rifle to his granddaughter and crossed quickly to Jean-Marc in a manner of welcome and aid.

"Master! What good fortune has brought you to my door? I would have thought you'd go directly to the manor house. You've clearly been traveling some distance." Raymond Bruen, the gamekeeper, spoke with growing concern as he observed the condition of Jean-Marc's companion. "Is she ill, Master?"

"She's been through much. But I believe quiet and rest are what she needs most... Yet I'm not assured she'll get what she needs at the manor. People are intent on intruding in our affairs, and I'm concerned they may not be far off," Jean-Marc replied.

Quickly all business, Raymond opened his massive arms to receive Solange from Jean-Marc's care. Holding the young maiden now, Raymond could not help but observe her overpowering beauty. As Jean-Marc climbed off the horse, Raymond turned to his granddaughter.

"Christine, take the horses into the barn, feed and water them. Unsaddle the first, but leave the second ready to ride if needed. Then, as before, keep an eye out from the meadow."

The young girl of twelve did as she was told, as Raymond carried Solange into the humble cabin and Jean-Marc breathed a small measure of relief, knowing nonetheless his journey was far from complete.

It did not occur to him that the possibility of finding his quarry hiding in plain sight would be presented to him without effort. His agents who originally came to Rennes Les Chateau—the small village where the leather worker resided who crafted the saddle left behind in the Soubise Palace—had simply asked the wrong questions and used the wrong method of inquiry.

The earlier action resulted in a body needing to be hidden, and now any further helpful information from the saddlemaker was an impossibility.

Yet as his group made their way again to the village, while watering their horses, the bishop had muttered in frustration to one of his men that he remained determined to find the Marquis Jean-Marc Baptiste de Rennes no matter where he might hide.

A devout young maiden tending to a small herd of sheep, much impressed with his church raiment, and who overheard the pronouncement, asked in pure innocence if 'Your Grace' had not found the marquis at his château, which lay in the high ground just south outside of the village. So, when Fortune opened its purse to him, the bishop took the advantages offered without question.

Even without the traditional support of Brother Jerome, the bishop felt he had laid the trap effectively and with suitable foresight. With his force strengthened by ten riders from his Spanish Inquisitorial enforcement unit, and remaining hidden in the line of the forest, he had positioned a small detachment of his troops a short distance from the target of his imminent assault.

He directed his men to identify all possible routes of

escape from the château and secure them before he made his approach. Now assured the trap was airtight, and mounted on the best steed in the group, the bishop rode at the point of his column of armed men, all of whom had orders to chase down anyone trying to escape and firm instructions to kill anyone not matching the marquis's description. He made it clear, as well, that no word must get out that the bishop was here, nor the nature of his business.

Arriving at the front door, as his minions closed in on all the other doors and the estate's stable, the bishop knocked loudly and imperiously, and then tried the front latch, which was unlocked. As he entered, followed by a phalanx of his men, he found a much-surprised servant and maid en route to answer the door.

The bishop gave them no chance to inquire about his business before he loudly demanded that the Marquis Jean-Marc Baptiste de Rennes be surrendered to him immediately, or grave consequences would befall all in the household. Beside themselves with apologetic confusion, both the servant and maid begged the bishop to understand that the marquis had not been here in the château for many months and they were uncertain where he was or when he might return.

Infuriated, the bishop beat the servant until he collapsed on the marble floor, and following the beating, the wounded man cowered at the cleric's feet until a small impatient hand gesture from his captor finally permitted him to stand again. Determined to capitalize on his command of the château, the bishop ordered his men to search the building along with the entire grounds and he demanded the servant take him to the marquis's chambers.

As the bishop inspected the elegantly appointed halls, finally arriving at the marquis's well-stocked library and adjoining laboratory, the cleric could not help but sense the entire château appeared to be more of a museum than a dwelling.

Everything in it seemed more in place for visitors to experience than where someone centered their life. The library held most of the great works that might fill any well-appointed nobleman's book collection. The selected statuary and paintings, while well-chosen and tasteful, were effectively run of the mill for those of titled station.

He found nothing unique or arcane, which is what the bishop sought, something that held the promise of clandestine secrets. Searching through the workshop, too, resulted in the same experience. It was a well-stocked laboratory for standard investigations of a wealthy aristocrat inclined toward general scientific inquiries.

Included in the atelier were some of the marquis's inventions and apparatus for demonstrating magnetism, electricity and static electricity, hydraulics and a rudimentary steam engine. Bishop Antonio del Julia y Sangresante paid little notice to two scale models of hot air balloons suspended from the ceiling in one corner of the lab. Instead, he hunted for any hint of a concealed door which might reveal something occult and hidden. With the servant by his side, the bishop interrogated the man with implicit threat.

"Where are his secret passages? I demand you tell me! To withhold any information from the Holy Church will have the severest of consequences for you and your entire family."

"Your Grace, if he has such things in this house, I've

never been privy to those secrets. I cannot tell you what I do not know," the servant replied with extreme deference and respect, more than fear, as he quietly nursed the fresh cuts and bruises on his face.

"How often does he frequent this place?" the bishop demanded brusquely.

"Once a year for a month or more, Your Grace. The marquis has many properties across the continent. This is but one of them," the servant replied dutifully.

A thought occurred to the bishop and he turned to his next in command. "Put all the horses in the stable. Keep them saddled. I want men on the third floor of the château, facing in each direction watching for an approach from any route. Inform my Spaniards in the forest to come here to the stables. It must appear as though the château is as always. It may be we arrived ahead of him, and we can then give him the welcome he deserves."

As his Spanish lieutenant went about executing the bishop's orders, the cleric sat down at the marquis's desk. After rifling through the drawers, he idly picked up a small bronze bust of Napoleon which sat there.

"And we have plans for you as well, my impetuous upstart who's incapable of learning the important lessons being taught."

And with that, the bishop stared out the study's window, across the lawn which gave a view of the entrance and the main gate, the wheels in his mind ever turning.

Solange lay sleeping deeply in Christine's small bed as Jean-

Marc and Raymond gazed on her with protective concern.

"So she is the last in the line, Master?" Raymond inquired.

Jean-Marc nodded. "So many were hunted through the centuries, it became imperative for the line to go underground and concealed. Even that measure provided no guarantee. Her mother was not as fortunate."

"She is so very beautiful," Raymond observed, more in a fatherly and respectful manner.

"Too often more a curse than a blessing," Jean-Marc replied. Then with a sense of purpose renewed, and energy restored, he turned to Raymond. "There are things I need for her wellbeing. I must go to the château."

Raymond's brow furrowed with concern. "I saw flocks of startled crows rising over the forest earlier today. They were along the approach to your château. By their agitation and formation, I took it that a body of riders was on the road, possibly heading toward your home. That's why I told Christine to be on special lookout before your arrival."

Jean-Marc nodded thoughtfully. "I anticipated this would be the case. Nonetheless, I must go. I fear Solange's welfare is at stake, since the riding here after her treatment was likely the worst thing for her; but at the same time, it was the only alternative."

"Father! Four riders approach!" Christine's voice called from the meadow.

Jean-Marc quickly stepped toward the window, his eye squinting slightly to scope the four riders approaching more than a quarter of a mile away, where the forest's edge gave way to the bottom of the pine-rimmed meadow.

Upon recognition, a slight smile crossed Jean-Marc's

face. Raymond studied his master's relaxed manner with curiosity.

Lt. Jean-Luc Glastre remained nonplused by Jean-Marc's lack of surprise at their arrival. It was as if the marquis had expected them. Jean-Marc welcomed the riders warmly and directed Raymond to provide refreshments for the men as Christine took the horses into the barn and tended to them.

In the cabin, at the rustic table overlooking the meadow, Jean-Marc sat with the lieutenant as two of his men sat by the doorway outside eating and drinking; and the third stood out in the meadow, bare-chested, washing himself in the stream. Jean-Marc studied the young officer with a light smile.

"You appear somewhat confused, Lieutenant," Jean-Marc observed.

"Our arrival here occurred only by virtue of a man dressed as a shepherd, who claimed to be on a pilgrimage, and yet seemed to know exactly who I was and how to get to you. And he quickly healed me of a very serious head injury I sustained outside your apartments in Toulouse. And he did it with a simple laying on of hands which gave such heat. I had privately feared the wound might ultimately be my undoing. And while you know very well you're being pursued by a coldblooded individual of astounding powers who will stop at nothing to achieve his infernal ends, you seem calm and at peace. I am unaccustomed to such strange behavior and phenomena."

Raymond took note of the lieutenant's revelation

regarding the Shepherd with Jean-Marc. "The Master has taken to the road."

Jean-Marc nodded knowingly, turning his calm gaze back to the young officer. "There is more to heaven and earth than is dreamt of in your philosophy, Lieutenant. And it appears one of the reasons you're here now is to live and learn that fact."

Lt. Glastre seemed troubled by other thoughts. Jean-Marc saw this. "More weighs on you than my immediate challenges, Jean-Luc."

"I have orders from the Emperor himself, sir. I'm not sure you'll like hearing what they are," the lieutenant confided.

"Oh, I know what they are, Lieutenant. And you'll ultimately report back to him what took place now and in the following of this day. My dear old friend Napoleon will ultimately understand that our reuniting was not destined to be. He and I now travel very different paths. I helped him when it aided the larger design of things. That work is complete. Anything I might do for him now would not change his future. It has been set. I think on a deeper level he knows this already. He must carry through the actions he has set in motion for reasons of his character and habit. These traits were long his strengths, but I now fear they've become his liability. He is indeed a very proud man. His good works on behalf of mankind are already complete and will live long after him. His endgame will play out within the year. I have a feeling, Jean-Luc, that your good works have only just begun, and in ways you could not begin to imagine," Jean-Marc revealed with enigmatic purpose.

Lt. Jean-Luc Glastre's eyes narrowed in anticipation

while his brow revealed serious concentration. This last day since Toulouse had completely transformed his view of what was normal in the world, and he sensed his loyalties of the moment, as well as the foreseeable future, were inexplicably migrating permanently toward the marquis's needs first, and Napoleon's second.

"**A** rider at the gate, Your Grace," the voice called down from one of his men, this one watching from the third floor facing the front of the manor. "He wears a blue velvet jacket and wide-brim black hat, Your Grace."

Below, in Jean-Marc's study, the bishop stood, crossing to the front of the château, where a window offered a line of sight on the front gate of the property. Indeed, a rider of Jean-Marc's appearance approached, shoulders slightly stooped as though he had traveled long and his horse moving slowly, at a casual pace. There seemed no awareness of imminent threat within the château, and he continued on toward the main entrance of the estate.

"That's him! We have him," the bishop announced. Calling into the residence, he commanded his men. "I want five men on horseback now, around back, in case he tries to flee. The rest of you stand ready to seize him as soon as he passes through the door. Vignon, maintain watch on the third floor."

As the bishop's forces obeyed the command, the rider advanced to a short distance from the main door. Pulling his horse up, the rider seemed on the verge of dismounting as he glanced up to survey the château with body language suggesting an air of relief and satisfaction. His face, however, remained obscured by the tilt of his hat brim from the windows on the first floor and by the angle of regard the rider took while he gazed at the front of the grand dwelling. Inside, the bishop fidgeted impatiently, eager for his trap to finally spring.

In the grand kitchen of the château, inside a large fireplace equipped with a massive iron spit for roasting, currently not in use, one of the thick bolts—which lined the edges of the great iron plate behind the spit—slid horizontally along a small groove, now revealing a hole.

A glint of light from the kitchen revealed an eye peering through this hole, allowing the observer inside to gain a perspective on the quiet of the kitchen. Finally, after a period of assessment by the observer within, well-oiled hinges allowed a section of the iron panel to swing inward ever so slightly, to permit better listening to what transpired inside the grand manor.

"He's about to get off his horse! Make ready! Signal those in back to prepare to ride around front," the bishop ordered his men in as loud a rasping whisper as possible.

Outside, in front of the château, the rider had finished his casual survey of the property. At the moment he committed his weight to the left stirrup to dismount, something caught his attention in the floors above him. Without pause, he immediately remounted and turned his horse, preparing to ride away.

"He must've seen Vignon! Quick, get him! Everyone go! Now!" the bishop shouted, as he ran to the door with his men.

The iron portal behind the roasting spit in the fireplace opened further, Jean-Marc appeared, carefully climbed out of the hearth and exited the kitchen, then silently padded along a back service hall to the entrance of his study, and finally to his laboratory.

Through the workshop's window he saw five of the bishop's riders swiftly galloping by from the back of the manor, heading to the front of the estate. In response, he shifted his position, to assure he remained invisible from outside. Once the riders passed, he went straight to one of the shelves to fetch an earthenware urn which he placed under his arm; and then he silently exited out the way he came.

In front of the château, the bishop cursed the departure of the rapidly escaping rider who had just passed beyond the front gate, heading to the thick forest beyond. The bishop's first three riders of the group were more than fifty yards behind.

Then as the horsemen sped off in pursuit, the bishop turned to see the servant and maid of the household, with their guarded and involuntary smiles. The bishop's eyes narrowed with a sense of seething intuition. He turned back into the dwelling, seizing the maid harshly by the hair as he did, leaving the servant to follow, begging for mercy.

Riding like the wind, Lt. Glastre led his pursuers off on a wild chase through the forest. Coached by Raymond and Jean-Marc, he had a good strategy for his line of escape, though he knew in this weather, tracking him would not be difficult for the committed pursuer.

But he understood his role was to draw attention away from the château so Jean-Marc would have a chance to retrieve the substance he required from his laboratory.

And as he galloped on, steadily building distance from the bishop's men, he had a remarkable reflection. He realized he felt a quality of joy he had not experienced since he was a boy.

Since he had been healed by the mysterious man on the trail—and since he found the determination inside himself that he would indeed help the marquis over and above the command of Napoleon—Jean-Luc felt almost giddy. Emancipated. Seeing the dappled light of the sun through the trees on the path ahead made him feel a profound sense of transported elevation.

Far behind him, his pursers shouted at each other angrily, each jostling for the lead, all intent on capturing their prey, with a special reward for the first to bring him to ground.

Jean-Luc, however, felt only a strange sense of enlightened detachment. Despite his extensive training and skill in the saddle, in both battle and peacetime, he rode his horse as though it were some sort of a magic carpet, feeling a bonding kinship with his mount he had never quite had before. After passing a small rocky ridge which broke the line of sight from the bishop's men, and as he and his steed cut off the trail, through the underbrush of the forest, seeking to broaden the distance from those hunting him with lethal intent, he experienced a quiet joy and excitement.

Descending the narrow spiral stone staircase which linked the back entrance of the large fireplace to an ancient subterranean passageway located there, Jean-Marc recalled the numerous times he had traveled these limestone steps, dipped with use through the centuries. Indeed in times of emergency through the ages, this passageway had been used as an invaluable refuge.

The base of the stairway opened out onto a sizable grotto. Here he retrieved a lantern from a stone table, which he had left burning low during his ascent into his captive château. So familiar was he with the stairway route that he had been able to traverse it earlier in complete blackness, by the touch of the walls and knowing the count of the steps which led up to the thick iron latch and which in turn opened the secret door into the rear of the kitchen's roasting fire pit.

With the lantern and earthenware urn in hand, he made his way through this cavernous chamber, where the lamplight revealed ancient brown, black, red and white prehistoric cave paintings of an eons-old drama. Black silhouettes of primitive spear-wielding men hunted fully colored bison, as well as a herd of large wide-antlered deer: both species long-extinct from these environs and the world.

Long ago, before the rise of civilization, this place had been a sacred space and a site of manhood initiation for Cro-Magnon tribes from the epoch directly following the last Ice Age.

Coming to the end of the high-ceilinged grotto, Jean-Marc arrived at a junction where three passageways opened before him. He took the left and continued on at a quick and easy pace. The network of natural limestone cavern passageways, along with the high panoramic promontory upon which his estate was situated, was why he had first acquired this property and maintained title to it, through various successive identities, since the Visigoths reigned in the land following the fall of the Roman Empire.

He now heard rushing water, which told Jean-Marc he was approaching the entrance of the cavern. As he came within a few feet of his destination, baffled light from the outside illuminated the passageway. He dowsed the lantern and placed it in a carved niche in the wall, hidden in the shadows, where it had been created centuries ago expressly for this purpose.

Jean-Marc crouched very low to navigate the irregular zigzag nature of the passageway, almost a crawl space at points. His course finally grew lighter as he neared the entrance where the sound of rushing water magnified with each approaching step.

The final exit from this subterranean realm entailed sidestepping around a vertical stone wall which brought him to a moss-covered rock recess behind a waterfall fed by a thick rushing stream. Executing the exact footfalls required to exit out to the other side, he finally emerged dry and in the quiet dappled daylight of a remote forest glen.

A casual turn to survey the route of his passage revealed that for anyone who might chance upon the small entry side of the passageway under the fern-shrouded waterfall would not see the slightest hint of the ageless cavern refuge which laid hidden behind the rushing cascade of water.

Jean-Marc deeply appreciated rare sanctuaries such as these. And this one remained unknown even to the longest-living inhabitants of the area. It had provided a venue of safe respite for him and his master through the centuries. Both had used one of the smaller grottos in the complicated network of limestone caves for their periodic 'long sleep' during which they had—for lack of a more fitting and accurate word, since the language of mankind had no knowledge or need for such a term—to hibernate.

These long sleeps traditionally lasted between five and seven years, and to assure a secure location from intruders was critical. And this had been one such place for centuries. Now that the bishop had discovered it, however, Jean-Marc had doubts about the reliability of its security in the years to come. With a trace of sadness, Jean-Marc knew he would likely never return to this place.

Refocusing on the priorities before him, he headed into the thick forest, with the urn in hand, and made his way to Raymond the gamekeeper's hut, less than a half hour's brisk trek away through wooded and rocky terrain.

Upon his return to Raymond's dwelling, Jean-Marc set about taking the dark brown powdered contents of the urn, mixing them with mountain spring water, brought the solution to a brief boil and let it simmer for almost an hour. Then he poured it into an earthenware cup and took it to Solange, who slept lightly in Christine's small room.

He woke her gently and explained she needed to drink what he offered her while still warm. She drank it; and before long, she stirred with invigorated life.

"What was in that, Master?" Solange inquired, as she felt energy coursing through her veins.

"A dried and powdered extract of mushrooms and other rare compounds found only in these mountains. It's one of the reasons I chose a home here. The active elements in the mushrooms will provide a unique boost of your energy for the next four hours, which is critical for us all. We need to move, and we must move quickly, Solange. Do you feel up to the challenge? Can you ride?"

"I think so," she said with grateful disbelief as she stood and found herself enjoying a vitality she had not felt since before the transformation.

She made an observation to Jean-Marc as she looked out the window across the meadow, where Christine sat over a hundred yards away on a log by a stream sparkling in the sunlight. "It's quite remarkable, Jean-Marc. I see details of the girl's clothing. I can even see her eyes moving, her nostrils flaring, her lips pursing," Solange's head tilted slightly, as she listened to something. "And in the distance, I hear a stag calling to his mate."

Raymond, who stood in the doorway, was quite impressed. "I've prided myself on perceiving the sounds of the forest which others cannot, and even I failed to hear what you just heard."

Jean-Marc nodded casually. "This is just the beginning of your journey of discovery, Solange. Under ideal circumstances, I'd say we should go out into the forest to explore and give you an opportunity to get more familiar with your new gifts. Unfortunately, our circumstances are urgent and time is of the essence."

Solange nodded with complete understanding as she got up and strode purposefully into the front of the hut. "Of course, Master. I am ready. But I cannot get over the sensations. It seems my blood pulses with a fire of some sort. I feel stronger, and the clarity and speed of my thinking is something I've never experienced before."

Jean-Marc nodded and smiled slightly as he began to make ready their final arrangements for departure.

As Christine brought Jean-Marc and Solange's horses around to the front of Raymond's hut, Lt. Glastre rode toward them across the meadow and pulled up alongside their horses.

"My man Sauveur has led the majority of the bishop's chasing force on something of a wild boar chase. He's staged to be relieved by my second, dressed in the same way, with a mount matching the first. Hopefully the ploy will lead them far away from here. However, by my observation, the bishop has kept a significant number of his men in reserve."

"He's not a fool and always keeps his options open," Jean-Marc observed as he helped Solange onto her horse. "We must make haste now. Our only true opportunity to escape this place cleanly remains about an hour's ride away."

Jean-Marc mounted his own horse, and after thanking Raymond for the assistance, the three were on their way, riding swiftly across the meadow.

The bishop stood in the kitchen of the marquis's château with the servant and his wife seated before him in chairs, bound with rope.

The bishop had ordered two of his Spaniards to build a fire in the expansive roasting pit. One of the men had an iron poker in the flames which he turned a few times, and finally checked it for its readiness. Seeing the iron tip glowing red, the bishop nodded with approval and gestured for it to be given to him. He brought the fiery point to the maiden's face, mere inches from inflicting serious permanent damage. She sobbed with panic and fear as her husband pleaded with the pontiff.

"Please, Your Grace! We've not seen him in almost a year, and we do not know where he is," the servant declared with sincere conviction and desperation.

The bishop merely stared blankly at the man and moved the iron closer to the woman's cheek. As the proximity of the heat raised blisters on her skin, she cried in helpless pain.

"Her cheek can heal, with time. But the place I intend to direct the point next is her eye, and then her other eye. The choice is yours, knave."

The bishop raised the poker, brought it closer and aimed it at the trembling woman's right pupil. The servant shouted out with helpless beseeching anguish. "Please no! I may know something that might help you!"

The bishop stared at the servant. "Speak," he commanded impatiently.

"I have been truthful to you, Your Grace, despite my loyalty to the marquis. What I did not tell you was that he sent a message to the château. It came the first thing this morning, by pigeon. He made a request."

The bishop's eyes narrowed with interest as he lowered the red hot poker from the woman's face. "Go on."

"As I am sure you know, the marquis is considered to be a natural philosopher of the highest order. His methodical and systematic inquiries into the mysteries and wonders of nature, including magnetism, electricity and the properties of hot gasses are beyond anything I have ever known..."

With rising irritation, the bishop lowered the poker back into the fire, heating his tool of torture in the heart of the flames.

"It sounds to me like you're stalling, you shameless pig. So much of my precious time has been wasted with this pursuit of wild geese. So, once this poker is red hot again, I'll finish the job without hesitation, and with a savoring pleasure. And I'll now include you in my branding exercise, since you've been foolish enough to think you can play with my patience. You have no idea of the number of souls I've dispatched to oblivion. You and she are nothing in my grand scheme of things," he informed the servant with imperious disdain.

Flustered, the servant protested fearfully. "No, Your Grace! Please! I provide this information so that what I'm going to tell you makes sense. Please!" the servant repeated, looking deep into his eyes, and then to his wife's trembling body.

"Go on," the bishop replied, leaving the hot poker in the fire, ready to do his worst.

"At times, the marquis has made a gift of some of his machines. At others, he sent word ahead to have some of his equipment delivered to another location so he might be able to put on a demonstration. Such a request was made this morning. When it came, I didn't know if it was meant to be delivered as a gift, or if he planned some personal utility for it. All I know is that Jacques and Tristan—both loyal men attached to the service of the household—responded and packed the equipment up to have it taken for a delivery to a destination at the exact time the marquis called for."

The bishop stood staring out the window, frowning. He then stared at the servant.

"Exactly what equipment was ordered? What is the location and the time?" the bishop demanded.

The servant shuddered with fear, glancing from side to side, vainly seeking some hope of respite. He knew his next decision would determine either the fate of he and his wife, or that of his generous an inspiring master. Either option filled him with an unavoidable dread.

Montségur
The Pyrenees, France
21 March, 1815 AD – Late Afternoon

Jean-Marc, Solange and Lt. Glastre rode single file, along the downward path of a steep, narrow and rocky trail through the forest. The riders needed to let the horses take their own time choosing their steps along this circuitous stony course. Solange remained preoccupied with thoughts, and after weighing them for a while, she finally spoke, choosing her words carefully.

"Will my father be joining us, Jean-Marc?"

Jean-Marc's manner was somber. "Solange, your father stayed to defend our safe way out. Because I was with you, the last I saw of him was in the laboratory, and he gave us the margin of safety to be where we are now. Gaston knew where we would be going. It may be he chose a different route to reunite with us to avoid being followed. But I cannot truthfully tell you where he is. The men he faced, and one in particular, were all extremely dangerous. Your father knew this as well and he'd have it no other way than to stand in their path."

"My father faced countless dangerous men and situations in the past and he always came home," Solange observed, hoping for the best.

Jean-Marc comforted her. "Your father's more than an invaluably resourceful man and an indomitable warrior. He knew what was at stake with our exceptional circumstances, Solange—especially with his daughter's life in the balance. I'm sorry I can't tell you more. I can tell you he knew our need to keep moving, to escape these lands which are no longer safe. He also knows of all the other properties I own. If and when it's possible, we'll get word to each other once our sanctuary is secured. We have well-established secret channels of communication."

Solange nodded thoughtfully. "I was never able to say goodbye to my mother. She departed on one of her trips, assuring she would return in due course. But she did not. Her ship never arrived in port. It's only my imagination that tells me where she is. It brings me little comfort, Master."

Where the path widened out onto an open meadow, Jean-Marc pulled his roan back slightly, so they rode side-by-side. He extended his free hand to hers, holding it with sincere empathy.

"What we do know is the great works both your parents contributed to for the welfare of mankind. I've known them both as magnificent people. They'll always live in my heart as immortals."

Solange nodded with appreciation, and striving to maintain her emotional equilibrium, she spoke. "If I recall correctly, Jean-Marc, you spoke to me while I drifted in and out of consciousness during our ride here from Toulouse. It reminded me of my mother, when she used to read to me while I slept."

"For some people, this manner of transmission is an effective one. With the scant amount of time we had, I believed this might be an effective way to keep your deeper mind awake and alert while your body went through such drastic adjustments," Jean-Marc offered.

"I understand this aspect of knowledge conduction and I am thankful for your use of it… I've been thinking about the Cathars—what my mother told me about them, and what you added to that understanding."

"And…?" Jean-Marc inquired.

"Their story is very much part of our story, yours and mine, isn't it? When my mother shared their story, she remained careful to present it more from a historian's perspective, one conveyed without emotion or taking sides. She simply told the facts and let me surmise the balance of truth, and the reality of horrors these people who called themselves Christians unleashed on a fundamentally humble, devout and peaceful population, whose only offence was a reasoned disagreement in theology with the Church of Rome. There was no mean or evil spirit in their difference of opinion. Despite how Church historians and their supporters vied to mischaracterize their practices, theirs was a sincere and devout path to a direct relationship with God. The Cathars' very existence, however, threatened Rome's monopoly on souls."

"You said you understood this as more a story which directly involved both you and me, Solange. Tell me more of what you see there," Jean-Marc encouraged her.

"You told me my mother comes from an ancestry very ancient and very important. I think some part of this bloodline story was part of the Cathar story as well. Is that right, Master?"

"Yes it is, Solange," Jean-Marc confirmed.

"And something happened at that time. Something that changed everything," Solange ventured.

"Yes, that's true… Others called us the Cathars—the 'Pure Ones'—but we referred to ourselves simply as 'Good Christians.' Within the movement, at the very center, it had been viewed as His return, though I'm sure history books will continue to deny that. They dismiss the Cathars as heretics and slander them as perpetrators of ugly infernal crimes, just as the Templars were years later. But what remained undeniable was that the spiritual landscape of this region transformed to something new, exciting and revolutionary. People's attitudes about philosophy, history, governance and art all transformed radically. The first spark of the Renaissance was born here. The heart, mind and soul of man emerged from the shadows, out of the Dark Ages, and into a new domain of knowledge and possibility. The Kingdom of Heaven was at hand, in stark contrast with the tortuous Hell on earth forced upon other faithful communities by Rome. The Cathar teaching echoed the Christian Gnostic values and perspectives which rivaled Roman orthodox dogma institutionalized centuries before.

And here these teachings found fertile ground, possibly because of the local history of Septimania—the ancient royal princedom of Jerusalem—which had pure direct roots to the heart and soul of the Holy Land. This region was, of course, also the traditional location identified as the site of Mary Magdalene's landing in southern France after the Crucifixion."

"The Magdalene tradition here is like no other place in the world. Her unmistakable and resonant influence is found everywhere across southern France."

"Indeed it is, Solange. And add to that the later Visigoth influence which laid under the current of the native culture, which embraced an Arian Christian faith—part of the Old Original Christianity from the tradition of Joseph of Arimathea. Its foundation and widespread establishment was in place here well before the Nicene Creed outlawed all other forms of Christianity competing with the Roman model."

"And the Roman Church kept insisting its message was the original one. That no Christian message preceded it."

"Correct. All these older influences promoted a different view of a man's relationship with God. And for the Cathars, founded in ancient Christian Gnosticism, His Good News provided the tangible deliverance of that kingdom. The Kingdom of God was indeed at hand for them. Here in Languedoc it was Heaven on Earth," Jean-Marc revealed.

Solange processed Jean-Marc's statement as she added what she already knew of this subject. "But the Pope and his Vatican hierarchy would have nothing to do with it. Your Kingdom of God threatened their stranglehold on the hearts and minds of the people of Christendom. The one at the forefront of this change had to be stopped, and *he* was my ancestor," Solange spoke, piecing the story together as she rode.

"The threat of the possible existence of the *Desposyni* could not be ignored. He *and* She had to be stopped," Jean-Marc said, modifying Solange's observation.

" '*Desposyni*.' My mother taught me about them years ago. They're 'the brothers of Jesus'—the bloodline of Joseph and Mary who survived the Crucifixion—James, Simon, Joses and the other Judas. I thought they all perished within decades of the Christ's ascension, leaving no heirs.

"There are two views of the *Desposyni* tradition. The first is as you described, the more public and traditional version. The second is the suppressed, true and original meaning: that they are the direct descendants of Jesus. Try as the Church did, stamping out the message could never be completely achieved," Jean-Marc replied and studied her meaningfully.

"The descendants of Jesus and Mary Magdalene," Solange uttered as larger wheels in her thinking turned, and her eyes widened. "It staggers my mind."

Jean-Marc continued, "This possibility was the ultimate existential threat. And the ruthless Albigensian Crusaders hunted the Cathars mercilessly, for years, with the Inquisition exterminating all their supporters, burning all their writings, until the last of the faithful were ultimately cornered in their final key refuge, where it all ended… Montségur."

And as the three riders arrived at a bend in the trail, where a line of pine trees broken by a rock outcropping gave a panoramic view across the valley, Jean-Marc pointed to a solitary rocky peak. At this distance, the ruins of a fortress could be seen at the crown of the stone mountain. "That is where it ended for so many."

"That's where his story ended?" Solange asked reverentially.

"No, Solange, it's where his wife Marie's story ended." Jean-Marc revealed with pensive reflection.

"The leaders of the crusade could not tolerate that anyone might defy the Church of Rome by answering to a different holy hierarchy than their Apostolic claim or holding beliefs different from those they demanded were the uncontestable Articles of Faith. Their version of the 'Good News' of the gospels on this depraved crusade was terror, death, destruction and pillage. It certainly gave credence to the Cathars' original position that two gods existed, not one, and that the pontiffs of Rome worshipped the dark one—*Rex Mundi*, 'King of the World'—ruling over the materialistic, power-based, chaotic world, bent on crushing any glimmer of hope of a direct relationship with the good god, of spirit, love and peace, in heaven, who Yesu represented. The Vatican's opulent and luxurious lifestyle, rampant with obscene privilege, granted favor to those who paid the right price. Those offences, along with the Church Fathers' enforced insistence on worshiping the Roman symbol of torture and execution—the cross—were considered proof of which god the Pope was aligned with."

"Joshua and Marie… Husband and wife…" Solange murmured. "Yesu and Mary…"

"And in Roman Church documents, *their* children were referred to as the *Desposyni*. As long as their bloodline survived they remained a true threat to the Vatican. And

485

indeed if they had any children, their line would trump any claim of an apostolic legacy. Any proof of their existence endangered all claims of legitimate apostolic succession. The entire bloodline had to be eradicated at all costs. Wiping out and eliminating any record of their existence has been a prime mission of theirs for centuries," Jean-Marc explained.

"*Desposyni* a threat? They should've been welcomed, honored and protected," Solange observed.

" '*Desposyni*' is Greek for 'Heirs of the Lord,' descendants of the bloodline of Jesus, through his mother. The term didn't exist until after the time of Christ and the legacy was recognized as being a problem. This ultimate royal bloodline posed a direct threat to the papal claim of supremacy in all things Christian. And the thought that Mary Magdalene's legacy might be fused with their Savior was an abomination to them. Its very nature suggested a fundamental invalidation of their position of women in the church, because Mary stood as a dominant and central figure in conveying Yesu's original message, as was revealed in the suppressed Gospel of Philip. And during the Cathar chapter, Yesu's true message encouraged the complete recognition of her leading role," Jean-Marc explained.

Throughout their ride, Lt. Jean-Luc Glastre trailed behind them, listening to the exchange with a sense of respectful but brittle disbelief, growing agitation and now finally reflexive indignation.

"What do you mean by Rome's 'dubious claims of apostolic succession?' Saint Peter is buried below the very cathedral in Rome which is named after him. It's from his personal leadership of the Church in Rome and tragic martyrdom there where this apostolic institution began. It's an unbroken chain of succession from Peter to the present Pope. This remains historical fact, sir," Jean-Luc claimed emphatically, disclosing his time-honored Catholic upbringing.

"That is indeed a centuries-long *tradition*, Lieutenant—one which began with Tertullian's writings in 250 AD. He was the first to claim Peter was in Rome, with nothing else but his statement and thin air to substantiate it. However tradition does not constitute historical fact. There are no records from the time to even suggest he visited Rome, and much to discourage that perspective. He's never mentioned in the Acts of the New Testament which chronicle St. Paul's tenure in Rome, supposedly at exactly the same time Peter should have been there. Furthermore, Peter is buried in the first Christian cemetery of Jerusalem. His tomb there is clearly marked. Paul, *not* one of the original apostles, and a self-appointed one at that, was the only one to go to Rome. His journey there was to face charges for his implication in fomenting civil unrest and the murder of a prominent Jewish high priest of the Sadducees—Jonathan Annas—in Jerusalem," Jean-Marc replied casually as he guided his horse around a tight rocky corner on the trail.

"Saint Paul implicated in a murder? This is simply not possible, Monsieur! The man was a saint, carrying the Word of God to the people! You go too far, sir!"

"He carried a message to the people which he claimed was from God, but which remained fundamentally of his own creation—'revealed' to him directly by God. He repeatedly ignored and even contradicted the teachings of Yesu and the original Twelve Apostles. He never once even directly quoted Yesu in his teachings to support his own

487

message. And as far as being implicated in murder, the Bible itself attests to his leadership of those who stoned the first Christian martyr to death in Antioch—St. Stephen. That was before Paul changed his name from Saul. In Josephus—the contemporary historian of the age—the murderer of Jonathan Annas was identified as 'The Egyptian.' In the Acts of the New Testament, Paul was interrogated and specifically asked if he was 'The Egyptian,' to which he refused to answer directly. The next thing chronicled in the Acts was Paul being sent to Rome to face charges, employing his privilege as a Roman citizen to avoid facing trial in Jerusalem. And when shipwrecked in Malta, and bitten by a snake, observers claimed it was proof he was a murderer, echoing their understanding of why he was being conveyed to Rome in custody. Despite their prodigious efforts to do so, the Church Fathers could never successfully obliterate the real story. Vestiges of the truth remained." Jean-Marc informed him. "Indeed some even implicate Paul in the stoning death of his principal rival for leadership of the Christian community, Yesu's brother, head of the Jerusalem Church, Saint James the Just—exactly the same way St. Stephen died."

"But Christ had no brothers or sisters," Jean-Luc insisted.

"You've learned well the Church's Articles of Faith, it would appear, without question, Lieutenant. But are you capable of learning the truth?" Jean-Marc replied in an off-handed challenging manner.

"It's all too incredible. And what you're saying about the Cathar movement representing the True Word of Jesus, why that's completely imposs—"

Yet something in Jean-Luc held him from finishing his damning declaration. He had seen enough in the last day to know—on a much deeper level—that there might be much more to the people he rode with, and the story he was involved with, to make rash statements of what must pass for traditional reason in a world where the Sciences of Man continued to uncover new revelations that compellingly challenged the long-accepted Church doctrine. And he was no man of science, nor letters. This much he knew: to make definitive pronouncements about what was possible, and what was not possible, was indeed unrealistic and untenable, and could in actuality really only be expressed as an opinion, not fact.

Jean-Marc noted Lt. Glastre's disquiet of mental conflict. "Jean-Luc, I truly appreciate you maintaining control of your reflex to judge things you're not yet ready to understand. It's encouraging and commendable. I see great things in store for you and your descendants."

"My descendants?" Jean-Luc replied with unexpected and engaged curiosity.

"Yes, that is certain. I have seen it."

"But how could you see such things?" the young lieutenant wanted to know.

"That's for another time, I'm afraid." Jean-Marc stated as the trio reached the edge of the pine forest-ringed meadow and a nearby rocky outcropping which gave way to the top of a grassy knoll leading to a much wider trail a short distance below them. "But first we must extricate ourselves from a gathering storm. We have company," he continued.

Arriving on the knoll, a panoramic view of the valley

sprawled out around them. Following on his spoken point, Jean-Marc gestured into the distance to their left, and to the north, where the high ground they had just descended from extended in a vast amphitheater-like configuration which went more than two miles above and behind them into the distance. Midway on this mountain slope, at a patch of trees and rock, stood the location the marquis indicated with his gesture. Lt. Glastre frowned, unclear exactly to what Jean-Marc had referred.

"Excuse me, but do you see something I do not, sir? I have extensive experience with reconnaissance missions, spotting the subtlest enemy movements in the distance. But here, I confess, I see nothing."

Solange smiled knowingly as she turned to the cavalry lieutenant, as she only now recognized that this young man was an individual of inherent, yet somewhat unrefined quality. "You'll get used to it, Lieutenant. He has powers of seeing at great distance which will astound you and defy belief." She looked in the direction Jean-Marc indicated and was suddenly galvanized with urgent concerns of her own. "My God! There must be more than twelve of them, Master."

"Thirteen. One's currently behind a tree. We must make haste or all will be lost. The one leading them authors the design of our eternal undoing, the one with the unique blue and green eyes. Study his face now, quickly, while you have the opportunity. I dare say he's doing the same to you."

And after a brief pause for Solange to do as instructed, and with the open ground nearby below them, Jean-Marc spurred his horse and trotted down to the wider trail, leaving his companions to also hasten their speed as best possible. Their destination was the solitary rock mount a short distance ahead of them: Montségur.

The bishop, of course, possessed the same power of enhanced sight as Jean-Marc and Solange; and as soon as his quarry hit open ground providing a broader view, he spied them immediately. The cleric ordered his men to accelerate their pace down the still steep and rocky trail with the greatest speed possible. The mixed company of Spaniards and sundry mercenaries rode with a vengeance, knowing success would bring them promised rewards from their merciless leader; and failure would result in consequences none of them wanted to consider.

Having just recently acquired an understanding of what the Marquis Jean-Marc Baptiste de Rennes planned, it had become crucial for the bishop to intervene now, before it was too late. Showing marked impatience, he shouted at his company to press on to Montségur with the greatest urgency.

For all that he cursed Brother Jerome's missteps in the past, now in the middle of an urgent action, the bishop privately rued the absence of the man who had delivered so robust and emphatic actions on his behalf though the centuries. And now in this crucial action he rued the absence of the monk's ruthless and brutally efficient support. For now, it was all up to the bishop to provide both the intelligent decisiveness and forceful ruthlessness of action in equal and effective measure.

"For King, Country and your Holy Church! They must

not make it to the ruins of the castle! Everything counts on that! I'll reward any man who captures the marquis with a hundred gold *soldi*! Another hundred for the book he carries!" The bishop challenged the mounted troops at his side as he pointed across the canyon to where the trio of riders made their way down the grassy knoll to the road below them.

In an instant, the front of the bishop's pack broke into a barely managed risky trot, down the rocky winding trail, striving to reach a wider expanse where they could let their horses gallop full speed.

The bishop watched as his wave of riders jockeyed for the forward position in the column which would give them the best advantage once flat, unforested ground became available to push their horses into a full run.

And then finally, once the trail met an open pasture, it became a mad race toward the trio more than a mile ahead of them.

Having seen their pursuers' actions, Jean-Marc and his companions galloped as quickly as possible toward the bare rock mountain peak which stood ahead of them. The small, barren castle of beige stone perched atop Montségur stood in mute witness to strife through the centuries, offering hopeful refuge once more to those in dire need.

As Jean-Marc and Solange both knew, the imposing and solitary bare rocky crag of a mount they approached was rich in charged emotional history for the region.

Here the Cathar movement fundamentally ended with

492

the burning of over two hundred Cathar faithful at the mountain's base. People locally accepted and loved as being 'Good Christians'—yet whom the Church of Rome branded as heretics—had held out against a force of ten thousand crusaders in a siege which lasted ten months and resulted in the collective execution of these people whose only crime was seeing their relationship and belief in Christ as being different from the rigid dogma enforced with militant uniformity by the powers of the Vatican.

Returning here after so many years certainly had its poignant associations for Jean-Marc. Yet the choice of the location for the marquis was not because of the history of the place.

Its location at the base of the Pyrenees range possessed particular characteristics specific to the locale itself, and which he deemed strategically fortuitous and hopefully advantageous. Yet as they galloped through the small highland village, well ahead of their pursuers, and reaching the base of the *poq*—the local term for 'mountain peak'— where the precipitous narrow craggy trail led up to the only access to the solitary redoubt, Jean-Marc could not help but recall the tragic history of this landmark.

Their horses struggled up the steep, tortuous rocky trail, where loose stones made the passage a perilous one, the route shrouded with a thick stand of pine trees offering temporary cover from their pursuers. Finally the trail became simply too steep to ride on horseback and Jean-Marc signaled that his companions should now dismount and lead their steeds up on foot.

As the trio continued, the stone foundation vestiges of the centuries-old former Cathar village habitation, more like rock rubble—too easily missed by the unobservant eye—came into view on either side of the trail.

In 1244, this site was where many Cathars lived before retreating into the mountaintop redoubt itself, and Jean-Marc could not help but sadly recall the doomed lives of the hopeful inhabitants—whole families who lived for the dream of a new land blessed with a faith that answered their beliefs with a loving support.

It was a dream that ended as a nightmare. This place represented the last significant vestige of a once great and vibrant movement in these exotic Occitan lands. Despite the fact that small isolated outposts of Cathar resistance were subsequently hunted down and extinguished in following years, the critical mass of the movement sustained its most profound and decisive mortal blow at Montségur.

While the castle they now approached was not the original fortification which stood during Cathar times, this hallowed pinnacle upon which the citadel itself stood, was revered in the ancient lore of the Holy Grail. Tradition recorded the first structure to stand here was the Holy Grail castle, where the Fisher King—of Wolfram von Eschenbach's *Parzival*—dwelled in ancient times. And indeed the mysterious Cathar treasure which was rumored in the outside world to have successfully been carried away under the cover of night—through the Albigensian crusader lines before the tragic surrender of the doomed faithful—had been the Holy Grail itself, the sacred Cup of Jesus Christ from the Last Supper.

Jean-Marc, of course, knew exactly what the treasure was, having accompanied it that dark night, rappelling down the steep windswept rock face of Montségur, on a very long, sturdy rope.

And while the 'treasure' had been preserved, another equally valuable treasure had been lost that next day in the bonfire of Cathar 'heretics,' because, despite being entreated by the faithful to take the chance for escape, Marie could not allow those who had been faithful to her and her husband for so long to die alone.

She would not accept the offer of safe escape, but insisted the message be conveyed to her husband to continue the mission they had worked so hard to sustain. Her husband, the Shepherd, never got over the tragedy, despite his mastery of body, heart and spirit. She had been his partner, his advisor, his very soul.

Solange, too, experienced emotional reflections as they approached the legendary citadel. Despite the fact the structure of the stronghold which now stood ahead of them was a fortress that had been built over the torn-down Cathar castle, she knew the stone used to build it was the same, and the enduring resonant symbolism for all who beheld the place was equally profound. Solange recalled, as well, other stories her mother shared with her which now conveyed a unique and powerful resonance for her. She recalled the stories of Mary Magdalene's arrival on the southern shores of a land which would later be known as France, near Marseilles, in the Roman Province of Narbonensis.

As tradition recorded, Mary Magdalene touched shore in a rudderless boat in the company of personalities from the Bible: Martha, Lazarus, Mary Jacob, Mary Salome and Saint Maximin, all of whom who would ultimately be credited with different roles in the conversion of 'pagan' Gaul to Christianity, the Christianity before the Roman Church's orthodox dogma—the Original and True Christianity.

Solange remembered how her mother told her Mary Magdalene also arrived with a blessed child in her company, a child of sacred royal birth: Sarah. When the story was shared with Solange in her youth, she felt a peculiar curiosity for it, since it was so at odds with the traditional Vatican-based story of the proliferation of Christianity.

Solange also reflected on the original destination of Mary Magdalene and her companions as well as the location further west on the coast of the Mediterranean—the Hebrew Principality of Semptimania, where the powerful House of Arimathea, headed by Joseph, had considerable holdings. Because of his extensive trading network in the Roman Empire, he enjoyed powerful influence as well. And Solange remembered her mother told her how Joseph of Arimathea had been the group's protector and helped to set them up in various locations around the province while he himself afterwards traveled to southern England—to Glastonbury—to establish the first foothold of early Christianity in those lands, also accompanying as guardian, another sacred royal child, a boy.

What held compelling fascination for Solange then, now held an arresting sense of revelation. She quietly felt a deep heartache for her mother and the journey of knowledge Solange was never able to complete with her. Never knowing her mother's final fate, as was also now the case with her father, for whom she had a grave foreboding, Solange felt a sense of disorientation and loss, the feeling only accentuated by the new alchemical influences coursing through her body.

The rocky path became narrower and almost impassible even on foot. Looking out over the rocky terrain around them, and judging the remoteness and singular access of their destination, the lieutenant's veteran concern of military position gave rise to expression.

"We may be able to defend this position as long as our supplies last, but there's no escape from this place. Sir, we're trapped here. Are you sure this is where you wanted to make your last stand?"

As they trekked on slowly, leading their horses, Solange turned to Lt. Glastre, whom she regarded with unguarded warmth, and replied, "The marquis would not choose this location unless he had a good reason."

"Your seasoned observation and concern is duly noted and appreciated, Lieutenant. However, you're still a man who's inclined toward making certain assumptions about situations without seeing all the influences at play. It's only natural. I know as well it's the product of your best intentions," Jean-Marc said.

The marquis then took hold of a hunting horn, which had been slung over his shoulder, brought it to his mouth, and blew it loudly. After a short pause, another horn blew back in reply, signaling to Jean-Marc's group that someone inside the ruins of the castle expected them.

Jean-Marc directed Solange and Jean-Luc to move as quickly as possible on foot up to the rocky entrance of the imposing ancient fortification which finally came into full view above them through the trees.

There, Lt. Glastre breathed a sigh of relief to see his

three men waiting for them. As planned, they arrived here only if they had succeeded in shaking off the bishop's men who had been pursuing their tag-team while disguised as the marquis. His man Sergeant Auzac— who had been tracking the bishop's party—was also here, having encountered the trio on their way here to the mountain. One man now scouted from the parapet, and the two others had constructed a barricade of fallen trees from the forest, with which they left a small passageway for the three new arrivals to pass before they closed it off against the onslaught that would come before too long.

Once inside, Jean-Marc took note of two large sheets of burlap material which lay open on the stony ground with rope strewn under it on all sides, suggesting this material had originally been employed for packaging bulky objects of some nature. Indicating it to the lieutenant's men, he inquired, "So my solution is all in place then?"

Sergeant Sauveur Auzac, the lieutenant's second in command, answered, shaking his head slightly revealing a mixture of doubt, reluctant fascination and respect. "It is, sir. Your men, Jacques and Tristan, are extremely capable. Though judging by the force on the move toward us, I'm not yet convinced it will work."

Gazing out to the west, where the sun slid down toward the mountainous horizon, Jean-Marc seemed to calculate something as he replied to Auzac. "Timing is the key, Sergeant. That, as well as a reliable observation of the local conditions I've conducted over the years."

Solange and Jean-Luc remained intrigued and somewhat mystified by Jean-Marc's remark. As the marquis turned and led them into the wider expanse of the ruined castle's courtyard, their leader's plan became more readily apparent. Jean-Marc's two assistants, Jacques and Tristan, were stationed in place.

Upon sight of the marquis's solution, Solange burst into involuntary laughter, and Lt. Glastre's eyes widened with wonder as Tristan looked up. Seeing Jean-Marc, Tristan waved and reported, "All is in readiness, My Lord." Jean-Marc nodded his grateful approval.

A large balloon, with colorful decorations festooning its side, stood before them. With a wicker passenger basket capable of holding at least four people, it had been inflated with the benefit of a combustion device housed below the opening of the balloon, providing hot air which gave the craft lift. The balloon remained tethered by a rope tied to a large stake in the sandy soil on the floor of the castle grounds.

"This truly is a *deus ex machina*, sir. I commend you. I pray it works!" Lt. Glastre said with an incredulous laugh.

The bishop cursed his troops' unfamiliarity of the terrain. This gap in local knowledge slowed them down, taking wrong turns in culverts that originally seemed to lead straight across the plain, yet which he knew Jean-Marc had led them into with a strategic delaying purpose.

And now with the mythic ruins of Montségur finally looming above them, one of his men had tumbled from his horse on the steep incline of the rocky trail causing the rider directly behind him to also fall, resulting in a broken arm which took the second rider completely out of commission.

Caring only for the critical mass of his force, the bishop assessed his troop numbers for the logistics that lay ahead of him, recognizing the timing of his attack—which must be immediate and effective—was the issue crucial to his success.

Ignoring his injured rider, Bishop Antonio del Julia y Sangresante ordered his men off their horses to deploy against the ruined castle fortification, still some distance up the mountain from them, and which presented a daunting refuge for his men to assault—given his limited resources and Jean-Marc's benefit of the high ground and advanced knowledge of their coming assault.

Just as the bishop's men began to meet armed resistance on their approach toward the entrance of the redoubt, something caught the cleric's eye in the mountain valley below and behind him. A lone rider galloped at full tilt in their direction.

As the bishop glanced in distraction at the figure, a small smile spread across his face. Though the eye patch obscured his facial features because of the low position he adopted to facilitate his gallop, there was still no mistaking the monk's robes and the massive muscular frame within them. Brother Jerome was headed toward them, and he would be here within moments. The bishop's spirits quickly rose as the new options of assault presented to him immediately multiplied with advantageous favor.

A seething rage coursed through Brother Jerome's veins. All he wanted was the death of Jean-Marc, whose actions had so confounded his master, the bishop, and who now stood directly responsible for the loss of his eye through his proxy, the fat old Army veteran.

The monk had been left with the mendicant nuns at the small infirmary of the Eglise des Jacobins in Toulouse, the birthplace of the Inquisition. After a short deep sleep, however, he roused, and before long was ambulatory, much to the surprise of his caretakers. But his reawakening was not without him taking his covert rejuvenating and voracious refreshment from one of the smaller nuns—in a storage closet—which would be the topic of horrified and mystified discussion for decades to come.

Because the bishop had never seen the severity of a wound such as the one the monk sustained to his eye—which refused to heal as quickly as they both experienced for centuries past—Sangresante decided that leaving him in the care of the nuns was the most sensible short-term solution.

Word was left for the monk, however, should he revive, where the bishop's ultimate destination was. And within an hour of rising from a complete coma-like unconsciousness, Brother Jerome rode at full gallop, headed south for the regions near the city of Foix, where the Marquis Jean-Marc Baptiste de Rennes was now known to have his château—information of which had been conveyed immediately to the monk by benefit of a carrier pigeon from the bishop.

The monk pushed his horse at full gallop until it was ready to drop, stopping at local farms along the way and demanding a replacement, with pay. On one occasion along his way to join the bishop, the monk happened upon a farm where a lone lad cared for the livestock of the farm, and

Brother Jerome availed himself of the nutrients within the boy, leaving him drained of life and blood.

Feeling additionally replenished with vital energy, the monk rode on, but the failure of his eye to heal properly only deepened his rage and his determination to have unholy revenge. At the marquis's château, he got the coordinates of the bishop's whereabouts; and now he was finally racing to his liege lord and ungodly collaborator in immortality.

As the monk arrived on the *poq*, he pulled up his chestnut mare, jumped off and began to scramble up the steep rocky trail with a lion-like ferocity. Before long, he joined the bishop, who pointed urgently at the fortification where his men were harried with gunfire from defenders behind the barricade at the gate.

"You must join the assault and break through the barricade before the marquis can escape. He has a plan, and the advantage is his! Time is of the essence, Hieronymus! Strike now or all is lost!"

Brother Jerome knew the bishop well enough that this was not the time to ask questions for more details, despite the fact that, from what he observed as he rode up, this solitary rocky crag seemed to offer no possible avenues of escape.

It may be, however, that the bishop became aware of a hidden subterranean passageway, or some other piece of intelligence. Without inquiring further, Brother Jerome jogged up the steep incline to where the bishop's forces had ducked behind rocks to trade pistol shots with the defenders.

A lull in the gunfire ensued. Casting caution aside, the

Parabolani monk sprinted straight for the barricade, intent on barging right through the structure, clearing a path for his allied forces.

At this moment, his aggressive advance on the position provided Brother Jerome a better view of what might be behind the barricade. He saw two things. It was now deserted, and two small columns of smoke rose from either side of the makeshift barricade which blocked the entrance to the castle.

Only a step further revealed to Brother Jerome the source of the smoke came from two fuses leading deep into the piled-up hastily assembled wood that made the barricade in front of the entranceway. Before he could react, however, an explosion erupted. It blew the barrier into a tangled chaos and forcefully hurled Brother Jerome ten feet backward where he landed momentarily stunned on his back.

At this same instant, a strange sight loomed over the parapet of the ruined castle, above the attackers and Brother Jerome, who struggled to regain his clarity of focus. Ascending gracefully over and above the parapets of the castle now, a colorfully painted and ornately designed hot air balloon appeared. Festooned with Napoleon's imperial crest, the eagle in a blue field, topped by a royal crown ensconced in a wreath and draped in an ermine cloak, decorated with iconic bees, the fantastic craft rose further above them.

Low silhouettes of a few passengers in the large, open, colorful passenger gondola below were visible, but not clearly identifiable. One of the passengers, however, came into view at the gunwale of the gondola—Lt. Glastre. With a pistol in each hand, the determined cavalry officer carefully aimed at the attackers and fired one shot, then another, as the bishop's dragoons scrambled for cover. Jean-Luc was handed two new pistols from comrades out of sight—and he took two more judiciously targeted shots—as the balloon rose higher.

The obscured angle of perspective for anyone on the ground made it impossible to see who else might be in the large wicker gondola of the airborne craft. Rising higher, the airship caught a cross wind which quickly moved it out over and beyond the steep and forbidding rock precipice which defined the north side of the mountain refuge.

Seeing this, the bishop shouted to his men, gesturing desperately. "Quick! Back to your horses! Don't let them get away! Pursue them! Follow this vehicle of Satan!"

The bishop's gang ran to comply with the orders, dashing pell mell down the steep rocky zigzag trail through the thin forest of pine trees to their horses some one hundred yards below them, to re-engage with the chase.

Along the way, one Spaniard tripped and fell forward on the rocks without enough reaction time to break the fall with his arms, and struck his face full force on the sharp stones. He did not get up and now lay inert on the path.

Scrambling around him, the posse members otherwise ignored the gravely wounded comrade as they dashed off down the rocky dirt track to pursue the balloon. The bishop followed right along with them, determined to keep as close to his quarry as possible.

"Shoot at the balloon itself! Bring it down!" he shouted as they rode on in pursuit of the escaping prize.

As he finally stood, recovering from his close proximity to the blast, Brother Jerome, however, found himself focused on other things. Something did not seem right to him. Avoiding possibly being seen through the gateway of the fortress, he scrambled into the underbrush which gave him vertical access to the highest point on the stone parapet, and he began to climb up the face of rough stone masonry with strong experienced ease.

Inside the rocky courtyard of Montségur, Jean-Marc and Solange stood by a second balloon, much smaller than the first, and without any markings. It was inflated, tethered and ready to fly and originally had been out of sight behind the larger balloon when Solange and her companions first arrived inside the castle.

Jean-Marc intently observed a staff that had been installed by his assistant Tristan at the highest point of the fortification. It had a small red cotton cloth tied to it, and this small banner fluttered lightly in the prevailing breeze. As Solange climbed into the passenger basket of the balloon, she glanced at Jean-Marc with a questioning look.

"Should we not ascend now, Master? The force has been distracted and drawn away. We can make our ascent without opposition."

"All in due course, Solange. We're waiting for the wind to change. Just at sunset—I have observed in the past—the prevailing breeze changes from that of a gentle western flow, which would take us on a course following the lieutenant's balloon, to an eastern wind off the mountains which will take us in the opposite direction, to the sea. I just need to see the indication on the flag. Otherwise the bishop's men, who are in pursuit of the first balloon already, will be well-positioned to take us easily."

As he watched the flag, Solange grew concerned, urgently needing to see the wind change. Her apprehension turned to primal fear when she spied a dark figure appear at the top of the wall opposite them, at the long end of the irregularly shaped, five-sided, oblong courtyard: Brother Jerome had just climbed over the parapet and scowled at spotting them.

Instead of jumping down to the floor of the courtyard, to challenge them from ground level, he began to jog around the stone parapet toward them, maintaining the high ground advantage.

Jean-Marc calmly noted the direction of the wind on the makeshift flag had finally changed. The red banner fell limp as the original prevailing breeze died. And as it did, he also sighted Brother Jerome just as Solange called his attention to the intruder.

"That's it! Cut the ropes on your side, Solange, quickly! Everything counts on our speed now," Jean-Marc exclaimed, noting Brother Jerome's low jogging advance along the top of the wall.

The tether ropes were cut. Released from its restraints, the balloon began to rise slowly as Jean-Marc jumped into the small passenger basket gondola, joining Solange.

As the balloon rose, however, Brother Jerome loped easily and quickly along the top of the wide uneven ramparts of Montségur castle, on an interception course where the balloon would have to rise and pass closest to the stone walls of the castle.

Seeing the monk's plan and vector of pursuit, Solange was distressed. "I don't think we're going to make it, Master!"

Studying the closing distance of the advancing monk and their rate of ascent, Jean-Marc turned and smiled to her with surprising calm. "We do our best, and we can do no more. I think we'll be fine. I have one more trick left to lighten our ballast and slow him down."

Jean-Marc then reached into the bottom of the balloon's basket and pulled out a large and unwieldy leather bladder-sack—the size of a bushel basket—holding a liquid of some sort.

He quickly heaved it with expert ease as well as considerable strength and accuracy to the top of the rampart closest to them, where the savage monk approached and which he needed to cross to reach them. The sack burst open and spilled out a thick, viscous oily substance which splashed for almost ten feet across the crest of the rampart—just as the monk reached it.

Unable to stop himself in time, he trod onto the slippery surface and fell, though not off the top of the wall. Instead he reacted quickly, slapping his hands down, letting his legs slip to either side of the wall, as though he had mounted a greased horse. Lightened by the release of the dead weight of the heavy oil sack, the balloon accelerated its rise, cresting the top of the battlements, just as the monk struggled to get back to his feet.

Scrambling like a simian, with his two hands moving on

the stone parapet to maintain balance, the monk finally reached the dry sure footing along the wall beyond the oil slick. He scowled with rage, redirecting his purpose at his rapidly escaping quarry. He began to run again at the ascending balloon, which had not yet completely cleared the confines of the courtyard.

Just as the new prevailing breeze hit the flag, and the balloon began to be carried away from the wall in the opposite direction of the 'Napoleon' balloon, Brother Jerome reached a flat stretch on the wall. The monk bolted into a sprint and leapt out with startling force over the sheer precipice of the wall, which gave way to an even steeper rock cliff dropping off for hundreds of feet below.

With astounding strength, the monk's soaring leap took him much further than any normal being was capable of; and with equally impressive strength, he successfully grabbed onto one of the rope tethers hanging from the balloon.

As the abrupt addition of his heavy weight forced the balloon to dip in the air, it threatened to bring the craft down altogether, so heavy was the monk's weight against the balloon's lift.

Seeing this, Jean-Marc quickly came to the edge of the passenger basket with a knife, intent on cutting the rope. As he leaned over, however, Brother Jerome hauled himself up by one arm, with superhuman strength, and grabbed with his free hand the strap of the canvas bag slung over Jean-Marc's shoulder.

The force of this action pinned Jean-Marc against the edge of gondola. Held by the strap, Jean-Marc struggled against being pulled over the edge by the monk. Thinking quickly, Solange grabbed the knife from Jean-Marc's hand and hastily cut the strap from Jean-Marc's shoulder, freeing him from the monk's weight. As the bag slipped away, Jean-Marc scrambled quickly to grab at the contents in the shoulder bag itself.

"The Book!" Jean-Marc cried out.

The Book only came out part way from the bag; and as the monk slid down, Brother Jerome grabbed at the tome, getting hold of the front cover and a few pages of the ancient fragile artifact, causing it to rupture, tear open, and fall apart in the open air just below the gondola.

As Brother Jerome plummeted alongside the sheer drop of the cliff—a few parchment pages clutched in his fist—he bellowed in rage and finally disappeared from view in the forested shadows at the base of the cliff.

Jean-Marc and Solange gazed helplessly out at other parchment pages of the Book, torn open by the monk, as they blew in every direction. While the balloon ascended in the steady wind which proceeded to convey them to the east, they soon sighted the Mediterranean coast coming into view in the distance, bathed in the rose-colored reflections of a waning day.

Seeing this airborne engagement from a distance, the bishop yelled out to his men, now well advanced toward the west, in pursuit of the first balloon.

"Stop! Come back! Recover the Book! Recover the pages!" the frantic cleric yelled out in desperation.

Riding after his men, the bishop continued to shout at

them until they heard him. They then broke off their pursuit of the first balloon and redirected their energies to the fluttering pages in the distance now spreading out in the evening breeze across the countryside, as the light began to set on the western mountains.

In the Napoleon balloon, Lt. Glastre and Jean-Marc's assistant, Tristan, as well as Sergeant Sauveur Auzac, viewed the developments with relief for both themselves and for Jean-Marc's wellbeing. From his vantage point in the balloon, Jean-Luc saw his three other men safely making their way down the cliffside by rope, away from the bishop's men, with the assistance of Tristan's associate, Jacques.

Jean-Luc reflected on the failure of his original mission— to deliver the marquis to Napoleon. But as he watched Jean-Marc's balloon drift further away from the direction their balloon was headed, he believed deeply as though in a picture far larger than the one Napoleon lived in, that the work the lieutenant had performed to support this mysterious man was far more important, more sacred somehow; and it had only just begun. He also had distracting, lingering thoughts about something Jean-Marc said to him about his own progeny in future generations, and the important work they were destined to perform.

Far in the distance on a lofty rock promontory—a number of miles away in the high country of the Pyrenees—the Shepherd watched and he nodded with satisfaction. As he raised his hand casually, palm facing the west, the west wind seemed to pick up and gather a gentle directed force, a protective breeze that would help deliver Jean-Marc to his ultimate destination beyond the shores of the sea.

The End

HISTORICAL NOTE

The setting of this novel is a time and place that witnessed historic and seismic cultural change with repercussions for the entire western world, and by implication world civilization itself. Following Napoleon's brash attempt at creating a far-reaching empire, and the royal houses of Europe's collective response to stop him, the revolutionary ideas Napoleon represented and fostered could not be suppressed. Once his charter for the Universal Rights of Mankind had been codified, accepted and embraced by his people, the genie was out of the bottle.

Following the chaotic madness of the French Revolution, Napoleon emerged providing a vision and a workable system of rule for a population transitioning away from a monarchy. A new order had been established, a model for other neighboring countries which could be ultimately embraced by people of all classes. In his wake, the dominant and centuries-old Hapsburg dynasty hosting the Holy Roman Emperor, along with the Church of Rome's infamous Inquisition, had been functionally retired from history. And with them a new era of promise and possibility emerged. New discoveries in science, nature and exploration only accented that sense of a brave new world coming into formation.

A majority of historical elements are employed in this book, woven with inventions of my own. Historic events referenced include: Napoleon's extraordinary escape from Elba on March 1 and his historic march to Paris, arriving on the first day of spring; the surrender and change of sides of the royalist troops outside Grenoble; Napoleon's seizure of the Vatican Archives and housing them at the Soubise Palace in Paris (along with the curious missing *J* section); and the heads of Europe meeting at the same time in Vienna to decide France's ultimate fate during his escape and march north.

The French salon society depicted in this book is based on historical record. These gatherings hosted the latest display of scientific knowledge and artistic innovation. Such elite assemblages also bore witness to members of different secret societies who attended to exchange views. Some historians contend the French Revolution was planned by the secret societies, such as the Freemasons, whose presence and influence in the salons was well established.

The state of philosophical and religious developments in the book—with the temporary resurgence of the Inquisition, which Napoleon had extinguished years before, as well as, the rise of Hegelian philosophy, which ultimately led to provide the foundational roots of both Communism and Fascism—was part of the reactionary and psychologically repressive landscape of this time. Of curious note, this forced infusion of Hegelian philosophy into Prussia's educational system, after the humiliating defeat by

Napoleon at the Battle of Jena, was the byproduct of sobering assessment by the Prussian ruling princes of their Germanic troops not obeying orders blindly, but instead, demonstrating autonomous and independent (albeit poor) decision-making that led to Napoleon ultimately being victorious over the German principalities. This strict education model, later imported to the United States, remains the foundation of America's public education system today.

The description of the Albigensian Crusade during the 1200's—the first Latin European Christian against Latin European Christian crusade, with the tragic culmination on Montségur—is true. The general description of the Cathar way of worship, their organization, the tradition of the *perfecti* and their traveling in pairs to spread their teachings, are based on historical fact. The Shepherd and his partner Marie are my inventions. The connection of the Cathar tradition with the ancient Gnostic Christian beliefs has been noted by numerous scholars.

The existence of Septimania and its hosting of a Jewish principality closely tied to Jerusalem during Roman times, and its exact geographical overlap with the early Mary Magdalene tradition in what was later to be Southern France, are fact. The representation of Montségur as being the site of the Fisher King's castle has been written about for centuries by various researchers. The Fisher King—first depicted in Chrétien de Troye's closely studied medieval text *Perceval*—is depicted as the holder of the Holy Grail, and some sources say the brother-in-law of Joseph of Arimathea. The traditions of Joseph of Arimathea—in whose sepulcher Jesus of Nazareth was entombed, the one

514

who caught Jesus's blood in the sacred cup, who was also credited with bringing the original pre-Roman Christianity to Southern England, as well as his being directly connected with protecting the bloodline of Christ—are historical fact. The term *Desposyni*, direct descendants of Christ, appears in the Catholic Encyclopedia.

The less flattering side of Saint Paul's history are all based on published research from numerous authors and academic scholars including *Paul and Jesus* by Dr. James D. Tabor. This book also depicts St. Paul in open conflict with the Apostles of Jerusalem. Insights into St. Peter's story in history are also based on published research, including one source contesting the saint's final resting place.

Historical figures include the two Monsignors Marini, who were the Church of Rome's caretakers of the Vatican Archives at the Soubise Palace, and of course, Napoleon.

One of my inspirations for writing the *Sub Rosa* series, the storied Count de Saint Germain, is also an historic personage, albeit one who remains clouded in mystery and speculation. His claim to immortality and his meeting with the Countess d'Adhémar depicted in the salon at the beginning of the story are taken from historical record. The meeting with the countess at a different social gathering of that period was placed here for dramatic convenience. The Count de Saint Germain had numerous documented pseudonyms, many of which are cited in the novel. His personas of Marquis Jean-Marc Baptiste de Rennes and Father Baptisti are my inventions.

The lost tradition of the study of the Seven Liberal Arts and elements of the alchemical process, including the importance of the double-stop of E-flat and G chords, are all based on published writings and research. Sources for these include: *The Seven Liberal Arts*, by Paul Abelson; *The Golden Age of Chartres – The Teachings of a Mystery School and the Eternal Feminine*, by René Querido; *The Renaissance of the Twelfth Century*, by Charles Homer Haskins; *The Elements of Alchemy*, by Cherry Gilchrist; *The Origins of Alchemy in Greco-Roman Egypt*, by Frederic Muller; *Alchemy Discovered and Restored*, by Archibald Cockren.

Graham Hancock and Robert Bauval's *Talisman* provides compelling insights into the Cathar story as well as revealing research into the hidden legacy of Paris and its ancient Egyptian spiritual roots from Roman times of hosting a center of worship for the Egyptian goddess Isis on the island where Notre Dame now stands. And indeed the name of Paris is derived from Pharos-Isis, Pharos being the island at ancient Alexandria where the famed Lighthouse of Alexandria stood. This detail proves a deeper insight into why Paris has been referred to as the 'City of Light.' Readers of *Sub Rosa – Sanctuary's End*, the first installment in this series, will recognize other historic connections.

Anyone who has read this book or my first will recognize a driving passion and theme for me is depicting stories of lost knowledge and hidden history, all woven into factual historical research. It's often said that the victors write history, which I think is true. But in that process, too often the truth itself is mangled and contorted to the agenda of those victors who protect their power and privilege. My stories, however, meant to be fast-paced and entertaining historical thrillers, *could* be true as well.

The *Sub Rosa* cycle will continue in a new era and setting with *Sub Rosa – Thy Kingdom Came*.

ABOUT THE AUTHOR

An honors graduate of Amherst College, his first professional writing credit being the *Sherlock Holmes Radio Theater*, Barry wrote creatively for animation, television and film. His produced television credits include: *Star Trek: The Next Generation*, *Hunter*, *Beast Wars* and *War of the Worlds*. Barry also wrote a range of projects for location-based entertainment including Universal Studios' *Star Trek Attraction*, Chicago's Adler Planetarium *Tour of the Universe*, as well as, the Davy Crockett one-man show *Ridin' into the Storm* for the Texas State History Museum's Spirit Theater. Barry also wrote for major computer games including Electronic Arts' *Command & Conquer* and *Lands of Lore*.

Beyond the creative content field, Barry developed computer-based management training courses, served as a marketing consultant in the automotive industry, and worked as an editor and writer for Glencoe McGraw-Hill where he authored three ten-chapter professional communications curriculum workbooks (on Technical Communications, Cross-Cultural Communications and Dynamic Listening). He has written for magazine publications ranging from communications technology to the martial arts. He is also a black belt sensei in both *Karate* and *Toshin Ryu*—Japanese weapons. Barry has worked for the last eleven years as a Solutions and Product Marketing Manager, and a white paper author, for a leading global communications technology company. He lives in Southern California with his wife, two children, and two dogs.

To learn more about the author, visit:
www.patrickseanbarry.com